THE BONES IN THE ORCHARD

GRAVESYDE PRIORY MYSTERY, #3

PATRICIA RICE

PLEASE JOIN MY READER LIST

Please consider joining my newsletter for exclusive content and news of upcoming releases. Be the first to know about special sales, freebies, stories from my writer life, and other fun information. You'll even receive a thank-you gift. Join me on my writing adventures!

To Join, Please Visit —
https://www.subscribepage.com/ricehr

AUTHOR'S NOTE

I read my first "Regency" in elementary school after I picked up a copy of Jane Austen's *Pride and Prejudice* at a Scholastic school book fair. Later, as a young, working mother, I worked my way through entire library shelves of Regency romance. I have written my fair share of those romances since then. And while I might have occasionally pondered references to curates, vicars, tithes, and so forth, I've never really had to do more than understand context and translate it into "clergy" and "money."

And then I started writing this book. I had to learn far more than I ever wanted to know about the mistreatment of impoverished curates during the Regency era and earlier. Reforms were made later, but wow, one had to be desperate or obsessed to survive as a curate if one didn't have a wealthy patron to provide a true living.

I want to thank Brenda S. Cox and her book *Fashionable Goodness: Christianity in Jane Austen's England* for straightening out some of the convoluted research I found online. Any flaws in this story are utterly mine and no one else's. I created an impossible situation, then had to dig my way out of it!

For those readers unfamiliar with the quirkiness of Regency marriage laws. . . People could not marry unless their intention to do so was announced in the church, in the parish where they lived, three weeks in a row. Otherwise, they had to ride to an archbishop, usually in London, and fork over a lot of money for a special license. Have pity on my desperate manor inhabitants with no income to pay the wages of a clergyman for their neglected chapel and no easy means to travel elsewhere.

And, as always, the manor and its location are completely from my imagination and my knowledge of small towns in general. You will not find Gravesyde Priory on any map!

For those readers who have difficulty with names (of whom, I am one), there is a character list at the end, plus a *partial* family tree on my website, https://patriciarice.com/wycliffe-family-tree-2/ That tree keeps growing as I write!

ONE

May, 1815

"THERE IS NO SUCH THING AS A PERFECT MAN," CLARE Knightley muttered as she picked her way through the wet grass carrying a basket of the first spring rosebuds.

She had told Captain Huntley that she loved roses. Did the vexing man bring her a bouquet? No, he had wondered if it were possible to grow more roses and promptly set out muddy pots of rose branches.

Her beloved was an engineer. A gardener, he was not. She sighed at the line of dead stalks and proceeded up the front steps, until she heard a horse cantering up. They had so few visitors in these rural environs, that curiosity had the better of her. She waited on the crumbling limestone stairs.

As a city girl, she knew little of horses. This one was black. The rider wore black, although his neckcloth had wilted, and his knee boots had acquired a layer of road grime. Overlong dark hair curled against the cloth—not a family member, then. Was he in mourning or just overly dramatic?

1

A large man, he swung down and made a sweeping bow with his tall hat. "My lady, dare I hope, my cousin?"

"No, you may not," she told him with assurance, taking an instant dislike to his familiar manner. This close, she could see his beard had been crudely shaved, his shirt cuffs were worn thin, and his coat had a decided sheen of wear.

Poverty did not make him a villain, she reminded herself. But it didn't make him a family member either.

"Is this not Wycliffe Manor?" he asked, pretending shock.

"Of course it is. There is a sign right by the drive you rode up. How may we help you?" She shouldn't be rude, she supposed. She simply didn't like the way he looked at her, then studied the sprawling gothic manor as if he'd possess it, if he could.

She could tell him the decrepit place ate money like a pig eats slop, but she politely refrained.

"My apologies if I have set off on the wrong foot, my lady. I am Duncan Reid, grandson of Lord David Reid, the late earl's brother. I am only back from India and just heard of the earl's will. Is Captain Huntley available?" His winning grin vanished, and he glared at her in stern disapproval, as if she might be a maid loitering on the master's lawn.

She really did not like his attitude—but now her dislike intensified. The man was a blatant liar and fraud. She turned up the stairs to the massive entry. Carved in good English oak, the manor's doors were works of art, but like the rest of the place, sorely in need of refurbishing. "He will not see you unless you have come with a letter from the estate solicitor verifying your claim. Good day to you, sir."

Quincy had a door open before she need reach for it. Over six feet tall, barrel-chested, and still muscled for a man in his fifties, the former boxer glared menacingly at their visitor.

"I demand to see Captain Huntley," the fake Mr. Reid shouted.

"If you are in need of employment," the butler intoned,

"please use the servant's entrance at the rear." He nodded in the direction of the stable yard.

"We need a footman," Clare called sweetly from the safety of the house as Quincy's very large son, and their only footman, crossed the vestibule carrying a massive, rolled-up carpet. Spring cleaning had commenced. He trotted down the stairs with his burden.

The visitor showed no interest in hard labor. Despite his probable assumption, the inhabitants of Wycliffe Manor did not lead lives of luxury and ease.

To Clare's delight, Hunt strolled around the corner, covered in his usual filth from working on the coal retort in the medieval crypt/dungeon. Her fiancé was a tall man, broad-shouldered, and despite his slight limp, he crossed the lawn with a military stride. Simply looking at him gave her pleasurable palpitations.

He'd seen her, and his protective instincts had him eyeing the visitor critically.

The fake Mr. Reid ignored the disheveled captain's air of authority and foolishly turned his back on him as if he were no more than a gardener. "I am a *Reid* and demand to see whoever is in charge, at once!"

Clare's beloved grinned devilishly and glanced at her, as if asking permission to handle their unwelcome guest as he wished. It had taken him a while, but the American captain had learned about the Reid family's eccentricities. Although Hunt had been named one of the heirs due to marriage lines, he was not related by blood, thus, he was the *only* heir with dark hair. And the only adult male at all, as far as the lawyers had ascertained, which was why they accepted him, despite all appearances to the contrary.

Genuine Reid heirs had several distinctive features besides blond hair. This impostor possessed none.

"We've need of a head gardener," Hunt said in crude

imitation of the vernacular, although in his American accent. "Come 'round to the back, if ye're applying."

"I am not a gardener or footman!" the pretender shouted. "I demand to see Captain Huntley!"

Clare left the cat to play with the mouse and carried her roses in to make a bouquet. Hunt might not be romantic, but they suited so well that just his rare smile thrilled her. Had she not accepted his invitation to this crumbling fortress, she'd never have realized that she didn't need to wear fancy gowns, glide about ballrooms, or hide who she was to find a good man.

Hunt not only accepted her tart tongue but *admired* her career as a novelist. Clare had not told anyone else except her best friend, Meera, for fear it would destroy her reputation and harm her nephew's future. Sharing this secret joy and heavy burden, and finding acceptance instead of the shame she'd feared, had been a marvelous relief. She might love Hunt for his understanding if naught else, but there was plenty more to the captain than that.

Wearing an apron and mob cap as if she were a housemaid, Meera emerged from the great hall covered in dust and cobwebs. The manor had been left empty for fifteen years, since the death of the last viscountess. Finding servants had been their task these last months since Clare and Meera had arrived.

"You are not supposed to be on your feet," Clare scolded her best friend. One of the many reasons they had brashly accepted Hunt's invitation to this rural abode was to escape the father of Meera's unborn child. The scoundrel was dead now and buried in the manor's graveyard, but the babe was large and Meera wasn't.

"A little exercise is good for me." With a Hindu mother and a Jewish father, Meera had been given opportunities Clare's aristocratic background had not allowed. Meera had studied as an apothecary under her parents' tutelage, but a new law prevented her from attaining a license because of her gender. She knew as much or more than most male physicians, which made it difficult to argue with her about healthy practices.

"If we are to have weddings here, the hall needs to be clean," Meera insisted. "We need a proper housekeeper, though. I don't know how to clean the chandeliers."

Weddings, plural. Clare and Hunt had only met a few months earlier and were doing their best to be proper and circumspect, waiting until a clergyman might be found. Without a clergyman, it was impossible to have banns said in their local church, as required by law. And since the church was naught more than walls with rotting thatch, the distant rector had not seen fit to send anyone, despite their pleas. They'd all have to move elsewhere to marry.

But given the rashness of her cousin, Lady Elsa, and the Honorable Jack de Sackville, the man she'd known since childhood, proper and circumspect wasn't to be expected. They would be anticipating their vows, if they had not already. Only Lady Elsa's interest in establishing the manor's kitchen and Jack's launching of his newly purchased stable kept the two apart much of the day. The nights, however. . .

"To have a wedding in the manor, we'd need special licenses from the archbishop," Clare reminded her friend. "It might come to that, if Jack can summon the time to ride to London and Hunt can find the coin."

"Jack and Elsa are threatening to return to their homes to have the banns cried," Meera warned. "They still have residence there."

"Hunt has written to everyone he knows about our need for a clergyman. Unfortunately, he's an American and not an Anglican and knows no one in the church. I've asked the aunts for their aid, and they're looking into it." The Reid family had female aunts and cousins aplenty, just no adult males. Clare proceeded down the corridor with her roses. "We must be patient."

So perhaps Lady Elsa's estate in Newchurch was their best choice. Clare hated to see them leave. No cook for the month it would take to read the banns and arrange the service. . . They would all have to travel a day's ride or more to celebrate with the newlyweds, and they had no carriage. Hunt's negotiation for a used one had fallen through. Uncertain whether her fortune would survive her bank's default, even Elsa couldn't afford a new one.

By noon, Clare had the roses in vases, scenting the family parlor. Cleaned up and ready to eat, Hunt stomped down the corridor. He checked to be certain no one was about, then swept her up in a hug and planted kisses all over her blushing cheeks.

"I love being allowed to do that," he said, once she was breathless. "Will you believe, after I dispatched the first rascal, *another* fool showed up declaring he was the parish curate and his *wife* is family? We will have to station the hounds and a gatekeeper on the drive to keep out needy hordes now that word of the earl's will has leaked out."

"A curate?" She pounced on this glimmer of hope. She dared a kiss to his bristly jaw, then took his arm as he aimed for the smaller dining parlor where a cold luncheon was laid out. "Do curates carry papers to verify their identity? Shouldn't a rector or vicar send one with recommendations or some such? It would be lovely if a clergyman could just materialize on our doorstep!"

"I'm new to your customs and ownership of mansions and have no idea. Have you heard nothing from our noble relations?" He handed her a plate to fill.

Starting early and working hard all day as they did, they'd come to rely on these brief mid-day meals to last them until dinner. Being rural, they could set their own hours without need of worrying about visitors, who really ought to announce the day of their arrival. Apparently, the good weather had dispensed with that nicety.

Clare frowned as she filled her bread with meat and cheese and took a spoonful of preserved fruit. If they started having regular callers. . . Visitors would have to bring their own picnic baskets. The few pantry staples the former care-takers had put up were nearly gone, and the village market was limited.

"You have seen how irregularly our family corresponds. It's as if I am the only one bequeathed with the ability to put ink on paper. If we are very fortunate, one of them will stuff a parson into a carriage and send him. . ." Realizing what she was about to say, she looked at Hunt. "You said the second visitor claimed to be a *curate* and his wife is a relation to the earl?"

He poured ale into his mug and pulled out a chair for her.

Before he could answer, Meera and Walker wandered in to fill their plates. Walker was Hunt's African steward and best friend. Although Walker and Meera spent as much time arguing as they did working, they had fallen under the romantic spell of the manor. Clare hardly ever saw the two apart these days.

As if conjured by her thoughts, the scent of jasmine wafted through the room. The estate grew no jasmine. The late Lady Reid had favored a floral French perfume that clung every-where, years after her death. Or her ghost lingered.

"Who claimed to be a curate?" Meera asked. "That dreadful man who insisted he was an heir this morning?"

"We had two visitors. I did not meet the second." Clare waited for Hunt to explain.

He was more interested in his food, but he swallowed hastily when they all waited in anticipation. "Older, garrulous gent, shabby, driving a pony cart. No sign of said wife. No papers. Just said he was the perpetual curate assigned to the parish."

7

"If he was assigned to this parish, it must have been during the viscountess's time, and that was fifteen years ago." Clare frowned. Lady Reid had had no money of her own to provide a benefice or upkeep for any church. The village had been deteriorating since the earl's death nearly thirty-five years ago.

Hunt shrugged. "I didn't ask. I just told him to come back with documents. He rode off more cheerfully than the first fellow."

Carrying a plate of freshly baked biscuits, Lady Elsa Villiers entered in a cloud of vanilla and spices. After setting down the tray, she doffed her apron to join them, as she had not when she'd first arrived, while hiding from her bullying brother. In the manor's protection, she had finally come out of hiding, if not entirely out of the kitchen.

Like any good cook, the lady was not svelte, but she was most certainly a blond Reid heiress. She helped herself to the luncheon she'd prepared and took a seat next to Clare. "Who are we discussing?"

"The villains showing up at the door, claiming to be heirs," Walker offered. "I think we should have voted to keep the curate, even if he is a fraud."

"A curate? Would that be the fellow the maids are nattering about?" Lady Elsa looked up eagerly. "I sent Marie to fetch greens at the market, and she came back all atwitter. Her grandfather said the curate has returned. Could it be true? Could we actually hold a wedding in the village?"

"Have you seen the chapel?" Walker asked disparagingly. "The roof has fallen in and pigeons roost on the rafters."

"And we are unsure as to whether we can use the manor's maintenance trust to repair it. The bank insists it holds the mortgages, and they are in the names of people who have long since moved away. Although. . ." Hunt rubbed the scar over his blind eye. "A chapel and parsonage usually belong to the church, so they shouldn't be mortgaged."

"The trust probably would not approve of tithing to the church from our maintenance fund. And we don't have any other income to tithe. But if the *manor* owns the property, and the earl once provided the benefice. . ." Clare worked her creative mind around the possibilities. "Perhaps if this person really is a curate, he would know?"

"Well, there is one way to find out." Meera finished her soup. "We must go into the village and see if the gentleman has lingered."

Meera wanted to check on an Anglican clergyman? Clare tried not to raise her eyebrows, but she was pretty certain the look Meera and Walker exchanged was significant.

Oh my, *three* weddings? They definitely needed a church, one way or another!

TWO

PATIENCE UPTON TIED HER LOOSE APRON OVER HER BAGGY
brown gown and scowled at the pigeon droppings on the
once-lovely chapel's stone floor. A whole orchard of fruit and
nut blossoms beckoned her up the hill, and she had to clean
guano. Life simply was not fair.

"Cover your face with a handkerchief," her mother
advised. "Bird droppings can make you ill."

Her mother was a normal-sized woman. At forty-seven,
Henrietta Upton had gained a few pounds over the years, but
she'd always been sturdy, and her figure suited her.

Patience, however. . . glanced down at herself with regret.
Tall, like her father, she'd never gained an ounce since adolescence, except in one specific area. She blamed her top-heavi-
ness for her inability to walk without stumbling. Obediently,
she tied a handkerchief over her nose and mouth and picked
up the broom her mother had packed in the wagon.

She was always obedient. She had little choice. Her
parents were her home. Since leaving Gravesyde Priory after
the death of the viscountess, when she was only eight, they'd
wandered from temporary post to temporary post. She would

only have time to make a friend or two before they were gone again.

Dust and straw filtered down as her older half-brother industriously repaired holes in the chapel's roof. She sneezed as she swept.

She remembered Gravesyde Priory with fondness. The lady at the manor had allowed her to run free on the grounds, following her gardener about, allowing her to borrow books from the library. Well, allowing her parents to borrow books so they could teach the village children, and that included her.

Paul leaned through a hole in the roof to call down, "Company coming down the lane. Tidy up pretty!"

Patience rolled her eyes. She was wearing her worst gown, and she was covered in filth. "I'll change into my silks, shall I?" she called back.

"You shouldn't sass your brother, lass," her mother scolded. "He's taking time from seeking his own parish to help us. It's up to us to convince the new lord that we belong."

Paul was the best of men, probably too good. He ought to be escaping her father's madness and finding his own position now that he was ready to be ordained, but he'd wanted to see them settled first.

"You are a Reid and do belong," Patience said fiercely, removing her apron and mobcap.

"Not on the right side of the blanket, dear. Let us not repeat that old history. Your father is the one who belongs. He was given the perpetual post decades ago. It's his for the taking." Nettie uncovered her gray hair and removed her apron.

Except the new lord had turned her father away for lack of documentation. Papa wasn't much on official paperwork. Which meant he hadn't consulted the rector. She doubted that

11

the chapel had ever provided much of a living, or her father wouldn't have left in the first place.

She wouldn't complain—too much. Her father was a good man. He meant well, anyway. It was just. . . well, he lived in the moment.

It was May. She needed to be digging in the dirt, planting a garden to tide them over the winter—should they be allowed to stay for a winter. With a sigh, she shook out her skirt as best as she could, wiped cobwebs off her sleeves, and removed her old gardening gloves.

She could do nothing about the fine hair spinning about her face like cobwebs or her unwieldy boots. At least, she knew where her feet were in the ugly things, and she was unlikely to break any toes.

She stepped outside into what should have been lovely sunshine. Except the tidy yard she remembered was now overgrown and shaded by thick yews and a forest of weedy beeches that had seeded themselves. A few tulips by the chapel door had survived neglect in a sunny spot, interspersed with forget-me-nots that had spread in the fertile soil. Lilacs and rhododendrons spilled over what once had been a stone walkway. She would need a ladder and a saw to even begin clearing the jungle to allow people to reach the church without having their hats knocked off and their gowns snagged.

Picking up her hedge shear, humming to herself, she traversed the path, cutting the vines and brambles grabbing her from the overgrown bushes. If she did this often enough, in a few more trips, she wouldn't have to fight her way through.

At the end of the tunnel of shrubbery, an elegant party studied the chapel's deteriorating picket fence and the overrun yard with doubt, quite rightly. If Patience had worn those delicate muslins and beribboned spencers, they'd be in tatters by now.

And then a dashing gentleman in a long-tailed coat and splendiferously embroidered waistcoat joined them, and she fell through the broken gate she'd meant to open.

A strong arm in an impeccable glove caught her before she landed on her nose. "Gentle, mademoiselle, this forest is not a place for delicate toes."

Delicate toes? She wore boots. She tried not to gape. He was *taller* than she, a situation that seldom occurred. He spoke with a deliciously French accent, in a mellow voice that could make a weaker woman vaporish. And beneath that elegant top hat. . . dark curly hair, long-lashed eyes, and a face of angles and curves to make an angel weep. His square jaw was just the perfect proportion to his square cheekbones. . . Oh dear.

A rogue, beyond any shadow of a doubt. And a flatterer. Her boots were *not* delicate.

Blushing, Patience straightened and shook him off. Her hands were improperly bare, so she tucked them behind her back. "Thank you, my lord," she murmured. Etiquette had been drummed into her from an early age, even though she often failed at it. Was this the new lord of the manor? She must keep her tongue in her head.

"Just plain Mister Henri Lavigne, I fear, a relation of the late Lady Reid." He gave the French pronunciation of *Onree*.

A mister, not a lord. But then, Lady Reid hadn't had sons.

"And these are Miss Clarissa Knightley, great-grand-daughter of the late earl, and her companion, Mrs. Meera Abrams. We were told a priest had moved into the neighborhood?"

Patience recovered enough of her equilibrium to bob a curtsy and surreptitiously study the interesting visitors. The gentleman with the French accent was no doubt Catholic and didn't understand Anglican differences. Would Miss Knightley be the new lady of the manor? Mrs. Abrams certainly would not. She had no look of the family at all.

Given her brown complexion, the companion did not appear to be English either.

Hiding her fascination, she bobbed another curtsy. "Pleased to meet you, sir, miss, madam. I am Patience Upton. My father is the curate assigned to this parish." She glanced over her shoulder, but her mother had not followed her out. "I am not at all certain it is still a church since he's been gone so long," she murmured in apology.

The pretty blond lady in a lacy blue bonnet considered the wilderness of a yard. "I was not even aware there was a church in there. We have only recently arrived and have spent most of these last months setting the manor to rights. I suppose now that the weather has improved, we should explore more."

"Is there someone on the roof?" the shorter, darker lady with the large nose asked in what sounded like horror, studying the rotting peak just visible above the trees. "That cannot be safe!"

"My brother," Patience explained, hiding her embarrassment. "We have learned to do repairs ourselves since it is so often difficult for a parish to afford them. My father is over there as well."

"The *priest* is on the ladder?" Mr. Lavigne seemed amazed.

"They're both men of the cloth. My brother has been ordained as a deacon and is ready to move up, but he has not found his first post. He is here to help us settle in. I would ask you to come in for tea, but I fear you would destroy your garments on brambles, and we have not unpacked our china." She did not inquire into whether her family had any right to take over the parsonage. She left that to her father. He'd barreled his way into positions more often than not.

"Then we should ask you up to tea!" Miss Knightley declared. "Captain Huntley is an officer who likes everything legal and on paper, but I shall assure him that your family is welcome. Will around four today suit? Since you will not have had time to set in provisions, I will ask Lady Elsa to prepare a good-sized meal so you might take some home."

A *lady* prepared meals?

Overwhelmed, Patience was uncertain as to how to reply. Properly, she should refuse. But the lady was right. They had nearly nothing to eat. And they did need to make a good impression on the manor's owner.

She bobbed another curtsy. "That is gracious, thank you. It will be a pleasure meeting everyone."

They said their farewells and ambled off. Patience watched as they stopped to speak with several of the villagers, then took a footpath up the hill to the manor. She closed her eyes and tried to breathe freely again, wishing she could be as boldly confident as her father.

She didn't know how to take it that a handsome rogue like Mr. Lavigne had not looked upon her with disdain, even after she'd nearly fallen into him. Were the other occupants of the manor so. . . worldly? Could she pray she wouldn't drop her tea in her lap or fall into the tea table just this once?

Before she turned away to announce their invitation, she noticed a big man all in black glaring at the party heading up the hill. Why was he so angry?

"YOU INVITED THE CHARLATAN TO *TEA*?" HUNT ASKED IN incredulity when presented with a great hall adorned in bouquets and china vases. He'd spent the day in the cellar monitoring the coal retort. Perhaps he needed to spend more time governing the ladies.

"We do not know he is a charlatan. He believes that the position still belongs to him. That is what *perpetual* curate means." Clare held up one of Hunt's grandmother's diaries.

15

"We are looking. In her journals, the viscountess does mention having tea with the curate and his family a time or two. As a Catholic, she did not attend the Anglican church, but she knew everyone in the village. She calls him Mr. Upton and says he has two lovely children and is teaching classes."

"That does not mean he is *this* Upton," Hunt protested, but he recognized the gleam in his co-general's eyes. She was determined to have a clergyman.

He was desperate for the same, if the truth be told. Trying to keep a respectful distance wasn't working very well when he knew Clare relished his embrace as much as he did hers. She was a quiet, unworldly spinster, and he wanted to give her time to be certain of a one-eyed ex-soldier. But in close proximity like this, he wanted the right to kiss and. . . more.

"Better yet. . ." She removed the spectacles she used for reading, and her blue eyes sparkled with mischief. "I don't know about the rest of the family, but Miss Patience Upton is definitely a *Reid*."

"There is no Upton on the family tree! We are not going down this road again, Clare." And this was why he wanted her so badly—she shook up his boring life. Obviously, he needed a challenge. "It's bad enough we're taking Lavender on the basis of her looks, but a curate's daughter. . ."

Adolescent Lavender had shown up on their doorstep a few weeks ago, all Reid dimples and blond curls, declaring herself the granddaughter of one of their aunts. She'd quickly settled in as a seamstress and one of the family, even though her name was not legitimately on the family tree.

"Lavender's grandmother acknowledged her," Clare reminded him. "But of course, we have to make inquiries. Only, Miss Upton has hair almost exactly like mine. Blue eyes, dimples, widow's peak, the odd earlobes, and she wasn't wearing gloves, so I could see her backward thumb! So many distinctive characteristics, can there be any doubt?"

Hunt pinched the bridge of his nose. "The Reids are a large and prolific family. Their bastards are no doubt scattered under every hedgerow. Are you planning on collecting all of your unclaimed family because the known ones are too rude to respond to our invitations?"

"Why not? Hasn't everyone so far been useful? Well, except Bosworth, our nasty banker, perhaps, and he may come around yet. It's not as if marriage makes your bloodline more genuine. Go wash up. They will be here shortly." She shooed him off.

Grimacing, Hunt took the marble stairs up to the family floor, where he encountered Walker, wearing a respectable coat and neckcloth, on the way down. Walker meant to attend this tea? Had the world turned on its head? More likely, he wished to strip the pretension from the visitors by making them take tea with a black man. As the son of emancipated slaves, Walker could be perverse when he chose. Hunt didn't blame him.

His friend and steward took in Hunt's filthy attire and shook his head. "Pretend he's a real curate, if he's willing to fix up the church. We can discover his credentials later."

Walker was attending tea because he *wanted a church*? Hunt raised his eyebrows. "*Et tu*, Brutus? You aren't even Anglican."

"Neither is Meera, but we want her child to have a name so the babe does not end up dispossessed like Lavender. That requires a marriage certificate." He glared defiantly at Hunt.

Hunt rubbed the scar on his temple. He and Walker had gone to school together under the tutelage of Walker's adopted parents. When the university refused to accept an African student, Hunt had attended the army's engineering school, where they accepted Walker as his servant. They'd studied together, gone to war together, come here to find Hunt's heritage together.

17

Walker had no English heritage to explore. But marrying Meera. . . His friend would have a future in a different world than they'd grown up in. Hunt couldn't argue with that. And Meera would be a brilliant wife to match Walker's intelligence.

"The two of you never stop arguing." Hunt felt he had to offer the devil's advocate position.

"It is called conversing. You should try it sometime." Walker continued down the stairs, leaving Hunt to the tender mercies of his new valet.

James, the peg-legged former batman, had adapted to Hunt's ability to collect every bit of filth and grime the house had to offer. Engineering and mechanics weren't a gentleman's purview. Hunt had never had to mind his clothing before. The valet accepted the challenge. He had dinner clothes laid out, all neatly mended and pressed as they'd never been before. A man could grow accustomed to such niceties—except for the lack of control over what one wore.

"Breeches, James? Really?" Pulling off his coat, Hunt glared at the offending garment in disdain.

"Company to tea, captain. A parson, I'm told. Would be nice to hear the good book preached again." James picked up the clothes Hunt discarded, examining them for rents.

Clare had been reading from the prayer book every Sunday, since Hunt's one eye required spectacles he had yet to acquire. He wasn't much of a churchgoer, but he couldn't argue the valet's position. Sunday was a half day off for the servants, and they liked to dress up and gossip the same as everyone else.

He was going to have to accept the garrulous old potential curate for now, unless Upton proved to be a true villain. They'd run across a fair share of scoundrels these last months since their arrival. Surely a villain would not bring a wife and children.

But the manor's occupants were convinced that the

impossible map the old earl had left would lead them to the jewels once worn by Clare's grandmother. Word of wealth traveled, even in these rural environs.

Hunt didn't want to be the one to send a curate fleeing down the road with a flea in his ear.

THREE

"*BONES*? IN THE ORCHARD?" HENRI LAVIGNE GAZED INTO HIS brother's mirror to straighten his neckcloth. As the younger son of a French count, Henri had been sent to his aunt in England to keep him safe from the revolution and to learn a profession. University had not suited him. Traveling and meeting people as a peddler had. But now...

He lived in a manor bursting with interesting people and entertaining stories. *Home* was an enlightening new concept to explore, until he succumbed to wanderlust again. He was singularly useless and purposeless, but he might lend a hand here and there to earn his keep.

Bones in an orchard weren't part of his life plans.

"I suppose the original priory was called Gravesyde for a reason." Arnaud, Henri's older brother, yanked on his boot and stood. "Perhaps there was an ancient cemetery, and the earl planted the orchard on top of it."

"Rather rude, yes?" Eager to go down and meet the visitors, especially the deliciously tall, golden beauty who dressed like a ragpicker, Henri opened the chamber door and tapped his toe impatiently. "Perhaps you should not mention this in front of guests?"

The eldest, and raised as the nobleman he never became, Arnaud glared at his brother's impertinence. "I am not an *imbécile*. The ladies do not need to hear of bones."

Henri laughed. "You *are* a fool if you think they will not. But I should like to meet this person who claims to have known the earl and viscountess. If he speaks the truth, he will have stories."

Leaving his larger, more proper brother behind, Henri took the stairs down two at a time. He could hear animated feminine chatter in the cavernous great hall. The guests had arrived. Having spent the better part of his youth in the masculine environs of school, he'd enjoyed his freedom as a peddler to speak to ladies young and old, rich and poor. He found them far more interesting than dour gentlemen who regarded him as a dangerous freak. Yes, he liked fancy vests and flirting. That did not make him any less a man. The English were just too boring.

With Napoleon rampaging across Europe once more, he might never see France and its charms again. He crushed that thought.

The ladies smiled up at him when he entered. The older, fatter gentleman with the pendulous jaws and sparse gray hair must be the priest. A younger, shorter man with auburn hair stood behind him, engaged in conversation with Jack, the horse-mad ex-soldier. Perhaps that was the priest's son, the one who had been repairing the roof? He needed to adjust his thinking to Anglican ways. What exactly was a curate? He certainly did not wear a priest's robes—or even a clerical collar.

As Clare introduced him to their visitors, Henri sought out the lovely miss they'd met earlier. She'd done her best to fade into the shadows, sitting far from the fire and lamps in a dull gray chair that matched her gown. Was she in mourning?

"Miss Upton?" He bowed in front of her after acknowledging her elders, who also wore dark colors. "Would you care to visit the gallery? We have a lovely art collection, and Miss Lavender has set the local ladies to fashioning buttons and clothing. You might be interested."

Lavender usually loved showing off her fashion business, but the usually talkative adolescent was casting interested glances toward the young gentleman. Ah, the clergyman's son had caught her eye.

Miss Upton, too, seemed indifferent about deserting the company. Henri was unaccustomed to disinterest. Well, perhaps curate's daughters were more proper. He accepted her excuses by carrying her a plate of Elsa's confections. Those, the lady couldn't resist. She still showed no interest in conversing with him, but he would persevere.

Arnaud and Hunt entered together, both built large and dark and more like brothers than cousins. They motioned the curate to stay seated, waited for introductions, bowed properly to the ladies, and shook the gentlemen's hands. Only Henri could see their tension. They did not trust the guests.

He did not care one way or another whether the church was rebuilt or burned. He might have been baptized Catholic, but he'd been born a heathen. He rather thought the pretty lady might not appreciate that sentiment. So he took a tiny sandwich from the tray and tossed the fireworks the more polite folk were avoiding.

"So, Mr. Upton, you served the chapel when the viscountess lived here? She was my great-aunt, you know. I don't remember meeting you." Henri had not visited often. As heir to a comte, Arnaud had been in France and had visited even less. The curate's reply might be entertaining, if naught else.

The fat gentleman in the shiny, worn breeches and frayed stockings complacently finished chewing, then took a sip of tea before looking up and locating Henri. "You were a rapscallion even then, refusing to sit still. Your aunt spoiled you."

Well, just about anyone could deduce that.

The gentleman rolled on without waiting for a response. "The lady was gracious enough to allow Paul and Patience use of her library. There were few volumes suitable for children, but Patience enjoyed the illustrations of flowers, and Paul found the sermons edifying."

"Were you with my grandmother in her last days?" Captain Huntley asked stiffly. Henri's cousin did not warm up quickly to strangers.

"Indeed, indeed, it was sad. She wasted away with few visitors, although I wrote everyone she knew. They were few, I fear. My wife tried to help, although the old housekeeper did not appreciate her interference. At the time, I truly believed the lady perished from loneliness." Mr. Upton helped himself to another plateful of sandwiches.

Well, that set a pall over the gathering. The old man certainly knew how to substantiate credentials with a good story.

Henri scooped up a scone, winked at the young lady hiding in the shadows, and added a few choice tidbits to a plate. "I believe our aunt was melancholy by nature and missed her home. I was old enough in her last days to know that she fretted over family, like Arnaud, left behind in war-torn France, but the earl left her nothing to assist them."

He carried the confections to Miss Upton's chair, since she could not easily reach the tray from the shadows. "What do you remember of your early days here, Miss Upton?"

"I'm sure I cannot say," she whispered, shrinking back in the chair, forcing him to set the plate on a side table.

"Cannot or will not?" he teased. "Do you remember me?"

She shook her head, and a spill of fair hair settled over her unadorned ears.

He didn't remember her, either, but that meant nothing. He'd spent his few days here stuffing himself with food and running wild.

"As far as I am aware, my grandmother did not correspond a great deal with family," Hunt acknowledged. "She wrote in her diaries more than she wrote letters. Were you here when she first arrived?"

"I was, indeed." The curate chuckled, apparently in fond memory. "Gravesyde was my first position. The chapel was ancient even then. The benefice had been set in much earlier days and had become almost worthless as expenses increased. I told the late earl I could not afford a wife under such conditions. He donated an additional meadow to the church to be rented out. The rector was quite pleased and doubled my salary."

Good gracious, the man must be a Methuselah. Henri regarded him with a little more interest but let the ladies continue the questioning while he calculated dates. The earl had died in 1781, nearly thirty-five years ago! But he supposed a young man, with a little experience under his belt, might have been in his early twenties then. That made the curate around sixty, not exactly ancient.

"None of us had the pleasure of meeting the earl or her ladyship," Clare was saying. "It is marvelous to hear them come to life through your stories. Were you with the earl, too, when he died?"

Henri knew that Clare was digging into ancient mysteries. His great-aunt's diaries had led them to discover murder and deception. With so many deaths at the manor, they had all wondered if her early demise had been natural. Or the earl's. Henri doubted if this bluff clergyman would have noticed.

"Aye, I heard his prayers from his deathbed. We had no physicians, you understand, and his lordship refused to call any from London. In his day, the manor bustled with servants. The whole village turned out when Lord Wycliffe was laid in his crypt, but few of his family attended, since he had only sisters and daughters still living. Some of their husbands who lived nearby rode in. They spoke with the

24

bankers and solicitors and closed the house down. It was a sad time all around."

They had surmised all this on their own. The curate could have done the same. But Henri was inclined to believe him. Upton simply did not strike him as an imaginative sort. He just related what he'd seen, without speculation.

"But you were still here when our great-aunt arrived a few years later," Arnaud said. He'd been standing in the background, listening, as was his way. He'd not known their aunt as well as Henri had, since he had refused to leave France until he had no choice.

"Yes, yes, I was. The village was still active and needed me. We'd hoped some of the family would return. Those were difficult days." Upton looked pensive as he sipped his tea. "And then the viscountess returned and we hoped. . . But she had no funds of her own. That's when optimism fled and the young people began to leave."

"But you stayed on," Mrs. Upton said proudly. "You knew she needed you."

The curate grimaced and set aside his teacup. "Well, no, she did not particularly. I had no powerful friends to grant me a better living. And then I married, and my wife, Paul's mother, wished to stay because of her parents. He still has family hereabouts. Lady Reid never attended our little church. She was Catholic, and I asked an old friend of that persuasion to visit. She was grateful for that, I believe."

"Who planted the orchards, Father?" Miss Upton asked. "I remember making applesauce from the harvest when I was a little girl. We spent days cooking and stirring."

Henri prevented his eyebrows from soaring. Now there was an excellent insight that could not easily be made up. And considering Arnaud's discovery of bones. . .

"The earl, my dear. The trees were already planted when I first arrived. He asked me to bless them. I thought that strange, but I was too new to argue. There were those in the village who muttered about graveyards and ghosts, but the superstitious will do so." The vicar lumbered to his feet. "Now, if you will excuse an old man, it's been a long day and I need a rest."

The ladies appeared slightly vexed that their storyteller left so soon, but there was nothing they could do but offer their farewells and send servants scattering for wraps and the promised supper basket.

Henri followed the captain as he escorted the Uptons to the door. He liked knowing what was happening in his new home, and for some odd reason, a young lady who hid herself piqued his curiosity.

But she carried out the basket of food without acknowledging his existence.

~

"BLUE EYES, WIDOW'S PEAK, ODD EAR LOBE," CLARE RECITED IN excitement. She loved discovering new family. "Although Mrs. Upton's hair is turning gray, it's most definitely blond. She is the Reid in the family. I wish we could have her story."

Like her, Elsa and Meera were scanning the viscountess's diaries of her return to the manor. It was a tedious job reading through the volatile lady's temper tantrums and old menus. They had succeeded in finding few other mentions of the young curate.

"Does being related to us make any difference?" A slow reader, Lavender worked on her sewing instead.

Dinner had been a gabble of speculation, none of it satisfactory to Clare's mind. The curate had not provided documentation, only promises to speak with the rector, who apparently lived a day's journey from here. The men were not pleased.

"Jack hopes the curate might better interpret the earl's map marking the location of the jewels, but he doesn't want to mention it until we know for certain he's not an impostor." Elsa held up the diary she read to the light. The sun had set some time ago, and lamplight did little to illuminate the faded, thin handwriting.

"The fewer who know of the jewels, the fewer miscreants will show up at the door." Meera tossed aside her book and picked up another.

"The promise of riches incites needy relations and frauds to crawl from the woodwork," Elsa agreed. "If we find Clare's family sapphires, she should probably lock them in a vault or put them in a trust for Oliver."

The theory was sound, but not the actuality, Clare knew. "If Jack is correct, those sapphires are worth a king's ransom. I could not possibly accept that responsibility. And it would be very hard to say who deserves a finder's fee when we all have searched. Should they be found, and I still have doubts about that, I might like a sapphire or two as keepsakes, to go with the one my mother left us, but other-wise, they should be included as part of the manor inheritance."

"Arguing over what we do not have is not useful. What is it the men are keeping from us?" Elsa asked. "I saw them whispering over whiskey. They've learned something, unless they're scheming ways to be rid of the curate."

"You were so busy fretting over whether Anne would take the roast out in time, I didn't think you'd noticed," Clare teased.

Elsa was having some difficulty adjusting to being a lady instead of hiding in the kitchen as cook. She still spent a great deal of time below stairs, teaching her assistants, creating menus, and overseeing her more difficult recipes. But if the lady wanted to spend time with her fiancé, she had to partici-pate in family affairs.

Elsa could not replace the older sister Clare had lost to an Egyptian riot, but she was enjoying her cousin's sensible company and hoped Elsa would someday learn to leave the kitchen.

"I tend to notice if Jack is not talking to me about his search for the perfect stallion for his new stable," Elsa said dryly. "And they were *whispering*, not shouting as they do over how the army should stop Napoleon."

"Bones." Lavender spoke unexpectedly. "Arnaud is learning about the orchard. One of the trees toppled in the spring rain, and there were bones in its roots."

"And you know this how?" Clare set aside her volume to study her younger cousin.

The fashion-obsessed adolescent shrugged. "People gossip. A worker tells his wife, his wife tells her neighbor, and soon, my sewing circle is abuzz. They'll imagine entire skeletons and the ghosts of prior earls before long."

Clare rolled her eyes. "I did not think there were that many people left in the village to gossip." Her thoughts momentarily wandered to her novel and how she might use this scene. . . when another thought occurred. "How long ago did they discover the bones?"

Lavender waved her hand casually. "Oh, I think the first ones turned up a week or so ago. They've been digging up more ever since."

"And no one has told us?" Meera was irate. She set aside her book as if to storm off to demand explanations.

"I don't think Arnaud has mentioned it to anyone until recently. The sewing ladies have been whispering for a week, but they didn't have any confirmation either. We are not privy to the minds of men."

Clare did not speak what she was thinking.

The Uptons and the fraudulent Duncan Reid both arrived as soon as the rumors had spread.

FOUR

Patience brushed away the bees buzzing around the scarf she'd draped over her straw hat and returned to clipping back the rhododendron. She'd already cut baskets of lilacs for her mother to deliver to the village ladies she remembered from her prior residence. Strangled by vines, the rhododendrons were past their prime. She could attack them with a vengeance.

She often took out her anger at herself on shrubbery. It was quite satisfying to wallop a towering bush into place while castigating herself for being so hen-hearted. The handsome gentleman had *flirted* with her yesterday. He'd brought her sweets and offered a walk in the gallery and what had she done? Sat there like a great lump of coal.

Yes, of course, he was a French rake no doubt following the tradition of seducing the parson's spinster daughter. Since she'd developed a great heaving bosom at the tender age of fourteen, she'd been fending off scoundrels. He could scarcely have seen what she'd hidden, though. She assumed he must be bored and not actually tempted by lust. But since she had no intention of falling for Mr. Lavigne's charms, she could have at least taken the opportunity to see an art gallery!

Humming an uplifting psalm, she stepped higher on the ladder and swung her hand shear to scale the bush down to a manageable height. In the opening she cleared, she could see her father speaking with a lanky man in farmer's attire. Her father appeared his usual imperturbable self. The farmer scowled. In curiosity, she strained to hear.

"Just because I left the village does not mean you do not owe the tithes you promised, Mr. Bartholomew," her father said in the implacable manner he used to empty the pockets of his parishioners. Curates earned only a tiny salary, a minuscule percentage of the parish's tithes. Beyond that, they lived on the generosity of others. "You committed a grievous sin, and you must atone in this lifetime, unless you wish to suffer in the next."

"You're naught but a money-sucking parasite, Upton!" the man protested. "It was self-defense, and you know it."

Oh, dear. Her father was at it again. No wonder he'd insisted on returning to Gravesyde—where he knew everyone and all their sins. They'd have chicken on the table tonight and lamb on the morrow, if he made his rounds of all the village's sinners. He wasn't collecting *tithes*.

Fortunately, there did not appear to be many folk left for him to extort.

She ducked back down, but her tattered fichu caught in an unclipped branch. Tugging fiercely at the stupid fabric with one hand, holding the shear and the ladder in the other, she tottered.

An aging rung split, throwing her and the ladder off balance.

"Miss Upton!" a male voice cried in alarm.

Startled, she lost her precarious grip and tumbled backward, directly into the arms of the charming Frenchman.

Her concealing scarf continued clinging to the top of the triumphant rhododendron.

While grateful that he'd prevented a nasty fall, she flushed at what she'd bared and hastily struggled from his hold. The instant she was on her feet, she swung around to face the shrubbery, attempting the impossible task of pulling her bodice over her cleavage.

The gentleman's elegant coat landed on her shoulders, and blushing more that he'd noticed, she tugged the fabric about her with a sigh of relief, which immediately broadened the gap of the lapels. "I hate me," she muttered, attempting to right a tailored coat not meant to fit her shape.

"So in an attempt to rid yourself of yourself, you flung yourself backward into the abyss, all flags flying?" he asked in amusement, placing one foot on the rickety ladder and reaching up to retrieve her fichu. His waistcoat was a lovely blue satin in the back, prettier than anything she owned.

"I apologize for disturbing your morning walk, Mr. Lavigne." Stiffly, she attempted to hold the coat, take the fichu, and dispose of the shear at the same time. "But I do not thank you for frightening me into your arms."

That was churlish of her, but she wasn't feeling particularly appreciative. Or even pleasant. She still wanted to shoot the bushes and anyone standing. Humiliation washed over her, on top of the already ingrained mortification that seethed inside her at all times.

"Ah, yes, I can see how my using your name might be a terrifying experience. My sincere apologies, Miss Upton." His amusement was evident in his voice. She did not need to turn to see it in his expression. "Are you quite all right? That bush seemed to be winning the battle."

Without a word of warning, he picked up a shearing knife, climbed the unbroken bottom rungs, and whacked all the new growth down to a reasonable height. He then moved the ladder to the next section and proceeded to repeat the process —in his shirtsleeves.

Patience lost her tongue watching masculine muscles beneath thin linen and a silk waistcoat. She'd thought the

Frenchman slender compared to the other men at the manor, but. . . She gulped. His shoulders must be twice the size of his hips.

She glanced down at herself. It wasn't her *shoulders* that were twice the size of her hips. She hastily attempted to fluff up the torn muslin scarf and tuck it in securely, but it was quite destroyed.

"You should not be ruining. . ." she finally dared to speak, but he waved her to silence, holding a finger to his lips.

She could hear her father speaking on the other side of the hedge. Could she simply evaporate now? Could she be any more mortified?

She took the coat off and held it out in hopes that he would climb down. She would have flung it at him, but she feared he'd fall while catching it, and that would be her fault too.

Looking down on her, Mister Lavigne's eyes danced with amusement. Not lust, she noted. Amusement. He dropped back to the ground to don his coat. In a hushed voice, he asked, "Is that how your father persuades his parishioners to their duties? Extortion?"

"Persuasion," she said through gritted teeth. "People do not voluntarily contribute to the betterment of all. To be fair, when the church is prosperous, he gives his largesse to the needy."

"A different form of trade." He nodded his understanding. "Do you know this Blackstone he argues with?"

She shook her head. "I remember few people here from my childhood."

He tugged his short-tailed country coat into place and indicated the pails of flowers she'd gathered. "I have come to ask what I might trade for some of your bouquets. The ladies admired their beauty yesterday. The manor grounds are somewhat. . . neglected."

"Oh." He actually had a purpose here besides embarrassing her. Naturally. "They might have them for nothing. I hate seeing them go to waste, but the chapel is scarcely ready for adornment, and these bushes simply had to be cut back. I thought perhaps I could make some sachets with the blooms."

"Sachets?" His dark eyes lit with interest. "The pretty things ladies put with their clothes to always smell of spring?"

She watched him warily. He did not seem to be poking fun at her. He even lifted a lilac bloom to sniff it appreciatively. What manner of man was this? "Yes. I save scraps from our sewing to make pouches for the dried petals, add a few herbs and things to preserve them. . ."

He beamed as if she'd just given him sunshine and roses. "Most excellent! I shall trade you my services as an incompetent gardener shearing back these bushes, if you will provide me with sachets I might sell to my customers."

Too shocked to be shy, she gaped at him. The gentleman did not seem to be the least abashed by offering physical labor in return for her meager pouches of dead blooms. "Customers?" was all she managed to ask.

"I am a peddler," he said proudly, testing the rickety ladder and moving it to the next bush. "I will sell your sachets for coins that will allow me to buy other trinkets and pocket the profit for my humble bank account."

"But. . ." Gentlemen did not work for a living! A peddler? Patience shook her head, ridding herself of the cobwebs her brainpan must have accumulated in cleaning. "You are the son of a French count, the ladies said."

He shrugged his impressive shoulders and removed half a foot of vine and bramble. "There are no more counts or kings, just death and poverty. Someday, perhaps, France will emerge from ruin to become a new frontier like the Americas. But for now, we must eat."

She had never properly given thought to how French

refugees must survive after fleeing their homes. Her father's parishes were very small and isolated. She had never met anyone from outside the country. People struggled to survive everywhere. How did one do so without a home? At least, Mr. Lavigne spoke English. How would one survive without knowing the language, having no home. . . ?

The handsome gentleman became a little more real. "But surely, if you are related to Captain Huntley, you need not worry about food on the table?" She could not stand here watching him work. She picked up her buckets.

"They cannot put clothes on my back. A man must contribute his share, as you say, to the benefit of all. I am not very good at much except trading. I am very good at that. How many sachets will trimming this hedge be worth to you?"

This was the most unusual conversation she'd ever had with a gentleman. She completely forgot to be shy or miserable while trying to work the numbers in her head. She had only sold sachets at village fairs to support the church. She supposed this was not much different. She named a number.

He nodded agreement. "Eminently fair. We will see how much ladies will pay for them and perhaps come to a different agreement later. I will set on my journey on Monday, if you can have a few samples prepared by then?"

"It takes time to dry the petals, but I should be able to do that. You really mustn't do too much from that ladder. I'll ask Paul if you might borrow the one he is using to reach the roof." Which was where her father *ought* to be, not bilking poor people of their meager possessions.

SWEAT DAMPENING HIS NECK, HENRI LOOSENED HIS LINEN, NOT daring to discard his neckcloth with the jacket he'd long since cast aside. The *demoiselle* had not returned with a new ladder, but he did not want to embarrass her more if she should.

A parson's daughter had fallen into his arms like an angel from heaven to shatter his simple life.

Towns were filled with willing women. Suddenly, none of their charms compared to those of the lovely Miss Upton. *Mon Dieu*, beneath that diffident demeanor and virginal innocence, she hid a bounteous beauty most women would have displayed proudly. Insanely, her modesty appealed to him.

This woman deserved a respect he could not afford.

Parson's daughter, he reminded himself. Proud and proper female who probably quoted scripture and was very dull indeed. He'd recover soon enough.

He whacked the bushes with frustration. It wasn't as if any decent woman would look twice at a homeless, itinerant peddler. Not that he was looking for a decent woman, he reminded himself. A *convenient* woman would be useful about now.

Speaking of women. . . The angry one on the other side of the hedge did not shout, but she conveyed a level of repressed fury none of the curate's other parishioners had exhibited. Even the curate kept his voice down so Henri could not make out the words. A personal problem, perhaps?

"Leave, ye old fool, stay away as ye were paid to do." Her last words carried as a black bonnet and shawl stalked away.

Interesting.

It wasn't many minutes later that angry voices again rose from beyond the hedge. This time, the curate spoke rather sharply for a man of peace. Unashamed of eavesdropping, Henri continued trimming. After all, he was being paid in sachets. A man had to perform his duties.

"I told you, I don't have anything to give, you old bastard!" a deep bass shouted.

Henri couldn't place the voice. Perhaps one of the farmers Hunt had lured back with promises of work?

"Then give your time," the curate advised, using a paternalistic voice now. "Everyone must pay a penance for their sins. They are uncovering the bones as we speak. Both the church and the parsonage are in need of repairs. If you will lend a hand for an hour each day, the world shall be a better place."

Henri's ears sharpened. This was the man who knew about the bones?

"Better for you, mayhap!" the man roared. "My time pays for a roof over my own head!"

"Would you like me to explain the danger your soul is in?" Upton asked in a decidedly unctuous manner.

"No, damn your hide, you know I don't believe in such! You're no better than a thief. I don't have to take this. Go ahead. Prove it." The unseen man didn't appear around the hedge but apparently stormed off in a different direction.

That was a considerable amount of ill will with which to start a new position. Well, return to an old one, as it were. How did the old curate know the sins of others? As far as Henri was aware, the Anglican church did not hold confession. He now had a new perspective on the priests of his youth. Had they used this sort of extortion?

He should have a word with Hunt about their potential new curate—before someone decided it would be easier to rid the village of the old man rather than bend to his will.

And then they needed to learn more about the bones.

FIVE

"I'VE FINALLY FOUND A MATCHED PAIR," JACK TOLD THE MEN lingering over whiskey after dinner. "The mare is already breeding. I should have more time to work on that map now."

Hunt grimaced and studied the odd collection of lines and notes that didn't constitute any kind of map with which he was familiar.

From one of his journeys, Henri had brought back a unique adjustable eyeglass Hunt could use for his one eye, one that magnified at different sizes. He was still learning its uses, but being able to read the fine print on a map was a relief after these past months of fearing he'd never read one again.

Not that the earl's eccentric map had any print. The bumpy square resembled a child's drawing.

"We cannot tell from this whether we're looking at the attic over the new wings or the old or if it is even this manor," Hunt argued. "All we can tell is that there is a great deal of space instead of rooms and that there is an X *outside* of the wall. It doesn't make sense."

"All the attics have a great deal of open space," Arnaud pointed out. "If the map maker was the earl, he might have been too old to remember how servants' rooms or school-rooms are situated and just left them out. The X could be in one of the undrawn chambers. What is to our benefit is that the viscountess did not make any changes to the manor's interior, so we don't have to beware of new walls or anything of the sort."

"It's either that or we have necklaces dangling in the vines outside the house," Jack complained. "Where are the windows?"

"The earl might have not been in full possession of his faculties when he drew this," Walker reminded them.

Hunt grunted at his friend's admonition. "I'm persuaded the old man simply meant to taunt his heirs. I am more interested in what we are to do about our new curate and the church. The women will chew off our ankles until we decide."

He would start gnawing off his own body parts if they did not settle this marriage business soon. He spent too much time imagining Clare in his bed as it was. Once he'd bedded her, then perhaps he could have his mind back. He wondered if Walker felt the same, or if he was simply making a marriage of convenience.

Henri cut up an old apple and ignored the map. "I have learned we are in the Bishop of Hereford's district. We might have to write there to verify Mr. Upton has the curacy to this parish."

"Hereford?" Hunt groaned. "Learning church districts is as bad as learning county ones. Hereford is way down in another county. We can't expect to take up residency there for a month!"

"Visiting the archbishop for a special license might be easier," Henri agreed. "From what I've heard, Mr. Upton has most likely lost every position he ever had for extortion."

"Extortion? Whom is he extorting and why?" Hunt wasn't entirely certain he wanted to know. He'd agreed to act as magistrate for this tiny exclave, but he hated being judge and jury.

Henri shrugged. "The curate threatened a man with bones being uncovered and his soul being in danger."

Hunt groaned. "The man could have been a lazy gravedigger."

Henri nodded but continued, "His victim told him to prove it, so he doesn't sound too concerned. I cannot precisely blame Upton for not waiting until people volunteer their aid. He has a family to house, after all. But it's odd that he's returned after all these years, provided he is who he says he is."

"Clare would say that he is here to claim any inheritance due to his wife. I'm more inclined to believe the bones have left someone ripe for extortion." Not wanting to hear more, Hunt stood. "Unless you can identify his victim, we should join the ladies to work this out. Or forget the entire matter and enjoy the evening."

"Play charades?" Arnaud asked cynically, standing. "I shall leave you to it. I have an actual commission and would like to finish before Henri leaves on Monday."

To Hunt's dismay, the ladies had not lingered in the parlor. He strode down the main corridor, checking various workplaces for the women, finding nothing.

Walker joined him on the marble stairs, looking equally puzzled. "Blue salon?"

"We'd hear them, but perhaps they're all reading." Hunt strode up the stairs with only a twinge from his injured knee. These months of exercise had greatly improved the torn muscles. At least Clare wouldn't be marrying a cripple, for what little that might be worth.

He noticed Walker didn't offer to return to his office to write the rector. Did that mean he wasn't eager for a clergyman or that he was more eager to see Meera? This courting business was awkward.

They found Oliver's tutor reading a volume on mathematics in the blue salon. At Hunt's question, Mr. Birdwhistle nodded toward the ceiling. "I believe the ladies are on a treasure hunt. I said I would sit here until Miss Knightley returns so I might see that Master Oliver remains in bed."

Given her nephew's tendency to roam, Hunt appreciated the tutor's willingness to help outside the schoolroom. He thanked the young man and returned to the hall where he hoped one day to install additional lighting. The flickering oil lamps did not suit his limited vision.

"Upstairs or back to work?" he asked Walker in resignation.

"Upstairs. It is always entertaining to hear what new theory they've developed. And we have yet to take a good look at the new wings. If only the village had more visitors, we could turn the east wing into an inn. It's useless otherwise." Walker started for the attic stairs.

"Unless one populates the manor with children and staff," Hunt reminded him. "They tend to demand rooms other than the nursery."

"Meera will need a nursery come autumn," Walker reminded him. "The manor will be its own village should we hire everyone we need."

"Or the bank will own it by winter," Hunt corrected. "I think we can win any lawsuit over the fraudulent deeds and erroneous mortgage documents, but it will drag on forever and legal fees must be paid out of our empty pockets."

Walker didn't reply. It was a weight they both carried. The treasure hunt wasn't entirely purposeless.

CLARE FINALLY MANAGED TO SEPARATE MEERA FROM THE OTHERS so they might talk privately, as they once had when it had been just them. Her friend was *enceinte* and really shouldn't be climbing stairs or around attics, but curiosity won out.

"Do you have something you would like to tell me?" she whispered as Meera helped her measure a room using an old pole Hunt had marked up. "Like why you and Walker want a church?" She examined the copy of the map they'd made and tried to determine if the shape matched the storage room where they worked.

Meera noted the measurement and did the calculations to compare it to the map's dimensions. She didn't look up—a certain sign that she feared disapproval. "Walker has asked me to marry him so the babe will have a name. I have agreed. We don't want a child to feel unwanted as Lavender does."

"Your child will never be unwanted!" Clare protested. "Marriage is for a lifetime. Can you come to love Walker? What happens if he wishes to return to America?"

"It's not as if I haven't asked myself those same questions," her friend replied defensively. "And given that I thought I loved a scoundrel, I cannot think I'm a proper judge of emotion. But Walker is a good partner. He has no interest in stealing from me."

The father of Meera's child had turned out to be a blackguard who only wanted her pharmacopeia and had turned violent when she'd run away with it. Meera had reason to be cautious.

Clare pounded a little harder against the wall, seeking a hollow place. How did one ask the hard questions that Meera and Walker surely had asked themselves? "Do you think the curate will consent to marrying a Jew and an African?"

Meera looked up and beamed. "Walker researched the law in a book from the library. If he claims to be Jewish, we do not even have to have banns read, since we do not belong to your church. We just need the registry and the certificate."

"It might be a little hard to convince anyone that Walker is Jewish," Clare said dryly. "But then, I cannot feature how they could argue either. It's not as if we could produce a rabbi."

"Exactly." With satisfaction, Meera began measuring the next wall. "All we want is to have the marriage registered so the baby has a name."

"And you don't anticipate a marriage bed?" Clare daringly asked, knowing her friend's passionate nature.

Meera cleared her throat. "That will not be a problem. He is quite good."

Oh dear. Clare didn't know what to say to that. It wasn't as if Meera could get with child *again*. And if she was already a fallen woman in the eyes of society. . . "Just don't let Lavender know," she finally said. "She mimics everything we do."

From across the dormitory area, Elsa cried in frustration, "None of these measurements match the drawing, Whoever drew it did not measure anything, I'm quite convinced."

Heavy boots on the stairs warned that the men had discovered them. Clare stood and dusted herself off. Meera finished her calculations and waved the page at Walker when he entered. "Elsa is right. The dimensions do not match here or in the wings."

"You don't think we've already checked that?" Hunt asked in exasperation.

"The earl must have been soft in the head," Jack declared. "Or the map is for one of the manors he sold."

Henri took the sketch and turned it around in his hands. "Could it be for outside? The gallery or the great hall? I know the dimensions are wrong, but if he was just sketching, he has drawn a large open space with a few alcoves. They could be anywhere if he didn't measure."

"I don't want to hear that," Clare said with a sigh. "It looks so simple. Has anyone had any luck in translating the other codes in the paintings? Perhaps we need them all."

"We're working on it," Walker promised. "There just aren't enough hours in the day to play at puzzles."

So very true, Clare had to acknowledge. Just finding time to work on her novel was a challenge. And then there was persuading the men to *talk* to them. . .

Taking Hunt's arm, she led the way toward the stairs. "And what have you decided to do about the bones in the orchard?" She loved the way they all squirmed when she dropped conversational bombs. Men! One would think they believed they were the only ones with ears in their heads.

"It's no doubt an old graveyard from priory times," Jack said dismissively. "They should be reburied in a proper cemetery. We won't need a coffin for that, will we?"

Elsa rapped him over the head with her copy of the sketch. "Should we not determine if they are new or old bones first? Meera, can you do that?"

Clare almost laughed at the collective masculine sighs of frustration when her apothecary friend agreed to take a look.

SIX

ON SUNDAY, PATIENCE'S FATHER HELD HIS FIRST SERVICE UNDER the almost-repaired roof of the chapel. She crossed her gloved hands in her homespun skirt. If she hid in the transept, she was out of sight of the rest of the parishioners. There used to be a small altar, candles, and flowers there. Now there was naught but a gaping hole in the floor she covered with her big boots.

Her mother had produced one of her embroidered altar cloths in green for the days of Pentecost. Lilac bouquets filled the musty room with the fresh scent of spring.

Her hands itched to dig in the soil, but she needed to till the ground first. She'd managed to remove the worst of the vines and brambles, but the soil needed improving after the spring rains.

She'd heard the words of the sermon a thousand times, enough to know her father hadn't started tippling before he began. He swore he'd quit once they settled here. Perhaps he might, as long as her saintly big brother was around to ease the pressure. After that. . .

She sighed and studied the congregation. Along with their servants, the ladies had come down from the manor, even the

Jewish one, interesting. Only two of the gentlemen had accompanied them: the tall captain and his slender cousin, Mr. Lavigne. She tried not to study the Frenchman as he dutifully listened to the Anglican prayers, but he had such a lively expression!

She tore her gaze away to survey the women of the village. She did not know them yet, but there seemed to be a good representation. She hoped their gloves were thick enough to avoid splinters in the hastily resurrected benches. Paul had been working night and day to put the chapel to rights. Unlike their father, her brother never allowed a minute to go to waste.

Only a few men from the village attended, and their expressions were sour. Patience sighed. She knew her father achieved a great deal of good with his methods, but they did create an atmosphere of hostility. She fought an uneasy shudder.

After services, while her father greeted his flock on the church steps, Patience slipped out the back door leading to the parsonage.

Mr. Lavigne was studying the rough patch of ground she'd cleared for her garden. He glanced up as she attempted to skirt through the shrubbery, and his expression lit from inside. She could not put it any other way. Her foolish heart opened with a missish joy she did not experience in church.

"Miss Upton, is this your garden? You have accomplished so much in so few days! I am ashamed of my remissness in my duties. I should have done this so you need not harm your fair hands."

Fair hands, indeed. Callused, grimy, overlarge, mayhap, but fair had naught to do with her hands. That took the air out of her bubble of joy. She regarded him with suspicion. "The sachets are almost ready. What may I do for you, sir?"

"I must find ways to be useful," he reminded her. "If I till your soil, will you reward me with some of the produce when it is ready? And then you might be free to accomplish tasks I cannot."

She blinked. She was familiar with neighbors trading favors. And her father had certainly taught them all how to pry coins and food out of one hand to feed another. But no one had ever addressed her directly about her own tasks. She had simply learned that the more she accomplished, the more there was to do. To be offered a trade of tasks. . .

She thought of her poor blistered hands and considered options, but they all required hard labor when what she wanted was access to the manor library. And orchard.

"I cannot think what other task I might take on," she admitted, forgetting to be shy. Her old pelisse covered her decently, so she did not fret over her appearance. "I am not good at needlework. I can teach children their letters, but you have no use of that. Gardening is what I do."

He nodded solemnly, as if pondering the dilemma. "But delicate ladies such as yourself should direct beasts of burden, not work as one! I cannot easily sell your flowers, but if you have produce—berries, perhaps?"

"There used to be strawberries and blackberries. I've not had time to see if any vines still live. I was only eight when we were here last." Reminded of former delights, she lifted her best Sunday skirt and crossed the wet grass to a weed patch lost in ivy.

He followed. But he seemed as interested as she in uncovering treasure, so she lost herself in the hunt. She crouched down to dig among the leaves and vines. "Look. Here is a strawberry leaf. Here are more. It's probably too late for this spring, but if I can clear this back—"

With a strength she didn't possess, he ripped out a large handful of ivy from the damp soil, uncovering a variety of weeds and a few struggling strawberry plants. "Like so?"

She attempted to imitate his yank and nearly fell on her bottom when a long root came loose from the muddy soil. He caught her elbow, and together, they merrily ripped and tore to uncover the bed.

By the time the manor ladies discovered them, they were both covered in dirt and weed stains.

"Strawberries!" Mr. Lavigne crowed at the ladies" exclamations. He pointed out the cleared bed and the few straggling plants, one or two even bearing tiny green berries, as if he had discovered gold. "Miss Upton has the magic to turn this waste into wealth!"

That was overstating the situation dramatically.

Miss Knightley studied the greenery with doubt. "I am a city girl. I have only seen strawberries in baskets or on the table. But if they can be raised from mud—"

"We could pay Miss Upton for her produce out of the fund that feeds us, correct?" Mr. Lavigne asked in excitement. "And there may be other treasures buried in here of which we are unaware."

The brown-skinned lady nodded. "I have only grown vegetables and herbs, but if you can recognize summer fruit among the weeds, it would be wonderful for all. I wish we knew more of the trees the earl planted."

There it was, the opportunity Patience longed to grasp. . . But tongue-tied and shy, she did not know how to reach out and take what she wanted.

"Do you know aught of orchards?" Mr. Lavigne asked, as if reading her mind.

Patience nodded, still searching for words, intimidated by the ladies in their graceful gowns and pretty slippers. Although they did seem to be wearing pattens, didn't they?

She took a deep breath, felt the Frenchman's gaze drop to her breasts, and cursed herself. She'd forgotten to be self-conscious until now.

Nodding stupidly, she adjusted her bonnet scarf to better conceal her pelisse bodice. "Lady Reid allowed me to follow the gardeners, and I have worked in orchards since," she finally managed to say, without saying what she wanted.

"So you're familiar with what is growing on the hill?" the plump lady cook in a lace-covered pelisse asked. "I am desperate to know what we can expect come fall. I could order jars. . ."

Jars, she understood. "The kitchen used to put up fifty jars of applesauce and released the rest to the village. The nuts depended on the crop size. Lady Reid mostly sold those to pay the labor, I believe. They had a few cherry, plum, and pear trees, but I don't think they produced a great deal back then. I was a child, but everyone explained very patiently when I asked questions. The pear trees seem to be suffering though. There used to be books—"

Sighing, she cut herself off. The ladies wouldn't be interested in her chatter.

"The library has more books than one man can read," Mr. Lavigne declared. "You should come find the books and tell us of pears and plums. Education is a fine thing!"

Miss Knightley nodded. "I have always wished I was more knowledgeable in *useful* matters. If we are to return people to the village, we need to know everything. Please, visit our library and the orchard, tell us what to do, if you can."

Those words opened the clouds on her horizon and let the sun pour down. Patience bobbed a joyful curtsy and tried not to sound too eager. "If you don't mind? The trees need tending now, while we can see the problem spots."

For the first time since she'd met him, Mr. Lavigne's smile dimmed, and he looked hesitant. "Do we need to consult Hunt about. . ." He gestured helplessly.

"Bones?" Patience asked—impatiently. "It is all about the village. Do you think I've not seen untended graveyards before? My father has plans to bless the poor souls before they are reinterred."

48

"That is decided then," the lace-covered cook announced. "Miss Upton, we need your help. Please consider the manor open to you at any time."

"Especially since she is obviously family anyway," Miss Knightley said in that dry, pragmatic tone that demanded attention.

Oh dear. Patience winced.

～

AFTER CHURCH, HUNT PACED THE TREE-SHROUDED LANE LEADING to the chapel and parsonage. He'd done a bit of reading since the curate's arrival. He now had a grasp on the *perpetual curate* designation. If it was true that Upton had been appointed, then it was for a lifetime—and paid only what Upton received from some distant rector.

From the looks of the church and parsonage, any income from a benefice was not being spent here. If the curacy had lands to rent, they weren't being rented. Much of the land in the area lay fallow for lack of labor.

Given what he'd read, the chapel had no doubt once belonged to the priory, and hence, the manor. He had to assume the hovels were now his responsibility.

He finally caught the curate scurrying down the path, tugging off his vestments on the way.

"Upton, a word, if I might?" Hunt asked, stepping from the hedgerow and startling the man.

The curate stopped in his tracks and tugged at his neck-cloth. "Of course, my lord, I am at your disposal," he said, a trifle nervously.

"We have written to Hereford to verify your position," Hunt warned him first. "The villagers confirm your identity, but they cannot explain the fiduciary responsibilities involved in our positions."

Hastily fastening the buttons of his ancient coat, the curate nodded knowingly. "Of course, my lord."

"I am not a lord, Upton. I am a mere retired army captain. Please call me Mr. Huntley." The last thing he wanted to be was a lord. "Do you have any knowledge of how the church here is maintained?"

"Originally, in medieval times, it belonged to the priory. The monks provided liturgy for the churls here in the village rather than invite them inside their fine church. The first earl assumed full responsibility for the village chapel and built a parsonage after the reformation. History is complicated," he said apologetically.

The man knew history! So perhaps he wasn't quite the wastrel his red-veined, bulbous nose indicated. Hunt nodded for him to continue.

The curate gestured at the thatched cottage. "Centuries of progress took the earls away from this rural backwater to more prosperous locales, but they continued to support the chapel. I assume the rector or bishop has records. As I said the other night, after centuries, those funds are meager. The rector receives the rents, but he lives in Hereford. He hired me as his curate rather than make the journey."

"So the church is responsible for your salary?" Hunt found this system inefficient and in need of clarity.

"In theory, but the rector is responsible for a number of small churches. Since so many people left the village after Lady Reid died and the manor closed, he does not consider us worth funding." The curate looked rightfully frustrated.

"Ah, I begin to see. So you moved on to feed your family after the village deteriorated, and now you're back. Why?" That had been the question Clare had posed.

Upton waved his pudgy hand dismissively. "Politics. The church is as political as parliament. My family has fond memories of Gravesyde, and this is my assigned flock. Now that they are returning, so must I."

Hunt still didn't have much confidence in the unctuous curate, but if Upton was legally appointed, he would suffice to register a marriage. "The trust we inherited from the late earl only mentions maintaining the manor. But if the church and parsonage are manor property, then they are our responsibility. Maintenance does not cover your salary, of course, unless we hire you for repairs."

The clergyman's rheumy eyes lit with relief. "Caretaker, sir. We are caretakers of the property. My daughter has already done a tremendous job on the landscaping, and my wife is a domestic goddess. My boy has repaired one roof and will start the other tomorrow. If they might be paid for their services. . ."

"I will speak with the solicitors, of course. The ladies wish to have services again. You maintain the parish registry and can perform marriages and baptisms and the sort?"

"Of course, of course." He brushed at a few dried tea stains on his coat. "I left the official register in Hereford and will be happy to retrieve it."

Hunt thought he looked a trifle anxious in making this declaration.

He hoped he'd receive a quick response from the rector. Parish records might tell them more of the orchard graveyard.

SEVEN

Henri returned from his peddling circuit on Wednesday afternoon, much sooner than usual. These days, he spent more time selling buttons, toys, and Arnaud's paintings to merchants in Birmingham than traveling the back roads. He enjoyed watching the seasonal changes in the countryside and talking with the farmers and merchants he met, but now that the manor was filling up, and he had his own bed and good company, he enjoyed coming home equally well.

Unfortunately, there wasn't much for him to do in Gravesyde. He had no particular talent beyond talking and no desire to hoe fields for a living. But the changes his new family created in the ancient manor inspired him. And the curate's daughter. . . Well, she was out of bounds, but it was like watching a shy fawn grow into a confident deer when she talked plants.

Drawing her out enough to make her talk of libraries and orchards had been entertaining, far more satisfying than casual flirtation.

As he drove his cart up the rutted manor drive in the late afternoon gloom, he studied a tall plume of smoke rising from one of the chimneys. They seldom set fires on a warm May day. Had the captain finally stoked the coal retort?

The stench emanating from the cellar as he drove the cart into the stable yard indicated something foul burned. The stable hands were so busy staring at the chimney that he had to tend to his own horse.

The plume of smoke died back as he crossed the yard. Entering the side door, he met no butler or footman. Had his cousin asphyxiated the servants?

He picked up his step entering the main corridor. . . and ran into the entire household gathered, staring at the wall. . . the oddly illuminated wall.

A single lamp attached to a pipe flickered and danced, throwing shadows and light across the dark hall nearest the parlor, at the base of the marble stairs.

"*Mon Dieu*, he's done it!" Henri stared in fascination just like everyone else.

"But will it explode?" Arnaud asked, warily studying the flame.

Henri smacked his brother's arm when the ladies expressed alarm. "Do oil lamps explode? They do not. It is no different. They have these all over Birmingham. They stink, that is all."

Hunt trudged in through the front vestibule, looking tired and filthy but triumphant. He nodded in satisfaction at his experiment, then traipsed back out muttering about piping.

"They lit Westminster Bridge a few years ago," Claire said. "It was a glorious sight. I never thought to see these *inside* a house!"

"I wonder if they'd be dangerous in the kitchen?" Lady Elsa wandered off, presumably back to her baking since she was covered in a wide apron and flour.

Henri enjoyed the inventiveness and the company, but when one was poor, money mattered more. He had a purse of coins and needed Walker's attention. Lavender's sewing and button ladies would be eager for payment once they turned away from the new marvel.

Predictably, always-eager Lavender woke first from her fascination with the lamp. "Henri! Did you bring me pretty muslins and more button forms?"

"The lads should be unloading the crates as we speak. You might direct them before the rain starts." He caught Walker's eye, and they departed to traipse down to the steward's office at the rear.

"Good trip?" Walker asked.

"Entertaining, as always. I found an outlet for Miss Upton's sachets. If we can manufacture them in larger quantities, it will provide a tidy profit. I don't think she is much interested in spending all her time sewing though." Henri jingled the purse in his pocket. "She might enjoy growing flowers to provide the scent."

"As we add seamstresses to Lavender's shop, we could set them to sewing the pouches during slow times. The key to bringing people back to the village is work. Every little bit helps." Walker took a seat at his desk and accepted the receipts Henri produced.

"Flowers in summer, fruits in fall, perhaps." Henri stacked the coins on the desk with the receipts.

"Only if we keep the manor, which requires keeping the village," Walker added, presumably so Henri didn't become too elated by his success.

He refused to be pessimistic. "What would anyone else do with this monstrous edifice? The maintenance alone costs a fortune, and that's without adequate staff. Just imagine having enough coin to keep it up without the trust fund!"

Walker shrugged. "Some folks have more money than sense. Others have wealthy trusts of their own. I prefer our idea of the manor as a source of income for the community as well as a roof over our heads. But I suppose if one is rich as

Croesus, a man might hire the entire village to slave for him."

Henri pushed a small portion of his coins across the desk. "That would pay the meager wages of a full staff for a year." He shoved another stack next to it. "This is what they have earned in a *month* our way. With this, they can soon afford to pay rents, should we ever fix up the houses to make them habitable." He picked up a few coins and put them in his pocket. "And I still get paid."

Walker nodded agreement. "The problem, of course, is that we're providing the gallery free of cost. If we ever had to charge rent. . ."

Henri shrugged. "We will earn more as we become known and our market grows. I have seen how they do it in town, start small and grow large. We can do it, if we wish."

Jack wandered in, still smelling of the horses he trained, his dark hair falling uncombed across his brow. "Did you find that hock salve I asked about?"

Henri nodded. "It's in the cart. Expensive. Are you sure you can't make your own?"

Walker spoke before Jack could. "You should ask Meera. The salves she uses for people are efficacious."

"Efficacious!" Henri crowed. "I like that word. I must remember to use it. My sales are very efficacious for putting coins in our pockets."

"Your glib tongue is very efficacious for making coins." Jack grinned. "You reading dictionaries to improve our education, Walker?"

The studious steward shrugged. "If a man does not continue learning, he may as well be dead."

"He does not want to appear to be an ignorant American," Henri whispered loudly. "I revel in being the ignorant Frenchman, but Walker is too proud."

Walker threw a paper wad at him. "Get out, the lot of you. I've books to prepare."

Henri wandered out in the company of a baron's horse-mad younger son, intending to find the horse salve. . . until he heard a familiar feminine voice. He slapped Jack on the back, directed him to the side entrance and cart, and continued to the small family parlor where the ladies entertained friends.

The manor had a formal withdrawing room but its furniture had been carted elsewhere.

Henri hid his delight at discovering Miss Upton balancing a teacup in a gloved hand while perching on the edge of a frayed silk chair, jumpy with discomposure. Clare glanced up at him in annoyance, rather like the older sister he'd never had. Except she was some years younger. The lady of the manor had higher standards than his.

Ignoring her disapproval, Henri bowed and remained in the doorway so her guest wouldn't flee. "Ladies, a pleasure! Miss Upton, you are *très élégant*. May I say your sachets were a great success? The merchants would like many more. We should discuss this when you have time."

Instead of being pleased, she widened her lovely periwinkle blue eyes in alarm. "More? It took me *two days* to make those!"

Pleased that he was learning the trick to keeping the lady from hiding her charms, he pulled the coins from his pocket. "I hope this is adequate recompense for your hard work." He set the coins on the table beside her.

Her eyes grew wide at the sum. "My sachets never earned that much!"

He grinned. "It is all in how one sells them. As I said, we should discuss this. I know you can grow the flowers, but you cannot possibly be expected to sew for a large order. There are others. . ."

"Miss Upton is a *lady*," Clare scolded. "She might make a few sachets for church bazaars, but she is not a seamstress. You should speak with Lavender."

Great-granddaughter of an earl, Miss Clarissa Knightley

had been raised as a lady who never lifted a hand to work. Lavender Marlowe was also a descendant, except her mother had been an unmarried maid. She had no family trust for support and must earn a living sewing. As a French egalitarian, Henri disdained the difference. But he would not offend Clare's sensibilities. . . too much.

"I will leave you ladies to the refinements. Perhaps there are not enough flowers to dry?" He put on his best concerned expression.

"There are always flowers in spring and summer," Miss Upton said impatiently. "And lovely leaves in autumn. That is not the problem. You would make more profit from the orchard, and you do not have enough labor to raise flowers *and* fruit."

Ah, the lady had a brain as well as beauty. Perhaps propounding his economic theories was not for polite company—

A rapping on the front door knocker, accompanied by the wild yanking of the bellpull interrupted any further discussion. Shouts ensued. Henri bowed out and hastened toward the enclosed vestibule at the front. The ladies would follow, no doubt, but he would be there to protect them from noisy intruders. As would his brother Arnaud, the massive butler Quincy, and his large footman son Adam. . . So, maybe he was not so necessary.

He did not catch all the visitor's words but heard Arnaud shout at him to find Meera. An accident then. Meera was as close to a physician as they would find anywhere outside Birmingham.

Henri dashed back to the infirmary where the little apothecary kept her herbs. She might be outside in the garden. . .

She'd apparently heard the shouts and his running footsteps and was already packing a bag. Henri helped her with her shawl and carried the bag as she unquestioningly followed him to the front, her brow furrowed in concern.

They arrived just in time to see the flutter of Miss Upton's ancient skirts as she ran out. Calling for her hat and shawl, Clare greeted them in relief.

"It's Mr. Upton. He's taken a fall. Henri, may we take your cart down so Meera doesn't have to run down the path?"

They'd just acquired a man of the cloth and a church, and they might lose him already?

In the gloom of a cloudy spring evening, Clare clung to Hunt's arm and tried not to weep as Meera pulled a sheet over Mr. Upton's large, prone form. They'd barely had time to meet him, had not even asked him to cry the first banns. And now. . . *his poor family*! What would they do?

Grimly, Miss Upton led her weeping mother inside the parsonage. Surrounded by a muttering crowd, the curate's son remained equally stony-faced. The poor man had yet to find his first position and now. . . he had a mother and sister to support. Ever creative, Clare wanted to solve the problem —except there were too many unanswered questions and a crowd to disperse.

"How did this happen?" Hunt demanded of the curate's son, looking up at the parsonage's thatched roof where presumably his father had been working. A ladder lay fallen across the shrubbery.

Paul—Mr. Upton—glanced at the villagers crowding around and gestured at the parsonage. "Perhaps we might go inside. . ." He nodded at his father's form beneath the linen. "Is there somewhere we can take him first?"

"Devil took him," one of the farmers said, spitting at the ground. "'Bout time." He strode off, muttering.

"Got what he deserved," a black-clad woman muttered, before hobbling off.

The others murmured among themselves. None came forward to help.

Clare shivered at the black cloud of—dislike? hatred?—emanating from the crowd. What had the garrulous old curate done to enrage an entire village?

The remaining women wrung their hands in their aprons, shook their heads, and glanced toward the parsonage. Clare assumed they wished to comfort the new widow. At least Mrs. Upton was held in respect.

The loss of the church just as they thought to have it back. . . It was as if hope had died. She couldn't restore hope, but she might disband the—mob? The male murmurs were becoming hushed, angry whispers. Another weeping old woman in black turned her back on the crowd and intelligently escaped to an ancient gig. Mobs could turn ugly.

Henri and young Mr. Upton lifted the body into Henri's cart. The crowd parted to let them pass.

Charity began at home. Clare called to Henri, "When you reach the manor, would you ask Lady Elsa if we might have a basket of food for the family's dinner?"

That stirred the women, at least. One of the older ones shook her husband's arm until he quieted. "The family didn't deserve this, they didn't. I'll bring down some rashers and bread for the morning. Annie, you've some eggs, do ye not?"

The women gradually wandered off, discussing meal arrangements. Clare elbowed Hunt and nodded in the direction of the men glaring at young Mr. Upton. The worrisome black cloud had not dispersed. "I think you need to listen to what they're thinking. There is animosity here."

Hunt sent her a puzzled look but unable to do anything else for the deceased, he crossed over to talk to one of the men he knew. Clare studied the position of the ladder and the roof but couldn't see how the man had managed to fall without grabbing at the uncovered rafters or loose thatch or some-thing. . . Nothing appeared disturbed.

Following Clare's gaze, Meera nodded understanding and slipped into the sideyard to examine the ladder.

One of the village women sidled up to Clare to whisper, "He didn't never go up that ladder. His son did all the work. Someone did for him, they did." She scurried away at a call from a man, presumably her husband.

Oh, dear, no, she didn't want to go through this again. First, the housekeeper, then that wretched gentleman on the road. . . One would think Gravesyde a thieves' den.

Keeping an eye on Hunt, who shook hands with rough farmers and slapped the new blacksmith on his broad shoul-ders, Clare crossed over to Meera. "They're already talking murder," she whispered.

"I think they're right," Meera said with a sigh of regret. "We found him face down. One does not easily fall off a ladder face down. It might be possible if he slid feet first from the thatch and simply knocked over the ladder on the way down. . . But the blow was to the back of his head, not the front, and he's lying parallel to the building. That doesn't make sense in any scenario."

"Except someone hitting him from behind while he was facing the backyard, not the roof. Oh, dear." Clare discreetly glanced around the narrow area between the parsonage wall and the overgrown hedge. The curate had been a relatively large man. "There isn't much room. If he wasn't working on the roof, why would he be here? He didn't have hedge clip-pers, did he?"

"I suppose they could have been taken, but I don't see any evidence of trimming." Meera stooped down to examine the trampled ground. "Too many people back here to pick out footprints."

They both studied the hedge wrapping around the yard.

"Only two ways in, where we just entered from the front

of the cottage, and possibly through a gate at the back." Clare glanced up. "Or perhaps over the roof?"

"Or from *inside* the parsonage," Meera added grimly.

The ladies had been at the manor. Where had young Mr. Upton been?

EIGHT

TOO SHOCKED TO THINK, PATIENCE HELD HER WEEPING MOTHER.
They'd only just come home. . .

In despair, she glanced around at the parsonage's meager
furnishings. Her mother had always made a home anywhere
they lived. Familiar pillows adorned the rotted horsehair sofa.
A colorful crocheted blanket lay folded over a rocking chair
they'd brought with them. Her mother's favorite porcelain
vase held the last of the forget-me-nots and tulips.

She thought she was weeping more for the loss of this
home than for her own father.

Paul finally entered, leading Captain Huntley and Miss
Knightley. She needed to fix tea. Releasing her mother,
Patience gathered her skirts, but the lady waved her to stay
seated. What should she do? Her mother needed tea. . .

The little apothecary entered behind them, glanced about,
and headed directly for the kitchen.

"Meera sent for some soothing herbs," the lady explained.
"She'll fix the tea. You just sit there and comfort your mother
while the men talk in the study."

"No." Nettie shook her head adamantly. "I want to hear
what is said. Sit here." She pointed at the empty sofa.

Paul grimaced but waited for the captain and his lady to take a seat, then settled in a cracked leather armchair. "I don't know where to start," he said.

Her brother was two years older than she, but lacking their father's impressive height and weight, he seemed very young and uncertain—and maybe a little frightened? She ignored a frisson of fear and contemplated their non-existent future.

Paul had an education and career. Patience did not, unless she could forge one here. Accustomed to thinking of only one day at a time, she fought to formulate her fear and hope into words.

As the apothecary carried in the tea, Patience let the words emerge. "Might we. . . Would it be all right if we stayed a while longer? Until we know. . ." She gestured helplessly. There was nothing to know. They had no other home.

"You are not to worry," Miss Knightley said firmly. "You are a welcome addition to our community, and we will not allow you to suffer. We will think of something."

Even though Patience fully comprehended how impractical that promise was, and that the lady was simply being nice, relief flooded through her. They had a little time. She accepted the teacup and sipped and tried to clear her head.

Her father was dead.

The man who had controlled their lives, uprooted them from one home after another, who kept them fed and housed on promises and lies. . . was no more.

Paul murmured polite phrases and accepted the tea with gratitude. Patience thought he might be more than a little intimidated by the physically imposing captain.

She had talked with Miss Knightley enough to know the lady was genuinely kind, if a bit brusque occasionally. She understood that. The lady had a lot of responsibility on her hands, but she meant well. The captain was an unknown factor.

"The village has been using the graveyard behind the manor," the captain said, setting aside his teacup once Mrs. Adams took a seat. "We will pay the gravediggers. There is a communal coffin. . ."

Paul vehemently shook his head. "I can make a coffin. It's the least I can do. We are strangers to you, and you have been all that is kind. We can't take charity."

"As I told your father, we believe the late earl's trust is responsible for the chapel and the parsonage. We will reimburse you for all your efforts to restore them. We really do wish to have a clergyman here, and for that, we need the church." The captain said that with almost a growl, obviously unhappy about the situation.

"Let us stick to funeral arrangements for now," Miss Knightley said gently. "There is too much to take in for the moment. How long will it take to make a coffin? Give us a time so we may arrange the gravediggers."

"You may not find anyone willing." Her mother finally spoke, wiping at her eyes. "My husband was not well-liked."

And there it was, the enormous specter overshadowing the room.

"He did what he had to do, Mother," Paul remonstrated.

Miss Knightley rose. "He was a man of the cloth and deserves our respect. The grave shall be dug, if we must do so ourselves. Let us leave so you may mourn in private. Miss Upton, if you would visit at your convenience, we'll talk about the future."

The future? She had none. Not yet. But her resolve was firm.

Patience saw the company to the door. Once they'd departed, she turned to her family. "I don't wish to leave Gravesyde Priory."

Her mother wept. "I don't want to lose you!"

Paul stood and uncovered her father's hidden brandy

bottle. "I'm not leaving until I know who murdered our father. I'll write the rector at once."

Murdered? Patience gulped and let the possibility nagging at the back of her mind emerge. Paul was right, her father couldn't fall off a roof he'd never been on.

HUNT TRIED TO ADMIRE THE BRIGHT GLEAM OF HIS NEW GASLIGHT as he descended the marble stairs before dinner. Unfortunately, he knew how much work it would take to run piping throughout the house, and that his retort had only the most rudimentary filters. More experimentation was required—for which he billed the trust. If the bank took the manor away, he'd have a small nest egg set aside, at least.

He would not have time for retorts and piping while planning funerals and. . . investigating murders, apparently.

Everyone gathered in the shabby family parlor before dinner for drinks and conversation. He'd come to enjoy these moments. They didn't replace an evening in the tavern with his fellow soldiers, but he was learning to appreciate the insights of ladies. So he had to listen when Meera and Clare insisted that the vicar had been murdered. He didn't have to like it.

"Captain, you will write whoever in your church can hire the young Mr. Upton as our curate?" Meera asked the moment he entered.

The women had been plotting.

"It's the perfect answer." Clare handed him his snifter of brandy. "His poor mother and sister will not have to move again, and we can cry the banns immediately!"

Jack lifted his brandy glass in salute. "I shall ride into the next county and meet this rector personally, if that will speed the process. I can even castigate him for neglecting the souls of Gravesyde's parishioners and admonish him for allowing a poor scholar to go hungry if he does not provide him this opportunity. Although I daresay any salary attached to the chapel is minimal."

"Ask him why the late Mr. Upton turned in his register and left in the first place," Clare added dryly.

Well, he should have guessed that everyone was more concerned about marriage than murder. Hunt kept his chuckle to himself. He was far more interested in that as well. He'd never been averse to the married state. He'd simply never found an opportunity—or the right woman. Now he had a woman, he still didn't have the opportunity.

"Perhaps you'd best not mention the possibility that the last curate was killed when you demand a new one," he suggested, sipping the brandy he'd poured.

"Murdered?" Henri glanced up from his conversation with Walker. "Upton was murdered?"

"It appears so." Meera nibbled at one of the crackers Elsa baked at Hunt's behest. "If I were to conjecture, he was to meet someone in that rather hidden side yard, perhaps in hope of gaining one of his extortion payments. When he prepared to depart, that person hit him over the head with a hard object. It may only have been in anger or frustration, but the blow was vicious enough to crack the skull. We do not know how long he lay there, but it was enough to cause brain bleeding and possibly led to heart failure. Without a surgeon who might perform an autopsy, we shall never know."

Henri ran his hand through his thick curls. "*Mon Dieu*, that poor family. A monster with such a temper should not roam the streets!"

Hunt added cheese to a cracker and sipped his brandy before replying. "I talked to some of the people gathered there and made a note of their names. As Clare pointed out at the time, there was a good deal of hostility toward the curate. They were not exactly mourning his demise. But other than to mention that they heard father and son arguing, they did not trust me with their secrets."

"I'm here to attest that fathers and sons argue," Jack offered. "I will not believe Paul killed his father over a squabble. I can talk to the stable lads. They gossip like old ladies."

"One of those old ladies suggested murder," Clare offered. "And another had harsh words. Perhaps I should learn who they are."

Henri angrily threw back his whiskey. "I overheard the curate several times. He appeared to be doing what the Scots call *blackmailing,* extorting protection money from his parishioners to cover past sins. The only name I heard mentioned, though, was Blackstone. He threatened another with bones. The only one I saw, though, was an old woman in a black bonnet. She could have been anyone."

Hunt frowned. "A woman would need a long arm or a long weapon. He was tall. I suppose it's conceivable but seems unlikely."

Adam, the six-foot-plus footman, announced that dinner was served. They moved as an informal group to take their usual places in the main dining room.

Still tidying her hair, Lady Elsa hurried from the kitchen to join them. "Have we discussed replacing Mr. Upton yet?"

Marriage was the main subject on the lady's mind. Hunt understood that. He was equally frustrated.

He let Jack handle his bride-to-be, while he turned to Clare. "How is Oliver settling in with the tutor? I see he has been persuaded to eat in the schoolroom?"

"They go along famously. I have told Mr. Birdwhistle that he might join us, but he is more interested in teaching Oliver not to eat under the table."

Hunt snorted. "That only works if there is just the two of them. If we introduce him to a table with strangers, he'll be gone again."

Clare's nephew was only seven, but in Hunt's estimation,

Oliver was on the genius end of the scale. Child prodigies often did not fare well in communal situations. The boy had come a long way these past months, but he still did not socialize.

Clare nodded agreement. "I know, but we must start somewhere. I think he does well when there is only a few of us, but all of us at once. . ." She glanced down the table of laughing, chattering family and friends. "He is too young yet."

Hunt nodded at the far end of the table where his unattached French cousins dug into the provisions with gusto. As penniless refugees, they'd gone without for too long not to appreciate the hearty fare Elsa provided. "We do not need the boy about when discussing murder. Henri seems exceedingly grim."

On his left hand, Meera glanced up from her conversation with Walker. "He would be the best of us to make inquiries in the village. The idea of a killer wandering the street gives me cold shivers." Since she had recently been stalked by her angry lover, the pragmatic apothecary had a right to fear.

Walker covered her small hand with his large one and sent Hunt a glance that he interpreted well.

Any threat to a woman with child would raise Walker's defensive hackles, but one to the woman he loved? Hunt still wasn't certain that was their relationship, but the two were close enough to want to marry.

Their discussion had captured the attention of others.

"I can talk to the staff, if Jack talks to the stable lads," Elsa offered. "But I don't think any of them had reason to kill a poor curate. They were looking forward to Sunday services."

"Most of them aren't from these parts or are too young to have known Upton when he was last here. If he left after Lady Reid died, that was nearly fifteen years ago." Clare bit into her roll with a frown.

"So we narrow the suspects down to those who were adults and lived here then?" Henri suggested.

"Not necessarily." Hunt knew he'd regret suggesting this. "I imagine the man collected enemies in every town he ever lived. We have been drawing people from all around the area with our offer of employment. I'm afraid we'd have to look at anyone over the age of thirty who is even passing through."

"Like that unpleasant fellow calling himself Duncan Reid?" Clare asked.

"Let us just pin it all on him and be done. I don't want to be questioning Lavender's ladies." Arnaud filled his plate again.

At the sound of her name, Lavender looked up from a diagram she'd been sketching. "Questioning? My seamstresses? They'd quit!"

"No, they wouldn't. They'd gossip," Arnaud corrected. "That's all they ever do. You won't even have to question them. But the nattering will drive me mad, and I'd have to question just to *fermer leur bouche.*"

Clare snickered. They'd all been brushing up on their French from translating Lady Reid's diaries. . . and to interpret Arnaud's attempts to conceal his rudeness.

"We want them talking, not shutting their mouths," Hunt remonstrated. "You will simply have to absorb the tittle-tattle until we find our predator. I don't want any more deaths on my watch. Not even a little threat."

They'd suffered more than that not too long ago when an irate clerk shot at Jack. War and poverty apparently stimulated violence in men's souls.

"Are there still soldiers camping in the north field?" Jack asked, apparently recalling the incident.

"We've found places for all except the most hardened tosspots. If we had someone to tell us what to do about the orchards, we might even be able to catch some of them early enough in the day to be sober for manual labor," Hunt said.

"Managing a hoe or shear with one arm or one leg might be difficult unless they're willing to practice," Meera reminded Hunt. "They might not be employable, except for using weapons."

That silenced them. Every man at the table, except Henri, had been a soldier once. But unoccupied men could mean trouble, which is what they were hinting at.

"If they only have one leg, they can sit and stuff dried flowers into Miss Upton's sachet pouches," Henri suggested. "If they have only one arm, they can still carry boxes about. We must find employment for them before the winter."

Arnaud glanced down at his hand, the one missing a finger. He'd had to learn to hold an artist's brush without it. "They might prepare my canvases and apply base coats to the toys the ladies are painting."

Hunt was a cynic. He didn't wish to introduce potential killers to his home. But his family was right. Everyone deserved a chance to make a living, and idle hands gave the devil work.

He'd not expected this second chance after war had cost him the sight in one eye and nearly crippled him. He could easily have been one of those homeless, unemployed soldiers.

Jack had been training a pack of hounds to secure the grounds with the aid of one of those soldiers. With more people moving in, some apparently violent, it might be time to hire a bailiff.

NINE

HENRI HAD NEVER USED HIS GOLDEN TONGUE FOR DETECTING killers. He most likely would have been a very bad spy. He knew how to talk about his merchandise to obtain the best price. He knew how to ask general questions to open up conversations.

Lying and deceit. . . He'd never practiced. He'd never needed to. His family had sent him to school in England to learn better English, not deceit.

He approached the parsonage thoughtfully the morning after Mr. Upton's demise. He'd rather not ask pointed questions and let a killer know they suspected the curate's death hadn't been an accident. He also didn't want to upset the victim's son if he didn't realize his father had been murdered.

Paul Upton was just climbing down from the parsonage roof. He wore what appeared to be his father's old clothes. They hung on him as if he were a scarecrow, tied with rope in the middle and folded up at the hems. The lad was barely as tall as his sister. He must take after his mother. The late curate had been a large man.

"You've thatched roofs before?" Henri asked, pumping a tin cup of water to hand the sweaty young priest.

"Aye, whatever it takes to earn an honest coin." Upton gulped the water gratefully.

As opposed to his father's methods?

"Although someone stole my legget last night," Upton continued. "I'll have to make a new one."

"Legget? What does one look like?" Henri glanced at the ground, but the only tool he saw was a long, knife-like one, presumably for cutting the straw.

Upton shrugged. "I build my own. Mine's a cross between a hammer and a mallet, I suppose. I wanted to finish up and put my tools away before I start on the coffin, but I can't find it."

Mallet? Perhaps one that could have been used to bash his father's skull? Henri refrained from speaking that aloud, but the other man looked uncomfortable enough to have realized it at the same time—if he knew his father's death wasn't accidental.

To ease the moment, Henri picked up the long knife and started trimming the overgrown hedge. "I earned my way through university with peddling. Carpentry could not be much easier."

"Huh." Upton wiped his brow with his shirt sleeve and eyed Henri's fancy neckcloth and tailored coat skeptically. "You don't look like a peddler."

Henri acknowledged that truth with a grin. "Now that I earn more selling in the city, I dress the part of prosperous merchant. Once you have a paying position, you will do the same. Miss Marlowe is very clever at sewing vestments and the like."

"Miss Marlowe?" The young man looked interested for half a minute, then frowned. "I might as well take up construction. I'm good at it. I have very few connections to offer me a position, and none of them are likely to want a parson whose father was murdered for extortion."

Ah. "So you think that too?" Henri shot the gentleman a considering look.

Upton shrugged uncomfortably. "I am not blind or ignorant. My father pushed limits he should not have. And he definitely did not fall from a roof he never climbed on."

"You are not demanding justice?" Henri asked, thinking the son seemed oddly dispassionate.

"If I had his position here, I'd call down hellfire and brimstone for solving problems with violence and hope someone confesses. As it is, I cannot see what anyone can do."

"The Lord would indeed have to work in mysterious ways if you can extract a confession with a sermon." Henri continued trimming the hedge. "But the ladies want a church. For that, they need a priest. I am Catholic. I do not know your ways. Can we hire you, like your father?"

The young man sighed and studied Henri's handiwork. "Much as I would love that, and so would my family, I suspect my father has soiled this nest too badly. There had to be a reason he originally left here and did not retrieve the register from the rector when he returned."

Because he'd been *paid* to leave, as the old woman had implied? Uneasy at questioning, Henri refrained from relating the incident.

"Do you know this rector?" he asked instead. "Might you ride over and speak with him directly? Would it help if the captain sent a letter with you asking that you be named our curate?"

Henri refused to believe this earnest young man would kill his father unless forced to the brink of madness. The mallet, opportunity, and their argument were not enough evidence. Perhaps if he knew more of the late clergyman. . .

"My father hired the horse and cart that brought us here. I have none of my own." The young man looked embarrassed. "I have been trying to work up the nerve to ask if I might borrow one so I might do just that, but I thought to finish the coffin first."

"Ask, and ye shall receive!" Henri replied, happy that he was making some progress. "We have horses. The ladies want you to stay. You will have as many letters as you like. This is not a problem."

Upton looked relieved. "I will write for an appointment."

That was an opening Henri could use. "Let us do that now. Your father kept a desk? With papers and pens for his sermons, perhaps?"

"It is not very organized," the would-be curate apologized. He started toward the back, then remembering himself, ushered Henri toward the front door. "My mother will fix us tea. She's at sixes and sevens, not knowing whether to unpack or pack."

"In her grief, she should do whatever feels right. It is not as if anyone is waiting to use this place. How long will it take to build a coffin? It is best to lay him to rest so she might move forward, *oui*?"

"I had to promise to build a table for the wood cutter in exchange for the planks I need. Once I have the boards, I can build it overnight." Upton led the way inside.

Henri looked about for Patience, but of course, she must be in a garden somewhere. Only the widow occupied the parsonage's dreary front room. She bustled off to fix the requested tea while Upton led him into a cluttered study still filled with unopened crates. The desk appeared untouched. *Zut.*

"I apologize for the muddle, Mr. Lavigne." Upton gestured at the crates. "Other things seemed more important than unpacking books."

"Call me Henri." He studied the clutter. "Mr. Lavigne sounds like my big brother. We are informal here."

The young curate opened a crate and rifled through it.

"Then please call me Paul. I cannot be my father right now. It hurts too much. The crates are not fastened."

Not daring to hope he'd find extortion notes, Henri rummaged through another crate, setting books on an empty bookshelf and quickly skimming correspondence before opening another box. He scarcely noticed when Mrs. Upton returned with the tea. He wasn't a tea drinker. But he was enjoying this part of detecting. His curiosity was insatiable.

A few moments later, a scent of lilac wafted through the room, and Henri instantly glanced up.

Miss Upton lingered uncertainly in the doorway. Wisps of fair hair framed her long face, not intentionally, he was certain. She brushed them aside while she found her tongue. She was dressed in black, which made her seem much too frail.

"May I help search?" she asked. "I packed most of the crates."

"Stationery," Paul said curtly. "He did have some?"

"Very little. He wrote his sermons in notebooks. I packed the good stationery between larger books so it would not wrinkle." She crossed the room, crouched down to examine a stack of crates, and pointed at the bottom one. "This one, I think."

Henri helped the curate's son haul the crates to a new stack, then left him to open the one indicated. He moved back to give Paul room, but the lady held his attention. Well, a lady as comely as this one would always hold his attention, but he could not dismiss her nervousness.

"Is there aught we can do to help you or your family?" he murmured, blocking her retreat by leaning against the bookshelf.

She reached into her apron pocket and toyed with an object there. "Is the captain the justice of the peace for the area?" she whispered while her brother swore at the mess in the crate.

75

"The village has elected him so, yes." Which might not be entirely legal, but they had solicitors who were supposed to be speaking with the Lord High Whomsoever to verify the position. "May I give him a message?"

He'd much rather walk the lovely lady up the hill to the manor to deliver it herself. He'd enjoy the company, only he was no longer a callow youth. He could be a gentleman when needed.

She removed a battered leather notebook from her pocket. "Would you give him this, please? I believe Papa might have been killed for it."

She knew too? Henri snapped his jaw shut and took the book he'd hoped to find.

Extortionists had to keep notes of who, what, why, when, and where, did they not?

$\sim$

AFTER MAKING CERTAIN PAUL HAD HIS LETTER-WRITING TOOLS, the elegant French gentleman tucked the little notebook into his pocket, and offered Patience his arm. "You must show me the work to be done. Did you not say you knew about orchards? We need expert eyes examining the trees. Let me be your beast of burden so you are free to use your pretty head."

The foreigner was beyond annoying, but he was too charming to set down. She let him lead her outside where they wouldn't be overheard. "Please cease the flattery. We know I am no expert and not pretty." She hoped she'd managed to conceal her exasperation.

"I am the one who determines who I think is pretty. And if I do not annoy you with my flattery, you will not speak with me. You are not shy when you are angry." She thought she heard a smile in his reply.

Startled by his insight, she shot the handsome gentleman a quick glance and saw no mockery in his dark eyes. He had the longest lashes. . . With a sigh of exasperation at herself, she directed him toward the chapel yard, enjoying a companion taller than she. He gazed about with interest, not pressing her to respond.

She finally found her tongue. "I am no expert. I have no schooling beyond the gardeners I followed like a lost lamb. What I *can* do is read and see where there is a blight or bug. I look at the blight, look at the book, compare it to what I know, and then hope I find a solution. But there is much experimentation involved. I do know, however, that the trees need pruning. I cannot do that."

This was a much better topic than the notebook she'd given to him. An intelligent man who had overheard her father's arm-twisting, he had not been surprised. She was well beyond embarrassment by now. However wrong her father's behavior, he had not deserved to die alone and in pain.

"The captain is having difficulty finding labor, skilled or otherwise. Perhaps, if your brother takes up the position of curate, he might learn of those who could use the extra work. But after you determine what must be done, we would still need someone to direct the laborers, and that is a chore not for a lady." He sounded quite firm about that.

"I am *not* a lady," she said with equal firmness. If she didn't look at him, it was easier to speak her mind. "I have toiled in the field the same as any laborer. I have followed the gardeners about wearing my brother's clothes, and they forget that I am female. Introduce me as Mr. Smith and allow me to wander your orchard as your head gardener, and I will see what I can do."

He pondered that as they stopped beside the garden they'd weeded earlier. He toed a patch of grass, crooked his head, and studied the field, not her. "I cannot like it."

She knew that. Men never did. But standing beside him, both facing the dirt from which good things grew, she did not have to be shy. He wasn't even looking at her breasts. She *preferred* concealing them beneath overlarge men's coats. When men treated her like a man, she could accomplish a great deal. "It is the only way I know. No man takes orders from a woman."

"Then they are fools." He finally tipped his hat over his eyes and turned to her. "They would have to be fools to think you are a man."

Now she felt the warmth of his gaze, and for a change, she did not feel it was so terrible to be a woman. She did not mind when he *spoke* to her as if she were an equal. "We all see what we want to see, I suppose."

Following her thought, she cringed a little. "Do you think my father *wanted* to see sin, and that was why he knew so many sinners?"

"To that, I cannot speak. But if you insist on being what you are not, I will walk with you when you view the orchards," he announced. "You may dress any way you wish, but I will see you are treated with respect. A lady cannot punch a rogue in the snout if he deserves it."

She chuckled at his charming vehemence. "Have you ever punched a man in the snout?"

He actually had to think about it. "I am more likely to aim for the soft belly. If I do it right, I knock the breath from them and have time to retreat to my pony and depart. But I do not make good customers that way."

"You use charm instead. I like that." And she was being the veriest pea goose to talk this way. But he hadn't laughed dismissively when she'd explained herself. That had somehow made it easier to converse.

"I am all charm and no substance, my brother says. But he has more substance than any family needs. So I am the beast of burden. When do you wish to view the orchard? I do not know what is involved in funeral arrangements and helping your mother. My family all died while I was far away."

He made her ashamed of feeling sorry for herself. "You have a great deal of substance, monsieur, to have survived so well on your own while so young. If charm is your defense, I'd say it works well."

He swept off his hat and bowed, revealing glossy black curls. "Perceptive and flattering, mademoiselle, thank you. You are to call me Henri, as your brother does. I am your servant. Point me to the task, and I shall undertake it."

"Not in those fancy clothes. Today, we mourn. You will take the notebook to your friends so they may dissect it as I cannot. I will stay with my mother. Perhaps, after the funeral, we will know better what our positions are." She had already told her family she did not mean to leave. She simply hadn't determined how she would stay.

"I shall abide by your wishes, for now." He returned his hat to his head. "Do you have family hereabouts? I understand your brother's mother was from here."

"Father never said much about them, and I do not recollect ever visiting." She scrunched up her nose, trying to remember long-ago conversations. Or perhaps, curses. "I don't believe he was on friendly terms with them."

"But now that he is gone, perhaps, they would like to know their nephew or cousin, especially if he becomes curate. It is good to have family, I have learned." He offered his arm to return her to the house.

She was becoming much too used to accepting his muscular strength as a support she did not need. She wrapped her fingers around his sleeve anyway, pretending she was one of the delicate ladies from the manor. "You might look their name up in Papa's black book," she said dryly. "It's Corcoran. For all I know, he might have used extortion to persuade the family into allowing him to marry. It wasn't as if he had a ha'penny to his name at the time."

TEN

CLARE SAT IN THE LIBRARY, COPYING OUT EACH PAGE OF MR. Upton's notebook and handing the copies around the table. Even Oliver took one so he and Mr. Birdwhistle could work on it.

"Initials are fairly meaningless," Jack argued. "We need someone who has lived here all their life to decipher them."

"Look at the dates. Should we start on the most recent, even though they probably aren't local? The local ones most likely date back fifteen years or more." Clare passed more sheets to Arnaud and Henri. Lavender, with her reading problem, looked over Oliver's shoulder.

"I'd like to see the church register." Hunt glared at his pages through his monocle. "It might be possible to match some of these older dates with deaths or marriages."

Clare stopped her copying to study the man she adored with all her heart, but whose overactive brain left her gaping. "You think Mr. Upton performed services for people who might have killed him?"

"Or he buried people he knew had been murdered. As a female, Lady Reid could not assume the role of magistrate, which only compounds the problem that we have. Since under England's ancient districting, we're an exclave of Shropshire, the law in Birmingham doesn't care about us. That basically means Gravesyde's only law for thirty-five years was in a district a day's ride away or more." Hunt rubbed his scarred temple.

Clare knew the criminal problem haunted him. The village had only recently chosen him to act as their magistrate, but he was American. He knew nothing of English law. He could claim manorial rights for taxes and small crimes, but murder belonged in the hands of lawyers and judges.

Except Gravesyde had no lawyers or judges. "If a curate suspected a crime, to whom would he turn?" she asked.

"The rector," Elsa answered. "A curate would have reported the crimes to the rector, who would have the ear of a magistrate."

"But as we have already ascertained, if the rector is in Hereford, any magistrate in that area would have no authority in the jurisdiction of Shropshire. And the closest magistrate is in Staffordshire, not Shropshire." Hunt glared at the notebook pages as if they were personally offensive. "And it was probably a bit awkward to trespass on Lady Reid's authority without her permission. Only the earl had the power to ask that Gravesyde's district be changed. He left us a tangled web."

"Through which villains and Mr. Upton might have fallen." Clare sighed and thought of all the petty crimes that might have gone unpunished. "It is a wonder the town is not a cesspool of lawlessness."

"Who says it isn't?" Arnaud asked cynically. "It's just that we're so isolated, there is no longer anything to steal and no people left to steal it."

"The manor was left untouched, despite being guarded only by elderly caretakers," Henri remonstrated. Henri had chosen cheerfulness to balance out his brother's pessimism.

"The village believes the manor is haunted." Giving up on

PATRICIA RICE

the notebook, seventeen-year-old Lavender returned to working on her sewing. "I have had to tell my ladies that the scent that often perfumes the gallery is from sachets I've added to the furniture to cover musty odors. They swear it is the late viscountess."

"The caretakers probably encouraged the superstition as a deterrent," Clare suggested.

"The lady helped me find her books." Oliver piped up unexpectedly.

This was the first Clare had heard of his talking with a. . . ghost? She wasn't certain how to respond. Her nephew had been the one to find Lady Reid's diaries, the ones that had revealed some of the horrid secrets of Wycliffe Manor. She didn't dare question her normally non-communicative nephew. He'd simply leave the room.

Who knew what else the walls would relate if they could talk? She didn't want to disparage Oliver's odd notion, but she'd rather believe the lady was happily in heaven, along with the earl and the monks and everyone else who had died here.

"Her perfume reeks from the diaries." Hunt settled the matter with his pragmatism. "And if we let people think the manor is haunted, it might protect us from thieves. I have no objection to ghosts."

Clare shook her head in disbelief and directed the conversation elsewhere. "Besides the initials and dates, what do you think the abbreviations mean?"

"Some of them are numbers. Payments?" Jack suggested.

"That's what it looks like under the initials EC in 1789." Tired of copying, Clare studied the first pages of the notebook. "There's a pound sign and three marks after it, as if that amount might have been received three times? Isn't three pounds a rather large amount for a local?"

"Especially over twenty-five years ago," Hunt agreed.

"EC?" Henri asked, looking up from his pages. "In 1789? I

82

see why the register might be useful. Do we know when the curate married his first wife? I ask because Miss Upton believes her half-brother's maternal family is called *Corcoran*."

"An Irish name," Elsa said, glaring at her page of notes. "That might explain young Mr. Upton's red hair. But they are likely Catholic. How would Upton extort someone not of his church?"

"What abbreviations go with EC 1789?" Walker looked up from the pages spread in front of him.

"Capital R and lowercase *str*." Clare pushed the book across the table for Walker to examine.

Meera held up one of her pages. "In 1814, his notebook is labeled Stratford. The initials are SA, then R and *dtr*, followed by a pound sign and the number two, repeated three times. His price has gone up."

Looking alarmed, Mr. Birdwhistle, the tutor, scribbled on his pages and passed them back to Clare. "I think it is time Master Oliver finishes his schoolwork. If I may assist after that, please let me know."

Clare read his note aloud after the young tutor ushered Oliver out of the library. "*R may stand for rape and dtr for daughter. This page dates from the year I was at university. There was a scandal concerning one of the professors and his wife's daughter, who lived in Stratford. These are his initials. The date is the year before the scandal broke.*"

The gentlemen uttered curses. The ladies paled. Choking on bile, Clare closed the notebook and rose. "I think that is enough for one evening. I do not want to believe the people who live here are evil."

She fled for her small writing office. Hunt followed. He closed the door after him and took her in his arms. She buried her face against his strong chest. "I thought I would be raising Oliver away from the ugliness of the city."

He stroked her back. "There must be millions of people in the world, maybe just in England for all I know. They cannot all be innocent, or we'd not need the courts. The city simply holds higher concentrations."

"Not reassuring," she muttered. "A man who would. . ." She shuddered. "If *dtr* is daughter, would *str* be. . . sister? How can anyone *do* that? Could a rapist still be living here?"

"The EC person was in Gravesyde over twenty-five years ago," he reminded her. "They could all be long gone."

"Do you think Mr. Upton did *nothing* to stop the crimes? If so, the girl's family might have beaten him over the head for not bringing the criminal to justice. I would call it justifiable." She wept in rage at the callousness.

"This is why gentlemen do not speak of such subjects to ladies," Hunt said wryly. "Henri should never have given you that notebook. We should never have discussed it. And yes, I know, you'd have beaten me over the head for concealing it."

She choked on a laugh. "Rightfully so."

"And Upton might have revealed the crimes at some point," Hunt reminded her. "Birdwhistle spoke of a scandal. That means the authorities were warned."

"University towns have authorities." She lifted her head in realization. "Until now, Gravesyde had none, like the other small parishes where the Uptons lived. Perhaps a man of the church was the only means of seeing that a crime was not repeated."

"Let us hope you are right. I'd rather not think ill of the dead. But *we* need to deal with any local criminals now."

Clare nodded and wiped her eyes. "Sweeping crime under the carpet simply will not do. It festers and grows like mold."

"Let us start making lists of every family who lives here now and who might have lived here then. We will start asking questions at the funeral." Hunt had a martial gleam in his eyes.

ELEVEN

ON SATURDAY, THE DAY OF THE FUNERAL, THE LADIES OF
Wycliffe Manor watched the procession through the parlor
window. Miss Knightley—Clare—spoke over the rattle of the
cart carrying the coffin. "Would you rather I close the
draperies?"

On the sofa with her back to the window, Patience held
her weeping mother. She'd rather be outside, seeking signs of
guilt in those who attended, but her mother came first.

Unexpectedly, Nettie threw off Patience's arms and stood.
"I want to see him pass." The ladies made room for her at the
mullioned window.

Patience understood the reason ladies did not attend
funerals. Weeping and wailing distracted from the serious
business of burying the dead. And these women barely knew
her father, so there was no reason for them to join the men
following the cart up the drive.

She'd like to be there for Paul, speaking his first funeral
service over their father's grave. But he'd insisted she stay
with her mother. *Their* mother. Nettie was the only mother
he'd ever known, since his died in childbirth.

Taller than everyone present, Patience stood back,

watching the mourners over her mother's shoulder. They had visited with many of the villagers since their arrival, but they'd talked mostly to the women, not the men. She saw no one she recognized.

"Your son makes a fine coffin," the plump cook, Elsa, commented.

"Jesus was a carpenter," Nettie replied. "A man of the cloth needs a profession that pays the bills."

A lesson her father never learned, Patience recognized. He had been a talker, not a doer. Catching sight of the elegant gentlemen in funeral black unloading the coffin, she understood that the charming Frenchman was much the same. He talked and sold his merchandise. She supposed he trimmed the hedge but only because he wanted to look at her bosom.

But if his talking got her into the manor's library and orchard. . . She was as immoral as her father. Where was the fine line between seizing an opportunity and corruption? Better minds than hers would have to philosophize.

Instinctively, she hummed a hymn while saying a silent prayer as they carried the coffin out of sight, to the graveyard behind the stable, not far from the orchard. She'd forgotten about the bones uncovered there. Had the earl planted trees on the bones of the monks, just as his ancestor had built on the remains of their priory?

No wonder the locals claimed the manor was haunted.

"That is Bridget Corcoran, Paul's grandmother, there, in the black bonnet with the black roses." Nettie nodded at the window to a couple wearing better clothes than the rest of the company. "That must be her son Ted with her. He'd be Paul's uncle, then."

It was impossible to see more of Mrs. Corcoran than a middling-size stout figure in black, shoulders curved with age. Her son was a similar height, as was Paul. Patience knew she had inherited her father's height. Paul must have inherited his late mother's.

The Corcorans wore expensive hats, so she couldn't discern if their hair resembled Paul's lovely auburn.

"Paul's grandfather is deceased?" Clare asked, studying the procession.

"I cannot say. Daniel Corcoran was a thorn in my husband's side when we were here. Perhaps he chose not to come, although one would expect him to respect his own grandson."

Had their father given Paul's grandparents reason to want him gone? Surely not.

"May I be rude and ask how you came to marry Mr. Upton? You are so much younger, and I believe you are not from around here?" Lady Elsa offered a tray of tiny sandwiches as if she were a maid.

Patience took the tray and passed it around so the lady needn't do so. She liked the manor inhabitants, but she was uncomfortable in their presence. She preferred to remain silent.

"I was Lady Reid's companion for a while. Mr. Upton called on her occasionally. I was a spinster. He was handsome and had a lively young son who needed a mother. I was accustomed to a clergyman's household. The lady offered a small dowry. It was all quite straightforward."

Patience knew her mother's history. Henrietta Nelson was a bastard adopted by a vicar in the north country, not far from one of the late earl's many estates. The entire countryside believed the orphan to be one of the many Reid castoffs, like Lavender. She'd essentially been the vicar's servant, grateful for a roof over her head. How she came to stay with Lady Reid was a mystery.

It was a matter of opinion whether marrying Isaiah Upton was a rescue or another form of slavery. Patience vowed never to be forced into that situation if there were any way of avoiding it. If she could earn the position of the manor's head gardener. . .

She wasn't a dreamer. She would take one day at a time.

The last of the funeral procession disappeared from view. Clare led the way back to the sofas, pulling a bell to order fresh tea. Patience meant to take a chair in the corner, but the lady gestured for her to return to the sofa beside her mother. She tripped over the tea table, shaking the cups. Apologizing, she settled in embarrassment on a frayed cushion.

'Miss Upton, Patience, if I may. . ." Clare lifted her eyebrows and accepted a nod as reply. "Henri has told us that you may identify problems in the orchard. We don't know how much the village is dependent on the manor's produce, but we think any cash crop would be beneficial. Arnaud has offered to escort you. He's been reading up on fruit trees, but he has no practical knowledge. His estate was mostly grain and cattle."

"Arnaud?" Patience asked helplessly. She thought she remembered him as being the very large, grim Frenchman, presumably the older brother of whom Henri spoke. She wouldn't even be able to open her mouth in his imposing presence.

"The Comte Lavigne, Hunt's cousin. He was injured in the war, his estates destroyed, but he's an eminently trustworthy gentleman. Although I suppose we should send one of the maids with you, just to eliminate any hint of impropriety. Would you be interested in helping us?"

A French count. Patience closed her eyes and breathed deeply to calm her rattled nerves. Anything worth having must be earned, she told herself. "Of course, thank you. I cannot make promises, but I do know what to look for. As old as the trees are, you will need to start replacing them. I know how to graft on rootstock, but that should be done soon."

Unexpectedly, her mother spoke up. "I understand you do not have a housekeeper?"

All the ladies turned to her eagerly. Clare, as usual, was the one to speak. "We just buried the last one. We have had no luck in locating anyone with proper credentials. Do you know of someone suitable?"

"Me." Nettie brushed at a crumb on her black skirt. "I have spent my life overseeing households. This one is much larger than my foster father's vicarage, but if you have a few decent servants, I should be capable of managing them."

Patience thought she might fall over. She would grip her mother's hand, but they both held teacups. She didn't realize she was holding her breath until the lady responded.

"That is a most excellent opportunity for us, but I am not so sure about your family?"

Patience felt her mother's shoulders straighten. She knew that gesture. The deal was signed and delivered, at any cost. She panicked, not knowing how to behave as a housekeeper's daughter. A curate's daughter at least had some claim to being a lady. A housekeeper was definitely below stairs. She supposed, if she could be a gardener. . .

"I have no family but Paul and Patience. Should Paul obtain a position, he needs to have his own life. He doesn't need his mother treating him like a child. Patience," Nettie patted her hand, "Patience can be his cook and housekeeper until he marries. Perhaps, by then, she'll have found a husband of her own."

Not bloody likely! was her mental response. Gritting her teeth and forcing a smile, she managed a more polite verbal reply. "If I am to study the orchard, I would prefer to stay with you here, Mother."

Clare's brow creased in thought. "There are plenty of bedchambers, although Elsa already occupies the one closest to the service stairs. Perhaps we should open the new wing. . ."

Nettie put on her stubborn face. "A housekeeper must be below stairs, accessible to the staff she manages."

"But you are family!" Clare protested. "You belong here the same as we do."

Patience clasped her hands and bit her tongue. She knew the argument was futile. Her mother refused to accept the family that had cast her out.

As anticipated, Nettie shook her head. "I am no one but a housekeeper."

The little apothecary hastily stood, ending the argument. "The housekeeper's chambers are in the new wing, near the kitchen. They need refurbishing, as does everything in the manor, but I believe there is room for a family."

By the time the funeral ended, Patience and her mother had a new home in the manor's cellar.

IN HIS NEW ROLE AS DETECTIVE, HENRI GREETED ALL THE PEOPLE attending the curate's funeral. He had to work quickly, before everyone departed. To those who didn't already know Henri, the postmaster introduced him as a merchant selling goods in the city.

While the captain worked his way through the farmers, Henri talked to men who carved walking canes and ones whose wives knitted socks he might sell. He asked if they'd known Mr. Upton when he was last here. Some remembered him as a young man whose very young wife died tragically in childbirth.

The men attending didn't seem to harbor any resentments against the dead man, leaving Henri to assume Upton's victims were not here. Nor had these good people been at the murder scene.

Few ladies were present, but Mr. Oswald, the diminutive postmaster, finally introduced Henri to Mrs. Corcoran. She lingered on the edge of the crowd, watching the newly ordained clergyman. She wore a black shawl and bonnet similar to the woman's who had warned Upton to leave town, but then, he wouldn't know one drab shawl or bonnet from another. He'd only had a glimpse.

"Your grandson's grown to a fine young man," the postmaster declared, following her gaze to the young parson shaking hands over the grave. "You must be right proud of him."

A frown formed on her already wrinkled brow. "Paul should never have come back to this place."

Henri grabbed the opportunity and dived in. "We are trying to put Gravesyde back on the map. We hope if he stays, the congregation will grow. Wouldn't our chapel be a fine place for a new curate?"

She shook her head slowly. "No, tell him to leave." She pulled down her veil, lifted her head, and called sharply, "Ted, I'm feeling poorly. Let us go."

A fancy frock-coated gentleman—Ted?—turned around, studied Henri suspiciously, then took the older woman's arm. No one introduced him before he led the old lady away.

"He's all she's got," Mr. Oswald grumbled. "Her old man's been crippled up and can't work much no more."

"Does young Mr. Corcoran farm then?" The initials in the notebook had been EC, not TC. What was the father's name?

"Teddy raises sheep on his father's land, although there's them that say his da ain't really his da, if you know what I mean. Daniel Corcoran came from the Irish. He's a ginger. Their daughter had hair the color of a copper penny, just like young Paul there. Ted got none of his da's looks."

Daniel, not EC there, either.

"Corcoran's daughter?" Henri was good with names and relationships, but he wanted verification. "That would be the lady who married Mr. Upton?"

"That it would. Tragic such a lovely lass died so young. But that's all water under the bridge. May she rest in peace. Mrs. Corcoran might have the right of it. There's naught here for the lad." Mr. Oswald frowned. "Look what happened to his da."

Henri knew the ladies wanted the young curate to stay. And Miss Upton seemed eager to remain. Upton's killer may have waited decades for revenge, but why would his family be in danger—*unless the notebook was more dangerous than they knew?*

Henri hated to warn the others they might be risking lives if they held a wedding.

TWELVE

Hunt spent Sunday writing a recommendation for young Mr. Upton and a plea for his services, while his family prepared the young curate for the all-important visit to the rector.

What if he were assisting a killer? Isaiah Upton had died in his yard, most likely under a blow from his son's tools. And from all reports, his family was far more likely to harbor grudges than a village the curate hadn't visited in fifteen years. They didn't really know the Uptons. They could be sheltering a murderess in their cellar or a murderer in the parsonage.

The women did not listen to his cynical fears. They wanted a chapel and a clergyman.

So on Monday morning Hunt carried his interrogations to the locals—without success.

"No one knows a blackguard calling himself Duncan Reid," Hunt grumbled to Walker, unsaddling his horse after a wasted morning.

Before replying, Walker waited until they left the barn, away from inquisitive ears. "I dug around until I found the manor's ledgers for 1778-1781. The earl donated a large meadow to the church in 1779 so Upton could rent it out for income. He wasn't making up stories. Unfortunately, the orchard entries are mere notations of initials and amounts paid for trees and labor. Did no one ever use names?"

"Look for DR in both the notebook and the ledgers, just in case. Upton might have picked up the earl's habit of using initials. If this fake Reid was here when the orchard was planted and returns when bones are uncovered. . ." Hunt rubbed the scar on his temple. "Can we arrest someone for a decades-old crime?"

"If Upton knew about the bones, and this Reid killed him to conceal it, you can arrest him for killing Upton. I'd be happier if we found the mallet that Henri mentioned, but I suppose it would have been thrown in the stream."

"I spoke with a Bert Bartholomew. He has a small plot of land and ten children." Hunt aimed for the carriage entrance.

Walker stopped him. "The one Patience says she heard arguing with her father?"

"The one Upton threatened with grievous sin and who claimed self-defense, yes. He admits to nothing, but then, if he's a murderer, he'd not exactly say so, would he? He's a tall, sturdy man, with a definite chip on his shoulder."

"Clare has the notebook, but I don't remember a BB in it. Perhaps whatever his offense, Bert didn't count as a criminal in the curate's warped mind." Walker strode off in the direction of the kitchen garden, where Meera probably worked on this sunny day.

Hunt continued to the house. Quincy met him at the door and took his hat. "I would advise avoiding the great room today, sir. Domestic activity is in progress."

"Mrs. Upton proving her mettle already, is she? And Miss Knightley?"

"In the library, sir."

Hunt found Clare in the wing of the library overlooking the rocky west hill. He'd employed ex-soldiers to clear out the brush in hopes of exposing anyone attempting to access the manor from the river and highway below. The windows now had a view of spring green leaves dancing on the wind, with the occasional appearance of blue flowers among the boulders, if one looked close enough.

At his entrance, Clare sent him one of those blinding smiles that almost crippled him with lust, while heating his previously cold heart. Some days, he thought it might be easier to return to feeling nothing. Today wasn't one of those days.

He leaned over to kiss her, then examined her notes. "Blackstone?"

"Henri mentioned the name Blackstone as one of the men Mr. Upton threatened. I have talked to some of the staff, and Archibald Blackstone, junior and senior, used to live in the village." She showed him the late curate's extortion notes. "AB, 7/79, BW, shilling sign, two marks."

"BW?" Hunt thought about it. "Since we're assuming sin —beats wife?" He took a chair to rest his aching knee. "That's over thirty-five years ago, and we don't know if he's talking junior or senior, although if Upton was speaking with him recently. . ."

"Probably junior. And he's only recently returned to town too. Interesting." She ran her finger down the pages. "Here's another. AB, 8/81, BW, pound sign, three marks. Whatever BW is, this second offense has the same penalty as raping one's daughter, if we are reading this correctly. I think I wish to be a hermit."

"No, you do not. You're gnashing your teeth and wishing you could kill Upton all over again, then whip Blackstone out of town, if this is he. We are not that different." Hunt had watched the once-traumatized lady blossom from cringing miss to fierce warrior over a space of a few months. Experience changed people.

Perhaps he should regret bringing her here where the

wider world banged on their doors. Would she have been happier in the sheltered bubble of her missish townhouse?

Despite their rocky start, he didn't regret her arrival for a minute. "How about Bert Bartholomew?"

"BB?" She started on the last page and flipped backward. "Just more ABs. Here's one 3/91, S, pound sign and a five, with no marks."

"Huh. That's ten years after the last. One would think Blackstone would have left to avoid Upton's extortion by then. Instead, he is caught committing another crime? Not very smart. What sin begins with S?"

Walker entered, interrupting their speculation. He carried a few of the enormous ledgers Hunt had once used as kindling, until the lady pitched a fit.

"After Clare gave me the Archibald name, I started looking. AB first shows up as a laborer in the earl's records in 1778." Walker dropped the books on the table and opened to a marked page. "He's only paid in pence at first." He flipped open another ledger. "By the time Wycliffe died three years later, AB earned a steward's wage. All the entries are under orchard, though. And they end after the earl's demise."

Clare sent Hunt a triumphant look. "I told you the ledgers were valuable."

"Keeping warm is valuable too." Although he'd been burning them in frustration, not for warmth. Hunt slid the ledgers in front of him and fished the damned monocle from his pocket. It was better than being blind, he supposed. "We have no way of proving this AB is Archibald Blackstone. Are there any DRs in there?"

"Duncan Reid?" Clare returned to flipping pages. "He's not a Reid. He might have been adopted by one, but even the earl knew he wasn't a blood relation, or he would have left everything to his only male heir."

Which was not Hunt, despite the legal niceties. Hunt's natural grandfather was a French count, not Lord Reid, the murderous viscount to whom his grandmother had been married. "I still say blond, blue-eyed parents can have dark-haired children."

"They can, but not in this family. And then there are all the other traits, none of which the fake Duncan Reid exhibits. As we have no recorded marriage records for any Reid male besides the viscount, and all the other males died young, I think we can assume anyone who uses the name Reid is from an entirely different family. If he wanted work, why did he not present himself properly?" Clare sat back and glared at the books as if they'd offended her.

Which they wouldn't have if she'd allowed him to burn them. Hunt wisely did not mention that. "Perhaps he wished to make the bones disappear? He fears they can be identified? Not that there is much possibility of that."

"Meera is putting the bones together as we find them. I don't know how she knows, but she thinks they're from a young woman. She's found signs of abuse and believes a skull fracture might have been the cause of death." Walker exhibited no expression on revealing this.

Abuse? Someone had beat her? As in, AB/BW. . . beats wife? Hunt rubbed the scar over his blind eye and tried to keep up with the conversation.

"Meera's physician father smuggled her into autopsies and lectures as a man." Clare returned to flipping the note-book pages. "She has a London education and knows more than many physicians. Sadly, abused women are not a rarity in country or town."

"Is Meera the reason the curate's daughter took the notion of dressing like her brother when she went out this morning with Arnaud?" Hunt preferred dealing with the present over the past. "No neckcloth in the world would disguise a prow as fine as hers."

Clare rapped his hand with her pencil. "At least a time or two in their lives, most women dream of the freedom a man

97

possesses. Men won't listen to orders from anyone wearing skirts. Worse, they would stare, grab her, and say rude things. If she were alone, they'd consider her easy prey. Men are beasts."

"Some men, maybe, not all," Walker said stiffly. "They simply need to be educated."

"Do I need to go out there and educate them?" Hunt asked. "If the lady knows aught of orchards, I don't want to lose her."

"Let us see how Arnaud handles the situation. Should I leave these ledgers here?" Walker prepared to depart.

"Yes, please, unless you need them to uncover more secrets of the orchard?" Clare had her hands on both books.

"I'll read the ledgers in here if I need anything in them." Walker departed, leaving Hunt alone with his intended.

Except they were never alone. Oliver might slip under the table at any moment. Servants darted back and forth around the corner and on the other side of the wall. Even the outdoors crawled with people.

To prove his point, a maid arrived to announce luncheon had been laid out, and a few minutes later, Miss Upton and Arnaud entered.

"Do we cut down all the apple trees and use them for firewood?" Hunt asked, just to make the tongue-tied curate's daughter speak.

She looked indignant at his suggestion, but true to form, Arnaud spoke for her. Clare was right. Men talked to men.

"Half a dozen or so are suitable for firewood, including the one that fell, revealing bones. We found more than bone." Arnaud produced an oilskin-wrapped package from his pocket.

THIRTEEN

WITH PROPER HOUSECLEANING UNDERWAY ON TUESDAY morning, Clare was left to deal with the mystery box. Everyone had examined it last night, without coming to any conclusion. She wished she could retreat to her desk and scribble on her latest novel instead. Writing provided great satisfaction, and in a round-about manner, paid Oliver's tutor.

But the meager contents of the wooden box Arnaud and Patience had uncovered should be returned to its family—once the family was identified. She had to assume the box belonged to the poor woman buried under an apple tree.

"Patience, I know you are no longer the parson's daughter and don't need to visit parishioners, but Paul won't return for a while, and the mystery of the bones needs to be settled. These small treasures belonged to *someone*." Clare poked at a thin silver necklace holding a tiny pearl pendant. A delicate bracelet of wire adorned in blue and white beads lay beside it, along with a tarnished silver spoon ring.

The curate's daughter poked at the sad remnants. "They are almost child-sized, except for the ring. Even then, her finger must have been very slender."

It fit Clare's finger, but she had thin bones. "Meera says it most likely would have fit the woman in the grave. I don't think this was an ancient burial from the days of the original priory."

"If they had nuns. . . ?" Patience obviously did not wish to make inquiries.

"Walker says the earl's history books show this was a monastery for men. And bones that old would have deteriorated a great deal more." Clare put the jewelry back into its rotting wooden box. "Lavender is talking to her sewing ladies, but they were too young when the trees were planted. We should talk to the older women who lived here then."

Reluctantly, Patience donned her black bonnet. Clare stuck with her straw. She had left her mourning clothes in London, hoping never to wear them again. She had lost all her immediate family except Oliver. Perhaps she had hoped that if she didn't have her blacks, no one else would die. She had been exceedingly naïve when she arrived at the manor.

Since she must now rent out her townhouse to help her uncle's failing finances, she needed to send for the personal items she'd stored away—a task for another day.

Their first stop in the village was with Mrs. Green, mother of Betsy, the first maid the manor had hired. The yard was still adorned in the colorful ornaments that Betsy's creative mind had built from scraps of nothing. Now that it was May, the whirligigs and lively scarecrows blended into the plots of tulips, peonies, and iris.

Crippled with arthritis, Mrs. Green was delighted to have visitors. Despite protests, she insisted on carrying out a tea tray. "Aye, young Mr. Upton that was, was oncet a handsome man. You have the height of him, dearie," she told Patience. "But more the fair look of your mam. She's a fine woman, deserves a good man of her own."

Since Mrs. Upton had just laid her husband to rest, Clare refrained from making a new match for her. She did, however, pounce on the gossip session. "Did you know Mr. Upton's first wife, mother of Paul? We hope he will secure the position of curate for Gravesyde."

The older woman patted Patience's gloved hand. "Your da was a good man. He rescued that poor child. She might have made a good wife, had she lived. Sweet little thing. The boy's uncle won't like having him here, I wager."

"Paul's *uncle*?" Patience emerged from her shyness to question.

"I don't suppose you met him. His mother makes over him, and he grew up prideful. Now he's claimin' he's got a gold mine, he's worse. He can go bugger his sheep." The old lady sat back and sipped her tea as if she were the queen after making that dreadful statement.

Clare choked on a response. Patience bit back what very much appeared to be a smile.

"Now, what can I do for you ladies?" Mrs. Green asked cheerfully.

"Gold mine?" Patience managed to recover her wits faster than Clare.

The old lady waved a frail hand. "Gossip. The family is all Micks. Daniel Corcoran came here with his wife long ago as I remember, bringing Teddy with 'em as a babe. They wasn't never poor, but they don't got gold mines. How's my Betsy doing at the big house?"

"Betsy is wonderful, Mrs. Green. We all adore her. She's been spending more time painting buttons lately, teaching the others how to do it." Clare made mental notes about Paul Upton's maternal family. They had been at the funeral, looking perfectly respectable. *Prideful* or not, she could see no reason they might kill the curate. She steered the conversation back to their original purpose. "We hope you can help us with something."

Patience took her cue and produced the small box.

Clare explained. "We found these and wondered if you

might recognize them? They seem to be quite old, and we'd like to return them to their rightful owner."

Mrs. Green fiddled around until she'd donned an ancient pair of spectacles to study the box contents. She poked a bony finger at it. "Reckon they's familiar. Can't rightly recall though. You asked Mr. Oswald yet? He used to take gewgaws when folk came up short."

Clare hadn't thought to ask the postmaster and owner of the closest thing to a mercantile the village possessed. "We'll do that. I only thought to ask ladies. I hadn't realized men noticed jewelry."

"Only if they need coins or they've brangled with their wives and need back in their good graces." The old lady cackled.

They left Mrs. Green after a cup of tea and crossed the street to the general store.

"I'm trying to recall my father settling a disagreement with gifts." Clare wrinkled her nose in thought. "I remember presents for birthdays and Christmas, not arguments. Anyway, these look more like children's baubles."

Patience shook her head and tripped on the step, grabbing the wall to prevent pitching into the store, as if practiced at the maneuver. "The ring is often what a servant will give his intended, silverware sometimes stolen from the lord's coffers. They snip off the spoon basin and file the stem down and bend it. When you're poor, you make do. A pearl is rare, no matter how small. One wouldn't give it to a child."

"I know so very little!" Clare mourned, pushing open the wooden door.

Mr. Oswald stood behind his ancient counter, totaling his postage book. He glanced up at their entrance and finished counting before greeting them. "What can I do for you, ladies? I just got in some nice threads from that young peddler of yours."

"Mrs. Green said you might be able to help us. We're

trying to return these items to their rightful owner." Clare took the box from the basket when Patience hung back.

He studied the contents and shook his head. "Ain't seen these in. . ." He wrinkled up his well-wrinkled face and thought about it. "Not since the earl were here, I'm sure. Thought the pearl was stolen when I first seen it."

"But it wasn't?" Clare prodded gently.

"Mighta been," he acknowledged. "The lad showed them to me. The ring were enough to pay his family's debt, so he didn't barter the pearl. He came and got the ring back later, said he was getting married. Working for the earl then, he was."

"What was his name?" Clare asked eagerly.

"A Bergstein, he was." Mr. Oswald stared at the ceiling in thought. "His da made trinkets and sold them from his pony cart."

Like Henri! Intriguing. "Bergstein?" Clare couldn't recall meeting any Bergstein.

The postmaster continued. "Aye, the lad's ma was sickly, as I recall. Looked like Gypsies but they wasn't. Oncet the da took sick, too, they made do with their garden patch and little Abe herding sheep and the like, until he and his sister were big enough for the earl to hire."

"Sister? Do you know her name?" Clare asked, trying to remember which initials in the notebook had *str* beside them.

"Nope, whole family kept to themselves. Only ever saw Abe."

"Might they still live around here?"

"Not so I know, no. His parents died about the same time as the old earl. Abe and the young ones left then, I reckon, like most everyone else up at the manor. Want me to take them things and apply them to your account?" Mr. Oswald eyed the pearl with interest.

Clare looked to the curate's daughter for guidance. The

manor didn't need funds for groceries. If the trinkets couldn't help them identify the body under the tree. . .

"We fear it is grave robbing," Patience said softly, twisting her gloved hands. "We wish to ask the family what to do with the box and the remains."

"Ah, the bones in the orchard." The old man nodded knowingly. Then frowned and studied the trinkets again. "How would Abe's things end up in a grave?"

Especially since they didn't think it was a man in the grave. "But this Mr. Bergstein never brought in these other bits?" Clare asked, hoping she might jog the postmaster's memory.

"The pearl but not the others that I recollect. The beads ain't worth much. The pearl could buy a family's groceries for a year. They never owed that much. Perhaps his ma stored them away?"

"Could it be his mother buried there?" Clare knew she grasped at straws.

"They wasn't Gypsies, but they was Jews. Don't rightly know where his folks got buried. Probably not in no Christian cemetery."

"That's sad." Patience took back the box. "The bones should have a proper burial if they belonged to Mrs. Bergstein. Abraham must have wanted the trinkets to remain with his mother if he buried her with them."

"Except he gave the ring to his wife," Mr. Oswald reminded them. "At least, that's what he said. He left not long after that. Don't remember a bride."

Perhaps he'd given the bride all his mother's trinkets? And then he *killed* her?

~

TUESDAY EVENING, SITTING IN HER MOTHER'S CELLAR PARLOR, Patience nearly knocked over her inkwell when Mr. Lavigne

—Henri—arrived at their door. Gentlemen weren't supposed to go below stairs!

"Your brother has returned," the handsome Frenchman said sternly. "You are to come to dinner with us, as he does."

That sounded like a command, as he'd obviously intended. She hastily righted the ink and set down her pen on the small desk. "Mother won't come. She has refused every invitation."

"That does not mean you must entomb yourself. Your brother is chaperone, *oui*?" Looking elegant in his fashionably knotted neckcloth, knit trousers, and polished dinner shoes, Henri was hard to refuse.

Besides, she was dying to hear what Paul had to say. And what Clare would report about the trinkets. Perhaps her Jewish friend had provided enlightenment on burials in their faith.

"I am in mourning, sir," she reminded him. "I have no black dinner gown."

He studied her bosom and grinned. She was learning that he knew when he was being obnoxious. She braced herself rather than cringe.

"As much as I long to see you in a dashing dinner gown, I will admit that it is unnecessary in this household," he said with regret. "Most of us are too busy to adhere to city rules. We eat when convenient and dress accordingly."

She knew perfectly well why he wanted to see her in a dinner gown. The single one she owned wasn't so fashionable as to bare her breasts, but it was closely fitted, and she hated wearing it. "Very well, if Paul will be there, and I can wear my Sunday dress, I will join you. Thank you for the invitation. At what time am I expected?"

He flashed his even, white teeth in a triumphant smile. She barely heard his reply over the stutter of her stupid heart.

"We gather in the family parlor about six. We eat when everyone arrives. Since Lady Elsa is often overseeing the meal, punctuality is futile." He bowed. "I am most pleased you will join us."

She had the impression he played his lovely accent for effect. She had heard him speak without it to men. Instead of despising his duplicity, her stupid heart fluttered more that he made the effort to charm her as if she were a real lady.

After he left, her mother carried in a pot of tea from the kitchen, sat on the faded sofa, and put her feet up on a stool she'd brought with her from home. "I hope Paul finds a church elsewhere. It can't help his career if it's known his mother is a domestic."

Patience tried not to roll her eyes. "You are a clergyman's wife and daughter. You are the only one assigning your reputation to a servant's position. Do you fear what Paul's grandmother said about us not staying?" Mr. Lavigne had informed them of the warning.

Nettie shrugged her plump shoulders. "Daniel Corcoran was always a difficult man, and Mrs. Corcoran lives in his shadow. I am comfortable here." Still wearing her apron, she sipped her tea while gathering her words. "I have always preferred staying home and keeping things sorted. I don't wish to have tea with ladies or deliver baskets to the poor. I wish to smash spiders and conquer dust."

"Which is why Papa called you a domestic goddess, I know." She kissed her mother's graying hair. "You defeat dirt and instill order. I miss him."

Nettie patted her cheek. "As you should, love. But now you have a chance to test your wings and fly. Wear the midnight blue. I don't think anyone here will object that it is not black."

Her unfashionable dinner gown. "It's silk, Mama! I will ruin it."

"Take my shawl. It's easily washed if you drip on it."

Cheeks heating that her mother recognized her problem,

Patience hurried back to the cubicle that held her narrow bed and limited wardrobe.

The blue silk had been handed down to her from a parishioner for a long-ago party. She didn't even know if it still fit.

Her undergarments were plain linen, but no one would know. The dress bodice was appropriately modest—but tight in the bosom. With a large shawl. . .

Eager to see her brother, Patience dutifully donned the silk with the silly cap sleeves. The skirt swished delicately over her hips—terrifying her that she'd step on the hem and rip it. She dared peek in the small mirror, grateful it revealed no more than face and throat. The blue did look pretty with her eyes. . .

She'd love to have a little pearl like the one in the box. Young Mr. Bergstein must have been grieving when he'd buried it with. . . The question was—who *had* he mourned? His mother? A wife? Mr. Oswald had only mentioned a bride and leaving town.

The orchard was a very strange place to bury anyone. She supposed he might have loved the trees. She was quite certain there was no Jewish cemetery, although the chapel should have some space set aside for non-believers.

Patience donned the delicate slippers she'd originally worn with the gown and wiggled her toes. The ankle ribbons felt beautifully light and frivolous, but the shoes had suffered the abuse of her big feet. Perhaps no one would notice. The ladies were eager to have banns cried, so Paul would be the center of attention.

It was past six by the time she arrived at the family parlor, clothed in her finery, feeling feminine and anxious in equal parts. She lingered in the doorway, studying the others to see how she compared.

Clare wore a lovely spring green gown, the low neckline modestly concealed with a colorful Kashmir shawl to ward off the evening chill. Lavender, of course, wore as many frills and laces as she could over her meager bosom. Meera always wore color—like a Gypsy, because bright colors looked well with her dark hair and complexion.

Patience breathed a little easier that she did not look terribly out of place. Daringly, she scanned the room for gentlemen, but only Mr. de Sackville and the captain were in sight, and they were lost in discussion.

She smiled in relief as her brother hurried down the hall.

Paul actually hugged her. That had to be a good sign that the meeting with the rector had gone well. Hope buoyed her onward.

As predicted, no one really noticed her after Paul's entrance. He almost appeared as if he belonged among the gentlemen. He'd had his hair barbered and wore a crisp white neckcloth. Who would do his laundry now?

Captain Huntley and Clare approached. She would have shrunk away from the towering, broad captain, but he barely noticed her existence. She felt marvelously free when a man did not stare. So she stayed at Paul's side, eager to hear if he'd be staying.

The men shook hands. The captain didn't even need to speak. Paul knew what he was expecting.

"Your letter did the trick, sir. I appreciate it. I am now the new curate of Gravesyde Priory Chapel."

Patience wanted to shout her joy as Clare did.

Mrs. Corcoran's warning muted her happiness. Why would Paul's grandmother not want him here?

FOURTEEN

THE MORNING AFTER THE NEW CURATE'S ANNOUNCEMENT, HENRI shoved his hands into his pockets, wandered past the stable, and down the lane toward the orchard. He should be driving into Birmingham with his goods and picking up orders, but Lavender's sewing circle wasn't quite finished with their garment order. And Arnaud had been in the orchard instead of finishing his commission.

Henri wasn't as inclined to spend his extra time helping with the parsonage yard now that Miss Patience wasn't there.

Instead, she was out with his brother, inspecting trees. They had spent most of dinner last evening discussing disgusting blights and bugs. She had looked magnificent in her blue silk and had actually *talked* to his brutish brother, who hadn't appreciated the effort she was making.

Henri had been forced to listen to young Miss Lavender natter about the lace she needed—for nightgowns. Now he had to carry the image of Miss Patience in lace and silk, with her lovely hair down—

The sight ahead dispelled that vision. He halted beneath a budding apple tree, fixated by all those feminine curves draped in an ugly broadcloth jacket three sizes too large for her slender form. From the backside, she almost looked like a very tall lad in his father's castaways. Almost. She wore a wool cap pulled over her golden hair. A few long wisps blew in the breeze around her rumpled neckcloth and slender throat.

She lifted her arm to point out a branch to one of the ex-soldiers bearing a pruning saw. She half-turned to point out another branch, and Henri grinned happily at the sight of linen and waistcoat hanging like sacks from her firm curves. Distracting, the fabric might be, but no man with eyes would believe she was male.

Just as Henri was about to make his presence known, Arnaud traipsed back from another part of the orchard. The lady eagerly turned in his direction, speaking excitedly. They had a long, involved conversation complete with expressive gestures.

So, the lady was only shy around him.

He didn't belong here. If the curate's daughter could bring his morose brother out of the black cave of unhappiness he'd locked himself into, Henri shouldn't interfere, not for a little flirtation.

Returning to the manor, he gave himself a good talking to. He was the younger, useless brother, the spare heir expected to earn his own way. And he was doing fine. He just wasn't pursuing the acceptable careers of military or ministry. It wasn't as if the English army would have a Frenchman or the Anglican Church accept a Catholic.

He liked talking, so peddling suited him. It would not suit a wife. Did he even want a wife? His head was most likely turned by all the happy couples at the manor. They seemed to complement each other well—and having a bed partner every night certainly had its advantages. So, he was a little jealous of their good fortune.

He should see if the new curate needed anything to speed up the weddings of the impatient couples. He might as well be useful.

And perhaps he could have a look at the church register now that the new curate had presumably returned it to the chapel. Other than learning if Bergstein married around 1779 to confirm what the postmaster said about the ring, he wasn't certain what to look for. But Hunt had thought it important to compare the register with the late clergyman's notebook.

He found the young curate in the churchyard, being berated by an older man, a farmer from the looks of him.

"I'll not be victim of your da's lies any longer! That book of his'n needs destroyin'. What's done is done and there's no changing it."

If the reference was to the notebook, here might be the reason the late Mr. Upton had been bashed over the head. Henri memorized the farmer's rough-hewn, bronzed features.

"And no matter how my Sara pleads, I'm not giving another fat hen to any church!" The farmer shook his fist in the clergyman's face.

Before Henri could intervene, Paul Upton caught the fist and shoved it away. For a slight man of peace, he had strength. "Mr. Bartholomew, I don't have the notebook. I don't need your hen. If you have repented your sins, the Lord has forgiven you. He might believe your repentance more if you actually attended church and prayed, but that's your choice, not mine. You might offer your wife a choice as well."

"She ain't goin' nowheres near this pit. Like father, like son, they say. You just keep outta my business." He spat on the ground and stalked away.

Looking harassed and less certain now that he was no longer threatened, the young curate glanced up at Henri's approach. "Do you think I'll even have a flock after my father threatened half the village or more?"

"The ladies will attend," Henri said with a shrug. "The manor's servants will follow their lead. I doubt anyone under fifty will know your father's ways. Find a wife who will feed the poor and teach the children—"

Paul grimaced. "And support her on what? The rector made it clear that the living provided isn't adequate to support even a curate. No one rents the chapel's meadow, and the portion he grudgingly offers as salary is miniscule."

Henri nodded understanding. "Wives are problematic without funds, agreed. The manor ladies won't let you starve, especially with your family to remind them. Hunt will pay you to see the buildings maintained. You'll find someone to rent the meadow. We all must start somewhere."

The other man picked up the shears he'd been using on the vines and weeds. "Thank you for that. The transition to being my own man while following directly in my father's footsteps is awkward. I appreciate the support. May I help you with anything?"

"The captain is interested in comparing the church register with our graveyard." That was only a tiny lie, a mere half-truth. "It seems disrespectful to leave graves barely marked and overgrown. We're hoping to put some of the ex-soldiers to work."

The curate almost managed a smile. "An admirable suggestion. And then my nosy sister can compare the names in the register with the initials in my father's notebook and discover who might want to murder him. My surmise is that everyone who lived here during the last decades of the last century would have happily done him in."

"But they didn't. Why? And why now? I doubt we'll ever know, but we might acquire a neat graveyard in the process. Do you know if there is a separate section for non-believers?"

"Like yourself?" Paul asked in amusement, leading the way across the shady, weed-patch lawn. "I believe the grave-yard at the Priory was originally established by the monks and used by the village ever since. So there are no doubt ancient Catholics, possibly buried beneath more recent Anglicans, but no non-believers in consecrated ground. The chapel once provided a small copse for non-Anglicans. I believe one of them bears the Bergstein name that my sister mentioned."

They pulled and cut back towering weeds and lengthy ivy until a few fallen stones came to light. Moss covered them, but Paul scraped it off on one of the larger monuments.

Bergstein, mother and father, 1780, it read.

"May they rest in peace," the curate said, as Henri crossed himself.

Where had Abraham Bergstein gone after the death of his parents and his employer?

And presumably, his wife?

EXERCISING HIS KNEE, HUNT AMBLED DOWN TO THE VILLAGE TO check on the new curate and his requirements for restoring the chapel and parsonage—and to discuss wedding banns. He found Paul Upton attacking a forest of vines.

"Do you think you can be prepared for a wedding service in three weeks?" Hunt stood back to examine the repairs to the chapel thatch—not that he knew much about thatch.

"If I am understanding the ladies correctly, there will be more than one service?" Mr. Upton, the younger, leaned against his hoe.

Hunt nodded. "We'll have to sort that out. I'm thinking one marriage a week might be best. The ladies may disagree."

"If the ladies manage all the fripperies, it is no difficulty for me to announce banns for three Sundays, then speak the service." Upton offered a small smile. "A wedding might even draw a little crowd. I need to convince people that I am not my father."

"I hope we have not placed you in an untenable position

by asking you to stay." Hunt frowned and kicked at a tree root. "We just thought your mother and sister. . ."

"You thought correctly. I cannot abandon them so soon after my father's death. He was a forceful man, good, in his own way. He leaves a hole in the fabric of our lives. I thank you for this opportunity and will do all I can to be what is needed here."

Hunt frowned but accepted the decision. "Have you inspected the register? Is all as it should be?"

"I have stored it in a safe place. Mr. Lavigne was here earlier to examine it. I don't know that he was enlightened."

"Henri was here? Did he say where he was headed?" Hunt wasn't entirely certain what to make of his younger, more amiable cousin. It was easy to ignore the ones who gave him no trouble.

"He asked after the graveyard for non-believers and was particularly interested in the Bergstein marker. I don't believe there is any of that family still about?"

Bergstein? The young man who'd sold his mother's ring and bought it back? Then buried it with bones? "Not that I'm aware of. Let us know what you need. Since the manor is now your family's home, come to dinner any time. Lady Elsa loves cooking, and hospitality is about all we can offer." Hunt tipped his hat and strolled back to the main lane through the village.

He stopped at the smithy to order more pipe for his gaslight project, then planned to return up the walking path to home. A group of men outside one of the abandoned inn buildings lured him from his goal.

"Used to come here of an evenin' to get away from the wife," one old man reminisced. "Decent, it were. A man could talk or smoke and none to say him nay."

"Bad brew," another old codger griped. "Blackie watered it down."

No sign hung over the door of the deteriorating half-timbered building, but Hunt gathered it must once have been a tavern.

"Did the place have a name?" a familiar voice asked from the interior. *Henri?*

The group of men separated, allowing Hunt to pass into the musty interior.

His young cousin was standing on what must once have been a bar, examining the rafters overhead. He grinned at Hunt's entrance. "They hung their mugs here."

"Kept kegs behind the counter," an old man said from a far corner. "We kept our own mugs here. I seen city taverns with booths. That'd be right warm in winter."

"A tavern?" Hunt asked, examining the walls of bare plaster and timber. "Wouldn't that require traveling customers?" Of which the village had none.

"To enjoy a pint or two in the evening?" Henri leaped down from the massive, dusty counter. "I know you lack imagination, Cuz, and you spend your evenings with your lady, but what of the rest of us? A place we can go after work. . . Not that I work, mind you."

Hunt might lack imagination, but the tone of Henri's voice opened doors. Henri was looking for a reason to settle down —and with his gift for gab and business sense, he'd be an ideal publican.

His bad knee prevented Hunt from climbing on the counter as his cousin had, but he was tall enough to examine the low ceiling. "A few leaks. The roof needs repairs. Tables, chairs. . . Not a problem. Probably need a license. The bank, however. . ."

"Bank ain't never owned this," one of the old men protested. "Bartholomews owned the inn long time back. Used to live here until they bought the farm. Only the tavern were left by then, and Old Blackie kept it operating, back when the lady was still here."

"Blackie?" Hunt tested the floor with his heavy boots

while Henri inspected beneath the massive bar. The late curate had argued with a Blackstone, but everyone said father and son had been gone for years. If one killed Upton, he was probably long gone again.

"Blackstones been here—"

"Since the monks died," a voice in back cried. "That's what he always said."

"Did the place have a name?" Henri asked again.

"Nope. We just called it Blackie's. Them's weren't good days. No work, the wives complainin'."

"Especially about the pennies we spent here," a voice cackled.

"The owner would be Mr. Bert Bartholomew then?" Hunt asked, hunting for practicality among the reminiscences. He'd met the farmer.

"Aye, he ain't got no interest in openin' it. He's got ten childern to feed."

"He could use the rent then," Henri said, almost to himself. "I know where to buy a few kegs."

"You'll need lamps, seats. We can scrounge the attics," Hunt suggested, falling under the spell of a tavern, like a real town. He missed sharing a mug with his fellows.

Henri brightened. "Let's visit this Bert fellow, shall we?"

The small crowd of old codgers cheered and led the way out of town.

Henri stepped back beside Hunt. "Bartholomew is the farmer Patience says her father threatened over a *grievous sin*. But Clare found no BB in the notebook."

Hunt pondered a moment. "Bert Bartholomew. Could he be an *Albert*? Another AB besides Abraham Bergstein and Archibald Blackstone?"

"So that's two, maybe three ABs. Let's see if this one beats his wife." Henri stepped blithely on.

Leaving Hunt wondering how a local magistrate could

remain objective when men he knew were hauled up for unspeakable, but all too common, crimes. He'd end up sending half the town to assizes, where the judges might be impartial but unlikely to care about the lives they destroyed with prosecution—the families left behind.

FIFTEEN

CLARE SPENT THE NEXT MORNING SEARCHING THE SPRAWLING, filthy attics for appropriate fixtures for a *tavern.*

"I never, ever, once dreamed I'd be furnishing a house of public drunkenness." She tugged a cloth off a collection of worm-eaten chairs and tables, probably dating back to the Tudors.

"The west wing has a billiard and smoking room for gentlemen. We only need open it up." Meera studied the stacked, hefty chairs and benches but did not attempt to lift them. "Why do they need a public tavern?"

"Because men are quite mad?" Lavender suggested, ignoring the useful furniture and examining trunks of moldering clothes.

"To balance out the church with a tavern? I suppose it is good to have another business in town." Clare swung down a substantial walnut chair and watched a leg fall off. She rubbed the filth off her hands onto her apron and grimaced.

"If Henri only runs it in the evening, he can still go into Birmingham with our goods, can't he?"

"You're starting to think like a practical merchant!" Clare regarded Lavender with admiration. "We should inquire."

"He will have to go into town for his ale." Lifting her oil lamp, Meera poked about in dark corners. The child she carried was just becoming visible. She shouldn't be climbing stairs, but curiosity ruled.

"Have you decided who weds first?" Lavender lifted an ancient silk from the trunk. Between age and the dim light, the color was difficult to discern.

"Jack and Elsa," Clare said firmly. "Or Elsa will abandon the kitchen."

"Walker and I don't need banns or ceremonies." Meera produced an ancient hanging oil lamp from a crate. "Mr. Upton says we just need witnesses to sign the register."

"Oh, you should have more than that!" Lavender cried. "We will all wear spring gowns and carry bouquets, and you should have a new hat!"

Mrs. Upton, their wonderful new housekeeper, arrived, huffing from the exertion of the stairs. She puckered her brow at the disarray. "This is dreadful. None of you should be in this pigsty. That is what staff is for."

Clare beamed at her. "You sound just like Mrs. Brown! She used to keep my family in order before my father died. It is a very good thing to have someone in the family who understands tidiness."

Mrs. Upton erased her frown. "It's what I know best and gives me a sense of accomplishment. Although we need more staff, at least another footman to run up these stairs. There is a Lord de Sackville at the door. He says his son invited him?"

No one had actually expected the book lover to leave his library! Oh, my, the baron was here, and she looked like a dustmop. "Jack's father, yes, of course. Have you sent someone to find Jack? Tell the baron I shall be right down. Ask Adam and Ned to haul down these chairs and tables when they have time, please? Meera can show them which ones."

"For the tavern?" Mrs. Upton's frown of disapproval

returned. "It used to be a wicked place, public drunkenness and bar fights. Quite disorderly."

And Mrs. Upton hated disorder. She must have hated Mr. Upton constantly uprooting her tidy home. But despite Hunt's doubts, one did not murder husbands over disorder. "Henri will not tolerate lawlessness. He knows the captain will close the tavern should that happen."

While Meera and Lavender discussed the sad lack of milliners and continued to peruse old trunks, Clare descended to her chamber to wash and remove her apron. Without a lady's maid, she couldn't do much about her dusty hem. She supposed she could have asked Mrs. Upton to help her with the buttons, but the housekeeper industriously returned to her tasks.

Clare checked the small mantel clock Hunt had repaired for her and realized it wasn't even noon. Lord de Sackville must have stayed in Birmingham to have arrived so early.

"Have you informed Jack of his father's arrival?" she asked Quincy once she'd run down the stairs. "And Hunt?"

"Mr. de Sackville is with his horses, miss. I have sent word. The captain is in the cellar and will be up for luncheon. I have sent tea to the library. His lordship insisted on waiting there."

"Most excellent, thank you, Quincy." Hearing voices emanating from the late earl's enormous library, she realized Oliver and his tutor must still be in there. That should be interesting.

The library's occupants barely glanced up at her appearance. Lord de Sackville was a slender gentleman in last decade's breeches and tailcoat, his graying hair brushing his collar. Spectacles perched on the tip of his nose, he stood at the bookshelves, riffling through pages, while Mr. Birdwhistle ran his finger down the library index, and Oliver dug through the stacks, looking for a particular volume.

Did she interrupt them? Curiosity was overwhelming, but they seemed so engrossed. . .

The tea tray arrived, and she gratefully directed its placement. Surely, once they saw food. . .

Oliver located what he was looking for, laid it on the table, and grabbed a scone, before returning to the shelves.

"Not with greasy hands, young man," the baron scolded, scarcely looking up from his book. "Finish eating, then wash. We really should be wearing gloves."

Finally noticing Clare, he nodded respectfully. "Your library is all that I've heard it would be. Thank you for allowing me to peruse it." He dived back into his book.

Well, that put her in her place. She took a *petit four*. . . She glanced down. A *petit four*? Elsa must have known her father-in-law-to-be was on the way. Time to drag the bride out of the kitchen.

Sending a maid to make up a room for the baron, Clare headed for the kitchen stairs, only to catch Elsa running up, wiping her hands on her apron.

"Is he in the library? Have you sent for Jack? Jack's father has always made me nervous. What do I say to him?" She hurried down the main corridor.

"Apparently, one does not say anything," Clare said with a laugh. "One leaves food in case he notices it. Go upstairs and change into something pretty for Jack. Perhaps Lord de Sackville will grace us with his presence at luncheon, but I wouldn't wager on it."

"No, no, of course not. He seldom leaves his library. I'm amazed—" She ran up the stairs without finishing the sentence.

Feeling like a clock mechanism with too many spinning wheels, Clare aimed for the informal dining room to see if enough plates had been provided, when Patience and Arnaud entered through the rear door, chattering. *Chattering.* Neither of them were talkers. Shy Patience was wearing. . . her brother's clothes?

Catching sight of Clare, Patience pulled off her gloves. "We are told to look for a Mr. Bergstein who knows about orchards. He is said to be back in town. Do you think he might be the man to whom Mr. Oswald referred?"

"*Abraham* Bergstein? The man who might have buried his mother's pearl with the bones?" Alarmed, Clare froze in place.

That would make three people who had returned after the bones were uncovered. Or rumored to have returned, since she had only met Upton.

Arnaud shrugged. "Should we find Bergstein, we will inquire. But he is said to be a fine orchardist. We need his knowledge. Is Henri about?"

Patience shook her hair out of her awful man's cap. "Arnaud would like to finish his painting, and he thinks Henri may find the gentleman."

Locating a possible criminal. . . Clare hated this. But if the jewelry box belonged to him, they needed to give it back. "Last I heard, Henri was at the tavern. We have a guest for luncheon. Will you eat before haring off in search of him?"

She didn't believe it was her place to warn a woman nearly her own age to take a chaperone, especially while hunting potential villains! Mrs. Upton had probably gone back downstairs. She might take her daughter to task.

"I'd much rather carry a lunch basket into town for Paul and Henri. I'm sure Jack and Elsa don't need my company." Apparently unconcerned about killers, Patience turned down the back hall for the service stairs, tearing at her man's neckcloth.

Arnaud silently took the marble stairs up, presumably to dress appropriately. He never missed a meal.

"Really, we may as well have horses perform in the hall.

This house is a circus and I don't wish to be ringmaster." Clare debated sulking in her office.

Fortunately, Hunt stomped in just then, wearing all his mud-encrusted filth. His smile at seeing her weakened her knees. She didn't object when he leaned over and kissed her from a distance so as not to ruin her morning dress any more than it was.

"I am told we have noble company. Do I have time to change?"

"I should hope so. You cannot sit down like that." She held him off and pointed upstairs. "I am not in the least certain that the baron will remember to eat. Jack does not exaggerate when he says his father never leaves his books. Only, it is our books that currently hold his attention."

"Excellent. Perhaps he can tell us where to sell them." Laughing, he dodged upstairs before she swatted him. "We could buy a carriage!" he threw over his shoulder before vanishing around the curve.

Although he was right. Precious volumes should not be left in the careless hands of this lot. Clare just feared the earl's ghost would return to haunt them if a single book left his library.

Or that they might be giving away the secrets to the jewels he may have hidden.

"I AM SIMPLY TAKING A LUNCH BASKET TO PAUL," PATIENCE explained to her mother as she stripped off her man's jacket and waistcoat. She wore her own shirtwaist beneath. The linen was thin and worn, but she could wear it with the riding skirt she'd been given in their last parish. The skirt was ridiculously long and not as good as men's clothes, but the fabric was far sturdier than muslin.

"You still need to take a maid with you," her mother fretted. "A woman alone is not safe."

"Then go down with me. You may insist on living below stairs, but you are not truly a domestic. You may come and go as the other ladies do." Patience wiggled into the riding jacket that matched the skirt. The outfit was more drab than dashing, but she had no desire to be noticed.

"There is no one to keep an eye on the kitchen staff if Lady Elsa takes luncheon upstairs. I must do that. If you would wait—"

"You still would not go with me. I know you too well. I'll see if one of the stable hands will accompany me. I do not like to ask them since I'm only a gardener with no authority." She tucked her hair into a straw hat with flowers that did not at all suit the outfit. But she hated stuffing her hair into a man's cap, and she owned no other.

A worried frown creased her mother's brow. "I don't know how you will meet a nice man and settle down like this. An earl's daughter might do as she pleases, but you. . ."

Patience kissed the top of her mother's head and started for the door. "I will not have to marry if I can live here and be a gardener." She ran out before another argument ensued.

She loved her mother dearly, but Nettie had been an impoverished old maid for too long to wish her daughter the same life. Patience wasn't at all certain, however, that marriage had improved her mother's position.

Loading up a basket with bread, meat, cheese, and pickles, she didn't bother stopping at the stable. The village was just down the hillside, less than a mile away. She patted the hound the new dog trainer was walking, waved at Ned, the deaf adolescent who ran the captain's errands, and took the walking path she remembered from childhood. She felt as if she'd finally come home.

Humming happily, she stooped to pick a bouquet of wildflowers. Before she could break one off, a massive hand grabbed her arm from behind and hauled her upright.. She emitted an *eep*, and a burly, black-bearded man shook her until she froze in terror.

"Pretty girls shouldn't be out here alone. You go back to that man of yours and tell him them trees got bugs because they never get winter washed, and the old leaves need raking and burning. They've been left too long without manure. And he should take better care of his woman or he'll lose her. Go!" He pointed back up the trail.

The second he released her arm, Patience slammed the basket at his midsection, driving him backward in surprise. She grabbed her long skirts and ran—down the hill, not up.

She kept running until she reached the village, where Henri was just emerging from his tavern and heading her way. She stumbled over a tree root and nearly fell into his arms. "A man," she gasped, trying to catch her breath. "A stranger! In the woods."

The men around him halted.

Henri held her as she gasped for air. His strong arms sheltered, but the fury in his voice frightened. "Did he touch you? I shall kill him if he so much as—"

She shook her empty head. She wasn't worth violence. "No, no, he told me to *manure the trees*!"

Now that she was safe, she sobbed and laughed over her foolish behavior. "I gave him your lunch and just ran."

"My lunch?" He managed to look murderous and sound amused at the same time.

She clung to him in hopes his rationality would calm her pounding heart. She feared she would have the vapors, and he was her port in the storm.

"Come, you must sit down and explain." Without releasing her, he signaled one of the men. "Will you look up the path for a man with a lunch basket? We don't want him terrifying the ladies."

Another took off in a different direction. Gossip would fly in instants.

Embarrassed, Patience tried to step away, but Henri wouldn't let her go. He was strong, and she was feeling ridiculously weak now that the incident was over. And his hold felt safe, unlike that of the mad man's.

"Come, let us sit you down. Someone will fetch your brother. You are unharmed, and that is what matters. Although I do regret the lunch." Arm around her shoulders, Henri led her into the low-ceilinged cottage he evidently meant to turn into a tavern.

"I brought enough for you and Paul," she babbled. "The manor is entertaining Jack's father, and I did not want to dress for a baron. I don't know why I gave him the basket." Once she was seated on a crude bench, she buried her face in her hands. She was such a ninny.

"We will follow the trail of bread crumbs and find him sleeping off the best meal he's eaten in his miserable life," Henri proclaimed cheerfully. "What is important is that you are safe, mademoiselle. What, exactly, did he say to you?"

Keeping her head down, she rubbed her brow and tried to recall. Now that he wasn't holding her, she felt even more foolish. "He kept telling me what to say to 'my man.' I don't know who he thought I was."

"He mentioned trees?" Henri drew her out.

"Yes. He warned me against going about alone and told me to winter wash the trees for bugs and burn leaves. I don't think he's right in the head."

"What does this man look like?"

She finally looked up, puzzling it out. "A bear of a man. Dark beard. Same height as me, but much wider and fearsome. I did not really look at him. I froze. And then I shoved the basket and ran." She glanced at her skirt. "I needed my hands to hold up all this wretched material."

"Which is why ladies do not go out unaccompanied," he

said sternly. "Perhaps, he did you a favor. What if he had been a really bad man?"

Patience scowled. "If I could have worn trousers, I would have kicked his shins and punched his snout. I hate skirts." She was too angry to be quiet.

"Ah, she is back. I may sympathize, mademoiselle, but I would much rather be the gentleman who escorts you. Do you think, perhaps, he has been watching the orchard and has seen you with Arnaud, and that is to whom he refers?"

"I don't know. I just want him caught and questioned. If he knows so much about the orchard, he should be working in it and not frightening me into an early grave." She stood and shook out her riding skirt to steady her nerves. "Now we will all have to go back and forage whatever is left from the buffet."

"First, we will go to your brother and reassure him and send someone to the manor with word of trespassers. And we'll ask for another lunch. Mrs. Ingraham will eat it all otherwise." He took her hand on his arm and strolled into the lane as if into a ballroom.

She had to laugh at the reference to Lavender's grand-mother. The plump lady did enjoy her food. But she pulled away to peer into his dark cave and study it as she hadn't in her state of panic. "There are no windows!"

"In the back. It is shuttered, the glass broken. At night, it is no matter. It is very shabby, I know, but it does not cost much. It is an experiment. The captain is fond of experiments, so I will try too." He waited patiently for her to return outside.

"I believe the whole family likes to experiment." She took his arm again. Why did she find it so easy to speak with this interfering man who spent so much time annoying her? "Perhaps science is contagious."

He laughed. "Perhaps so. You are experimenting at being a man?"

Well, at least he was amusing while roasting her. "I am a

gardener. I wish to be treated as such. I can think of no other way of accomplishing it. But no, I do not wish to be a man." Especially when he made her feel very much like a woman. It was rather unsettling but not unpleasant.

"That is good. I do not want you to be a man either." He gestured at the parsonage, where her brother was running out the gate, looking worried.

"Patience! What happened? Are you all right?" Her brother rushed up, then stopped to study her clinging to Henri's arm.

She quickly dropped the arm and hugged Paul. "I am quite fine, just feeling foolish because I lost your lunch basket. We are looking for a man called Bergstein who used to work in the orchard. We have heard he's returned. Have you met him yet?"

"Bergstein?" Paul glanced at Henri. "The family whose graves you found?"

"Possibly a son. The earl's records show an AB working in the orchards when the earl was here, so he'd be in his fifties or older. We were thinking AB might be Blackstone or Bartholomew, but there were so many more people living here then. . ." He gestured helplessly, then turned to Patience. "Who told you about this person?"

"One of Arnaud's pruners. Mr. Oswald did not think any Bergsteins were still about." Admittedly, a man who might have buried a pearl in an orchard with bones did not seem like the best man to seek.

"I should start visiting and learn my parishioners," Paul admitted. "I've been hiding, fixing what I can with my hands."

Patience nodded at the general store. "Mr. Oswald knows everyone. He may know where the family used to live."

The men seemed reluctant. Impatiently, she strode up the steps, not stumbling on them this time. "Mr. Oswald," she called to the old clerk and postmaster behind the counter.

She'd been told he was once a teacher, but she didn't remember him. "You remember telling us of a Mr. Bergstein?"

"Abe? The man you saw in the woods?" he asked. "He don't like people much."

They all three stared. Henri spoke first. "How do you know she saw him in the woods?"

"Only man ever wears a beard except them soldiers, and they's all too crippled to bother a lady. Last I heard, Abe's got all his limbs." He pondered that a moment, then returned to counting the cash in his drawer.

Abraham Bergstein was the earl's orchardist?

"He is the only Bergstein around here?" Paul asked.

"So far as I know," Oswald said without looking up.

"How long has he been back?" Patience asked. "You didn't mention it the other day when we talked about him."

Oswald squinted at her. "Ain't rightly seen him. It's just gossip."

Patience sighed in exasperation and tried to recall all the entries in her father's book. AB had beaten his wife. Another AB had an S after his name. Stealing? Stabbing? She didn't know how her father's mind worked.

But according to Mr. Oswald, the pearl buried with the bones had belonged to the *Bergsteins*, and if *Abraham* was the only one. . . She wished she knew more curse words. Or perhaps a magic spell or two.

SIXTEEN

"You want a man who might have murdered his wife working in the orchard?" Henri asked his brother as they loaded furniture into his peddler's cart late Thursday afternoon—when they ought to be dressing for dinner.

Since he'd begun hauling boxes and barrels instead of trinkets, Henri had removed all the shelves and drawers from the paneled horse cart. The ancient table and chairs from the attic just barely fit inside. He added a crate of battered tin mugs from the servants' hall that Elsa had provided.

"I want a man who knows the trees better than I do so I can return to painting." Arnaud heaved the last heavy chair into the load and threw in the broken leg. "And we don't *know* that he murdered his wife."

"And what about Miss Patience?" Henri shouldn't be angry with his brother, but sometimes Arnaud was thick as a brick. "He's a wild beast who terrified her."

"Once we have an orchardist in place, she can return to knitting or whatever it is women do. She shouldn't be out there pretending to be a man. Are you heading into town tomorrow? I'll have that oil done." Arnaud stepped back and dusted off his hands.

Henri wanted to take the chair leg to his brother's thick skull. If the dull wit did not see how shy Patience came out of her shell in his company, he wasn't one to enlighten him.

"Yes, if you've finished the work, I'll take the painting and Lavender's buttons into town and return with kegs. How good are you at painting walls? The tavern could use a good whitewash, if naught else." Henri stuck with tasks Arnaud understood.

He'd have to determine if Bergstein was mad on his own. Arnaud wouldn't.

"I'll go in with you, take a look. But crumbling walls don't hold paint. I could paint a tavern sign if the new curate will cut one out. Do you have a name yet?"

"Not Blackies." Henri was firm on not using the former owner's name.

"Hard to come up with a symbol for NOT BLACKIES."

Henry snorted. His high and mighty brother had made a jest. The world had come to an end. Or perhaps *le comte* was starting to heal.

They played with tavern names as the cart rattled down the drive, but they were French, and English tavern names were ridiculous.

"Red Bull, and I will paint a bull on your wall," Arnaud suggested as they pulled in front of the crumbling tavern. The sunny day had clouded over and threatened rain. "Although, if the roof leaks, paint is the least of your worries."

Before Henri could answer, a few of the old men who'd encouraged him arrived to help unload furniture. Henri hadn't sorted out their names yet.

"The new curate fixed some of them leaks," the bald one said, pointing at patches in the wooden ceiling.

"Ain't a half bad lad. Mary's son grew up right."

"She was always better'n Teddy. Never seen brother and sister so different."

Henri absorbed the gossip as he directed furniture place-

131

ment and checked the roof repairs. Thunder in the distance warned they would be tested shortly.

"Lad's a carpenter. Reckon he can fix this chair." The bald old fellow took a seat and tested the legs by leaning back in it. "George, you still got that old chair used to be in here?"

As Henri examined the whitewashed, wattle walls with Arnaud, men came and went, carrying in bits of memorabilia from the former tavern that they'd apparently appropriated for their own. Just listening, he learned about George, William, and Charley, the old codgers who'd once spent their evenings here. Questioning would only silence them, so he eavesdropped.

"A fresh coat of plaster should do it," Arnaud decided. "Come up with a name, and I can do a mural between the half-timbering, as well as a sign."

Henri produced a small keg from the cart. "All right, gents, where are your mugs? We need to christen this place. Do we call it The Monk's Tavern?"

"Monk's!" they shouted, grabbing their mugs from the bar.

"You want me to paint a monk on the wall?" Arnaud asked in incredulity.

Henri handed him one of his own mugs. "A beautiful woman with golden hair and periwinkle blue eyes. I'm not calling it the Maid's tavern!"

"Wise choice." Arnaud tipped his tin mug to Henri's just as the door swung open.

All eyes turned to the newcomer shaking raindrops off his hat. A man of slight height but husky shoulders, thinning dark hair with gray streaks, he didn't appear dangerous. He wore a gentleman's attire, and the other fellows grew silent, swinging their gazes to their mugs.

"Can a man get a mug on a night like this?" he asked, sidling up to the bar.

"Not licensed yet." Henri tried to recall where he'd seen the face. He poured a short one in a spare tankard and set it in front of the newcomer. "On the house. I'm Henry." He deliberately used the English pronunciation until he had the man's measure.

"Ted." He lifted the mug in thanks and chugged it down.

Ted. Henri had a memory for names. Teddy Corcoran? The young curate's uncle? Right, he remembered noting at the funeral that the young curate and the Irishman were of similar build, except Paul had his late mother's red hair, according to the gossips. Rumor had it that Teddy had coin. That made him welcome.

Thunder exploded overhead and a deluge hit the roof. Henri directed his attention upward, studying the stained places for leaks, wishing he'd thought to bring food. It could be a long night. Good thing the keg was almost empty.

The door abruptly crashed open, and a large fellow all in black staggered in, roaring. "You're stealing the tavern now as well?"

Henri winced. Arnaud stiffened. Corcoran simply sipped his ale. Settled in with their mugs, the other occupants regarded the newcomer warily. Henri searched his surroundings for a weapon, just in case. The man was a big brute, but there wasn't a lot he could wreck, he decided.

"Tavern's his'n, fair and square. We watched Bert sign it all proper," the gent named William called over a roll of thunder.

Unappeased, the big, black-haired stranger swung a massive fist at the keg on the bar. Henri snatched it from destruction, then ducked down to set it on the floor, keeping his head out of range as well. The drunkard bellowed and shoved off all the pewter mugs Henri hadn't hung yet.

Arnaud leaned against the bar, drink in hand, but the tension in his shoulders said he could strike at any second. Not wanting his big brother fighting his battles, deciding the stranger dressed in black was more inebriated than dangerous, Henri stood up out of reach. "Don't have a fire to offer, but have a seat out of the rain, sir. We're all friends here."

"No Frenchie is a friend of mine." The stranger leaned over the bar and breathed cheap gin in Henri's face. "You're one of them aristosnots from the manor, ain't you? Just wait until I get my papers and prove I have as much right there as you!"

Snot. Nice. The man had a way with the vernacular.

Arnaud sipped his ale and regarded the blustering bully. "The gentleman does look a trifle like us, does he not?" Since Henri and Arnaud were *not* related to the Reid family in any way except by marriage, he was being malicious. "Although twenty years older. Perhaps he was one of our great-aunt's lovers and that entitles him to the manor?"

The stranger pounded the bar. "I am Duncan Reid, grandson of David, the earl's brother! That makes the viscountess my great-aunt too."

Well, no, not unless there was a lot of incest happening, and perhaps a bit of time travel. The impostor needed a more accurate idea of their ancestry.

According to the family tree tapestry, the earl's younger brother had died half a century ago. Had the brother produced a son, he'd have to have done it in adolescence. Henri was quite certain the lawyers would never have missed a legitimate male heir in their decades long search.

The late viscountess had been French and her sister was Henri's mother. So, no, the drunkard couldn't claim the lady's side of the family either.

Henri gestured at an empty chair. "Well, have a seat, Lord Reid. Or is it Wycliffe? Tell us of where you've been since the last earl died."

"In India, as I told that American usurper. I come home to discover everything given to strangers!" He fell into the ancient chair everyone else had the sense to avoid. The back leg tilted, and he nearly slid to the floor. He was too pickled to notice.

Ted Corcoran settled in a dark corner, listening.

"You don't sound swell enough to be an earl's grandson," Old Man George called.

"He don't sound like *us* neither," Charley argued. Bald and average height, he'd brought his own chair and claimed his place beside the cold hearth.

"To be fair, *me*—I do not zound like any of you." Amused, Henri exaggerated his accent while studying the fake heir, but Clare was quite correct. Duncan Reid did not have the look of any of the ancestral portraits. "What did you mean, that this is your tavern?"

"It's Bert's place. Everyone knows that," George argued. A once burly man turned to pudginess with age, he'd asserted himself as the tavern authority.

"My da's family been here longer than the monks." The chair leg gave out, and the fake Lord Reid landed hard on the rough wooden floor. Cursing, he stood and slammed the chair into the hearth, shattering it into pieces. "Don' need this damn piece of shit. I'll get what's mine." Apparently having said his piece, he staggered out.

Arnaud stood and slammed the door closed after him.

"What happened to Blackie's son?" Bald Charley asked out of the blue.

Henri prevented his eyebrows from reaching his hairline. They'd said *Blackstones* had been here since before the monks. Charley was quick on comprehension.

"Old 'un died. Young 'un married and moved on, long time back," George the Authority answered. "Way back when the old lord were still here. Did summat to make his lordship angry, and he ordered him outta town."

"Blackstone's son?" Henri asked, pouring his brother the last of the ale.

"Archie, he was. He'd be near as old as me if he lives."

Short and stout, William had cropped iron gray hair and didn't sport as many wrinkles as George and Charley. Henri placed him in his fifties.

"Heard Archie Jr. got 'pressed into the Navy after he left here. Reckon he had a son after he left? Has the look of old Blackie, summat," George mused.

Henri was fairly certain the stranger's black hair was dyed with boot polish. His face had been weathered. . . The faux Reid could easily be in his fifties. He was heavy and muscular —from a life in the Navy?

"*Archie* Blackstone was the barkeep's son?" Henri asked, to clarify. Was this the AB in the curate's black books? The one who beat his wife or was guilty of S?

"Ay yup, but that fella don' look like the runt what was," William said, confusingly. "I'd best be off before the wife worries." He returned his mug and strode out, none the worse for drink.

"Does he have far to go?" Henri asked, listening to the rain on the roof.

"Nah, he's in town. The street will be running a river soon." George studied his empty mug with regret.

"If that's all the ale, I'll be off to home too." Gentleman Teddy lifted himself from the corner and drifted into the night.

Henri might need to keep a musket behind the bar. The faux Reid wasn't a runt and had a temper. Ted Corcoran might be a runt, but he had an attitude of defiance. It didn't take more than that to start a battle.

HUNT WASN'T AT ALL CERTAIN HOW HE HAD ENDED UP IN THE library after dinner when he should have been enjoying a leisurely brandy at the table.

Instead, he was listening to Lord de Sackville lecture on

the quality and content of ancient volumes, while Jack and the women took notes and created neat stacks of aging tomes. Even Walker had joined in, probably toting pounds and shillings in his head.

The earl's library was apparently worth a fortune—to the right people.

With his one weak eye, Hunt felt like Lavender, left out of the proceedings. He wanted to abandon the lecture to Jack and Elsa, drag Clare away to. . . what? Discuss coal retorts? Not likely. What did married people discuss?

Unmarried people discussed marriage. Now that they had a clergyman, he wanted to discuss dates. She would ask about guests. They would have to open a wing—

Quincy rapped on the door. The butler usually scratched discreetly. Hunt's head jerked up from where he'd been nodding off. The butler had a stout little man with him, holding a worn cap and looking awed and anxious at the same time.

"There has been an incident, sir." The stoic butler added an unusual hint of urgency to his tone.

Clare stood when Hunt did, apparently catching the nuance. The others remained captivated by the lecture—or riches—and paid no attention.

Hunt let Clare into the hall first, then closed the door behind them. "An incident?"

"The curate, my lord, captain, sir. Someone ransacked the church. The lad was still there. They broke his skull, just like his da's," the short, stout man said nervously, obviously straining to pronounce all his consonants.

Clare gasped. "Is he. . . ?"

"Breathing, my lady, miss, but bleedin' fierce."

Before she could even call for Meera, the apothecary hurried down the hall, followed by the footman carrying her medical bag. Quincy and Adam were efficient.

"Henri's cart is still in the village," Hunt warned her. "You cannot go out on foot in this rain."

"They're loading him up as we speak," the little man explained. "But the church is a right mess. The thief tore it all to pieces."

"I'll tell Patience and Mrs. Upton," Clare said quietly. "Meera, what will you need from the kitchen? Hot water?"

The women scurried off to prepare. Hunt would prefer to break heads, but first, he needed to catch the criminal. "I'll ride down, see what can be done." He glanced at the visitor. "Thank you, sir. I apologize for not knowing your name."

"William, sir, William Oswald, postmaster's brother. Pleased to meet you. I'll be off. The wife will worry." He returned the cap to his iron gray hair and hurried toward the carriage exit.

Hunt had worn his boots into dinner. They were comfortable, and he didn't care to impress a baron with fancy attire. He was seeing the benefit of staying prepared if he must act as magistrate or justice of the peace or whatever in hell he represented.

Quincy waited for orders.

"No need to inform the others just yet. Henri and Arnaud are already there. See that Meera has all she needs. I'll head down on my own." Hunt strode off for the stable.

He took Ned with him. The adolescent was eager to work. As a deaf-mute, he wasn't given enough work to occupy him. But he was a strapping, bright lad, nearly as strong as Hunt. If there were murderous thieves about, Ned knew what to do.

Henri, Arnaud, and half the village waited for him at the bottom of the hill. The lane to the chapel was only a brief distance from the manor drive. Several women were weeping, and Hunt's stomach lurched. Had the curate *died*?

Henri was already on the cart. Seeing Hunt's expression, he said, "The lad's alive. He must have interrupted the burglary. Let Arnaud explain." He whipped his patient horse into a trot, and the crowd parted to let him pass.

Gnawing on fury, Hunt rode up the lane. Once so overgrown that he hadn't even known the church was there, the hedges had been neatly cut back and the stone path unburied from years of debris. The new curate had been busy. Like the women, Hunt didn't want to believe a good, hardworking man could be a murderer, and he didn't wish to lose the lad to some criminal element he should have known about.

Arnaud met him inside the chapel. A bald, older gent and a woman of similar age were with him. Arnaud introduced them as Mr. and Mrs. Charles Jones.

"Used to act as deacon in the late Mr. Upton's time," Mr. Jones said. "The missus here helped with the flowers and such." He indicated the shambles around them. "This wasn't called for. The chapel never had more than pewter and a few gewgaws. Ain't even had that lately. Never been anything worth stealing."

"We were sewing cushions for the benches," Mrs. Jones said, wiping at a tear.

In the light of several oil lamps, Hunt examined the wreckage—benches overturned and broken, the altar smashed with what must have been an ax. . . Had they taken an *ax* to the poor lad? He peered into the darkness, but the curate hadn't unshuttered the windows yet. Anticipating destruction?

"This looks more like malicious vandalism than theft. A thief has no need to destroy benches." He entered the church to right an unharmed pew. "Would anyone have been out in this weather to notice strangers?"

He had a yard full of damaged ex-soldiers trained in violence. Hunt couldn't imagine any of them drunk enough to do anything this irrational.

The only thing of value the church might have possessed was the official register—and the former curate's notebook?

The notebook was in Hunt's desk. He didn't know where Paul had locked up the register.

Arnaud all but snarled, "The personage calling himself Duncan Reid did some damage at the tavern earlier. The men thought he resembled the late Archibald Blackstone."

Hunt pondered Archibald Blackstone. All he knew was that there was a father and son and the late curate had recently threatened one. A *Blackstone* was the fake heir? And the AB who beat his wife or committed S? Why would he call himself Duncan Reid? To hide from Upton? Except, even if no one else had, *Upton had recognized him*. That churned Hunt's instincts.

"The man calling himself Duncan Reid was a big man, black hair, bronzed as if he's been in the sun. Does that sound like your Blackstone? Why would he smash a church? Or a tavern?"

"That be him." Holding his cap, Mr. Jones tugged it in circles. "The old Mr. Upton that was, he was down on Blackie Junior pretty bad when he was just a stripling. The boy was wild, he was, drinking, fighting. Mr. Upton complained. Finally, the old earl told Blackie to leave town, or he'd have him hauled to assizes. If this be him posing as a lord, he ain't changed his ways, just his looks. Used to be a stripling, and his hair weren't ne'er black."

"Well, if Blackstone Junior did this, I'll do what my great-grandfather should have done." Hunt was only just learning his new judicial duties. It was good to follow the earl's direction in this matter.

"Why would this Blackstone claim to be a Reid when he was bound to be recognized?" Arnaud asked, righting overturned benches.

"Half the people around here are related to the Reids," Mrs. Jones declared with a humph of disapproval. "Centuries of the same families, above and below stairs, mixing in the manor. . . Young people are no better than animals."

Hunt winced. Clare's policy of accepting even illegitimate heirs had come back to haunt them. From the woman's glare, she was making a statement.

Blackstone believed he was a bastard of the earl's nephew? Even the banker, Bosworth, hadn't gone around claiming to be an heir, and he actually was fathered by a Reid —and looked like one.

Mrs. Upton, their new housekeeper, was also said to be one of the Reid family by-blows—and looked like one. She hadn't made any claim on the estate either.

Blackstone might be a little mad and a lot drunk.

"Do you have any notion where Mr. Blackstone resides?" Hunt began stacking the remains of axed benches beside the door. They were scarcely more than worm-eaten firewood.

"His da had a place out where young Mr. de Sackville keeps his horses. Field's been fallow since the old man died," the elderly Mr. Jones declared, looking militant.

"All right, we'll see if he made it home." Hunt gestured with his head at the door, and Arnaud and Ned followed him out.

"Drunkard could be lying in a ditch. On a night like this, we're not likely to find him," Arnaud argued sensibly as the rain poured off the capes of his greatcoat.

Hunt signaled Ned, then pointed at the lantern the boy carried. Ned nodded understanding and began searching the shrubbery. The boy had quickly learned to interpret signs.

"Did you see him with a horse?" Hunt examined the ground around the chapel. With so much shrubbery, a horse could only be concealed in a few places. He saw no dung.

"Huh. No. On foot, how far can he get? I rode down in the cart. I'll search the side of the road from foot. You go ahead." Arnaud took his lantern and started down the lane.

Before he got far, Ned whistled and gestured to the woods beyond Patience's garden plot where a scrap of paleness lay among the debris of dark, rain-soaked leaves.

They converged on the patch in the light of the boy's lantern.

A large, black-haired man lay sprawled in a puddle of muddy water.

Even from his horse, Hunt could tell Blackstone hadn't made it home safely.

Had there been a fight and the *curate* struck a fatal blow, before collapsing? Paul was young and strong and had been present at the time of both deaths. . .

SEVENTEEN

Outside the manor infirmary, Patience held her hysterically weeping mother. Nettie had raised Paul since he was a toddler. He was the perfect child, more so than her own daughter. Patience understood. Paul was their future. If anything happened to him. . .

The world would suffer as great a loss as his family. Her mild-mannered, hardworking half-brother was the best man she knew. She tried not to dissolve into tears for her mother's sake, but she couldn't imagine a future without her understanding, capable brother in it.

On top of their father's loss. . . It was too much to bear.

Patience held her mother while Jack held a weeping, terrified Elsa. The captain was still in town with Arnaud, searching for the vandals, and Clare was in the infirmary, helping Meera. Walker was outside, gathering an army. If prayers worked, perhaps all of the couples wishing to marry would keep her brother alive.

Henri paced up and down the hall, as helpless as she was. When her mother started babbling about never returning to this evil place and the ghosts of people past, Patience turned a lost look to him. "Would you help me take her downstairs? A bit of tea and a little laudanum might not be amiss."

Jack and Elsa immediately sprang apart, remembering their distress wasn't as anything compared to Nettie's.

"Let me do it," Elsa begged. "I'll make a nice pot of tea. I have some of Meera's soothing powders. I can try those. Jack?"

He gently pried Nettie from Patience's arms, and the trio traversed the back hall to the kitchen stairs. Patience was torn between waiting to hear about Paul and going with them. She hated standing here, doing nothing.

"Send someone up with tea for Miss Patience," Henri called after them. "We will be in Clare's office."

Jack waved acknowledgment. Startled, Patience didn't object as Henri grasped her elbow and led her to Clare's study just down the hall. His strength was somehow comforting, even though she knew being alone with him was highly improper.

"We must think, put our heads together. It will occupy our time while we wait. You are about to tear your pretty hand-kerchief to tatters." He seated her in the wing chair beside the hearth and began arranging a fire.

Patience glanced at the tattered cloth in her hands. It had no doubt been in sad state before she rendered it useless. "Why would anyone hurt Paul? He would give them the shirt off his back, if he could. Anything they wanted, they had only to ask."

"But he had naught to give," Henri concluded, striking a flint and setting it to the kindling. "They wanted something he did not have. Your father's notebook?"

"The captain has it," she decided after some thought. Then in alarm, she asked, "Will they hurt the captain next? Come here and hurt more people? We should burn it!"

Henri shook his head, then stood and took her hands. "You're cold as ice." He rubbed her fingers to return warmth.

"If I could stop this monster, I would. But good people don't think like bad ones. How would you let a monster know the book was destroyed if you do not know who he is? And we cannot even know that was his goal."

She shouldn't allow this intimacy, but his strength and warmth eased her churning thoughts, allowing her to concentrate on Paul. She prayed silently, promising God she would do nothing but good if he would only save her brother.

A faint floral scent drifted around them, dragging her back to the here and now. She reclaimed her hands and glanced around in puzzlement. "Do I smell jasmine? I once worked in a greenhouse where they grew exotics. Do you grow it here?"

Henri employed his Gallic shrug to good effect, drawing her gaze to his broad shoulders in their tightly tailored coat. "My great-aunt favored the perfume. Clare says her ghost haunts us. More importantly—do you know where your brother keeps the church register?"

She looked at him with confusion. "The register? Why?"

"That is another valuable your brother possesses. I think a thief did not get what he wanted, which is why he tore up the church. And if you think Paul would have given it to him if he had it. . . Then he did not have the book either."

She shook her head. "I don't think he would have given the register away. If my father did as he ought, the bishop should have a copy of prior years, so it is not so very valuable, but it is an official church and government document. He would have fought with a thief to prevent losing it. Besides, he didn't have it. He hid it here with us. Which is odd, now that I think about it."

Henri seemed to brighten. He arranged his greater size by sitting cross-legged on Clare's hearth to feed coal into the flames. "Not so odd. Very smart, I should think. Your father might have been killed for his little notebook, but it stands to reason he must have had proof for blackmail to work?"

Patience covered her mouth with her now-warm hands.

"Oh, my, of course! Father couldn't just stand up in church and say Mr. X stole the horse. He'd need proof."

"And he carried very little on him except his notebook. And that did not cause any trouble until he returned to Gravesyde, where the register resides." Henri didn't sound entirely certain of his reasoning.

"To be perfectly correct, all the churches Father served had their own register. But we were never in any one place long enough for him to cause much trouble. Gravesyde was his parish. This was where he lived the longest." Patience's thoughts raced. "And he was very reluctant to claim the register or visit the rector."

"But Paul did not have knowledge of the register's danger and brought it back here." Henri wrinkled his broad brow. "But what could possibly be dangerous about a record of births and deaths?"

"And marriages," she added, because she couldn't think of a reason either. Perhaps a burial after AB did BW? "I suppose someone might have believed there is only the one copy."

Henri followed his own train of thought. "So your brother obtained the register, and then, after all these many years, the church was ransacked. We will have to wait for him to wake to tell us exactly what happened, but right now, we should examine the register and the notebook together, look for anomalies?"

The warmth of the fire and the lingering floral scent acted as restoratives. Her mind was leaping like a frog's. This handsome gentleman was no doubt trying to distract her, but he could very well be right. Paul must have had some inkling of danger when he hid the register here—unless he hid their father's secrets.

Might they find her mother's ghosts by looking at dates and names of people long dead or gone? "My mother may know more than Paul. That may be the reason she is hiding here."

Henri nodded sympathetically. "Yes, I think so too. But we should not disturb her with questions just yet, *non*?"

"No, no, she's not coherent. If Paul recovers. . . Perhaps she'll be angry enough to speak. He's her pride and joy. Should we figure out who did this, the captain will have to spirit the culprit away before she finds out, or she might kill him barehanded. She is a model of efficiency and decorum, until someone hurts us, then she becomes a fierce mother bear. She once took a stick to a man who hit Paul."

Henri grinned in that manner that would have her swooning if she let it. "How did the man fare?"

"He ran off as if confronted with a mad woman, which she most certainly was at that moment. One does not hit *children*." Patience had been raised knowing that. No matter how rambunctious she and Paul had been, her mother found ways of dealing with them that didn't involve hitting.

"Until she is ready to talk, we must sleuth on our own. Perhaps if we make educated guesses, she is more likely to respond? I will fetch the notebook from the captain's desk, if you know where to find the register." He stood expectantly.

"My mother locked it up. I don't know if I can find the key, but I will try." Reluctantly, she followed him to the hall. He strode toward the study. She had to hurry in the other direction, to the service stairs and their small apartment off the kitchen.

Downstairs, Jack and Elsa were entertaining her mother at the kitchen table, surrounded by staff. A brandy decanter was at Jack's right hand. They'd found a better medicine than powders. Her mother looked a little flushed.

Patience slipped into their rooms, found the housekeeper's key ring, and sought the small, ornate one she'd seen her mother use on a drawer in her clothing cupboard. Nettie had

147

shown her the false bottom, so she knew where to look. She slid it out, found the large ledger, and put the key back. Then smuggled the book out under a layer of linen in need of washing.

As if understanding Patience needed secrecy, Jack and Elsa distracted her mother so she could slip by. The staff paid her no mind while they had a baron's son and an earl's daughter entertaining them.

She felt guilty enough breaking and entering. She didn't want anyone else to know the register was at hand, not if it was a reason for murder. She left the linens in the laundry room and rushed back up stairs.

She stopped at the infirmary first, nearly running into Lavender carrying a bucket of bloody cloths. She grimaced. "How is he?"

"He's coming around," Lavender whispered. "Meera says he'll be fine. She thinks someone hit him from behind, and he fell into something sharp. Head wounds bleed. She worries that the blow might have scrambled his wits a bit. He keeps falling asleep."

Patience sent prayers of gratitude to heaven. "Tell my mother, please? To lose him would be. . ." She had no words.

Lavender nodded understanding. "I'm going down now. Meera is very good. She'll make him come around."

Not wanting to interfere with the apothecary's good work, Patience hurried to the main hall. Really, she shouldn't be unchaperoned in the company of a veritable stranger, no matter how charming, intelligent, and helpful he might be. But she wanted to feel useful, and pruning an apple tree right now wouldn't find out who had hurt Paul or killed her father.

Henri had found another chair to set before the fire and added a table and lamp for the books. He had her father's notebook open and was taking notes. He stood and smiled, and her foolish heart melted thinking the smile was just for her. The fragrance of jasmine was so enticing. . .

"How is your mother? Did you stop by the infirmary?" he asked.

Unlike her, Henri always knew what to say, even if it was to stop her silly fantasy. Diffidently, head down, she reported, "Lady Elsa is giving Mama brandy. She's steadier, I think. And Paul is coming around. They don't know if his wits are scrambled, but he's alive."

"This is all excellent news. Sit. Let me take the book. I have warmed the fire for you. I am interested in looking for Corcorans." He set the book on the table and took her hand to seat her as if she were an elegant lady in silks.

She stumbled and nearly toppled into the chair, but his strong hand held her steady. "The Corcorans are Paul's family," she whispered in horror. "Do you think they. . . ?"

He gestured at her father's extortion list. "I am only attempting to connect names with initials. EC is easier than AB, of which there appear to be many. I believe Paul's grandmother is a Bridget and his mother was a Mary, correct?"

"His grandfather is a Daniel," she added. Reluctantly, she continued, "And his uncle is Teddy, short for Edward."

"Ah, I did not know that. Teddy for Edward instead of Eddy, how peculiar." He showed her the entry: *EC 1789 £ | | | R, str.*

"You think that stands for Edward Corcoran? That was before Paul was even born, while the viscountess lived here —" Patience shook her head, not understanding. Clare had said the *R* might stand for rape and *str* might be sister, but that was well beyond fathoming. "Paul's family is *very* respectable."

"We could be wrong." He pointed at the register. "Did Paul's uncle ever marry? See if you can find births and marriages for his family. Let us make this about your brother, for now."

"Paul? Why?" Puzzled, she turned the yellowing pages of the heavy church register. She recognized her father's writing on the last pages and carefully leafed to the beginning of those entries—1778. He truly had known the old earl.

"Let us just say, because I do not like a man who does not acknowledge family."

She thought he was keeping something from her, but the register was too much of a curiosity, so she studied that rather than question. "If I understand correctly, Paul's family is Catholic. It would be very hard for Father to shame them if they did not attend the chapel. But I suppose they must register deaths and such as anyone does."

She turned to the register pages from *before* her father's arrival. The village had been busy then: marriages and births outweighed deaths. The Corcorans didn't appear until 1774, with the baptism of Mary—Paul's mother?

Patience did a quick calculation. Paul had been born in 1790. His mother had been *sixteen*? And her father had to have been. . . in his thirties, easily.

She swallowed hard and started making notes.

EIGHTEEN

THE HOUSEHOLD DID NOT LEARN OF BLACKSTONE'S DEATH UNTIL tittle-tattle ran rampant below stairs the next morning. Elsa passed the gossip on to Clare, who sought Hunt to confirm it. Discovering all the men—except poor unconscious Paul—had vanished on mysterious errands, she ground her teeth in frustration. At what point would her intended start confiding in her?

In an act of silent rebellion, she settled in the library with her nephew Oliver, his tutor, Mr. Birdwhistle, and Jack's bibliophile father. The hush as they perused the sacred pages of valuable volumes, deciding which ones might best be sold, soothed her rattled nerves. *Another murder!*

It was bad enough that the last curate had been slain, the chapel ransacked, and poor Paul bashed insensible. But another death?

Clare simply couldn't bear it. She had come to the manor because she'd thought a rural abode would be a safe place to raise her nephew and quiet enough to allow her to write her novels. Instead, people were being killed right and left. They may as well be living in a thieves' den.

The fake Duncan Reid had been an unpleasant man,

certainly, but no one deserved to have his life cut short. The courts might decide a man was too evil to live, but that hadn't been a judge or jury stabbing a man to death in the woods on a stormy night—if the gossip was correct. It wasn't as if she had anyone to verify the maids' tales.

Could the impostor have cracked the new curate's skull? His father's as well, possibly? Why? Then still *another* person had stabbed the impostor? She hated thinking the village had *two* killers. So, perhaps there was only one. She shouldn't assume the fake Duncan Reid was a villain because she hadn't liked him.

She shuddered at her thoughts, then grimaced at the Latin volume she was supposed to be studying. She did not have a man's education. The book meant nothing to her. It was pretty. The leather was excellent, and the gold embossing was rich. The pages were a very fine linen and the printing ornate. But it was Latin. What good was a book most people couldn't read? She'd volunteer it for sale.

Even if the books earned a fortune, they could not replace a man's life. Money could not buy a clergyman. . . Well, perhaps it could. Should Mr. Upton recover, they might have to offer him a generous stipend to stay and perform services in a place with an assassin running about, one that seemed to dislike his family. She wouldn't stay, if she were him.

Lavender peered around the door and gestured at her. Not certain whether she wanted to return to the drama, Clare frowned, but her cousin seemed to be smiling. Well, her young cousin was almost always smiling these days.

She pushed back her chair and left the bibliophiles to their work.

"Mr. Upton is speaking," Lavender whispered. "I don't dare disturb the captain. He has returned from the village and is roaring and swinging his walking stick as if he'd chop off heads. But Meera thinks he ought to hear what Mr. Upton has to say."

Clare couldn't reassure the girl that Hunt was all roar and no bite. Hunt was quite capable of beating a man with a stick or heaving him out the door. He wouldn't treat Lavender that way, but it was easier to confront him than explain. And she'd like to beat his head about with a stick, just a little.

She knocked briskly, ignoring the shouting within. She had come a long way since the days she dived for cover at any loud noise. Without waiting for a response, she shoved open the study door and strode in, prepared to yell for attention.

Hunt was sitting calmly behind his desk. Jack was the one roaring. One of the ex-soldiers she didn't recognize was bellowing back.

Hunt glanced up at her arrival. The way he acknowledged her, even when he was busy, stirred her blood. She offered a smile as a result, and he was out of his chair before anyone else noticed her existence.

"We are looking for the men who were at the tavern," Hunt told her. "Edward Corcoran's parents say he's gone to town; that does not mean we believe them. And I want to talk to this Bergstein, even if he wasn't at the tavern. I'll have soldiers scouring the woods."

"We have soldiers?" she asked as he stepped out, closing the door behind him.

He shrugged. "Ex-soldiers, one-legged, one-armed, half-blind ex-soldiers."

Ah, the homeless men camping on the back lot that he was employing as best as he was able. "Who is Jack yelling at?"

"Almost everyone," Hunt said with a chuckle. "He is very frustrated that the banns will not be announced on Sunday unless young Paul rises from his sickbed. He wants the dog trainer to send the dogs after the culprit."

"And the trainer is telling him the rain washed off the scent? Poor Jack." Clare took Hunt's arm and tugged him down the corridor. "Men enjoy being bullies too much. But good news—Paul is talking. Come along and be quiet for a change."

He grunted and retaliated by sliding his arm around her waist and nearly hauling her from the floor as they hurried to the infirmary in the back of the house. She felt much better already.

Patience was almost forcefully hauling her mother from the room. Patience was tall, and her mother was not. The younger woman had her arms around Nettie's shoulders, whispering in her ear. Their new housekeeper's hands were rolled into balls, and she was red-faced and weeping.

"They don't look happy," Clare murmured.

"I think Mama Bear is ready to kill," Hunt murmured back.

"Mama Bear? Is that an American saying?"

"Something Henri said." He let her enter first and followed on her heels.

Clare wished she'd had parents willing to kill for her, but her mother had been an invalid, and her father had been disinterested in anything except making money. If she ever had children. . . She cast a glance at Hunt. Should they finally marry, there would be children. What kind of parents would they be?

If they stayed here, they'd have an entire village to assist them.

And killers to stalk them? Perhaps welcoming strangers into their midst was not a wise choice. If Mrs. Upton had a temper. . . She could not think like that. If they did not welcome newcomers, how would the village survive?

Meera was helping the patient to sit. Hunt took her place. He wasn't as gentle, but he soon had the curate sitting up and sipping from a mug.

Clare hugged her weary friend. "You must rest. It isn't good for the babe you carry to wear yourself out."

"I slept for a while. But if someone could sit with him, I'd like to freshen up and lie down properly for a bit. And thank Elsa for providing meals. I never knew an earl's daughter could be so thoughtful." Meera tucked a black strand of hair back in place.

"It all depends on how one is raised, I suppose. Elsa appears to have been brought up by cooks." In amusement, Clare sent her friend off, then joined Hunt. She supposed it wasn't proper for her to be in a man's sickroom, but at this point, who knew what was proper? Murder certainly wasn't. If Hunt wasn't sending her away, she was staying.

"Can you tell us what happened?" Hunt asked.

The patient touched the bandage on his forehead, then rubbed his thick auburn hair in back, wincing. "Not entirely." He closed his eyes as if his head hurt, which it probably did. "I was in the parsonage study, writing Sunday's sermon, when I heard a commotion in the chapel."

Picking up a bowl of cooling porridge, Clare took a seat beside the bed and offered him a spoonful, as if he were an infant. The slender curate wasn't tall or intimidating. She couldn't imagine him going after noisy intruders. "And you went out without a weapon?"

Paul took the bowl and another spoonful while he thought. "I assumed some animal had gone in and couldn't escape. I've seen it happen. Deer, in particular, are nosy creatures."

"I suppose that's reasonable now that the doors are unlocked. They do not fasten well." Clare sat back and watched to make certain he ate.

"How would you drive out even a deer? Do you own a weapon?" Hunt asked in exasperation. "The village has been lawless for decades. It is not the quiet place you may remember."

"I don't remember it as quiet," Paul said dryly, between spoonfuls of porridge. "I might have only been ten or so, but I learned early that the viscountess had no authority. There

155

were brawls and stabbings, and when I was bullied, my mother wept for us to leave. As I recall it, by the time our benefactress died, the only people in the village were the elderly and the incompetent, which includes the drunkards and indolent."

Clare wanted to know more of the history. Hunt was more interested in the present. He intruded on the reminiscences. "What happened when you went to the chapel, unarmed?"

"I heard muffled shouting and thought it might be a drunken brawl. I'd only just opened the door, entered, and saw the wreckage of all our hard work, when I was slammed from behind. That's the last I remember."

"Someone outside hit you?" Hunt asked.

Paul wrinkled his brow. "There was no light. I'd gone in far enough to see if the windows had been damaged. They're old and quite irreplaceable."

Sitting behind the patient, Hunt rolled his eyes.

Clare refrained from swatting him and offered, "You saw wrecked benches, came further inside, and glanced up to the windows?"

"Yes, I believe so. I'm not sure what I hit going down." He rubbed his brow. "The broken edge of a bench?"

"That's where we found blood," Hunt agreed. "So whoever was in there was probably by the door when you entered. Did you have any sense of height?"

Paul started to shake his head, winced, and rubbed it instead. "Just pain. If they had a tool to wreck my benches, it could have been anyone, large, small, male, female. . ."

Clare leaped ahead to ask, "Was there anything at all in the chapel worth stealing?"

He didn't shake his head this time, but his grimace reflected his answer. "Not a thing. The register would have been the only valuable, and I had my mother store it here. I replaced it with an ancient church financial ledger in hopes of preventing this kind of damage. Apparently, I underestimated the stupidity of thieves."

Clare exchanged a glance with Hunt. In the dark, the thieves wouldn't have been able to tell one book from another. They needed to see if the false book was still there—and if not, find out who had it now.

AFTER ASCERTAINING WHERE PAUL KEPT THE FALSE REGISTER IN the chapel, Hunt sent Ned down to see if it was still there. While he signed the correspondence Walker had prepared asking for the aid of someone with judicial experience, and petitioning to have Staffordshire annex the manor property, Hunt acknowledged Henri's arrival. His younger cousin held a handful of papers and looked a little bleary-eyed. Henri preferred talking to paperwork.

"Have we found anyone to claim the impostor's body or even identify him as a Blackstone?" Hunt asked, setting aside his pen.

"Arnaud and Deacon Jones searched the old Blackstone farmhouse. There is evidence someone has been staying there." Henri shuffled through his papers and placed one in front of Hunt. "They found this. It appears to be a document from the navy concerning one Archibald Duncan Reid Blackstone."

Hunt whistled, pulled out his monocle, and studied the paper. "I don't believe the navy has ever spent much time researching sailors they impressed. He could have made that name up all on his own."

"It gives date of birth as 1759 in Gravesyde Priory." Henri slapped another paper on the desk. "Patience and I stayed up half the night searching for familiar names in the official church registry. We didn't go back that far. I just asked her to

157

look it up when I saw the navy paper, and she copied out the entry."

Hunt read the bold scrawl. "Archibald Duncan Blackstone Junior, baptized son of Archibald Blackstone and Lilith *Reid* Blackstone, April 23, 1759." He frowned. "The Reid is part of his mother's name, not his."

Henri shrugged. "He may have claimed through his mother's line, but unless he has offspring, it's little matter to us now. Then there's this."

He set a paper with a long list of entries on the desk and pointed at one. *Archibald Duncan Blackstone, Jr. married Naomi Bergstein, November 13, 1778.* "That's while the earl was still alive and planting orchards." Henri slumped back wearily.

"It doesn't tell us anything," Hunt warned, although his gut twisted in suspicion. "Has anyone found the bearded Bergstein fellow yet?"

"There are enough abandoned buildings that he could live in a different one every night. He could hunt rabbits, steal a few carrots and potatoes from gardens, and no one the wiser. But if he's watching Patience and Arnaud in the orchard, we may need to patrol it with dogs. I'm supposed to be in Birmingham. I need to hit the road."

"Go." Hunt glanced down the list at the other familiar names. "I'll ask around about the rest of this list."

"I may not be back until tomorrow. Can you tie up the ladies so they don't go anywhere until then?" Henri shoved up from the chair.

Hunt snorted. "Tell them you won't bring back fabric for new gowns for their weddings unless they stay in the manor?"

Henri offered a faint smile. "I'll blame it on you. I don't want my head ripped off."

As Henri departed, Hunt scanned down the list his cousin had apparently prepared using the register and Upton's extortion notebook. Under Archibald Blackstone Jr.'s entries, he'd copied *AB 7/79 BW* and *AB 3/91 S* with a question mark.

S—for stabbing? Except Blackstone had been the one stabbed last night. Might that mean Abraham Bergstein wielded a knife, and he was the *AB 3/91 S* Upton was extorting? Although Stealing was just as likely as Stabbing.

1791 was ten years after the earl died, during the reign of the viscountess, when poverty and lawlessness had been on the increase. Lack of wealth and power had tied his grandmother's hands. He could almost feel her frustration.

Hunt worked his way through more names. The farmer called Bert with ten children was an *Albert* Bartholomew, another AB. He wasn't born until 1770, so he was unlikely to be *AB 7/79 BW* but could easily be *AB 3/91 S*. The feminine hand had recorded that note with a question mark too.

They had nothing else in the register for Bergstein— because they were Jewish? And as with Meera, the law did not require Jews to abide by church regulations essentially written by and for Protestants.

He started at the very top of the list to see what Patience and Henri had considered most important. . . and stared. The feminine hand had underlined the important parts.

MARRIED: ISAIAH UPTON AND MARY CORCORAN, DECEMBER 15, **1789**, BY ELLIOTT MARBLE, RECTOR.

BAPTIZED: PAUL DANIEL UPTON, SON OF **EDWARD CORCORAN** AND MARY CORCORAN UPTON, JUNE 8, **1790**, BY ISAIAH UPTON, CURATE.

The curate's son had been born less than six months after marriage? Not necessarily unusual, although the age difference would make Isaiah a dirty old man. But Patience had included a parenthetic comment: *The baptism is in the hand of Isaiah Upton.*

The late curate had very carefully recorded that he was *not* Paul's father, that Edward Corcoran. . . his wife's brother. . . was the natural father.

Patience had added *EC 1789 £ | | | R, str* without a question mark after the entry. If their speculation was correct, in his youth, Edward Corcoran had raped his sister. And Isaiah Upton had charged him three pounds—as punishment. Then he'd married the poor child.

A teardrop marred the neat printing.

NINETEEN

THE NEXT DAY, WHILE GRAVEDIGGERS OPENED A HOLE FOR THE
unlamented Mr. Blackstone, Patience crouched beside a
marker she'd uncovered in the manor's cemetery. Evidently,
the village had continued using the priory's original burial
ground even after the monks were long gone. It wasn't as if
the chapel had space. And the town was called Gravesyde
Priory for a reason, she supposed.

She smoothed her hand over the crudely chiseled stone.
Mary Corcoran Upton 1774-1790. At the age of sixteen, she'd
died giving birth to Paul.

After having been raped by her own brother? Isaiah
Upton might not have been the most honest of men, but he
took his duty seriously. Patience didn't think he would have
lied on official documents. But they might not be interpreting
his notebook correctly.

If they were right, however, Paul wasn't even her half-
brother. She'd done her crying last night. He needed her to be
calm now.

Still a bit unsteady on his feet, Paul held his hat in his
hands and murmured a prayer. Auburn hair fell over the

bandage that prevented his actually wearing the hat. Now she understood why they did not resemble each other at all.

Patience accompanied his prayer by quietly singing a hymn, then laid a bouquet on the stone. "We should ask Mother what she knows," she said as they placed flowers on their father's more recent grave.

"What would that serve? Do I want to confirm that I'm the son of a rapist instead of a good clergyman?" Paul asked bitterly.

"You're my brother, and he was our father in all sense of the word but one," she said firmly. "That does not change. If we assume the worst about that entry, then Corcoran is an unnatural father, at best. Papa had his faults, but he loved us without reserve."

"Then you think my *unnatural* father hit me over the head?"

Well, put that way, no. It did not seem reasonable. Why would he? If he was Catholic, would he even be aware of the register entry?

She had never understood how easy it was to commit murder with impunity. How many people could have been at the church, wielding an ax? All of them. She couldn't blame Paul's. . . father?. . . simply because Henri didn't like him. They could as easily accuse his grandfather of murder, or the old lady down the street. Some old lady had threatened their father, anyway. The initials in his notebook could as easily be women. They just happened to be invisible.

Patience glowered at the grass beneath her feet as they returned to the manor. Nettie was insisting that they must leave Gravesyde, but they had nowhere to go, and Patience wanted to stay here, where she felt welcome. Paul, on the other hand, had opportunities beyond a place that might have killed him.

"Will you stay?" She asked the question she knew everyone wanted to know.

"If they'll have me, yes." Paul sounded determined. "They're in desperate need of a church here. Someone must remind them of the results of sin and encourage their better natures."

"Mother keeps talking about evil," Patience said worriedly.

"The devil's evil is superstition. The truth is more prosaic —people listen to their baser natures if there is naught to stop them. Do we believe the devil makes us do it? I rather think it's a more human failing." He sounded a little more certain as they talked. "The Commandments are simple to follow, if one is taught to understand that they mean we can't be animals who can do whatever we want."

"Do you think Father was teaching right and wrong by forcing men to pay for their crimes monetarily?" She'd been puzzling over his behavior. She knew he was good at heart, but extortion seemed so. . . desperate.

Paul thought about it. "He didn't arrive in Gravesyde until just a few years before the earl died. Most of those first entries tended to be for pence, as if for minor infractions. So, yes, I believe he was attempting to teach a lesson at first. The earl was elderly and building an orchard and might have ignored petty misdeeds."

"Leave it to Father to exact justice and feed himself at the same time." She watched as Henri's wagon rattled up the drive. He'd gone to Birmingham to buy supplies and sell the village goods. Presumably, he took a share of the profits from other people's hard work for himself. How did that compare to her father's means of earning a living?

Paul watched the household spill onto the drive to help Henri unload. "We can assume the earl handled major crime until he died, so Father did not need to. It was only after the earl's death that everything began to crumble. Father had no other control than the pulpit and the pocket. Can we hope the captain will restore law and order?"

"With Clare by his side, one hopes." She sent her brother a glance. "Will you be up to crying banns on Sunday?"

"The sooner, the better, or I will be baptizing six-month babies come winter. Yes, I think Gravesyde needs us." His pace increased as they reached the yard.

Watching Henri's muscled strength as he swung heavy crates to the drive, Patience stumbled a bit and fell behind. Not until Paul hurried to aid Lavender in lifting bolts of cloth did she wonder what had set her brother to eagerly join the unloading despite his aching head. Surely he could not be interested in Lavender? She was much too young and frivolous. . .

Oliver and his tutor hurried out to see what Henri had brought. Patience caught the tutor glancing at Lavender as well, but Paul had reached her first. Oh, this was fun! Much better than hunting killers.

Humming a happy tune, she recognized the scent of jasmine wafting around the cart as she reached it. She really did need to find out if she could grow the vine here. If the countess had loved it, then they should provide her ghost with what pleasures they could.

Laughing at her foolishness, she caught a bolt of lovely pale blue silk taffeta as Henri heaved it from the back. Seeing her, he grinned and tipped his hat, then returned inside for more goods.

Lavender rushed over to *oh* and *ah*, taking the bolt from her arms. Patience turned to catch the next item. Henri lowered a light dressmaker's box labeled *lace* to her and heaved a heavier produce box at Paul. Teasingly, she offered to trade so Paul could take the lace into Lavender. Since he was staggering under the weight of the produce, he actually accepted.

"Not quite recovered, has he?" Henri called down as Patience handed off the crate to Jack to carry down to the kitchen.

"He's doing well enough to say he'll be crying the banns on Sunday." Patience stepped aside so he could swing down from the cart.

Henri reached in and removed another dressmaker's box, placing it in her arms. "I hope that means you will be staying and can put these to good use. Lavender should be able to make any adjustments you need."

Before she could find her tongue, he'd run around to his horse and was leading the cart to its resting place behind the stable.

Patience stood there for a moment, stupidly staring at the box. Henri had brought her a *present*? Or just one more item for the manor's cupboards?

One of the older seamstresses examined the name on the box, took Patience's arm, and led her back inside. "Let us see what cast-offs the old biddy sent this time. The material is usually very fine."

"The old biddy?" Patience stumbled over the doorstep but scarcely noticed as she righted herself. They hurried down the dark hall to the gallery. Henri had given this to *her*. To be adjusted. She was too confused to be excited. Or so excited, she was confused.

The enormous, two-story gallery had seemingly filled with women emptying boxes and examining bolts of cloth and exclaiming happily. Even the button makers had joined in to inspect all the accouterments of. . . wedding gowns, of course. Three brides needed new gowns.

While Patience. . . slipped to a quiet niche to open her box. She slid the string off and carefully lifted the lid to peer in as if a snake might leap out and bite her. No snake. No delicate silk. Foolishly relieved, she removed the top and puzzled over the contents.

An almost canvas-like fabric in a dirt-brown color lay on top. This would be tough enough for gardening if. . . She lifted it and gasped. A full-length apron! It had pockets and ties and where in the name of all that was holy had he found it?

Beneath it was a jacket and a. . . riding skirt?. . . of a sturdy brown nankeen. Perhaps she should have taken these to her room. They seemed terribly personal. . . which was why she should assume this was meant as a. . . uniform? Like the ones Lavender was making for the maids.

While she dithered, Lavender pounced, tearing the jacket from her grip and dancing about in glee. "Oh, look at how this is cut! It's old-fashioned, but very fitted. I can add a bit of braid. . ."

Patience shook out the matching skirt. Unlike current styles that included acres of trailing cloth to cover one's ankles while riding, this one. . . must be made for a much shorter woman. She stood and held it to her waist. It fell just to her shoes. Excitedly, she wondered if she might wear boots with heels so she did not trip. . .

Lavender dropped the jacket and shook out the skirt, examining it with a critical eye. "Someone has already taken in the seams and removed the excess. It would have had panniers or a hoop to hold it out. . . The woman Henri knows collects good cast-offs in the second hand market. She has an excellent eye. Henri must have told her to watch for a sturdy outfit."

She measured the gown against Patience's waist. "We'll have to take it in. It's much too short for riding, but. . ."

Patience finally understood, and her eyes widened. "It is made for *gardening*. I might move freely and not worry so much about getting dirty. And if I wear the apron over the jacket. . ." She lifted the two garments together.

"You can be a lady and not look like one," Lavender concluded with a grin.

The heavy apron with pockets hid her jutting bosom as the fitted jacket never would. Patience didn't know if she wished to hug Henri for noticing or slap him.

Either way, she blushed profusely.

HENRI CARRIED HIS RECEIPTS AND CASH IN TO WALKER TO record. Coming down the stairs after washing and donning fresh clothes, he'd heard the women squealing in excitement at the front of the house. He didn't dare venture near to see how Patience had taken the clothes he'd bought for her.

As fetching as her man's trousers might be, he didn't want men mocking her. Or judging her by her lovely curves. She could hit him with the box if he'd done wrong. Arnaud ought to be the one thinking of her comfort, but he doubted his brother had even noticed her anxiousness about her looks.

Of course, his brother had never made a living at reading people's expressions and moods. Peddling his goods down back roads, Henri would have starved had he not learned his customers.

"Any news?" he asked of Walker in his office, as they sorted personal from manor business and counted out Henri's commission.

"Meera thinks Blackstone's death was caused by a very long knife. The wound went straight through him. We found an ax nearby, presumably the one used to break up the chapel benches. As far as we can determine, it's just an ax one uses to chop firewood and not a murder weapon. Paul was to go down after he visited the cemetery to see if his ax is missing. I take it your arrival delayed him." Walker sat back in his desk chair and crossed his hands over his flat belly. "How does one use a long knife?"

Henri shoved his hands in his pockets and thought about it. "She is sure it was not a sword? How could one tell?"

"A rapier is thin, the wound was not. Broadswords and sabers are not stabbing implements. A sword is heavy and would be easier to swing and cut a person in two. Sabers are curved and this was a straight edge."

"So, a knife-blade-sized wound, straight through. . ." Henri wrinkled his brow. "I am not a weapons aficionado, but I have used a sword and a knife. It would take a great deal of strength to stab a man clear through. A long, thin—extremely sharp—blade would work best. Blackstone was a large man."

Walker nodded agreement with this assessment. "Hunt and Jack are talking to our soldiers, but Jack is familiar with British weaponry and cannot think of anything that resembles what Meera describes. I'm not sure they entirely believe her."

"They don't think in terms of farm implements. That's far more likely than weapons in these parts," Henri suggested.

"Hunt and I know what to tell workmen to do if they're building a bridge. We're not much on telling them which tools to use. And neither of us are farmers. *None* of us," Walker corrected, giving it thought.

"Except Patience!" Henri crowed. "She'll know gardening tools."

"And her brother knows carpentry tools. Didn't he say he'd locked up his? Has anyone checked them?"

"I shall ask. The real question is—why would anyone murder a lying vagrant?"

"Because he lied to the wrong person about the wrong thing?" Walker grimaced. "That might make any of the manor heirs suspect, except they seem intent on taking in anyone who seems to be family. I see no motive there."

"We need to know more about Blackstone. I suspect more than one someone didn't like him. If I'd been our new curate, I would have been tempted to run him through after the bastard nearly destroyed the chapel. I suppose they could have fought and Blackstone staggered out after knocking Paul down. Even the unlikely is possible." Jingling the coins in his purse, Henri departed Walker's office.

After that gloomy prognostication, he preferred to follow

the sound of happy feminine exclamations. Happiness beat ugliness any day.

The long drive into Birmingham might be lonely, but the result was reward enough. If he could buy a larger cart, his trips might be less frequent. . .

He'd still be an itinerant lout, but he'd be useful and well-fed. The days of eating over campfires no longer appealed. He must be growing old.

Patience practically danced out of the gallery before he reached it. She wore the ugly apron over her flimsy morning gown and broke into a huge smile when she saw him, then ducked her head, blushing. That she actually dared smile at him without persuasion, excited him in ways he shouldn't indulge—not if she preferred his silent brother.

"Thank you," she murmured, not looking him in the eye. "It is perfect. However did you find it?" She held out the apron like a skirt and swung around so he could see how nicely it engulfed her.

In his mind's eye, he could still see her enticing curves. "I saw a carpenter wearing one and asked where he had it made. We have charged it to the manor's maintenance account as a uniform, so now you must be our gardener."

She sobered. "Have they found Mr. Bergstein? What if he is a real orchardist and not a villain? He won't want my help."

"If you claim your place as a Reid heir, I don't think he has a choice. You will be his employer. But that is putting the cart before the horse. First, we must find the gentleman, then determine if he is a killer or knows anything of use." Henri offered his arm. "Would you care to accompany me to the captain's lair?"

She clasped her hands and lowered her gaze to the floor again. "I'd rather prove my usefulness. Meera is to show me what needs doing in the herb and kitchen gardens. We don't want her working too hard. . ." She gestured helplessly, reminding him that in a few months, the manor would house an infant.

Perhaps he shouldn't dream domestic dreams just yet. Infants were beyond his knowledge.

"Very well, mademoiselle." He bowed. "I shall beard the lion alone."

But, of course, Hunt had fled his study for the dungeon experiment, knowing no one would follow him. Henri was tempted to traipse down to the bug-infested crypt, simply to prove his wretched cousin wrong. Only, Clare was outside, trimming roses, and he stopped to speak with her. Which was when the young curate trudged up the hill in the company of the mute boy.

"Mr. Upton, you are supposed to be resting!" Clare cried.

Henri had last seen him unloading the cart, which wasn't exactly resting. The curate was not a man to sit idle.

Paul took a seat on the crumbling stairs and gingerly touched the bandage on his forehead. "The captain sent young Ned to hunt for the ledger. He said it was not there. I needed to see the damage and foolishly thought to verify his conclusion."

Clare signaled Ned, indicating drinking. The boy trotted off.

"And?" Henri prompted, surmising there was more to the story.

"I was reminded that I was interrupted while chopping wood a few days ago. I left my ax in the woodpile. It's no longer there."

"And that is what they used to break up the chapel?" Clare asked in horror.

Paul nodded and winced. "Most likely. Although, since they found the ledger and stole it, I don't see the sense in it. But that's not all."

He glanced nervously from Clare to Henri. "Perhaps I should speak to the captain. It is not for ladies to hear."

Henri snorted. He might be useless, but he knew people. "Almost-cousin Clare, would you like to step inside so we men might discourse upon delicate subjects? Or perhaps you would care to fetch Hunt?"

The lady waved her shears with a militant gleam in her eye. "Or perhaps *you* would care to dig Hunt out of his spidery dungeon while I tend the poor, injured curate?"

The poor, injured curate rubbed his nose and sighed. "I have a sister. I understand. I wished to be polite."

"Save it for the arrival of the antique aunts," Henri suggested. "What else did you discover?"

"Someone used the ax to break into my tool shed. My long eaves knife is missing."

"Eaves knife?" Henri immediately conjured the weapon Walker described. "Long, thin, very sharp?"

Paul nodded. And winced again.

TWENTY

CLARE RELISHED THE ABILITY TO HOLD HUNT'S GLOVED HAND AS they sat on the front bench of the chapel that Sunday. Soon, she would no longer be a sheltered maiden, but an experienced wife, allowed to hold her husband's *bare* hand. And more. She blushed and turned her thoughts to churchly ones.

In two short days, the men of the village had cobbled together enough benches for the tiny congregation—not so tiny on this day with two couples crying banns. All the manor's staff had turned out, as well as the village ladies, including all of Lavender's workers. The chapel rustled with bonnets and the creak of corsets on the older ladies. The few village men proudly sported clean neckcloths and slicked back hair.

She was fairly certain even Meera and Walker were here somewhere. They'd chosen to have a quiet wedding in the curate's office after services. Clare had wanted their best friends on the bench with them, but she'd been overruled. The murders had caused too much ugly turmoil. People always blamed strangers first, and Meera and Walker personified a foreign world beyond the understanding of the locals.

Their attendance might arouse suspicion best left undisturbed, especially with the rumors flying about Mr. Bergstein, and Mr. Blackstone's funeral announced. Clare had reluctantly agreed to control events by giving the gossips pleasantries like the weddings of two Reid heirs to talk about.

Patience and her mother watched proudly from the sidelines as the new curate preached his first sermon. Paul spoke of healing old wounds and building toward a better future. At times of dramatic change, such calming notes smoothed the transition.

Crying the banns gave everyone a happier topic than murders and funerals. The congregation left the chapel smiling and chatting.

Clare had never felt very visible in her London home. She didn't know how to handle being the center of so much attention. Elsa seemed at ease with it. She and Jack laughed and helped the parishioners make eager plans, while Clare and Hunt slipped away toward the parsonage.

Like her best friend, Clare meant to marry an American who knew almost nothing of her home and family. But in these past months, Hunt had adapted admirably, even learning to deal with his blind eye. He no longer shot bats in frustration or spoke of giving the manor back to the bank. He was building a war chest of tools and an army of people to protect his unexpected inheritance.

Clare simply needed to adapt with him, because she could not imagine a future without this stalwart, intelligent, understanding man at her side. He was the solid ground she could return to after her flights of fancy carried her away.

Mr. Birdwhistle led Oliver back to the house with the rest of the staff. She and Hunt waited for Mr. Upton to finish talking with his parishioners.

"There they are," Clare whispered to Hunt, nodding toward Meera and Walker waiting, hand in hand, by the towering rhododendrons.

Meera had agreed to a new gown, but only because her

old ones were in need of letting out to conceal her growing bosom and waistline. She'd chosen a wine-colored bodice with cream inserts and skirt. The ladies had embroidered maroon designs down the seams and added puffy silk roses at the hem. Apparently giving in to the bridal spirit, she'd added small white flowers to her upswept black hair.

Walker wore buff pantaloons and a navy coat over a waist-coat in the same wine and ivory as Meera's gown. Lavender could be very persuasive when it came to fashion.

"You both look splendid," Clare declared as they approached.

With Jack and Elsa leading the excited villagers in a different direction, they were left some privacy. Respecting the discretion of the soon-to-be newlyweds, even Patience and her mother conspired to free Paul to escape as quickly as possible. He hurried from the back of the chapel in his robes and led them to the parsonage.

"Do you have the register?" he asked, unlocking the door. "I hate that I cannot keep it in the church."

Walker produced the book from under the giant bouquet of flowers Meera held. "Give us time and we will secure a safe box like Hunt's in your office."

"We thank you for agreeing to do this," Meera murmured.

"It's a civil ceremony. I imagine even Captain Huntley could perform it, and it would be perfectly legal as long as it's witnessed. But I am delighted to be of service and see that everything is properly recorded in church and county records." Paul took the heavy register and laid it on his desk. "Did you have words of your own you'd like said or will the Anglican ceremony suffice?"

"We're not religious," Walker affirmed, setting a paper on top of the ledger. "But these are words with which we're both familiar, if you can use them?"

Clare loved that the young curate was willing to accept the needs of those different from his teaching. She squeezed

Hunt's hand, and he rubbed her palm with his large thumb in return.

Paul scanned the paper and nodded. "Excellent. Do you have rings? Should I incorporate your words into the usual ceremony then?"

With everyone's agreement, he read the service, then had them repeat the vows they'd written. Teary-eyed, Meera took Walker's hand, which shook only a little as he gazed upon her with what seemed like sincere adoration.

Hunt produced the rings. Walker's black hand carefully held his bride's brown one as he slipped on the gold band. Neither were given to expressing emotion, but in the moment, they radiated happiness.

Clare wept as her best friend tied herself for life to a gentleman so foreign to Meera's upbringing—but so close in mind and heart. Hunt held her and offered his handkerchief as the newlywed couple discreetly kissed once they were declared man and wife.

Who would have believed when they'd run to the manor in terror, that one day, it would lead to this?

They all hugged joyfully, then signed and witnessed the register and certificates Paul produced. Walker handed the curate a substantial purse, which led the poor man to relax and offer sherry to celebrate.

"I have asked around about Abraham Bergstein, but only Mr. Oswald seems aware of his existence, and that through word of mouth," Paul explained as they sat in the parsonage parlor. "It is rather akin to finding evidence of a myth."

"Jack has learned directions to where the family once lived, so he is not a product of Mr. Oswald's imagination. It's quite a way out of the village, closer to town. He will take a few men with him this afternoon to see what he can find." Hunt set his sherry aside. "We're missing too many pieces of the puzzle. There is nothing about Bergstein in the register except the marriage of what I assume was his sister. Why would he murder for it?"

"We do not know that he did any such thing," Clare insisted. "The box of jewelry buried with the bones might have been stolen. We have no motive for *anyone* to kill. All we have are initials in a book. We know Mr. Bartholomew hates the church and the late Mr. Upton. He is strong enough to have knocked over Paul and stabbed Mr. Blackstone, but why would he do so? Blackstone might have hated Mr. Upton, but other than searching for the register to prove he was a Reid, why would he demolish a church? And if anyone sought the notebook. . . it is worthless without the late Mr. Upton to translate it, and even then, it would require proof to substantiate any crime."

"People would not necessarily know the notebook is useless. Anyone my father extorted might have sought it," Paul said gloomily. "I should probably talk with my grandparents, see if they might help." He finished his sherry and grimaced. "I do not know how to talk with them about my mother."

"I don't think you should bring up anything they don't," Clare said in sympathy. "There is nothing we can change now."

She glanced at Walker and Meera, who nervously sipped from their glasses. Socializing was not their milieu, either, unless they were talking mathematics or medicine. "Elsa is preparing your wedding breakfast. Let us think on more pleasant topics today."

She stood, and everyone eagerly followed. Clare was well aware that they were avoiding the fact that a killer lived among them, and they had utterly no means of identifying him or her, proving guilt, or knowing if they might strike again.

If motive and opportunity were all it took, the young curate could have killed his blackmailing father to take his position. Or if his mother had the temper Patience mentioned. . .

Henri had reported an old woman telling the late Mr. Upton to go away as he was paid to do. . .

Even Clare's gothic novels weren't this complicated.

~

No one from the village had shown interest in attending Blackstone's funeral, and none knew about the private wedding ceremony.

So it was only the manor occupants at hand when Elsa produced tables of delicacies, and Henri broke out celebratory barrels of ale. After that, there was no keeping the wedding a secret. Once the staff learned the occasion, they joyfully joined in. On the whole, Hunt decided, the manor's staff did not much care if they commemorated a wedding or a funeral.

As the tables in the drive filled with food and the staff poured outside, one of the soldiers produced a stringed instrument he played like a violin and another played a flute. Everyone happily clapped and danced on this warm spring evening, filling the area by the stables where carriages might once have parked.

Once Walker and Meera joined in the dancing, Hunt had no choice but to ignore his bad knee and hold out his hand to Clare. She brightened like one of his gaslights, and his insides performed an unexpected tumble. Lust, he understood. This need to please his intended was new.

She was fragile in his arms, but she spun and stepped and flashed her ankles with a spirit one wouldn't expect from such a genteel lady. He had to remind himself that she wasn't breakable, and he need not treat her like delicate porcelain. He caught her waist and swung her off her feet, and she squealed in delight.

That certainly produced a surge of lust.

177

"I love that they have found a way to celebrate the marriage despite Meera and Walker's wish to be discreet," she murmured when they came to a breathless halt on the sidelines.

"You mean we're not engaging in pagan spring rituals?" Hunt glanced about and found the newlyweds swinging happily, arm-in-arm, to a new tune. Walker was actually smiling like a besotted fool.

"Celebrating," she said firmly, clinging to his arm. "Meera and Walker are always so quietly efficient and invisible, that we tend to forget their existence, like gears on a clock. On this day when they should be the center of attention, they have bent backward to be inconspicuous. I understand, of course. Meera has been treated so poorly in the past, and her condition opens her to gossip. And Walker. . ."

"Is a scholar and not a fighter and avoids conflict," Hunt concluded. "He is skilled at avoidance, even when bullies go out of their way to show their bigotry. I suppose it is to their credit that we don't suffer that kind of ugliness here."

Clare laughed. "That, and Quincy and Adam would squash bigots like bugs. It remains to be seen if Mrs. Upton can maintain the same control, but she's downstairs, and Meera and Walker are upstairs, so there shouldn't be much problem."

Hunt hugged her slender shoulders and relished the fact that she didn't pull away. "I've had the command of hundreds of rough soldiers but never learned the nuances of dealing with servants. I am starting to understand that there is a pecking order similar to the army's."

"Well, the manor staff hasn't completely reached that stage of organization. Mrs. Upton is new and duties are not delineated clearly, since everyone must lend a hand where it's needed. I cannot hope we'll attain the level of propriety our aunts expect. But surely they will notice a difference."

"I think I shall schedule pipe installation for the week they are most likely to arrive," he said wickedly. They had yet to send announcements, but he fully expected their elderly relations to descend upon receiving them.

She elbowed him, then nodded toward their new housekeeper and her daughter lingering to one side. "Poke your cousins into asking Patience to dance. She's betwixt and between and your soldiers don't dare approach her."

"She's taller than half the men here and most likely has denied them." Hunt glanced around for Henri or Arnaud.

"Rightfully so," Clare said with a touch of acid. "Their eyes wouldn't lift above her bosom. It's no wonder the poor girl is shy."

"Women ought to delight in their generous endowments," Hunt protested. He finally found Henri working his way through the crowd. Arnaud, as usual, was nowhere to be seen. "Watch. She will turn Henri away."

Patience and her mother observed the merriment from beside the garden wall, prepared to slip away through the gate. Henri produced a flower to show them.

Clare giggled. "Henri won't let her turn him away. He is seducing her right now. Look, she's actually talking to him. She has forgotten she is gawky and is caught up in the fascination of whatever they're discussing. Your cousin is dangerous to women."

"Well, I should hope she's sensible enough not to fall for his charms. He has a woman in every port, so to speak, and very little to offer in a way of livelihood." Hunt frowned and tried to imagine his roving cousin settling down with a family.

"They're adults and not our concern. Lavender, now. . ." She gestured at the adolescent happily dancing around a circle of admirers—including the tutor. "She needs parents."

"Do not look at me!" Hunt protested. "It is more than enough that I must be magistrate as well as engineer and detective and legal executive. I am not ready to be a father to an almost-grown young lady."

"Interestingly. . ." Clare inclined her head toward a man striding down the drive from the carriage entrance. "Arnaud has just arrived."

Hunt shook his head in amazement as Arnaud strode through the dancers to lead Lavender aside in earnest discussion—while Henri spun Patience into the fray. "It's a damned good thing we have a church and preacher," he muttered.

Clare laughed. "We need to invite young Paul when his head is feeling better."

"Or hold the dances on the village common and invite killers. Come along, my love, one last dance, and then we should retire the musicians for the evening. Danger lurks in the dark."

Hunt swung his intended back into the line but spent the remainder of the evening searching for furtive expressions.

TWENTY-ONE

"I AM GOING WITH YOU."

Finished checking his horse's girth, Henri glanced up to see Patience signaling a stable hand. She had donned the long-skirted habit she'd worn the day the black-bearded man chased her. She'd tied a white jabot with broad pleats around her throat, presumably to distract from the tailored fit of her jacket.

He could tell her that it was impossible to disguise her beauty, but he preferred to let her believe otherwise. If she was actually making demands, perhaps her disguise had given her a little confidence.

Jack was already on his spirited thoroughbred, letting it dance in the brisk morning air. "You most certainly are not. This is no mission for a lady."

Henri rolled his eyes and indicated the horse Patience should ride, letting Jack take the brunt of the argument. Unaccustomed to dealing with women, the soldier had not thought this through well.

"You are visiting Paul's family, are you not?" Patience strode toward the gentle mare the lad led out. "Then it most certainly is a mission for a lady. You do not ride up on an innocent household and start making demands. This is a *family* visit."

"Are you only shy around me?" Henri asked dryly, cupping his hands to give her a boost up.

She stumbled and caught herself on the sidesaddle, then tugged at her long skirt in irritation. "I am not shy."

"Tongue-tied?" he suggested. Despite her height, she was light enough to lift easily. She managed to seat herself, although not with the skill of an experienced horsewoman.

"Ladies do not speak with familiarity to unrelated gentleman," she said with a lofty lift of her chin, not looking at him.

She had *danced* with him yesterday, although she'd kept her eyes on her feet. He'd enjoyed himself and thought she had too. He'd hoped he was making progress. . . especially when his oblivious brother had spent his time arguing with Lavender.

"Miss Upton. . ." Jack pleaded. "We could be encountering a dangerous man."

"Oh, please. Edward Corcoran is no larger than I am and old enough to be my father. He still lives with his *parents*, for pity's sake." She sat still while Henri adjusted the stirrup.

"*Jack* is an unrelated gentleman," Henri reminded her, stepping back to make certain she sat comfortably.

"Lt. de Sackville treats me like an annoying little sister. He is not a gentleman." She turned the mare down the drive and took off before Henri could mount.

That made Henri a gentleman? What, exactly, was her definition?

"I'm not sure which of us just got told off," he muttered, swinging into the saddle and following.

The ex-lieutenant shook his head. "I can't think letting a lady meet potential killers is what Hunt intended when he sent us on this mission."

"But she has a point. Paul is her family, thus, his family is hers, in a roundabout sort of way. Besides, I see no way of stopping her short of tying her up." Henri wasn't accustomed to being left unprepared and uncertain. The lady turned his head in ways that prevented logical thought.

Not that Henri was much on logic, but he rather preferred to be in control, at least. Perhaps he'd been on his own for too long.

They led another horse for the curate's use. The Corcoran farm was a few miles distant, and the horses needed exercise. Jack talked about the stable he was renovating on his new farm, while Henri watched Patience sway in the saddle ahead of them. He hoped, perhaps, just a little, he was becoming more *familiar* to her.

He almost laughed when they reached the parsonage, and she produced shears to snip blooms from the tops of several large shrubs while she waited for her brother to appear. The flowers made a pretty bouquet she tied with a ribbon she'd evidently brought for the purpose. She truly was a clergyman's daughter, prepared on all suits for every occasion.

Paul had forsaken his robes for riding attire. He could not keep a hat on with the bandage on his brow, but he'd acquired a cap that gave him a jaunty look. He didn't even seem surprised to see his sister waiting on him.

"I am very grateful to have your company," he said, speaking to all of them. "I wish to be respectful to my grandparents, but I'm not certain I can offer the same to my uncle."

The one who might actually be his father, if they were interpreting the evidence correctly. Henri would hate to be the judge and jury on this one.

"Do we have any specific questions we wish to ask?" Henri rode beside Patience, behind Jack and Paul.

"Paul is simply visiting," Jack said. "I will stay in the yard and ask about horses or corn or anything that comes to mind, while watching out for Edward Corcoran. I assume you'll just keep Miss Patience out of trouble."

Patience ignored him, as she might a brother. Henri followed suit and let the lieutenant create his battle plans.

"Isn't the Bartholomew farm in this direction?" He had a map in his head from his peddling days. "He's the one Patience heard arguing with the late Mr. Upton, claiming self-defense. I don't know if he was the same person I heard shortly later discussing bones. That person definitely sounded hostile."

"No one sounds pleasant when being extorted," Paul said. "I don't know how to approach my father's victims."

"And it's a trifle difficult riding up and asking if anyone took an ax to benches out of spite," Jack added. "I cannot think of any other good reason for anyone to do so."

"It does appear to be an impetuous act," Paul acknowledged. "The villain found the ax and in a fit of anger, possibly drunken, attempted to demolish the church."

Except Blackstone died that same night, the faux ledger was stolen, and Paul brutally attacked. Why would any of their suspects want to harm a curate or kill an ex-sailor who had not been around for decades? An old grudge? Blackstone had a bad history. Since he didn't appear wealthy enough for anyone to rob, vengeance seemed the only motive. Perhaps Paul had interrupted a madman—and stabbed him in a fit of revenge?

Henri suspected the curate would have confessed, if so.

And then there was the woman who had claimed to have paid the late clergyman to leave. . . They had seen no record of that payment in the notebook. Perhaps he ought to look at church ledgers.

The Corcoran cottage was a reasonably handsome one, a two-story stone with a newly thatched roof and mullioned windows. The barn was large and recently painted. It did not have the look of a place that encouraged sexual depravity.

Henri winced as he realized he was assuming only poor people committed crimes. He knew better. Poor people had to make do with what they had and fight for what they wanted, perhaps, but wealthy people had the same urges. They just had better means of concealing their worst impulses.

Patience took her brother's arm as he knocked at the door. Jack rounded up the horses and went looking for a trough. Henri felt superfluous, but watching the two innocents on the step, thought he'd hang about anyway.

A stout, crisply mob-capped maid answered. This was no struggling farm family. Henri hoped they'd misinterpreted Upton's notes.

Paul tipped his hat. "We have come to pay our respects to my grandparents." He and Patience produced visiting cards.

Henri had never had cards made. Half the families he visited in his cart wouldn't have been able to read one and most would have considered them pretentious. If he planned to settle down and be a gentleman of sorts. . . Did he?

The maid took the cards and shut the door in their faces.

"Friendly," Patience commented dryly, holding the bouquet. "I am glad I did not bring food."

Henri wanted to spy as Jack was doing, but he refused to leave these two on their own. They sincerely seemed to believe all people were decent and respectable until proven otherwise. He could understand Paul hoping his mother's family would be welcoming, but Henri distrusted Edward Corcoran—who had been in town the night the curate had been hit over the head.

If Upton's notebook didn't lie, why would a father do that to his son? Blackstone was far more likely, had he not turned up dead.

The maid returned and bobbed a brief curtsy. "The mister has taken to bed, and the missus is with him. They are not accepting callers."

Henri was almost relieved. Patience handed over the bouquet with polite phrases.

"We are sorry to hear that. Is there anything we might do? A physician, perhaps?" Paul inquired.

"Prayers," the maid muttered, then once again shut the door.

"I wonder if we should send for Meera." Patience actually accepted Henri's arm as they followed the path back to the horses. "Although I believe Mr. Oswald said Mr. Corcoran can no longer work, so it may be a long-standing condition."

Or the man was a drunk.

"I suppose their son has to work in town to support them," Henri added, studying the empty pasture beyond the trees.

"More likely, my grandparents do not wish to know me." Paul frowned and kicked a rock.

Understandable, perhaps, if his father had blackmailed them. Although, it really made little sense for a wealthy Catholic family to care what a poor Anglican clergyman said. It appeared they did not even socialize enough to let gossip concern them. The late Upton's attempt to shame them had no doubt been futile.

"The Corcorans have a carriage and horse," Jack reported as they rode away. "Any help must be out in the field. I wandered about and not a soul asked what I was doing."

"I was here quite a long time ago when I first started peddling. They had no interest in my trinkets, so I never returned," Henri admitted. "Edward must be more than a sheepherder."

Patience was disappointed for Paul's sake but rather glad a possible rapist was not at home. Surely, they must be misinterpreting their father's notebook. Such a tidy farm ought to have properly brought-up owners.

Henri's frown didn't appear to agree with her.

"Did you not say Mr. Bartholomew lives out this way?" she asked, redirecting their gloom. "Should we not visit him as well?"

"And have him shoot at us?" Jack asked. "Wasn't he the one who told your father he'd have naught to do with the church? He doesn't sound welcoming."

"But his wife might be. They have children. She'll be wanting a school. I could talk with her." She couldn't teach older boys. They only wanted to whisper about her chest. But she loved working with little ones.

"I doubt he can afford a musket. Shooting is unlikely. Jack can talk to their field hands, if he has any." Henri nodded at a newly dried field prepared for planting. "I'm fairly certain that's Bert's land. His wife always had time for me when I came through."

"Will she remember you without the cart?" Patience realized how silly that question was when he quirked an eyebrow at her. She blushed. "Not too many Frenchman here," she answered herself.

He'd made her giddy with dancing yesterday. She seldom had the opportunity to be escorted by a gentleman, much less one actually taller than she was. He had seemed to be enjoying the company and music and not thinking lascivious thoughts.

Perhaps her own lascivious thoughts were to blame for her discomfort now.

Henri led them into a dirt yard filled with pecking chickens and a rooting piglet. The creatures scattered, and a barefoot urchin raced out to chase the animals toward a dilapidated pen.

"Is your mother home?" Henri called down from his perch.

Patience could imagine him doing this from his cart seat. He was naturally friendly, and she admired the ease with which he met the world. Would he return to peddling? She caught herself selfishly hoping he wouldn't and forced her attention to the business at hand. The child scampered into the house.

Henri and Paul dismounted while Jack rode into the fields to pry.

A weary woman in a flour-dusted apron and worn gray gown appeared in the doorway. Fading brown hair struggled from her cap. She bobbed a curtsy and studied them with interest. A young girl carrying an infant stood behind her, and a toddler peered around her skirt.

"Mrs. Bartholomew?" Paul took the lead, doffing his cap and bowing, revealing his bandaged brow. "I am Paul Upton, the new curate. This is my sister, and I believe someone you know, Henri Lavigne?"

She peered at them suspiciously, then brightened when she recognized Henri. "Mister Henry! We've missed your cart." Then remembering her manners, she curtsied again. "Wilt thou have some tea?"

"That would be so lovely, Mrs. Bartholomew." Patience waited for her brother to help her down, but he deferred to Henri, who admittedly, took her weight more easily, although his strong hands left her a trifle breathless.

Children crowded around as they entered. Patience ended up with the infant in her arms as the older child raced about the meager kitchen gathering cups and tea. She would have to send a food basket with more tea later. They could not possibly afford such an expensive item too often.

They certainly could not have afforded her father's extortion.

A toddler tumbled and wailed. Henri scooped him up and dangled a watch fob to divert his cries. Paul carried the teapot to the table.

It was chaotic but a far better welcome than the one at his grandparents' house.

THE BONES IN THE ORCHARD

Henri explained he no longer had much time for peddling, but he hoped to supply Mr. Oswald's store with the notions she needed. Paul invited her to services, adding that they needed ladies to help restore what had been neglected. Mrs. Bartholomew demurred, blaming lack of transportation and the children.

Returning the infant to his mother, Patience sat a child of about five on her lap, asked his name, then produced paper and pencil from her pocket to show him letters to spell it out. "The Corcorans have a carriage, do they not?" she asked, keeping her eyes focused on the paper. "Will they not take you up?"

"Oh, they're not one of us," Mrs. Bartholomew said hurriedly. "They's Papists, although I don't know they attend meetings or such. Irish, y'know. Bert won't have nuthin' to do with 'em."

"Ah, I thought perhaps he and Mr. Edward Corcoran might be of an age and neighborly." Henri followed her example and picked up another child to show them letters.

"They oncet was, I suppose," Mrs. Bartholomew admitted reluctantly. "Can't help but be, living out here. But then Teddy got Bert's sister in the family way, and Bert made him marry her right proper. Teddy didn't half like that. We tried to be friendly like, on account of Sally and all. But oncet she had the babe, she packed up and left for town, and we ain't seen her since."

Vanished? Patience recalled the bones in the orchard and recoiled. Hiding her alarm, she asked, "That's so sad. How long has it been since Mr. Bartholomew has seen his sister?"

"Oh, reckon that been twenty or more years back, when Lady Reid was still here. Bert was married to my sister then, and I was just a lass."

Her head reeled calculating all the dates and people. Had Bert and Teddy had a knife fight over Sister Sally? Did that

explain the AB 3/91 for S? But Sally was the one who disappeared. Did the initial mean *For Sally*?

Only then, she had to wonder what happened to Bert's
first wife. And if this was his first wife's sister. . . Her father
would have known any marriage between them wasn't legal.

The register. Had the marriage been recorded? And Sally's
death?

The answers had to be in the register—and someone had
killed to obtain it. Except the thief must know by now they'd
stolen the wrong book. They would be back to search again.

TWENTY-TWO

CLARE WAS REVIEWING OLIVER'S PROGRESS REPORT WITH THE tutor in the library when the visiting party returned. Lord de Sackville had taken himself off to the far wing of the library after Walker and Meera set up battle stations on the main table. Planning two weddings and sending announcements required much scribbling of lists. For inexplicable reasons, Oliver was showing Lavender a children's book he'd found. Young Mr. Birdwhistle's attention was divided between the two, she noted with amusement.

She heard Jack, Paul, and Patience bustle in via the carriage entrance. Henri and Hunt entered through the front moments later.

This must be serious if Henri had dug Hunt out of the dungeon.

The tutor hastily gathered up his materials, Oliver, and Lavender, and led them to quieter environs. Lavender didn't appear too upset about being excluded from the adult proceedings—not while she had Mr. Birdwhistle's company.

Clare, on the other hand, didn't know if she wanted to be an adult under these circumstances. The visiting party did not appear happy, which could only mean a killer was still on the

191

loose. She didn't mind planning dinner menus or parties, but manhunts. . . She'd rather join the children.

The party had discarded their hats but still wore their riding gear and boots and carried in the scent of spring air and horses. They brightened when Elsa and a maid brought in tea and scones.

Recalling the days when they'd had to answer the doors themselves and dig a cranky housekeeper out of the kitchen to be served anything, Clare allowed herself a moment of satisfaction for the quickness with which staff had been notified of arrivals and acted on it.

"I should go below and talk to Mother," Patience murmured, not taking a chair.

"She knows you're here." Instead of returning to her kitchen, Elsa took a seat at the library table. "If she wants to know more, she's free to join us. Sit. We want to hear your side of the story, not just the men's."

Clare hid a laugh at her cousin's bossiness. The lady knew how to run an estate. She simply preferred cooking. Bossiness was apparently useful in a well-run kitchen.

Jack kissed Elsa's cheek and claimed the chair beside her. Hunt pulled out the one beside Clare and sprawled in it in all his filth. Henri and Paul fetched chairs from the dining room. Paul sat at the end of the table closest to the door. Ordered to stay, Patience reluctantly sat on his right. And interestingly, Henri placed his chair at her other side.

"Henri tells me you have found the weapons?" Hunt took the lead while the others grabbed scones and poured tea. His hands were grubby from working with his pipes, so he kept them in his lap.

The weapons? Clare's insides churned at this news. She studied the visiting party—who were definitely not happy about their discovery.

The curate reluctantly took the lead. "Jack found my eaves

knife and legget in Mr. Bartholomew's barn with his other tools."

"How do you know they're yours?" Clare asked, because one dirty tool looked much like another to her.

"I made them myself. I had the blacksmith straighten an old scythe for the knife, and I made the handle to suit the length of my arm. I always initial my tools so I know which ones to take home if there is a party of us working. They are definitely mine. They've been cleaned and oiled and look better than I left them."

"Did you speak to Mr. Bartholomew about them?" Hunt demanded.

"He wasn't there." Jack threw back his tea and reached for another scone. "I spoke with men in the next field over. They say he's planning on repairing the thatch on the barn. They're not thatchers and knew nothing about the tools."

The late curate's daughter hadn't touched her tea. She folded her hands in her lap and didn't look up. "Patience, did you meet Mr. Bartholomew's family?" Clare asked, in hopes of persuading a fuller picture from her.

"She is caring for ten children, some of them her sister's. They are quite poor. We need to send a food basket and include some tea. I fear we drank theirs." She sounded defensive.

Ten children! To take away their wage earner. . . But if Mr. Bartholomew had killed two men. . . A man that dangerous might abuse those poor children. He could have killed others! What in the name of heaven did they do now? She understood why Hunt hated this.

Henri lifted Patience's teacup and forced her to take it. "Jack was out in the barn and not with us. He did not tell us about the tools until we left the house. It did not seem wise or useful to go back and ask his wife about them. We need to find and question Mr. Bartholomew."

"*And* my uncle," Paul added. "We cannot pass judgment

without learning more. We must find some way to enter the Corcoran house. We have solved nothing."

Clare watched Patience sip her tea and let the men explain. She might have to draw out her thoughts later.

"Bartholomew's wife said he'd gone into town and wouldn't be back until tonight," Henri explained. "The Corcorans wouldn't even speak with us, and there was no one about outside. They are not friendly."

"Do we station guards on the road to catch the two of them?" Hunt asked.

"The guilty would only ride over the fields." Jack screwed up his face in thought. "We need to draw them out. How?"

"Corcoran has already shown up at the tavern once. Bartholomew might not be averse to a drink before going home," Henri suggested. "If I open the tavern—"

"No license," Hunt reminded him.

"I've written to the authorities in Shropshire," Walker said from the end of the table. "They probably have no idea who we are, but as long as they can tax us, they ought to offer licenses."

"What if licenses are one of those laws covered by manorial rights?" Hunt studied his muddy boots. "I have been told I have the power to create and enforce taxes."

"And plead ignorance if you're corrected later," Walker finished for him. "I'll draw up a fancy certificate."

"And what will you do if Mr. Bartholomew and Mr. Corcoran show up?" the curate asked.

Clare waited expectantly, praying it didn't involve weapons and confrontation. She noticed Patience waited with anxious interest too.

"I'll question them as best as I can since I'm the one who will be there," Henri offered.

"And I'll post some of our ex-soldiers to follow them home, if necessary," Jack said. "Although I'd really like to find this Bergstein fellow as well. I don't like that he returned as soon as the bones were uncovered and felt free to frighten a lady."

"They're all of an age, aren't they?" Paul asked quietly. "Just young enough when Father was here to get in trouble together."

Clare put down her scone, no longer hungry.

All *three* men might be killers? Or was Paul pointing a finger away from himself. . . or his mother?

Did the men not consider a woman capable of a blow strong enough to take a big man down? The late curate's death might have been accidental, an angry swat of a large mallet, not necessarily with intent to kill.

But wielding a knife long and sharp enough to run Blackstone through might require a man. She didn't wish to experiment.

AFTER LUNCHEON, HUNT SADDLED UP. HE DETESTED ARTIFICE and preferred more direct methods of dealing with criminal elements, but he needed *facts*.

Walker mounted a placid pony, refusing to allow Hunt to ride out alone. "Planning on playing lord and master in your fancy pants?"

Hunt snorted. He was wearing old uniform trousers. "If the women have their way, we will add a tailor to our staff. Lavender is not allowed to measure men for new suits. I am to tell her if these are suitably comfortable, so she can rip them apart and use them as a pattern."

"They look fine for riding to me."

"Apparently, they are worn, and one pair is not sufficient. In my unofficial capacity of lord of the manor, I must have new everything. I suppose I should wear new for the wedding, at least." Hunt shook the reins and spurred his mount down the drive. "How is married life? Any warnings or advice?"

Walker controlled his pony and considered his reply. "I enjoy not sneaking about, but nothing else has really changed. I suppose, if anything, I feel I have a little more right to show my concern and question her if she's out of sorts. And to insist that we find a midwife."

Hunt considered that. "Do they *expect* us to show concern? I am not certain I will notice."

Walker chuckled. "They will make you notice, if you share a bed. I assume you do not mean to keep separate rooms."

"Clare might want us to move into one of those empty suites in the new wings. One more thing to think about," he said morosely. "It's a lot of work just to get a woman into our beds."

"Worth it," Walker declared. "When you find a good woman, it's like finding a gold mine, you stake a claim. Be a fool not to. Did you determine where this Bergstein lives?"

"Jack gave me directions to the parents' plot. No idea if it's his. It is nearer town than the village, so he may only visit occasionally, long enough to terrify Patience. I cannot decide what to do about him until I meet him." Life and death matters required a type of thinking for which engineering school hadn't adequately prepared him.

"It would be beneficial if Bergstein is just a misogynist and not a killer. Miss Upton appears reasonably knowledgeable about the care of the trees, but she is not a manager of men. And Arnaud truly does not want to do it."

"The ladies are likely to kill a misogynist if you put one in charge. You are assuming he really is an orchardist from a few initials in an ancient book."

Walker shrugged. "According to Patience, he seemed to care about the trees. And we need profits from the apples, unless you plan to sell the library."

"The sale of some of those volumes will pay the bank

enough to keep them off our backs another year, if I can pry them out of Clare and the baron's hands. Clare fears the earl will haunt us, and the baron wants to keep them for himself."

"Despite his inclinations, Lord de Sackville has generously given me a list of men who might be interested and promised to make accurate descriptions to include in my queries. I'm suggesting an auction. But paying on the mortgage won't buy a carriage or increase our maintenance budget to cover both staff and large improvements like gas lighting. Or new trees for the orchard."

"We need to hire someone more experienced than I to build a system sufficient to light the entire manor. I can only run a few pipes to the main halls. The budget definitely isn't large enough if we also decide the village is ours to repair. Do you think the funds are invested well enough to ask for an increase?"

"It's difficult to say. Since we insisted on moving the cash to the Bank of England and out of local hands, the solicitors are miffed and won't let us touch the principal. I'm corresponding with investors recommended by the marquess, but the returns aren't high anywhere. The manor really needs to sustain itself."

Hunt grimaced. "We can hope Arnaud and Jack crack the painting codes, or someone makes sense of the earl's not-quite-a-map, and there are jewels at the end of the rainbow."

"More likely shifty leprechauns." Walker nodded at the tavern as they rode by. "Henri already has his old men working. They really want that tavern."

"Taverns are mixed blessings, at best, especially if I must establish law and order. But as a gathering place. . . It beats church." Hunt studied cottages as they rode through town in the direction of the main highway into Birmingham.

He noticed improvements already. People had a few more coins in their pockets now that the manor was returning to operation. If he thought he could be useful, he was willing to put down roots.

For Clare, he had to. After finding her place here, she wasn't likely to start over elsewhere. After her disastrous experiences, she needed stability.

For her sake, he must lay to rest decades-old crimes as well as new ones. The village couldn't continue as a nest of killers and rapists. He'd never set out to be a lawman.

"The ladies won't agree with you about the church," Walker surmised. "But men and women, are of necessity, different."

"I wouldn't expound upon that theory in the company of the ladies, if I were you. Let's give these nags their heads and see if we can catch Bergstein at tea." It felt good to be on a horse again. His knee had given him trouble after it had been nearly blown to bits, but he had enough strength now to kick his mount to a gallop and not fall off.

The fields further from the village still appeared abandoned. People weren't rushing back to the farms from the factories. There was very little traffic once they reached the main highway.

Hunt studied Wycliffe's rock-studded, timbered hillside as they passed. Only the false towers of the manor loomed from this distance. The river demarking their boundary like a moat ran high with spring rains.

He supposed the isolation was a protection of sort. Wycliffe deer would never be poached from this side of the hill.

The lane he'd been told led to the old Bergstein place was several miles down the road, on the opposite side from the river. An overgrown hedge and untilled fields ran along the highway, discouraging entrance, but they found a dirt cut-through and a path that appeared to have been used recently, if horse dung and broken weeds were any indicator.

Walker unclipped the musket fastened to his saddle. Hunt

unbuckled his sword sheath. Gnarled tree branches leaned over the path, disguising the horizon.

A mile or so in, a clearing opened. Instead of a house, a caravan leaned to one side on a broken wheel. Once cheerfully painted, it had seen years of neglect. Upon closer inspection, the foundation of a bungalow emerged next to it. A charred chimney indicated it had burned.

Along the back of the property, a line of trees bloomed more healthily than the manor's orchard.

No one stepped out of the caravan to greet them, but a man's shirt hung on a line between two of the trees.

They either had vagrants, or Bergsteins still lived here.

TWENTY-THREE

WHILE WALKER AND HUNT CHASED GHOSTS, HENRI SPENT THE day restoring the tavern to usefulness. Instead of joining the others for dinner, he waxed the tavern bar with a concoction recommended by Mrs. Upton. The dark oak gleamed in the light of the oil lamp. One of the old gents had brought in a rickety rack for the mugs and tankards so he didn't have to climb up to install hooks in the overhead timber. The first layer of whitewash on the walls had dried, and the place already looked brighter.

Arnaud eyed the open spaces between the smoke-darkened wall timbers and had already charcoaled in a few subjects. Henri had insisted The Maid be painted directly across from the bar so he could admire her while he worked. He hadn't dared ask Patience to pose for it and hoped his thickwitted brother would think to use her as a model.

His newly issued "license" had been framed and hung beside the door. He'd already taken in a few coins from the old gents, who'd found their favorite chairs and drawn them up to the non-existent fire. He needed to have the chimney inspected before he attempted to drive off the damp.

He'd like to fix the back window and remove the board to

air the place out, but there was only so much time in a day. He'd brought in a stool for himself and practiced putting his feet up on the shelf beneath the bar while he polished mugs. He munched a sandwich from the basket Elsa had prepared for him.

Hunt and Walker entered, surprising the devil out of him. Henri dropped his stool to its feet and stood, reaching for his best tankards. He kept an eye on the old gents, but they merely studied the foreigners with interest.

"Did the ladies miss me at dinner?" Unwilling to discuss potential killers in the presence of witnesses, Henri merely filled the mugs with ale.

"The talk was of weddings and orchards, so no, not particularly." Hunt leaned an elbow against the bar, ignoring the other customers while lifting his tankard.

The captain was a large, impressive gentleman, one who understood that his presence attracted attention. He wouldn't impart anything he didn't want the world to hear.

Walker didn't have to be large. His skin color alone placed him under scrutiny. Henri didn't think he'd need the weapons he stored beneath the bar to defend a friend, but he was prepared to. He'd rather make Walker comfortable. Every man deserved a place to relax and converse.

"You've learned more of orchards?" He wiped down the already shiny bar. He knew they'd been hunting for Bergstein. The men listening would too.

"Patience told us we need new root stock so she can begin grafting new trees. Ours are old and won't bear much longer." Walker sipped his ale and spun a silver coin on the bar. "That hill isn't good for much else."

"But she says we don't have anything to create healthy root stock, whatever that is." Hunt sipped his ale.

"You need saplings to grow new trees," one of the gents called.

Henri bit back a grin as Hunt swung around, leaned his

elbows on the bar, and regarded the room. The young captain with his scarred visage and air of authority had just received the response he wanted—an invitation to join the old-timers.

Walker snorted into his cup and let the conversation go on without him.

"Did you find the Bergstein place?" Henri kept his voice low while Hunt and the others discussed trees.

"We think we did. Naught but a broken-down caravan there, so he's likely not living there all the time. But he has a small orchard of his own, better looking than ours."

"We have only to wonder if we're hiring a wife beater or worse if we find him. It might be better to write universities and ask if they know of any able agriculturalists."

"Fancy name for a farmer." Walker finished his ale but didn't ask for a second.

The door opened, and a silence fell as Ted Corcoran entered. Wearing the tailed coat of a gentleman, not a farmer, he signaled for a mug and settled in a dark corner. The conversation resumed.

Henri poured a mug and left it sitting on the bar. "I'm not a serving girl."

"Mighta fooled me." Corcoran reluctantly got up to leave his coin and retrieve his mug while looking Henri over. "Fancy duds for a man."

Since Corcoran's coat was a decade out of date and his fancy neckcloth stained with dinner, Henri took that with a cellar of salt. He wore silver buttons for a reason, and they went better with embroidery and silk than wool. Now that he had a laundress, he indulged in fine linen. And he knew how to find clothes second-hand and have them tailored. Ladies liked him fine.

"No harm in looking good," he told his obnoxious guest. "You work around here?" He was aware that Walker and Hunt listened, although they didn't appear to.

"Not if I can help it." Corcoran returned to his seat.

The old gents had begun reminiscing over the days when the earl had planted the orchard. Hunt encouraged them with an occasional question or two.

"I keep waiting for the other shoe to drop," Walker murmured, staring into his empty mug.

"Corcoran knows you're with Hunt. I think he's spying on us. He doesn't look the sort to cause a fracas," Henri murmured back.

"What happens after we leave? You be all right here?"

Henri grinned. "More than all right. He's twice my age and apparently doesn't enjoy physical labor. If he's carrying any weapon, it's a hidden knife, which has to be small. I have a double-barreled pistol and a shotgun. Want to calculate my chances?"

"And if his pals show up?"

"Pals? You think a man like that has friends?" Henri thought it over. "Bartholomew apparently was one once. I wonder if Bergstein or Blackstone might have been? That would be interesting."

As if conjured by their discussion, a tall, thin man of roughly the same age as Corcoran entered. With a lined, weathered face, he wasn't prepossessing, but his taut edginess warned of a temper.

Henri had met him once, when he'd shaken his hand over renting the tavern. Bartholomew didn't acknowledge him beyond ordering a pint.

In a fit of inspiration, Henri turned three mugs upside down on the bar, showed him a penny, then slid it under the center mug. "If you guess which mug has the coin, the drink's on the house." He shuffled the mugs. He had everyone's attention.

Bert pointed at the right hand mug.

Henri lifted the mug, uncovered the coin, and poured a half pint. "On the house. Any other takers?"

George, the tavern authority, removed himself from his

favorite chair to idle over. "Bert, how ya doin'? I'll take a try at that game."

Henri suspected Bert had stopped at the tavern before heading home—where he would learn a deputation from the church had visited. Given his angry conversation with Upton, he wouldn't be pleased. This might be their only chance to question him about the tools.

George guessed the wrong mug and paid his coin for a refill. "You still lookin' for help on thatching that barn?" he asked of the new arrival.

Bert nodded glumly. "Can't pay enough. Reckon I'll do it myself when I find time."

Hunt pointed at the mugs. "My turn."

Henri put George's coin under a mug and shuffled. "New curate knows thatching and carpentry, probably looking for work."

Hunt picked the correct mug. Using practiced sleight-of-hand, Henri slid the coin into his palm, then lifted the mug to show it empty. Hunt could afford to pay.

The captain glared, knowing he'd been had. Apparently conceding the game was an effective conversation starter, he added, "Curate did a good job on the chapel for a reasonable price, but someone stole his tools."

"Ain't got no truck with the church," Bert muttered. "Interferin' busybodies."

Corcoran spoke from his dark corner. "You're goin' to hell for what you did, anyways. Barkeep, I'll take another."

"Name's Henry." He poured a mug without offering the shell game and waited for Corcoran to drag his lazy hide to the bar to pay for it. "New curate doesn't preach hell," he added, just to stir things up. "But he swings a mean mallet."

"Legget," Bert corrected.

"Heard that's what killed the old curate," Deacon Jones said from his chair.

"Heard an eaves knife killed Blackie," George the

Authority added, taking his mug back to his chair. "Reckon the new curate learned better uses for his tools? It's curious his'n went missing right after them murders."

Bert stiffened this time but drank without speaking.

Corcoran half-stood, snatched his mug from the bar, and sat down again. "Heard Blackie was claiming to be an heir. Maybe the heirs did him in." He didn't look at Hunt.

Hunt simply held his mug out for another pour. It was the deacon who spoke up. "The Blackie we oncet knew would claim to be the devil himself if it put coins in his pocket. He never had two to rub together, but he ain't been about in years. Why would anyone waste time killing him?"

"Robbery, jealousy, and vengeance are the usual reasons," Walker said, not looking at anyone.

"You a lawyer?" William Oswald, the postmaster's brother asked skeptically, when no one else spoke.

"Just a reader. Wycliffe left a big library. Anyone here jealous of Blackie? Want to settle an old score?" Walker pretended to drink from his empty mug.

Settling old scores had probably killed the old curate, Henri reflected, but he preferred letting the conversation carry itself.

"Bergstein might have had a score to settle with Blackie, but if knocking up sisters called for killing, I reckon Teddy there would be dead a few times over." Bert finished his drink and walked out.

Hunt blocked the door, preventing a furious Teddy Corcoran from following him.

TWENTY-FOUR

"You've been fighting!" In horror, Patience studied the bruise on Henri's cheekbone as he entered the breakfast room. "I knew that tavern would be a terrible place. I'll ask Meera for a poultice."

She started to stand, but he pressed a hand to her shoulder and poured her more tea. The familiarity startled her into stillness. She had spoken to a gentleman as if he were her brother!

"I appreciate your concern, mademoiselle, but it is nothing. The captain and I had a small discussion with a customer and accidents happened. I assure you, I have suffered worse when Arnaud loses his temper and flings paintbrushes." He filled his plate at the sideboard. His appetite was obviously unharmed.

Clare glanced up from the notes she was scribbling. "Hunt came home glowering and went straight to his study. It was more than a small discussion."

"It involved sisters, present company excluded, and cannot be discussed in polite company. This is the purpose of taverns." Henri poured coffee for himself and appropriated the chair next to Patience.

Proximity made her nervous, but she was too intrigued by the topic to protest. "Sisters? As in Mr. Corcoran's? Paul's mother would, indeed, be an ugly topic."

"And apparently Blackstone's sister and possibly Bergstein's or someone else's. It was never quite clear." Walker entered with Meera, assisting her into a chair before filling her plate.

Meera beamed like the newlywed she was. Patience thought she understood the reason for honeymoons. The happy couple emanated a glow that made everyone else restive.

Patience was not unaffected. She inched away from Henri.

"An Abe was mentioned. I assume that is our missing Bergstein. It is possible all our suspects had sisters." Henri dug into his eggs.

"Should we be looking at their sisters as killers?" Clare asked with a hint of irony.

"Or wondering whose sister is buried in the orchard?" Patience was appalled at thinking this way, but it had to be said.

"If Bergstein had a sister. . . could it be her jewelry buried with the bones?" Meera asked.

"But Mr. Oswald said Abraham bought back the pearl for a *wife*. So he might have married someone else's sister?" Patience decided she'd had enough speculation. "I wish to see this orchard the captain says is down the road. May I have directions? I'll take one of the men with me."

"Don't be ridiculous," Henri said sharply.

He never spoke sharply. Patience jerked with surprise but laid her napkin down and rose anyway.

Henri flung down his fork. "Stable hands are not soldiers or gentlemen. If Arnaud will not go with you, I will. There are killers on the loose. Just because he knows trees doesn't mean Bergstein isn't one. If you are caught trespassing, you are giving him excuse to shoot. Trees cannot be worth it."

207

"I am forewarned now. We need root stock if the orchard is to be restored. I'd like to ask if he has the Paradise variety of apple." She already wore her riding skirt for the journey. She lifted all the foolish fabric and stumbled anyway.

She was built top heavy and would have crashed into the sideboard, but Henri was already on his feet and caught her before she did more than stub her toe. "Let me finish here and find my boots. Arnaud is painting the Monk's walls today, so I will take his place at your side."

"From the sounds of it, you need to take a few soldiers. What is Jack doing today?" Clare glanced up in concern.

"He has men coming to work on his stable. I will ask one of Hunt's army to join us." Henri hurriedly finished his coffee and toast.

Patience was accustomed to doing things herself. It seemed foolish to take an armed escort to visit an orchard. She'd always done fine carrying a basket of food.

If someone had saplings already rooted, she had a little money of her own to pay for them. The captain would surely reimburse her. She simply didn't want to impose. . . Or to let him know where she was going, because she knew she was being foolish.

Gravesyde wasn't exactly bucolic.

"They are just trees," she continued arguing later as Henri's armed soldier followed them through the village. "I cannot imagine anyone standing guard over trees."

Henri had buckled on a sword but did not appear to be carrying any other weapon. "You are assuming everyone is as rational as you are. A man who would hide in the woods, terrifying ladies, not making himself known to the gentlemen, is not behaving rationally."

"Perhaps he is *shy*," she retorted. She never spoke like this to anyone else, not even her brother. There was just something about this irritating Frenchman. . . She hummed to herself, calming her irrational responses.

"Or he is a hermit who shoots trespassers."

"How else am I to find out if he can help us if we don't ask?" she asked in exasperation.

"You tell everyone you know what you want and hope he hears and responds. He cannot live entirely in a world of his own. We know he must see Mr. Oswald occasionally for him to know the man has returned."

"Or Mr. Oswald can be a killer trying to point us away from himself. I do not like games. I prefer directness." Which was apparently a difference between them. Having a house-keeper for a mother was beneficial—she'd heard the gossip about last night's shell game.

"Directness can get one punched in the nose or shot at. We occupy different worlds," he asserted, almost angrily.

She pondered why he might be angry but couldn't fathom it. So she simply added her observation. "We are male and female. Of course we occupy different worlds. Women aren't threatened with punches, since we are easily intimidated by words and size. So we do not call attention to ourselves by speaking with unfamiliar men."

"Yet you are set to go out and introduce yourself to a potential madman!"

"Well, you and the captain didn't," she said with a shrug. "You said there was no one there. I simply wish to see the orchard."

And yes, she knew she was being foolish. But if she wanted to work in a man's world, she had to find some manner of doing so.

"More likely, he isn't there much. The caravan is hardly a roof over his head. Let Jack set a watch on the lane to let us know when he comes and goes." He rode beside her now that the lane had turned onto the larger main road.

He seemed a little less angry. Perhaps she had said the right thing for a change. "I suppose we must consider that, if he is not there again today. I will take his basket to Mrs.

Bartholomew then. I had hoped to visit her with things the children might need."

"Are you suicidal?" He was angry again. "Bert has murder weapons in his barn!"

"We could ask him how they came to be there." Now she was needling him, she knew. His temper was entertaining. She rather enjoyed conversing with a gentleman who treated her like a person and not a pair of breasts. She hummed happily while he stewed.

"Women," he muttered, apparently gathering he was being led down a garden path. "Now I understand why I have lived alone."

"If you don't attempt to understand us, then that is for the best," she agreed. "Is this the path to the orchard?" She reined in her horse at the small hedge opening with recently snapped branches.

He didn't respond but rode through the opening first, leaving Patience sandwiched between him and the soldier at the rear.

"You ought to carry the basket if you're in the lead," she taunted. "It is not human nature to shoot a food basket."

"It is if he's mad." He halted and held out his hand for the basket, presumably thinking it a good idea but too annoyed to say so.

"If he can grow fruit trees, then he is the right sort of mad." That didn't mean he wouldn't kill people, but she supposed almost anyone might do that with the right provocation. She was no one to judge, and she could not live her life in fear. She preferred believing kindness would be returned.

They rode into the clearing. No one shot at them. No one greeted them. The place appeared abandoned. The shirt she'd been told had hung on the trees was still there.

"Perhaps he's been murdered," she suggested, riding

toward the orchard. For reassurance, she sang a hymn under her breath.

"Perhaps he hides to prevent himself from being murdered," Henri countered, following closely and watching all around them.

Patience only had her gaze on the trees. "I cannot tell if he's growing the Paradise variety, but they are young and healthy. Look, he's started new ones." She pointed at a line of saplings distant from the orchard. "This is what I need to do, if I could buy a few from him to start. Seeds take too long."

"He may only return once or twice a year to see what needs doing," Henri suggested.

"More than once or twice. If it's dry, new trees need watering. And he knows the need for fertilizing regularly. Then there's the trimming and picking and grafting. . ." She pointed at a line of young trees that had been grafted to stronger rootstock. "It's much like taking care of roses."

She produced her ever present pencil and notebook and scribbled a note asking if she might buy the rootstock or any of the young trees. Then she rode over to the sadly neglected caravan. There was no block to help her down from the horse. "Will you place this inside for me?"

To her relief, Henri did not argue but swung down and took the note, disappearing into the interior. If Mr. Bergstein had been murdered in his sleep, Henri probably wished to know. Or *needed* to know. Patience doubted anyone would *wish* for such a thing.

He only looked impatient to leave when he emerged. "Shall we deliver the basket to Mrs. Bartholomew then? It does no good to leave it if Bergstein is only here once a week or so."

"Could we? You don't mind?" That had been her intention.

"It's probably an idiotic thing to do since her husband is storing murder weapons, but we can assume he'll be out in

211

the fields. Unlike Corcoran, Bert does seem to work, and those children ought to have more than they do." He swung back into the saddle and let their armed escort lead them out.

"One must wonder how the Corcorans feed themselves if they have no garden. I worry about Paul's grandfather. We have yet to see him out and about."

Henri shrugged as they reached the highway. "I daresay there is a garden. It just doesn't need to be near the house if they're not working it."

"It does if they have a cook. Perhaps we should find out who does the cooking for them?"

"An excellent thought. Not certain how to go about it, but—"

"Mrs. Jones does their cooking," the soldier threw over his shoulder. "We used to hang about her back door to deliver baskets to her customers. She'd give us what she didn't need."

Patience knew some of the homeless ex-soldiers still lived in a hollow by the river. Being a crippled ex-soldier himself, the captain was trying to help those he could and didn't begrudge the land and game the household didn't use to the ones who refused his aid. Sounded as if they had other sources of food as well.

She leaned forward to see their escort. "Mrs. Jones?"

"Deacon's wife. They be church folk and hold services in their front room. But people pay her to cook too." He cocked his chin in the direction of the lane where the Bartholomews and Corcorans lived. "They live down that away. He used to tutor and she was a cook at some big house."

"Amazing." Henri started down the lane they'd traversed the day before. "Mrs. Jones may be our best source of gossip."

"Which is why they belong to the church," Patience said in amusement. "They don't need to hang about taverns."

"Don't mock my tavern. I earned enough last night to buy

two kegs to replace the one I started with. In one night." He sounded as if he mocked himself.

Patience was suitably impressed. "It is a shame we do not have more highway traffic so you aren't taking the coins of poor local folk."

"The manor is offering work. The village is not so poor now. If they don't need funds for food, then they can put some of their coins in my pockets."

She studied him with curiosity. "Does this mean you wish to stop traveling?"

He glared at the horizon. "Yes. I would like to have done more with my life than sell buttons."

They had reached the Bartholomew farm. Patience didn't have time to question or even ponder his reason for establishing a tavern and giving up his peddling route.

Bert Bartholomew stood in the yard, aiming a musket at them. Apparently, he *could* afford a weapon.

TWENTY-FIVE

HUNT LEFT CLARE AND MRS. UPTON IN THE CHAPEL, DISCUSSING seating, food, and flowers for the upcoming weddings—which sounded more like an excuse for village festivities than a solemn ceremony. He supposed Gravesyde could use a little festivity.

The wedding announcements had gone out in yesterday's post, but there was little expectation that any of their numerous unknown relations would respond. Clare had simply hoped to entice more family to acknowledge the manor.

Family and festivities might be important, but he didn't much care if the lilacs would be finished blooming in June or if the scent of the roses might be too strong for the chapel. He was far more interested in what bed Clare wanted to share.

In the meantime, it wouldn't hurt to have a chat with the new clergyman. Hunt was beginning to suspect there might be more than one killer on the loose. Many people had a motive to want the old curate dead, even his family, but who would kill a worthless ex-sailor? Someone from Blackstone's past, perhaps, and that wouldn't be the much younger new curate, even if he could have stabbed the man before falling unconscious. Two potential killers made his head ache.

He found Paul industriously trimming trees, while giving advice to a young boy hoeing weeds in the dirt patch that was the churchyard. Teaching by example made better sense than preaching in Hunt's mind.

"We have persuaded your mother out of hiding," he told the curate on the ladder. "She's in the chapel with Clare. I want to ask her a few questions, and she might respond more readily if you're about."

Paul lifted his eyebrows in surprise but climbed down. "Fetch some water from the pump and cool down a minute, lad," he told his young helper, before loping after Hunt. "You think my mother is hiding?"

"It is one theory. She lived here for a decade. She knows the people better than we do." Hunt opened the chapel door to discover the ladies attempting to open a window shutter. The outside ones had already been opened, he'd noticed. "Is that wise?" he asked.

"There is no point in having something if one doesn't use it." Mrs. Upton glared at the recalcitrant bar. "We simply wanted to see how much light it would let in."

Paul crossed the small nave to kiss his mother's cheek. "How are you doing in your new abode?"

She swatted impatiently at him. "About as expected, staying busy. You need pillows at the altar for old knees. Have you found anyone to head a sewing circle?"

"I am working on it. Miss Lavender has appropriated most of them for her paying positions. I may be reduced to begging Miss Clare's aid in persuading them to work for free." He reached up and pried open the shutters.

Catching a ray of sunshine, the filthy window cascaded a rainbow of colors across the chapel. Clare murmured some platitude about petitioning Lavender, while admiring the ancient glass.

Hunt studied the artwork of a shepherd kneeling in a flock of sheep to tend a lamb, guaranteed to put a man to sleep. "Needs cleaning."

"Doesn't everything?" Mrs. Upton agreed with a sigh of exasperation. "I used to polish those myself. I'm too old for that now."

"Did any of the village ladies help you?" Hunt hoped to lead into the subject of his interest.

"Mrs. Jones and Mrs. Oswald, but they were getting on even then. The younger ones were all having babies. Right after I married Isaiah, before I had Patience, I organized a cleaning party where we looked after each other's children while we worked. But some of the men objected, and we didn't manage to do that again." She bent to drag a bench over to better inspect the window.

Hunt and Paul grabbed the bench and moved it for her. She was not tall enough, even standing on the bench, to reach far. Pulling a duster from her apron, she knocked out decades of insect carcasses.

"Why did the men object?" Clare asked, standing well back from the dust.

"Small minds, petty jealousies." Mrs. Upton climbed down and scowled at the mess. "We'll need to bring the staff down here to clean."

"Explain, please, Mother. I would like to know how to avoid whatever plagued Father's time here." Paul produced a broom from a closet and began sweeping.

Hunt really didn't want to believe the curate was capable of killing. A monster had stolen his tools, murdered two men, and taken the weapons with him. The question became—was Bartholomew that monster? Elsewise, how did the tools come to be in his barn?

Bert hadn't admitted to even owning them last night, which was a black mark against his integrity. He'd been one of those who had threatened Upton over extortion, so he had to be a suspect. But he'd only been a young lad when Blackstone left the village. Why would he kill him? Had Blackie known something that threatened Bert in some way? The bones on the hill might be an indicator of a major crime in the past. Could Blackie have returned to extort people, too, killing the old curate in the process? Damn, but he hated thinking like this.

Mrs. Upton took the broom and indicated that he open the window on the other wall. "Too many young hotheads back in those days. I don't see that problem now. All the young people are gone. Paul will be fortunate his parishioners don't all die of old age in the first year."

That was a jolly thought. Hunt pried open the bar holding the second shutter and opened it carefully so as not to fill the air with bug dust. "We're hoping to bring some of the younger generation home to work the fields and support their elders. Paul probably needs a wiser advisor than I am."

"That wouldn't be me." Mrs. Upton waited for them to move a bench beneath the second window—an angel overlooking a field of sheep and grain.

Definite theme there, Hunt reflected, studying the filth.

Clare held his hand while she admired the stained glass. "The women working with Lavender all seem pleasant. I suppose, back when the viscountess was alive, the manor still employed a houseful of locals and the orchard was maintained."

"There's that." Mrs. Upton swept the sill. "All the young folk had coins in their pockets and no law to say them nay. Lady Reid did not mingle and had no idea of goings on. And there was that dreadful tavern. You shouldn't allow your cousin to reopen it, captain. It only attracted ruffians."

"Only old men there, far as I can see, including Mr. Jones and Mr. Oswald, husbands of your loyal helpers. Henri can handle them. The Irishman seems to be the only one with quick fists." Hunt kissed Clare's gloved hand and began examining the benches to be certain none would collapse if some of the heftier members chose them.

"Oh, they all were quick with fists and knives." The housekeeper climbed down and began sweeping the debris. "Blackie Senior encouraged them. The more they drank, the more money for him. And if a fight broke out, they'd all buy each other rounds until it was settled. Horrible. Isaiah daren't break them up. They all turned on him if he tried."

"So, perhaps I should occasionally stop at the tavern, come to know the fellows, perhaps influence them to better ways of airing their grievances?" Paul suggested, producing a hammer and nails to mend anything Hunt pointed out.

His mother shot him a warning glare. "They would either hush up or you'd learn more than you should. I would rather you took a position anywhere but here."

For some reason, the bones in the orchard reared up in Hunt's mind. A woman had been abused. Upton had known of it? After the fact, one assumed, or the bones would be in the cemetery. One of those men had a secret. And if he'd killed once. . .

"Other villages are no different. If you mean to steer Paul away from knowledge of his birth, it's too late," Clare said quietly. "It's old news, and I doubt anyone will speak of it."

Well, that hadn't been where his thoughts had gone, but Clare was most likely correct on the cause of their housekeeper's reluctance. Chances were good Upton hadn't told his wife everything he knew.

Mrs. Upton bit her lip, looked away, and swept angrily at the floor. "That was Isaiah's affair. I simply want Paul to be happy."

The young curate hugged her and returned to pounding nails. He was a good listener and not much of a talker.

It was hard to tell how much his stepmother knew of Paul's true parentage, and Hunt didn't intend to ask. "Did you know the Bergsteins?"

"Gypsies, as far as I knew." She shrugged. "The parents died shortly after the earl, I believe, and the children grew up wild. I believe the viscountess might have employed several."

"How many were there?" Clare asked.

"Hard to say. The ones I knew were dark, handsome, and wild. Isaiah complained the boys were handy with their knives, and the girls were loose with their favors. Keep in mind, he'd been there a decade before I arrived, so he knew more of them. They weren't of our faith, and he had no influence over their behavior."

"And the Corcorans were Catholic and didn't attend his church either," Hunt added, trying to sort out a village from thirty-five years ago. "Were they wild too?"

"I only heard tales." Mrs. Upton said curtly. "Teddy Corcoran had just married about the time I met Isaiah, and of course, his sister, Paul's mother, had died the year before. If there were other siblings, I heard naught of them."

"Did Teddy Corcoran's new bride attend church here? She was a Bartholomew, wasn't she?" Clare straightened the benches Hunt disarranged.

"Bert and his wife attended, but I don't remember the sister that married Teddy." She wrinkled her brow in thought. "He was Catholic, of course. She had an infant, so she might have stayed home. And then she left him not long after I married Isaiah. Teddy was one of the wild ones who hung about the tavern, before and after his marriage."

"Who else hung about the tavern?" Paul asked, turning over another bench to check its legs. "I need to develop some plan if the young ones begin gathering again."

"Corcoran and Bartholomew were young hotheads who fought regularly. Blackie's son was gone by the time I arrived. The fieldhands, along with the Bergsteins, were involved, I suppose. Lady Reid had a steward, if I recollect, who was in charge of keeping them in hand, but as often as not, he was right there drinking with them. It's a small town with nothing productive to do in the evenings. You cannot be the law." She shook out the altar cloth and polished the candelabra.

"Then we must find useful occupation for their evenings," Paul decided. "If we put them to work repairing fences and roofs, there will be less time for idle argument and ale."

"That requires money," Hunt reminded him. "The manor has a limited budget."

"What if. . ." Clare began.

Mrs. Upton spoke at the same time. "They could share tasks together, as the wives did in my time?"

"Mr. Bartholomew needs his barn thatched. The church needs all sorts of work. Henri needs help restoring the tavern. . . I'm sure there are others." Clare clapped her hands in excitement. "We need a town hall meeting to discuss who needs what!"

Hunt bit back a groan. "After the weddings, perhaps?"

Impulsively, Clare hugged him. "We shall practice organizing with the weddings."

If it meant she'd embrace him more often, he could live with town meetings. Hunt hugged her back, then had to set her aside at the sound of horses riding a little too fast down the lane.

"They're in here!" a voice shouted.

"Henri," Hunt murmured into Clare's ear. "He and Patience went to visit Bergstein." He set her aside and strode out of the church. Everyone, naturally, followed.

Henri was already off his horse and reaching up for Patience, who was still carrying her food basket.

"I take it you didn't find Bergstein," Hunt said dryly, rescuing the basket while Henri manhandled the curate's daughter to the ground.

She appeared more irate than concerned about her less than graceful descent. "He *threatened* us! Mr. Bartholomew threatened us! All I wished to do was thank his wife for tea the other day. And he told us to go away and not come back. I have never. . ."

Henri hugged her shoulders and held a finger to her lips. "We are fine. He did not shoot. But I daresay I've lost a customer, although I cannot fathom why."

"To keep you from finding murder weapons?" Hunt asked, pointing out the obvious. "You were only supposed to go to the orchard!"

"But there was no one at the orchard, and we had food that might go to waste, and there was absolutely no reason for him to treat us like that. I hope he is not invited to the weddings. He is a nasty man." Patience brushed down her riding skirt. "It's been a very disappointing day. Mr. Bergstein has just the young trees we need. Must we camp on his lawn until he shows up?"

"You are not to go anywhere near either of those men, Patience Upton! What on earth were you thinking? This is highly improper. . ." Mrs. Upton turned her outraged glare on Hunt and shook her broom. "How could you let her. . ."

Hunt pointed at the soldier loitering at the gate. "They had an escort. They are adults. I am not anyone's father. I have my limits."

Their housekeeper burst into tears. Paul took her in his arms, shook his head, and led her toward the parsonage.

If they had another housekeeper gone mad. . . Hunt calmed his temper when Clare slid her arm through his. "I am only an engineer," he muttered. "What am I supposed to do?"

"We'll all go up for luncheon and discuss the next step. I fear we must confront Mr. Bartholomew somehow." Clare nodded toward Patience. "Will you walk with us? Henri can take the horses back to the stable."

"I'll take the basket to Mrs. Green first. Someone ought to have the benefit of a nice meal or two. And perhaps she can tell us more of Mr. Bartholomew. I shall be there directly."

Patience lifted her long riding skirt and started down the lane.

Henri rolled his eyes, handed the reins to the soldier escort, and ran after Patience.

"Meera and I could walk to the market without an armed escort in *London*," Clare complained. "We cannot go on like this, looking over our shoulders every second."

"We will handle it. Come along, we'll discuss it at luncheon, as you suggested." Hunt cast a glance after the arguing couple. "I think our new gardener is learning to speak for herself."

"Yes, well, she no longer has her father to speak for her. It's about time." She lifted her skirt and started down the lane. "Let us just hope we uncover no more bones. I don't think I can abide this much longer."

Clare had family all over the countryside that she could return to—leaving him here. Hunt couldn't let that happen. He'd string up every blamed man in the village first.

TWENTY-SIX

THE NEXT MORNING, THE MEN LOCKED THE WOMEN OUT OF THEIR council of war. Clare countered by calling Elsa, Patience, and Meera to their own council. Mrs. Upton refused to join them. Instead, she vented her fears and frustration by leading an army of maids and scrubbing all the guest rooms in anticipation of two weddings.

Clare hated to tell her that they were unlikely to have anyone but themselves and a few elderly, nosy aunts. If their eager housekeeper started demanding new linens, she'd break the news then.

"Hunt says we must stay in the house until they bring in all their suspects for questioning," Clare announced when they'd settled in with tea and cakes. "I am quite fine with that, if I could spend all day in the library or my office, but I cannot. There is far too much to be done in too short a time."

Elsa pointed at the cakes. "Taste, please. It's a new recipe I hope to serve at the wedding breakfast. And while I might love my kitchen, it is ridiculous to think we can hide for an unknown amount of time. Although, I suppose, if it's only a day or two, until we start receiving answers to our announcements, it might be reasonable."

"I have no purpose unless I'm outside, overseeing the gardens!" Patience helped herself to several cakes. "And if they hope to find Mr. Bergstein, they might have to wait until he has a day off from wherever he's working now. That could be a week or a month, we have no notion. We last saw him on a Thursday, but we cannot count on him showing up tomorrow."

Meera leaned back in her chair, sipping tea, her brow wrinkled in thought. "It does seem essential to have the killer caught before our guests arrive. Can you imagine the havoc if he decided to stab someone else while they were here? Your noble aunts will have the vapors, then all the titled jackasses would rush in and order the manor burnt down."

Elsa giggled. "Jack's father doesn't even realize there's a manhunt going on. Although," she grimaced, "the best of the London Season will be winding down soon. Unless my mother is marrying her marquess, she is likely to arrive at any time. She is one of the titled jackasses who would order the place burnt."

Clare bit back a snicker at the earl's daughter and the Jewish apothecary both using tavern language. Patience appeared a bit shocked, but if she meant to work with men, she must learn the vernacular. "I know our family is impractical, at best, but I don't think anyone would order arson. More likely, they'd find a way to return the manor to the bank. I, for one, am against that. What must we do to help the men round up our various suspects?"

"It would be better if we could prove which one was the killer," Elsa pointed out. "The men rush about with weapons and ropes and whatnot, but has anyone sat down and tried to make a case against any of them?"

Clare beamed and opened a writing box of paper, pens, and ink. "My thought precisely. I was thinking we could write down each suspect, where they might have been at the time of each murder, why they might have committed it, things like that." She'd tried something similar in her gothic novel, and it had helped tie up the ending. Perhaps the technique could be expanded to real life.

"You should be a barrister." Elsa tested her cake, wrinkled her nose, and continued, "Or do they just stand in court and argue that this person is too nice to be guilty?"

"It's not as if I'd be allowed in court to find out. Surely, men are capable of logical thinking. Eventually." Clare passed out papers and writing tools. She knew Hunt would prefer to have evidence laid out in front of him.

"But what if we're looking at the wrong people? Shouldn't we consider people outside of my father's notebook?" Patience didn't eagerly reach for paper as the others did.

Clare nodded and handed her a sheet. "Excellent thought. You start a list of other possible suspects, although I'm afraid you'd have to include your mother and brother. They both might have reasons we don't know for wishing your father dead."

"My father was not an easy man. I'd have to include myself as well," Patience muttered. "Perhaps I should not be here at all."

"Hunt suggested that we might be looking at two killers, one who attacked your father because of the notebook, the other who attacked Blackstone for something in the distant past. That Blackstone arrived at the same time as your father is problematic. If he killed your father, how would we prove it?" Clare picked up her pen but let it hover. "I'm not sure how to address that logically."

"I see why the men are out riding around, gathering people up." Meera glared at her page. "That's far more active than sitting about, philosophizing."

"It's not philosophizing. The captain can't send half the men in town to assizes. He needs evidence to present to the court. I will start with Blackstone Junior." Elsa dipped her pen in ink. "He was roughly the same age as Patience's father, older than Bergstein and Bartholomew and Corcoran, am I correct? Chances are good that Mr. Upton knew a great deal more about him than anyone else. He certainly knew he wasn't Duncan Reid. Blackstone could very well have been Mr. Upton's killer."

"Blackstone was overheard arguing with my father," Patience reluctantly agreed. "His father ran the tavern, and Mother says he used to run wild. The register shows he married a Naomi Bergstein, presumably one of Abraham's sisters. Do we know exactly when he left town or joined the navy?"

"And he was a liar and a manipulator, coming here and pretending he was a Reid just because his mother had Reid in her name." Clare produced the register, the notebook, and the certificate showing Blackstone's commission to the navy. "He was born in 1759, married in 1778, presumably after a youth of carousing and living off his father's tavern. Walker found an AB employed here until after the earl's death, which is about when Blackie joined the navy. The navy certificate is dated 1782—four years after Mr. Upton took up the position as curate but before Lady Reid arrived."

Patience hurriedly took down notes on her paper. "Papa probably drove him out of town with his extortion."

"He could be the AB/BW in 1779." Meera read through the notebook. "But Blackstone was presumably at sea by the time of AB/S in 1791."

"So the AB/BW in 1779 might have been the incident that drove him out of town," Clare speculated. "But that isn't something we can note. Let us just gather facts."

"I hate this." Elsa poured more tea. "The other men are all roughly ten years younger than Blackstone. They would have been little more than adolescents when he left. Why would they kill him?"

"On general principles," Clare said, wrinkling her nose in distaste. "He was a nasty sort. But let's look at our primary suspect, Mr. Bartholomew. He has the weapons that killed both victims and has a nasty temper. But what could his motive possibly be? And was he in town on both days?"

"He argued with my father the day he died. My father knew something awful about him. And he has a musket and is willing to use it." Patience rubbed a tear. "I hate this too. I don't think I can be very useful."

"But you are a witness to some of the people who threatened your father. We don't have many witnesses. What did Bert say?" Clare asked.

"Everything was so new back then. I cannot say for certain. I remember my father mentioning his name, but I really cannot remember what he looked like. Papa mentioned grievous sin and atonement, and Mr. Bartholomew called him a parasite. I looked up the word. I suppose if one considers money to be blood, he was, really." Patience scrunched up her brow. "I think that was when Mr. Bartholomew claimed it was self defense."

"So Bartholomew might have already killed in self defense?" Meera asked. "Let us hope he did not notice you there if that was the reason he killed your father!"

That silenced them.

Henri didn't wish to ride out with Hunt and the party determined to haul Bartholomew in to be questioned. He could not abide seeing that poor woman and her children in hysterics. He was a coward.

He might have offered to go with Arnaud and the soldiers to camp out at Bergstein's orchard, but he preferred the third choice—Edward Corcoran, simply because he didn't like him. They could all be wrong about the notation in Upton's notebook. Upton might have written down Corcoran's name as Paul's father out of spite. But just because Corcoran was a wealthy man did not mean he shouldn't be held to account like anyone else. He should be questioned too.

"It's better if I do this alone," he told Hunt. "I'll take my peddler's cart, carry some gewgaws, question Mrs. Jones, then move on to the Corcoran household to deliver their dinner, if all goes well. I don't think their son is someone we can drag in to question without good reason. Since he seems to travel, we don't even know if he was in town when Upton died. We need more information."

"He can't be arrested for ancient crimes," Hunt agreed gloomily. "If his family didn't attend services, then Upton couldn't force him to tithe. He has no motive for leaving his tidy nest and dirtying his hands against men larger than him."

"I wonder if Blackstone might have known Corcoran's filthy deeds?"

"As the son of a tavern owner, he knew all the gossip." Hunt rubbed the scar above his blind eye. "Like the late curate, a lot of people probably wished Blackstone dead. Those bones didn't bury themselves in the orchard. If Upton knew about them, then chances are, Blackstone and Bergstein did too, and that's why both of them returned. I wish Meera had said the bones belonged to monks."

"The monks are in the cemetery or the crypt, not in an orchard. Someone took advantage of a tree being planted, and that's the earl's time. Bert would have been too young. I'm wagering on Bergstein for the bones, at the very least. If he has an orchard, he no doubt worked in this one. Guilt may have caused him to leave the box with his victim. Prove that, and we may prove he did in the curate and Blackstone to cover it up." Henri tapped on his peddler's hat and strode out.

Which pretty much left Corcoran off the suspect list. He had probably never used a thatching tool or dug a hole in his life.

Blackstone would have made a much easier suspect,

except he was dead. If Blackie killed Upton, how would they prove it now?

Henri loaded his cart with trinkets and picked up the ex-soldier the Corcorans would recognize for meal delivery and struck out for the home of the good Jones folk.

Martha Jones was a gray-haired farm wife, saggy with age, engulfed in a worn apron. She greeted his arrival at the kitchen door with delight. "Mr. Henri, you haven't been by in forever! I heard you were staying at the manor now."

He tipped his hat and opened the cart side to reveal his wares. "That I am, Mrs. Jones, which means I needn't go out until I have the perfect goods for my customers."

He went into his spiel about the notions she preferred, sold her a few, then indicated the soldier. "This gent here says he delivers food for you. He's hurt his foot, so I took him up. No reason he should have to hoof it if I'm about."

"Oh, that's kind of you, sir! You really should attend our chapel, even if you are a Papist. I was just preparing the pot, if you'll wait a moment." She hustled inside and returned shortly with a container insulated in thick towels. "Mr. Jones could do this, but he's never about when I need him." She handed the soldier a basket of his own. "Just remember to return those so I may fill them again."

The soldier tipped his cap. "One of the boys'll be out first thing in the morning, ma'am. We sure do appreciate it."

They exchanged a few more pleasantries, and Henri was on his way. "Thanks for helping me," he told the man—barely more than a boy—poking through his basket to produce a meat pie. "We're trusting on your discretion."

"Mrs. Jones is like my ma was," his accomplice said. "Kinda reminds me of home. Soon's my arm heals, I'll join up to fight old Boney again. Ain't nothin' back home for me no more. I reckon the captain will write me a recommendation, right?"

From what he could see, if the arm hadn't healed properly

by now, it never would, but Henri nodded. "The captain's offered work to anyone who wants it, should you decide to stay."

Henri knew not all the former soldiers wished to give up their gin or freedom for the little the manor could offer. Not many good citizens would think to hire rough, disabled ex-soldiers. Maybe more wealthy nobles should fight on the ground with the men they sent to war, like Hunt and Jack had, so they'd have more sympathy for their plight. But that was his revolutionary youth speaking.

They rolled up the drive of Corcoran's house, and Henri pulled around to the rear. He surreptitiously studied the windows but saw no movement. He left the lad sitting on the cart where he could be seen and hopped down with the hot container.

The stout, stoop-shouldered woman who answered the door was definitely not a servant. She wore a decent bombazine with fine lace trim, a crisp cap adorned with black ribbons, and a heavy silver cross on a fine chain. She scowled at him, then glanced back at his cart. "We don't buy from peddlers."

"Only here to deliver dinner, madam." Henri doffed his hat and bowed. "Young man there hurt his foot, and I took him up. He didn't want you to go hungry. He says your husband likes a good tobacco. Might I show you what I carry while I am here?"

She glanced over his shoulder to the familiar young soldier, then stepped aside. "Leave the pot on the table. Hisself shouldn't be smoking, but Teddy smokes the same. Show him what you carry."

Henri left the pot where indicated, then fetched his tins, and looked to his hostess for direction. He was relieved to know Paul's grandfather was alive, at least.

She pointed at a door in the back of the kitchen. "He can't get up and down the stairs no more, so we set him up in the dining parlor. Go right through there. But don't try cheating him. My son will find you if you do."

Lovely. With a smiling nod, Henri made his way into a dark room, the curtains drawn against the last light of day. A solid old bed nearly filled one wall. It was so tall, the diminutive patient probably had to fall out of it to reach the chamber pot.

Henri pulled the door shut, conspiratorially pulled a flask from his pocket, and held it up. "I'm to sell you tobacco, but I thought a good Irishman like yourself might appreciate a bit o' caper juice to wet your whistle before we haggle."

The old man pulled himself up against the pillows. He still had a full head of silver hair, and his eyes twinkled at the flask. "Don't mind if I do. Woman won't let me have a bit of pleasure since I been laid up like this."

Henri handed over the flask and busied himself opening tobacco tins. "For your grandson's sake, I'll give you a good price. He's that worried about you, but he can't get past the gorgon."

The patient handed back the flask, and his eyes narrowed. "My grandson? Mary's boy? Or has Teddy got one he's not told us about?"

Did that mean he didn't know his son had fathered Paul? "You haven't heard? Our new curate is Paul Upton, Isaiah and Mary's boy, if I have it rightly. You understand I'm Papist, like you, and don't attend. But he seems a fine fellow."

The wrinkled hand holding the tobacco tin shook. "Mary's boy is here? He shouldn't have come back!" He set the tin on the table. "You tell him to leave this place. It ain't nowhere for him to be."

"His stepmother and sister are here," Henri said quietly. "He'd rather know you than run away."

The patient rolled his head against the pillow, closing his eyes. "Leave me a tin. She'll pay on the way out. You tell him not to come here."

"I'm sorry if I've disturbed you, sir. Would you like me to come back next week with another tin?" Henri didn't know how else to learn what was happening. It was evident Teddy wasn't anywhere about.

Daniel Corcoran pretended he didn't hear—until Henri had gathered up his supplies and headed for the door. "Day after tomorrow, they go up to town."

Henri tipped his hat. "See you then."

TWENTY-SEVEN

In the family parlor with the other ladies, Patience studied the notes on possible suspects and sighed. She wasn't accustomed to staying inside, doing nothing. "Really, it's like reading a novel. I do not like fiction. I want scientific fact."

Clare sent her a disgruntled look. "Scientific fact came about because someone said *what if?* One must start somewhere."

"But look at these!" Patience held up the pages. "William Oswald may be the same age as Blackstone, but he's half the size, and he helps at the church, for heaven's sake! Just because Henri says he left the tavern right after Blackstone that night means absolutely nothing."

"Corcoran leaving at the same time means nothing either," Clare conceded. "Except both of them had opportunity. Half the village might have been out and about at that hour, in the pouring rain, but so far, no one has spoken up but Henri."

Patience returned to her father's notebook. "If we have a town hall meeting, we should hand out copies of my father's notes and ask if they remember any of the incidents that might match the initials. If we are to convict based on this, we should know who everyone is, not just the ABs. This scribble

233

might be WO, but the crime was only worth a penny. And I suspect if the B represents the sin committed, it is no more than blasphemy."

Patience tossed the book back to the low table. "I shall go mad if we must stay inside much longer."

Meera picked up the book and riffled through it. "There are quite a lot of B sins. I cannot imagine the sinners cared a great deal if your father preached about their blasphemous ways. They're just paying up their pennies to keep him happy."

"To feed us," Patience corrected. "He was begging, if blasphemy is the sin. It's not as if the earl was likely to fine them." Unlike Paul, her father hadn't been an educated man. He wasn't too proud to beg.

The bell for the front door jangled. They all straightened eagerly.

So far, the men had had no luck in rounding up any of their suspects. Patience supposed being well-fed and trapped in the manor wasn't as bad as the poor soldiers camping out in damp fields, eating over campfires. She simply didn't see how anyone could be convicted on the basis of an old notebook and some stolen tools. It just did not seem reasonable.

Perhaps visitors could tell them what was happening out in the world.

A young girl in stiff apron and cap knocked. She bobbed a curtsy, handed Clare a card on a silver salver, and departed.

Clare glanced at the card and wrinkled her nose. "Is it a sin to tell a lie and say I am not at home?"

She handed the card to Meera, who passed it to Elsa, who passed it on to Patience, who looked at it blankly. "Mr. Bosworth?"

"Banker. He claims to own the mortgage on the manor and most of the village, even though Hunt has proved his deed is for the worthless west hill only. We are at an impasse. Bosworth says the viscount borrowed a large sum of money, and the loan has been accumulating interest. Hunt is taking him to court. They've come to an informal, temporary arrangement, but neither of them is happy."

A banker. Banks had money. Paul and the church needed money. If she was stuck in this house, she ought to be useful in some manner. Patience didn't think she'd be very good at talking to bankers, but perhaps she could learn a thing or two if she went with Clare.

Henri had been very close-mouthed about his visit to the Corcorans, which irritated her no end. Paul ought to be allowed to meet his grandparents!

So, maybe she could learn things from the banker that Henri didn't know.

Which was endlessly foolish, but when Clare prepared to meet their visitor, Patience rose too. She couldn't hide behind draperies forever. "Why don't I go with you? You may call me your assistant. If he's too demanding, you can say you have important matters to attend, and leave me to take notes."

Clare laughed in delight. "An assistant! A secretary. . . I love it. I feel very official and important now. Meera, you stay there and put your feet up. Elsa, do you have any poisoned cakes to serve?"

"That would only make him a patient or another corpse to be buried. I'll just send up tea, shall I?" As impatient with taking notes as Patience, Lady Elsa sailed down the hall in the opposite direction of the great hall where Clare had sent the banker.

"Well, let's see what calumnies he intends to cast today. If obsession is a form of madness, I do believe Bosworth is just slightly touched in the head." Clare lifted the hem of her muslin morning gown, took a shawl the butler handed her as she passed by, and entered the great hall.

Patience bundled her heavy shawl around her and followed. Clare was light and delicate, as a lady should be. Patience felt like an unwieldy giant in her wake. But at least she was warm in her woolens. The two-story great hall was never warm, even when a fire was lit, which it wasn't today.

The gentleman pacing in front of the windows was nearly as old as her father. Of middling height and weight, he wore an elegantly tailored coat of olive green with leather riding breeches and boots. Despite the long ride out here, his linen appeared spotless and stiff. He wore his faded blond hair a trifle overlong, raggedly covering his ears and not styled the way Jack and Henri wore theirs.

He bowed at Clare's introduction to Patience, then glared until they settled on the settee so he could sit. He flung a card on the low table between them. "What is the meaning of this?"

Clare didn't glance at it. Patience picked it up and recognized one of the wedding announcements.

"You did not wish to be made known of our marriage before it appears in the papers?" Clare waited for a maid to settle the tea tray on the table.

"I don't care about the d-d. . . wedding." Bosworth fell silent until the maid departed and tea was poured. "Who sends out w-wedding announcements with n-notices that a library is to be sold? You cannot s-sell the library!"

Interesting. The older man stuttered. Did he only do so when in a rage? If he fell into frothing over an invitation, that might be most of the time.

"Oh, well, yes, we can, actually." Clare sipped her tea. "We thought to save the heirs postage by informing them of our intent to marry at the same time as we informed them of our intention to sell a few of the books. We assume most have no interest in either event. It's simply a polite formality."

Patience admired the lady's temerity. Bosworth was almost steaming. Patience refrained from reaching for her teacup for fear of being scalded by his glare. She'd thought bankers were pleasant gentlemen. She daren't ask this unpleasant fellow for chapel funds, not in a million years.

How had her father dared to approach all and sundry, men even scarier than this?

"The library is a valuable part of the manor, and until you pay the monies owed, the bank owns the manor!" Bosworth slammed his cup down so hard, Patience feared he'd cracked it.

Apparently, Elsa had thought to send up the less delicate china. No tea leaked.

Patience pondered this drama over shelves of moldering tomes. She'd been told the library hadn't been added to for nearly half a century, so they were of little use for gardening purposes. She'd found a few on fruit trees, but the information was old. If Jack's father had found a few volumes valuable to collectors, why would a banker care?

Clare rose, forcing the gentleman to stand with her. "Really, this argument must be taken to the courts. Our solicitors will handle it. I have more urgent matters to attend. Miss Upton, might you escort Mr. Bosworth to the library where he may consult with Lord de Sackville about the value of the volumes we hope to sell?"

As Clare sailed off and Bosworth nearly bubbled with fury, Patience rose to bob a curtsy like a good secretary. She led the way to the formal entry of the hall and not the connecting door. Visitors were not family, after all. Or, as she'd been told, the banker was unacknowledged family. She didn't know the etiquette for bastards.

Oliver and his tutor were working at the front table. She was fairly certain Jack's father had taken over the table around the corner, facing the west hill—the land the mortgage deed covered. At least, living in Wycliffe Manor was more exciting than a parsonage. Assuming Bosworth wished to see the volumes to be sold, she led him to the rear wing of the grandiose library.

Lord de Sackville was seated in a leather chair, deeply engrossed in a thick volume. He didn't even look up at their entrance. Stacks of leather-bound volumes were aligned on the table in some order known only to the baron.

"This is a travesty," Bosworth muttered, opening the first book he came to, a treatise on Plutarch in Greek.

"Can you read it?" she asked, out of curiosity.

He glanced at the pages in scorn. "Of course not. But the earl valued it. His descendants ought to honor his choices."

"As best as I can determine, the earl honored wealth. If his library was a good investment, then he would want it put to good use." She didn't know where that had come from, except she found this man disagreeable and knew Clare and Hunt needed funds to help the village.

"You know nothing, you silly twit. These might be valuable for more than money." He sat down and began examining the next volume, also in Greek.

Silly twit, indeed. She ran her fingers down the exquisitely imprinted gold titles until she found one she recognized. Pleased, she flipped through the pages until she ran across familiar verses and began to read Psalm 23, in Latin, aloud.

He glared at her. "What is that gibberish?"

She set the beautiful Bible on the stack in front of him. "The Bible in Latin, with fabulous illustrations. Even I can tell it belongs in a vault. Shall I bring you pen and paper so you may make notes?"

He glowered at the stacks, then at the baron lost in thought in the corner. Finally, he returned to working his way through the books one at a time, flipping pages as if in search of something. "I am fine. Go away."

Which was when Patience realized what he was doing—hunting for the map that Jack had found. How very foolish. The baron had gone over every one of those books, as probably had half the household. They weren't selling any notes the earl might have hidden to a potential treasure.

Which meant the banker suspected the earl had concealed jewels and had no better idea of their location than they did.

238

And he was hoping the bank would acquire the manor so he might search himself? Without the family trust, it would take a fortune in jewels to maintain this place.

Before she could make herself scarce, a commotion in the hall drew her attention.

"I'm no killer! You can't arrest me on trumped up charges. If Corky put you up to this, I'll. . ."

"You'll what, kill us?" Hunt asked, less than solicitously.

Their voices faded as a door closed.

Bosworth looked up, alert. "They've found Blackstone's killer?"

"Or my father's. Did you know Mr. Blackstone?" Now that she thought of it, the two men would be much of an age. It was hard to think of old gray hairs as young once, but they must have been.

"Of course not. There has always been a criminal element in the village. As a property owner, I should be included in any legal proceedings." He stood and walked out, leaving Patience to gape after him.

Was she supposed to halt him?

"Read the Bible, lass," the baron unexpectedly said from his corner. "You have a most melodious voice, and clutch-fists like that aren't worth wiping your feet on. Would you read the full psalm for me, please? I lose myself too much in the written word and have forgotten how pleasant reading aloud can be."

Wondering who Hunt had caught and what the men were doing to him, Patience swallowed her fear and took a seat near the baron. She'd spent many evenings listening to her mother read. The soothing phrases might calm her jumping nerves now.

She had to raise her voice over the shouts on the other side of the wall.

TWENTY-EIGHT

HOURS OF DEALING WITH THE PROTESTING BARTHOLOMEW, THE damned banker, and the arrival of Bert's family had worn what patience Hunt possessed to ribbons. He contemplated the bottle of brandy sitting on his study shelf as Walker entered, undoubtedly with still another problem.

"What shall I do with the wailing wife and children?" Walker asked—probably sarcastically since dealing with families of killers wasn't the reason he'd accompanied Hunt to England.

"Lock them in the wine cellar with Bert? Put them in the crypt?" Hunt avoided brandy in times of crisis but getting drunk had its appeal. "Could we send the wailers home with Bosworth?"

He needed to sort the bastard banker out one of these days. He didn't need the constant interference. He wasn't in the army any longer. He didn't have to follow orders of bungling generals.

"Filled himself up on Elsa's dinner and is now guzzling your brandy and annoying the baron in the library. I believe your intended has opened the east wing so he must stumble down dark halls to find his room." Walker set the book he'd been perusing on Hunt's desk with a page marked. "All you can do is send Bert to assizes and let the court decide."

"I've heard horror stories. The court will hang him on general principles." He'd no idea taking up the reins of this dratted place would make him judge and jury. He'd simply wanted a home and something to keep him gainfully occupied.

"What chance have we of ever learning who killed whom? If we're to make the streets safe, throw the lot of them at the court." Walker played devil's advocate well. "I'll heave the wife and babes into the barn." He walked out, leaving Hunt to his gloom.

He didn't try to read the ancient print in the law book with his one bad eye. He was contemplating the brandy decanter when Clare slipped in without knocking. She was growing quite bold, which relaxed him enough to stand and hug her. The scent of his grandmother's jasmine perfume followed her in.

"You keep me from murdering people," he murmured into her hair.

"Or murdering yourself? I have come to see if I can help so you won't dream of sailing away to calmer shores." She snuggled into his embrace, which almost had him forgetting Bert.

"Tropical beaches would bore me, although I'll admit, running away has its appeal. Or perhaps I could become a power hungry monster shouting *Off with his head!* Except I know I'd lose you either way." He resisted kissing her. His lust was such that it would inevitably lead to complications, when he needed his wits about him.

"Most heirs to great estates learn their duties from child-hood. You cannot expect to step in and learn it all in a few months. That's why you have us. What is troubling you?"

He sat down in the leather chair Walker had vacated and tugged her into his lap—not exactly the best position for thinking. But escaping his circling thoughts helped clear his head.

"Bert had the opportunity to murder both Blackstone and Upton. He claims not to know Blackie but admits he has the weapons for both murders. He admits he argued with the curate, but he claims that by keeping his family from the gossips at church, Upton couldn't shame them. And any crimes in his notebook are too old to take to court. He has a valid point."

"How would our late curate have shamed him?" She rested her head on his shoulder.

"Our family man admits he was once a hothead who took a knife to Teddy Corcoran in a dispute over Bert's sister. If the notebook is correct, this was during Lady Reid's reign, when there was no law. Upton could presumably have reported the altercation to the rector in Hereford, who might have called upon some authority. He chose to fine Bert instead. And because Corcoran was presumably guilty of fighting and possibly wife beating, he didn't seek the law either."

"Corcoran was Catholic and not one of Upton's parishioners, so he didn't fear extortion. Or shaming." She followed his thoughts. "And because he had wealth, he might pay a lawyer. But Bert had to pay Upton or be remanded to a magistrate? Better the devil he knew rather than abandon his family? Bert strikes me as a man who takes care of his family, if they were fighting over his sister."

"He's poor. He hasn't a lot of choices. From our farmer's point of view, Corcoran deserved killing for whatever happened with his sister. Bert was young and had a temper. He's not expressing much regret even now. If Corcoran had been the one killed, I'd have no difficulty accusing Bert."

"He had no reason to kill Upton over an old crime everyone already knew about." She frowned, grasping the problem.

"And he had even less reason to follow Blackstone and kill

him. He said he went directly home, although, since we don't have clear time frames, his wife's word of that proves little. It's a work of a few minutes to walk from the tavern to the church and run a man through with a knife." He winced. "I'm sorry. I shouldn't have said that."

"I write gothic novels with scenes worse than that," she scoffed. "Are you concluding Blackie vandalized the church? That took considerably more than a few minutes, as does breaking open the tool shed."

"True." He pondered the time frame. "If Bert meant to follow and murder anyone, it would be Corcoran, not Blackstone. Given the disparity in size between the Irishman and the sailor, the two are easy to tell apart, even in the dark, so he couldn't have mistaken his victim."

She kissed his stubbled jaw. "From the descriptions we've received, Blackstone and the elusive Mr. Bergstein were much the same size and coloring. And we know nothing of the bones in the orchard that might have drawn everyone to return. For all we know, Mr. Bergstein came back to kill Blackie for marrying his sister and possibly beating or killing her. We need Corcoran and Bergstein to fill in the picture before you can charge Bartholomew. Come along. We should settle his family somewhere safe for the night."

"You think our killer might harm women and children?"

"Apparently, you do, since you've ordered us to pull up the drawbridge and batten the hatches." She gracefully escaped his embrace.

"Mixing metaphors, my dear." Relieved to have an excuse to jettison his thoughts, Hunt followed her out—

Just in time to see Henri bursting through the front door, looking harassed and fierce.

"I may be delayed. Do what you must with the family." With resignation, Hunt signaled for his younger cousin to join him in the study.

~

Clare hugged the rare, intimate moment with Hunt to herself as she sought out Patience, who was settling the terrified Bartholomews into the attic nursery. The curate's daughter always knew the most compassionate thing to do.

"I thought you meant to help us!" young Mrs. Bartholomew cried as she rocked the youngest and the others milled about anxiously, examining ancient, dusty toys.

"We *are* helping," Clare said firmly. "There is a killer on the loose, and you are not safe until we find him."

"My Bert is not a killer!" The young mother wept. "He's a hard man, but he has to be to earn the bread for our table. He never hurt no one!"

Well, yes, he'd stabbed a man he'd once considered a friend.

"The men will determine that. No one is being charged yet. They are looking for witnesses and evidence to present to assizes, where any final decision will be made." Hunt simply didn't trust a distant judge to make the right decision. "Until the killer is found, we are making certain your family is safe."

She inspected the cots a maid and Patience arranged and wished she were more confident that justice would be served.

"Do you know where Mr. Bartholomew acquired his thatching tools?" Patience asked, a little uncertainly.

The curate's sister usually only spoke when something needed to be said. Clare let her take charge.

"He didn't steal them! He found them in our brook, just where we take the cow to drink. It was like the Bible says, the good Lord provides."

So, the wife was unaware that the tools had been used to kill. But Bert knew it and had said nothing.

Having raised Oliver since infancy, Clare knew how to wrestle anxious children into bed. She opened aging wardrobes, shaking out old bedclothes, inspecting them for sturdiness and size.

"Then trust the good Lord to take care of your husband and let's settle these little ones down for the night." Clare handed out gowns to one of the older girls who seemed to be in charge of the youngers.

Patience inspected a shelf of books. "I shall read a story if you will all settle down."

Clare made mental notes of improvements to be made before Meera's babe arrived. And some day—for her own children? Not if killers regularly haunted the area.

She set aside the doubts she'd harbored since arriving in this desolate location. If she loved Hunt, she should trust his ability to take care of his family and be willing to follow him anywhere—as her sister had followed her husband.

And got herself killed.

At least, Gravesyde wasn't a war zone, exactly.

Eventually, the children settled in. Clare drew Mrs. Bartholomew into the nanny's suite, leaving Patience soothing the children with the lovely voice she seldom used.

"What will we do without Bert?" The woman collapsed in an ancient rocking chair. "How long will this take?"

Clare hid her relief that the chair did not collapse from disuse. "I wish I had answers. We can only ask questions and hope we find someone to help us."

The young wife rocked and wept. "I cannot take care of the children and the farm on my own. We'll go to the poor-house if my Bert can't come home."

Gravesyde didn't have a poorhouse. The manor inhabitants provided the village's only government, and they couldn't tax an impoverished population. Would Shropshire take Gravesyde residents? They'd resist. She didn't know who could afford to support ten children.

"Have you or Bert no family who might help?"

Bert's wife shook her head. "I only had my sister. Bert's

brothers would throw us out and sell the land if they thought they could have the farm. There ain't money enough to pay for help."

"I don't think they can throw out his wife and children if he owns the land." Clare hadn't sufficient knowledge to grasp what would happen if Bert should hang. It was too horrible to imagine.

The young woman kept shaking her head and weeping. "We ain't rightfully married. The law won't let a man marry his wife's sister. If he hangs, they'll take away the farm. Without Bert, we'll starve."

Clare rubbed her eyes. Of course. She knew that. She just hadn't wanted to think about it.

They lived in sin and didn't think they belonged in church. If Bert hanged—where were his greedy brothers? Would they have planted the tools? More likely, the real killer would have.

Could this all be about land instead of past grievances? She was too tired to work it out.

TWENTY-NINE

Patience finished reading the book, checked to see that the children slept, then slipped from the nursery. She had hoped to calm her roiling emotions as she read, but the knots in her insides had only tightened to painful.

If Mr. Bartholomew was hanged, those children would suffer immeasurably. They would most likely starve just waiting for their father's trial. And he might hang simply because they couldn't find enough evidence to prove him innocent. This was all wrong. Her father would have fixed this.

But she couldn't preach or threaten or even gossip well enough to learn more. She was singularly useless.

Downstairs was quiet. She found Clare and Meera in the family parlor, but the men were nowhere to be heard. Perhaps she should simply retreat to her room in the cellar, but it was early yet, and she was too upset. She needed to *do* something.

"Where is everyone?" she asked.

"Elsa is flinging flour in frustration. Instead of holding a town hall meeting that might include women, the men are hiding in the tavern, most likely plotting." Clare looked up from the notes she was writing. "Did you learn anything from the children?"

"I didn't even think to try," she admitted in disgust. "My father would have pried every sliver of knowledge out of even the smallest. I had always thought him a nosy old gossip, but I'm thinking now that he was actually all the law these small villages had. I'm not sure even Paul can do what he did."

"Perhaps the men are trying to do the same. Gossip isn't quite the same as gathering evidence and witnesses, but it might provide direction. We need to mix more with the women to learn what they know. Lavender sees them often, but she is too young to fully understand human nature. She's happily sewing lace on every piece of fabric she finds in anticipation of romantic weddings." Clare forced a smile.

That's when Patience knew she had to support the lady who had so generously taken them in and helped in every small way allowed to her. Patience had no money and no power to accomplish more than growing a garden. She might put food on the table, but anyone could do that. With time on her hands, she ought to be able to do more.

The village would have to find funds for a poorhouse if those children were thrown into the street. Men had all the money and power. Women only had their wits to persuade men to do what was right. Clare and Elsa were ladies who had to obey rules.

She was not a lady. She was the daughter of an impoverished, extortionist curate and wished to be no more than a gardener. She had to obey the law but not society's rules.

She didn't give herself time to think about it. The knots in her stomach actually loosened now that she had a direction of sorts. Knowing she could trust the men of the manor helped immensely.

She thought she might have gone a wee bit insane as she excused herself and returned to her room below stairs. Her mother was happily gossiping with Elsa and the servants in the kitchen—was she learning anything useful? Probably not. Most of the staff hadn't lived in the village until recently, when hired by Hunt, and these murders seemed rooted in the past. She didn't think help could come from that direction.

The older men in town had the answers.

Donning her daring dinner gown without her mother's help was a definite act of madness. Fortunately, the crucial fastenings were in front. She wrapped a gauzy scarf around her waist to conceal the unhooked back fastenings that she couldn't reach. She pretended the bow was fashionable. Men wouldn't know.

Remembering her inability to flee in skirts, she donned her men's breeches under the gown. She hoped she wouldn't need to run, but she foolishly felt more respectable this way.

Not looking at herself in the mirror, she donned a heavy black cloak and hood, picked up a lantern, and slipped outside into the twilight. She knew the path to town by heart.

She still traversed the woods in trepidation. The evening light didn't reach through the birch and spruce. *Jinglebrains,* she muttered to herself. *Nodcock. Daft gaby.* She called herself every sort of fool as she hurried down the path, keeping her mind from what lay ahead.

The children, she reminded herself. She did this for the children. And because she couldn't sit in warmth and comfort and do nothing. If her father could beg. . .

The tavern door was open to the stench of smoke and ale. Male voices murmured, but the evening was early. She wished they had a piano or fiddle. Oh well, if she was to do this. . .

The loud, smoky room stinking of ale fell into shocked silence at her entry. Even with her height and in a cloak, she couldn't disguise the fact that she was female.

A protest immediately erupted. To her surprise, her brother was here too. He and Hunt leaped to their feet.

"What is wrong? What's happened?" They were aimed for the door, taking her elbow to steer her out.

She should let them.

If she did, she'd spend the rest of her life letting men steer her course. How would she ever be head gardener if she couldn't make men do what she wanted?

A niggling voice said this wasn't the way, but in this case, she had no choice. Compassion sometimes required a boldness she must learn.

"We need to raise funds for Mr. Bartholomew's poor children and wife." She tugged her arms from their hold and turned to the bar. Unlike her brother and Hunt, Henri watched her warily. He didn't underestimate her. She liked that. "How much is a song worth?"

"Patience, this is ridiculous. Ladies aren't allowed in taverns." Paul tried to wrestle her out, but she wasn't small. He'd have to bodily haul her from the floor. He wouldn't.

He'd have to accept that she wasn't a lady.

"Farthing for a simple verse," Henri suggested cautiously. "Penny for the whole song. Sit up here." He patted the bar.

While Hunt and Paul protested, one of the older men grinned and provided a chair for her to step on. She climbed to the bar and arranged her cloak and skirt decently, feeling like a great fool but a modicum safer.

The old fellow held up a penny. "Can ye give me a round of *John Barleycorn*? My pappy used to sing it."

"I don't know many drinking songs." She wanted to be fair. "But I learn quickly. That's an easy one though. My father sang it."

"Patience, you cannot. . ."

All the men shouted Paul down as she attempted the first words of the song declaring beer would never die. Closing her eyes, she recalled her father bellowing the tune while working in the barn. That helped to steady her voice.

By the third verse, men roared in delight and stamped

their feet. Fearing a killer lurked among them, she tried to study her audience. Frowning, Hunt retreated to his table. Paul planted himself by her side at the bar. She recognized only the men from the manor.

Somehow, she must help draw out the strangers. She understood that was why her brother and the others were here—they were excluding the women from the meeting, just as Clare had predicted.

"Another, another," a different man cried, waving his coin when she finished the final verse with the unkillable Barleycorn still kicking. "I got a farthing. Maybe just the first verse of *Barbry Allen*?"

"No one can sing only a single verse of *Barbara Allen*," she protested with laughter. Under cover of her words, she nudged Paul with her boot. "Collect coins, will you?"

If the village curate approved of her singing by collecting coins, it almost sanctified her outrageousness. Maybe. No one else tried to throw her out, anyway. She sang the first couple of verses and someone else offered another penny to finish it.

"I'll throw in half a pint for each song you buy," Henri called when her song ended. "Gentlemen, let's spend our pennies on the babes!"

She turned and granted him a big smile for understanding what she hoped to do. She forgot to clutch her cloak closed. Henri's eyes widened when he saw what she wore beneath it. She hastily grabbed the edges and faced the room again.

She had Henri behind her, and Arnaud and Paul to either side. She could pretend this was no more than a church recital to raise funds. She used to do them as a child, until she grew up and the stares of men frightened her. But the manor occupants were gentlemen, in the true sense of the word.

Hunt and Walker and Jack blended into the background, watching the crowd. Even if they didn't approve of what she was doing, they gave her confidence. Covered head to toe in the cloak, she could hide her self-consciousness. She had feared her voice wouldn't be enough, but perhaps music was all she needed to produce the desired effect.

She sang a song that had men weeping. More pennies hit the bar. But how did she draw them out? Where did she start? The bones in the orchard?

Remembering a sad song about burying a lover in a lonely grave, she leaned back to Henri. "Give me some watered ale to wet my whistle, and I'll sing one for you."

"Keep 'em weeping," he murmured, doing as she asked. "This isn't lemonade. Careful."

As she warbled the old tune about bones and graves, making up lyrics she'd forgotten, a bear of a man entered—a bearded giant, a familiar one. She ought to be terrified, but she really wanted to kick him.

"A non-believer, a Papist, and a Jew walk into a bar. . ." Henri muttered behind her.

"Finish that, *mon petit frère*, and I'll punch you," Arnaud muttered back.

"A comte, a captain, and a peddler. . ." Henri raised his arm to fend off his brother's blow.

Undeterred by their antics, Patience continued singing, but everyone in the tavern had turned their attention to the newcomer. They stopped laughing and clapping, and she could sense tension rising. Were they really afraid of this man? Uncertain of how to keep the peace, she chose to distract by unfastening the strings of her hood, letting it fall back. Gazes slowly returned to her as she continued her sad song.

She despised being stared at, but if it would remove her father's killer from the streets, she could sacrifice a bit of modesty. Knowing some of the pins in her hair had loosened, she shook her head and let a few strands tumble while she finished the verse.

"There's truth in some of them songs," the stranger commented beneath the stomping call for another round.

"Traveling minstrels sang as a form of carrying news to villages around the land," Henri said. "Songs of Robin Hood hid words of rebellion."

"No one hereabouts to write a song about the bones in the orchard," Mr. Oswald called from his seat by the fireplace. The postmaster's brother had apparently grasped what was happening as well. Or perhaps he simply wished to agitate the newcomer.

"There should be songs about justice." The giant stranger set several pennies on the bar. "Got any like that?" This had to be Mr. Bergstein, the orchardist Henri had been trying to catch. What did she do now?

"The only justice is by our own hands." A man in a dark corner on the far side of the bar flung a penny to the bar. "Sing the *Hangman's Son*."

She couldn't see him clearly, but others evidently recognized him, including the giant, who turned in his direction. "Then someone should have put an end to you long since, Corky. How is it that Bert's the one who'll hang?"

Corky. Corcoran. Paul's father? Patience took a swig of ale, spluttered, and tried to recall songs of hangmen and justice. She couldn't. "Perhaps if the gentleman will sing a few bars, I could pick it up."

"Bert won't hang until we know he's guilty." Hunt intervened. "If any have evidence otherwise, speak it."

"Bert's a cold-blooded killer," Corcoran called out when no one offered a few bars of the song. "He tried to kill me once. Bergstein is no better."

Perhaps she ought to sing anyway, but Henri placed his hand over hers and gestured for silence while the men glared at each other. She'd wanted to draw them out, but the simmering anger was worrisome. She really didn't know enough about men.

"How is that?" Hunt asked, leaning back in his chair. "If

this is Mr. Bergstein, we've not seen him about until this evening."

"The black-hearted Gypsy is the one who buried the bones in the orchard," Corcoran said with a shrug. "Hated having his sister married to one of us. He and Blackie near killed each other back in the day. No reason Abe and Bert didn't work together to finish the job."

The newcomer—the black-hearted Gypsy?—sipped his ale, expressing no rancor, but he glanced at Henri and nodded at Patience. "Remove the woman. She oughtn't to be here."

That was the outside of enough. Before Henri could react, Patience slapped her mug down. Perhaps she'd taken too much ale, but she wouldn't be talked to like that again by this rude creature. "Women are left to pay for the messes men make. Why shouldn't we *hear* about them first? Mrs. Bartholomew is weeping her heart out because her husband kept tools that weren't his. Her children are terrified they'll be thrown into the streets. If you have something to say that might help, say it."

"All you sniveling cowards gonna let a female talk that way?" Bergstein didn't even glance her way.

He definitely needed kicking. "Do you have any ale to waste, Henri?" she asked. "Perhaps if I wet his head. . ."

"No fighting, Patience, or I *will* carry you out," he warned.

She thought he might. So how did she make this ornery bear of a man talk?

Henri, of the quick wit and tongue, solved the dilemma. "If Mr. Bergstein refrained from killing Mr. Blackstone decades ago, when he most deserved it, I fail to see why he should do so now. What new evidence do you bring us, sir?"

He was turning his tavern into a town hall meeting—as expected. Patience would dump her mug on him, except, in this case, she suspected only the men had the answers needed.

Bergstein ignored his ale. "Blackie was a blood-sucking

thatch-gallow, a tosspot, a wife beater, and a wastrel. He killed Naomi and told the world she fell. Blackie deserved to hang, but the earl threw him out before I could strangle the bastard. I buried my sister with the trees and trinkets she loved. Her death killed my ma just the same as if he put a hole in her heart. I came back to see if justice might finally be served, but someone did that for me."

The sorrowful giant knew where the bones were and what was with them. Patience thought he spoke the truth, so far as he was telling it.

AB/bw. *Archibald Blackstone* beats wife, Naomi. AB/s. *Albert Bartholomew* stabs Corcoran.

Abraham Bergstein wasn't one of her father's sinners. He was a Jew and not his concern at all.

"But if you didn't kill Mr. Blackstone—who did?" She had to ask.

"Only man in town with enough blunt to feed Blackie's blood-sucking—until he tired of it. Blackie's da was a barkeep and heard all the gossip and sottish confessions. You might want to ask what Blackie knew about whom. He was worse than the parson." Bergstein drained his mug and started for the door. He'd apparently said his piece.

Patience didn't catch the first move. She only noticed Hunt and Jack coming to their feet, fists ready. She swung around to see why.

The man in the corner had thrown back his chair. "You lying blackguard!" he cried, diving for Bergstein, knife in hand.

Paul was in the way.

Patience screamed—and without giving it a second thought—kicked her boot high, directly into Corcoran's weak chin.

THIRTY

SIMULTANEOUSLY CHEERING AND CURSING THIS COURAGEOUSLY insane female, Henri yanked Patience behind the bar. Paul lurched out of reach, holding his arm. Enraged, Corcoran staggered from the kick but came back, knife still in hand.

Before he could strike again, Hunt and Jack seized his arms and yanked him off his feet. Patience kept screaming, more in fury than hysteria, Henri thought. She struggled, and he had to fight his baser instincts to prevent glancing down at what her unfastened cloak revealed. Having a tavern erupting in chaos aided that endeavor.

Looking dazed, Paul pulled out a handkerchief and pressed it to his wound, which calmed Patience a fraction. She tensed as the old men leapt up, overturning chairs to escape the brawl. They shouted accusations and cheers as Bergstein drew his knife and dared them to release Corcoran. Hunt and his cronies could handle those two.

He wasn't needed here.

Wrapping the cloak around the beauty Patience concealed, Henri carried her out of the fray, leaving Hunt to deal with the melee. What she had done finally hit her. She was trembling so hard, Henri feared she couldn't walk. "Let us sit down over by the chapel. Paul is fine. The captain can stomp drunks. Please stop shaking before I have hysterics."

She gulped a laugh but clung to his shoulders until he set her down on a bench recently uncovered from the overgrown chapel shrubbery. She buried her face in her hands and kept shuddering.

Since he loved holding her, Henri wrapped his arm around her shoulders and cuddled her against him. "I had no idea you sing like an angel. People must have flocked to your father's church just to hear you."

She shook her head and didn't fight off his arm. "I don't like people looking at me. I haven't sung in public for *years*."

He worked that tidbit through his nearly empty head. Having all those lovely curves this close was not conducive to clarity. His tavern might be burning down, and he wouldn't care. "Then it must have taken a great deal of courage to come here tonight. Mind you, I am not saying I approve. Men are beasts, and ladies don't belong in taverns. But without you, I think we would have beat around bushes and never learned anything."

"I was stupid and foolish, and I got Paul hurt. Again," she muttered.

"He got himself hurt by protecting Bergstein. Or not moving fast enough. Maybe both. And you do realize it takes a stupid fool to be courageous, don't you? It's the very definition of war. A great many stupid fools run at each other with weapons. But until mankind changes, someone has to protect the helpless." He'd never given that much thought. He'd always thought his brother an *imbécile* for remaining in France and nearly getting himself killed. But Arnaud had been protecting his own.

She wasn't trembling as much, but she shook her head in denial of his wise words. "I wanted to be *useful*. And now I'll never be able to go out in public again."

"On the contrary, the whole village will wish to hear you

sing. Hide in a dark corner, if you must, but if you'll be singing at services, your brother will need a larger chapel to hold his congregation." He would have paid his entire night's earnings to hear her sing again, although he might have chosen different songs.

She sat up a little straighter and still didn't protest his arm around her. She probably didn't even notice. The evening had rattled his patient Patience.

"It's just singing," she protested. "Everyone does it. I'd meant to distract. . ." She let that sentence dribble away, thankfully.

Ah, she'd worn that gown to distract but hadn't dared open her cloak. Henri smiled and toyed with a loose strand of her lovely hair. "Other people open their mouths but don't produce the notes of a nightingale. Any time you wish to distract, simply sing, and the world goes away. If I could have you at the bar every night, I'd be a wealthy man. And I could hide you behind a curtain and say the same."

"Oh." She puzzled over that a moment. "I don't think I quite believe you. You are trying to make me feel better. I thank you for that."

Well, at least she'd noticed he was trying. That was a good first step. He'd concentrate on keeping her at Wycliffe before trying to work out how a homeless, itinerant peddler might keep a woman who wanted fields to dig in.

He quit thinking about it when she glanced toward the tavern, where the noise had dropped to angry shouts, no doubt from Corcoran. Even as they watched, Hunt and Jack hauled the smaller, older man out by his arms. Bergstein followed of his own accord.

Still slightly shaky, she stood. "I had better return to the manor. Mother is probably packing our bags already."

Alarmed, Henri rose with her. He had no right to continue holding her but took her gloved fingers. She'd gone to a tavern in gloves, a lady to the last drop. "You cannot go! We need you here."

I need you, he realized. She was his sunshine. He rose in the morning hoping to catch her smile sometime during their busy days.

He was supposed to be encouraging her for Arnaud, but he gave up that notion now. Arnaud wouldn't recognize a shining gem unless covered in paint and pasted to canvas. Patience deserved to be appreciated in all her complex glory. She might be better off marrying a banker or a. . . No. She held his hand. She'd come to *his* tavern and to *him* when she wanted to help. He might be worthless to everyone else, but he was *not* worthless to Patience. He simply needed to make her see that. Somehow.

"The manor does not need me in the orchard if Mr. Bergstein stays," she argued. "I suppose we should see what the captain decides about him. Perhaps, if I wear men's clothing, people will forget." She didn't sound hopeful.

"You are staying here," he said with certainty. "The manor needs your mother's housekeeping talent and your gardening expertise." I need to see you to keep breathing, but he couldn't say that. She would flee for certain.

"I behaved like a trollop. I will be fortunate if the ladies do not throw my bags out the door." Following his lead, she dragged her feet up the dark pathway.

"They will *not* throw you out, and that reminds me." He dug in his pocket and counted the coins using touch. "You earned nearly a shilling for the poor tonight. Paul might have more. So do not tell me you are useless!"

"That won't feed ten children for long. Perhaps we could employ the oldest if her father must go to trial."

He liked the sound of that *we*, even if he couldn't work out how to make her feel useful if money didn't do it. Money was all he knew. "We will work out something. Bert is *not* an innocent man. We told him those tools belonged to Paul and were used for murder, and he didn't say a word. And we still have no good motive for Corcoran to have killed anyone, other than his nasty temper. Same for Bergstein, although his temper isn't as bad."

Which reminded him to ask Hunt to keep them all locked up until he and Paul could go out and talk with *Corky's* father.

Henri was convinced that the elder Mr. Corcoran hid the secrets they needed to solve a few of these crimes. Perhaps Patience might notice him if he caught a killer.

Once he set his sights on a goal, he did not give up easily.

THE NEXT MORNING, HUNT TOOK HIS COFFEE AND HIS BREAKFAST plate and hid in his study. He pondered locking the door but knew it would do no good. Intruders would pound until he was forced to slip out through the library, which was always inhabited and no better than his study.

Being an engineer had involved papers and pen and measuring instruments and using his head for something besides a hat rack. Being master of a manor. . . involved not killing anyone who interrupted his breakfast.

Walker had the decency and sense to wait until he'd finished his coffee before walking in with reams of notes. "We had to put Corcoran in the crypt. The other two were fighting over whether to kill him and save us the trouble of taking him to court."

"Convenient that the place has multiple jail cells," Hunt muttered, donning his monocle and attempting to scan the pages of script. Walker's handwriting was excellent, and he always wrote large so Hunt could read easily. He just didn't want to.

"Wycliffes might have enjoyed being judge and jury, hence multiple jail cells," Walker said. "They didn't do as well in the nursery department. The attics are overrun with inquisitive creatures, big and small. The ladies can't keep them reined in and want to know if it's safe to send them home. There are weddings to plan."

"Keep them out of the woods." Hunt held up a letter that had arrived in the morning post. "I think I shall go hunting for the next few weeks."

Walker scanned the formal stationery and grimaced. "*Both* of them? Did London not provide sufficient entertainment? Aren't there supposed to be romps and balls and that sort of thing? Why come here?"

"Apparently, weddings are more interesting, and they've run out of family to control. That leaves us. Do you want to tell Clare? I fear she'll run far, far away."

"She is currently occupied handing Bosworth his hat and ushering him out of the library before he drives the baron mad. She has told him his chamber is needed for guests. Does she read minds? Does she know your aunt and great-aunt are arriving?"

Ignoring the ridiculous question, Hunt smiled for the first time that morning. "She's flinging the bastard out on his posterior? Without a pistol in hand? She's a quick student."

"She's made of stern stuff. She's told him he may attend when we auction off the books. Which brings us back to your housekeeper and gardener who are depart with him."

"Henri says if the Uptons leave, he leaves. I think the nightingale made an impression. And Clare might cry if she loses her housekeeper. We can't let them escape."

"That's your bailiwick, not mine. Just tell me how to handle the prisoners and whether it's safe to let the multifarious Bartholomews go home." Without waiting for a decision he knew wasn't coming soon, Walker walked out.

Hunt read through the statements taken from their prisoners, but while accusations ran rampant, evidence did not. He'd hang Teddy Corcoran just because he was slime, but there wasn't a shred of actual proof that the man had knocked up Bartholomew's sister and possibly raped his own, other than Bert and Isaiah Upton's declarations. Teddy had already paid the price for the one when Bert had assaulted him and forced him to marry his sister. Both crimes had been well over twenty years ago. Hunt refused to bring anyone up on charges that old.

He could hold him for assaulting Paul only so long.

At least, if Bergstein was to be believed, they now knew Bert's runaway sister and her babe had landed safely in Birmingham. Hunt supposed he should send Henri up to town to confirm that she wasn't bones in the orchard.

Presumably, Naomi Bergstein was the bones. And Blackstone, the man who had killed her, was also dead.

It was the *current* killer of Upton and Blackstone who most concerned him. Had Bergstein been Blackie's executioner? They had only his word that he was not.

Clare slipped in with another cup of coffee. She held her hand to his shoulder to prevent him from rising. "Paul isn't seriously injured. He wants to go with Henri to Corcoran's home to inform them that we are holding their son."

"I am not convinced that Corcoran wasn't trying to stab Paul under cover of threatening Bergstein. He didn't appear that drunk." Hunt had played and replayed the scene, but it hadn't made good sense.

"Don't tell our curate's family that. I am trying to convince Mrs. Upton and Patience not to flee. What exactly happened last night? Patience won't leave her room."

"She sang rowdy songs to earn money for the poor. I suspect she had a sound notion that doing so would drag good, solid Englishmen into weeping, which meant they got drunk, fought, and words were said. I'd like to give her a medal and a reward." Hunt sat back with his coffee and admired the flush on Clare's cheeks.

"Oh, my. From Henri's effusions this morning, I gather she sings well? Could she be persuaded to sing for our wedding?

I wonder if she can play the pianoforte?" Her thoughts obviously flew off in a different direction than his.

He handed her the vellum letter. "I daresay the aunts can play, if needed. We apparently will have family attending, after all."

She skimmed the letter and raised her eyebrows. "*Today*? They are coming today? Whyever. . ." Flustered, she didn't finish that question but jumped to the next one. "Mrs. Upton cannot possibly leave now! Oh, my. . ." She dashed off, leaving the study door open.

Henri entered next, dressed in his peddler's garb of old coat and scruffy hat. "I'm taking Paul out to visit his grandparents while Teddy is incarcerated. Don't let the bastard out until we're back, please. There's more here than meets the eye, I'm convinced."

"If it involves Paul, you may wish to take another witness. Are any of your tosspots available? The postmaster's brother or George, perhaps? Neutral parties." Hunt tried to think like a magistrate. He hated the notion of sending any man to prison or to his death unless he was a hundred percent certain he had the right criminal.

"Elsa has prepared a basket for the Corcorans. I thought to take Patience, but Clare is claiming they'll run away together?" Henri rubbed his shabby cap on his coat and watched the dust fall.

"Lady Lavinia and Lady Spalding are expected to arrive today. Don't let Clare run too far or I'll have to run too. Tell Patience she has to sing at our wedding. Women can't stand as witness anyway." Hunt sipped his coffee and contemplated the best place to hide. With Corcoran in the crypt, he couldn't play with his gas furnace. "Try Deacon Jones."

"Ah, right, that might work. We shall be on our way, posthaste." Henri clapped his cap on and sauntered out.

An inn, Hunt pondered. He could charge his guests by the room, extra for meals. Except inns made their best money from taverns, and Henri had claimed that. His cousin had the mind of a successful merchant. Besides, innkeepers had to smile at guests and Hunt preferred to growl.

Adam, their young footman, appeared in the doorway. "Captain, sir, the prisoners are shouting again. What do we do with them?"

Hunt practiced an evil grin. "Give them bad gin. Drunkards talk."

THIRTY-ONE

"Hunt says we are to take witnesses. Women can't stand up in court," Henri protested from the driver's seat of his cart. "Deacon Jones lives out that way. We will fetch him."

Clare squeezed Patience's arm to keep her silent. "If we cannot go with you, then take Elsa's basket. Their only son has been locked up and might be sent to trial. Even if the Corcorans are wealthy and not of our church, they should be offered the same compassion as anyone else."

"Mrs. Jones cooks for them," Patience whispered. "They don't deserve more."

"That is for your brother to decide. We have other decisions to make." Clare waved the men off, then dragged Patience back inside. She'd known they'd never let women attend the Corcorans, but at least she'd found a way to persuade Patience from hiding. She'd apparently used up all her courage singing last night.

She'd recover if they kept her busy. "Hunt's aunts are arriving today. They have powerful connections who can see justice done once we know the guilty party. Sometimes, women can accomplish more behind the scenes. We must choose our battles."

"Every day is a different battle," Patience replied gloomily. "After last night, no one will ever listen to me again. I would leave today to save you embarrassment, but I don't know where to go yet."

"I understand you were brilliant last night. Do not play the fool now, when we need you. We have an attic full of children and cellars full of furious men and the aristocracy arriving on our doorstep! Does this sound like a time to abandon us?" Clare thought about that as she tugged her victim down the hall. "Well, yes, I suppose, it's reason to run far, far away."

Patience chuckled, even if it sounded forlorn. "I shall retire to the nursery, then."

"Sing them nursery songs," Clare commanded. "Have them whitewash the walls and dust the furniture while they're at it. Anything, just keep them quiet until this is settled!"

With luck, Clare would keep Patience busy enough to forget her humiliation. Singing in a tavern was a trifle, under the circumstances. They had only two weeks left to organize two weddings that might include everyone from jokers to lords or a killer or two. And she'd been neglecting Oliver dreadfully.

Sending Patience to the attics, she hunted down her nephew in his favorite haunt of the library. To her amazement, the tutor and Lavender were apparently performing a mock trial with Oliver as the. . . witness? Defendant? And the baron as judge! She hovered in the doorway, listening to the arguments over the crime of stealing lace. A box on the table held a kitten and a bed of shredded. . . lace.

Oh dear. Clare fled. She loved that Oliver was emerging from his shell and learning to work with others. She didn't have time to regret that he didn't need her as much.

Meera and Elsa were in the infirmary, arguing over a healthy menu suitable for older ladies. Clare took the lists from their hands and wadded them up. "We are not catering to anyone. The aunts have the same position here as all of us, even less, perhaps, since they contribute nothing. Feed the hardworking men. Should our aristocratic guests do anything worth rewarding, which I sincerely doubt, ask their favorite meal—it will not be healthy, mind you. They likely grew up on sausage-stuffed partridges in cream sauce."

"We should reward Patience," Elsa declared. "She is terrified of her own shadow, but she faced a roomful of drunks for those poor children. I'll ask Mrs. Upton what her daughter's favorite dish is!"

"Patience is *not* terrified of shadows." Meera returned to mashing herbs for her concoctions. "That's Clare. *Patience* is uncomfortable being stared at. You must admit, her beauty attracts gawking."

Clare thought she ought to object to the insinuation that she was spineless, but Meera had seen her ducking under tables at so much as the crash of broken china. She hoped she was doing better these days. "Patience is modest, as a curate's daughter should be. But she is also a Reid and belongs here. I wonder. . ."

Clare pondered her thought as she ran upstairs to see how the rooms might be arranged for guests. The aunts had claimed suites near the stairs the last time they were here. Jack and his father now occupied those rooms. Should they put the aunts in the late viscountess's chambers? That would give them a parlor to share. . . But eliminated that choice as a bridal suite.

She found Mrs. Upton in the east wing, overlooking the drive and orchard. She had maids scurrying to and fro with fresh linens, dustmops, and scented polishing cloths. Under her supervision, Adam and Ned were carrying down carpets for beating.

She glanced up at Clare's entrance. "These mattresses

need airing and restuffing. How are we to do all this at a moment's notice?"

"We'll give the aunts choices. It's the best we can do. I'm quite certain their own mattresses haven't been aired in a dozen years. If they expect better here, they will have to contribute to the cause. What can they do if they disapprove of our housekeeping? Leave? Perhaps the dust should remain." Clare knew she sounded like her cross-patch sister, but with lives at stake, a few dust balls didn't matter. She was learning priorities.

Mrs. Upton managed a smile. "We should pay more attention to the bridal chambers? Have you chosen which suite you and the captain will share?"

Clare's cheeks flamed. "I'm sure they're all fine. Thank you for handling all this." She gestured at the east wing room which probably hadn't been used in decades, noticing the newly-washed windows had been propped open to allow in fresh air. "I am rather praying no one else will arrive. I am unaccustomed to house parties."

"Lady Reid would have loved it." The housekeeper smiled wider in remembrance. "She loved parties, but no one would visit this remote outpost. Think of this as a party for her, and it will be easier."

Even though the late viscountess must have been a terrifying termagant, she'd had a hard life and still tried to do what was right—if her diaries were to be believed. Clare nodded at this wisdom. "Lady Spalding is her daughter and Lady Lavinia was her sister-in-law. Install them in the viscountess's chamber and let her haunt them."

And then she ran upstairs to check on the attic nursery.

Surely, once Hunt had found the killer, life might go back to normal. She prayed that would be before the wedding.

~

HENRI STUDIED THE SITUATION AS HE DROVE HIS CART UP THE drive to Corcoran's comfortable home. A man given good parents, a solid roof over his head, and fields he could cultivate ought to have better things to do than engage in knife fights.

One hoped a man of Corcoran's middling age had graduated from molesting women. But if Bergstein were to be believed, Teddy spent his time in town, gambling and wenching, which was why he was seldom to be found at home, not because he was working.

At least, Paul had turned out well, even if his natural father was a flea-bitten mongrel.

"I'll let Mr. Jones out at the front door." Henri halted the cart in the drive to allow the neighbor to climb down. "Take the basket as your excuse for arriving, sir. I'll go around back while you distract the door guardian and see if Paul and I can slip in through the kitchen."

The elderly deacon touched his cap in agreement, then climbed out and carried the basket down the overgrown stone path. No one gardened in this household, apparently.

"You'll sweet talk the maid in the kitchen?" Paul asked with a faint smile.

"Aye, easier than your grandmother." Henri turned the cart around for hasty departure, if necessary. With Teddy locked in the crypt, he didn't expect trouble—just resistance.

Paul carried the tin of tobacco for his grandfather, leaving Henri to knock at the back door. No one answered. The house was too large and solid to hear Jones at the front. Henri lifted the latch—no lock held it. They let themselves into the kitchen, which was a mess of dirty dishes. Had they sent the maid home?

From here, he could hear the harridan talking with the deacon at the front. They were supposed to have him in here as a witness, but Paul was already hurrying down the hall to meet his grandfather. Oh well.

The old man had pulled himself up against the pillows. He looked relieved at Henri's arrival. "You seen the lad? He didn't come in last night, and herself is in a dither." He glanced with curiosity at Paul.

"I'm afraid your son got into a fight last night and is now cooling his heels in Wycliffe's cellar." Henri refrained from calling it a crypt. "I thought perhaps you might be interested in meeting our new curate, Paul Upton."

The old man's eyes narrowed as he looked from Henri to Paul. Then he gestured for Paul to come closer. "Push that mop of ginger off your face," he ordered.

Startled, the young curate took the chair beside the bed and held back the auburn lock of hair falling on his brow. "I've been told I look somewhat like my mother?"

"My Mary," the old man whispered. "You got her eyes, and there's the mark you were born with." He touched a mole near Paul's hairline. "I only got to see you as a babe, but I took note of that. I hoped you'd return."

"I've tried to visit, but I didn't appear to be welcome. I didn't want to intrude where I was not wanted." Paul took his grandfather's frail, wrinkled hand. "I am glad to finally meet you, sir."

The voices at the front door grew louder. The old man hastily removed his hand and pointed at the faded rug beside the bed. "Pull up the boards, quick like, before she comes in."

Henri shut the bedroom door, couldn't find a lock, and stood with his back against it, while Paul pushed the old rug aside with his boot. The floor boards were worn, and he had to go down on his knees to examine them. Impatiently, Henri dropped down to join him, finding the crack to slide his knife into. The board creaked and popped out. He left the honors to the curate and returned to preventing entrance.

Paul wiggled a large ledger from the small hole, returned the plank, and handed the book to the man in the bed. "That looks like one of the chapel's old accounting ledgers."

Like the one stolen the night Blackstone died? Henri bit down his curiosity as the old man flipped open the covers with hands gnarled from years of hard work. Yellowed documents fell out.

"The lad brought the book home t'other night, ripped out the writing, and said there was good pages for me to scribble out my will." A grim smile of satisfaction crossed his face as he handed the documents over to Paul, just as footsteps stomped down the hall. "Don't let herself have these, not at any cost. She protects the lad."

"The lad?" Henri finally had to ask. "Teddy?" Who had to be in his fifties and no boy.

The old man nodded. "He ain't mine. He's hers. Mary was mine. I tried to raise them both right, but he was a bad seed from the start. But you can't tell herself that."

The unlocked door slammed into Henri's back.

"What's going on there?" the harridan cried. "What have ye done, ye old coot? Gone and fallen when I said to stay put?"

"I'm fine, Bridey. These gentlemen come to see me." Sitting up straighter, he gestured imperiously for Henri to step away.

Taking the book and papers, Henri slid them under his trouser band, under his coat, before he eased from the door. He pondered the significance of Teddy not being Mr. Upton's son.

Bridget Corcoran burst in, her graying hair disarranged from its usual bun, her eyes red from weeping. "What are you lot doin' in here, botherin' the old fool? Out with ye! He don' need more tobacco. . ." Then she noticed Paul, and she paled even more.

"Mary's boy will look after you, old lady," Mr. Corcoran said with fondness. "You don' need to be protectin' me from me own grandson."

"You!" Mrs. Corcoran glared at Paul. "You! You're the reason my boy didn't come home!"

"Mary was ours too," the old man reminded her. "She didn't live to take care of us, but her angel has sent her boy."

"Her bastard!" the old woman spat. "Teddy took care of us all these years. You can't forget him for a bastard!"

"My parents were legally married, so I am not a bastard," Paul said quietly, taking a higher road. "I understand why my natural father cannot claim me, and I know I am not responsible for his behavior. Nor are you responsible for how he has chosen to live his life. We all have our crosses to bear. I hope I might make yours easier, if you will let me."

"*Natural* father," Bridget spat. "As if anyone knows how many she slept with. She was a whore looking for ways to escape the home we provided, thinking her looks made her too good for us. You don't come sniffing around, looking to take what belongs to my boy what stayed and worked all these years."

Henri winced, but this was not his fight. How did one tell a loving mother that her son was an incestual rapist too lazy to leave home?

"I'm not here to take anything away from anyone," Paul said with the soothing voice of a professional clergyman. "I only wished to meet my grandparents and see that they are being taken care of. The man I called father all my life wrote my natural father's name in the church register and sent it to the proper authorities, as is required. Should you ever wish to know who he is, it is there for you to see. I don't think my mother was old enough to willingly engage in sin, but that is of no matter today."

"What did you do with my boy?" she demanded, ignoring all the rest. "Where is he?"

Henri decided this was where he stepped in. "Edward Corcoran stabbed Mr. Upton here last night. There were witnesses. He is being held until the magistrate can decide what to do with him."

"Teddy stabbed you?" the man in the bed asked, proving his faculties were fully intact. "Teddy tried to *kill* you?"

"He was angry. It might have been an accident. But as you must be aware, there have been two murders in the village recently, one of them Mr. Upton's adoptive father." Henri lingered in the open doorway, ready to leave. He hoped they didn't need Mr. Jones as witness, because he apparently had not been invited in. "After last night's attack, your son must be questioned."

Henri had the notion that the motive for both attacks was contained in the documents concealed beneath his coat.

The old woman collapsed on the side of the bed, weeping. "My boy didn't do nothing! He were with me all the time! You tell that man I said so."

The old gent patted her hand and waved them away.

Would a mother's testimony hold up in court?

They let themselves out.

Mr. Jones was waiting cheerfully in the cart with the empty basket. "She told her maid she wasn't needed today, so she was most appreciative of the basket. Although you're taking away my wife's profits."

"Only this once," Paul assured him, climbing into the back of the cart. "Henri, do we need to drive out of sight before you give me the book and papers?"

"Or do we wait until we take them to Hunt?" Henri urged the horses down the drive. "I have a suspicion this is the book stolen the night you were attacked."

"Then shouldn't we look at it immediately? Could my grandfather be in danger?" Paul asked anxiously.

"I may be overly suspicious," Henri admitted. "Mr. Jones, will you act as witness that we took the book directly from the house without opening it? And that anything we find inside comes entirely from Mr. Corcoran, and not us?"

"Aye, I can do that. I cannot believe he's in any danger from the missus, but if it's urgent, then let us see it now." Mr. Jones pulled a pair of spectacles from his pocket.

Henri removed the uncomfortable cardboard from his trouser band.

Paul held up the outside of the ledger so they could read the label of 1801. "This is the book I placed in the chapel. I chose it because it was the last year my father acted as curate here."

"*Corcoran* stole the chapel ledger?" Deacon Jones asked. "Does that mean he is the one who struck you on the head the night Blackie died?"

"Him or Blackstone," Henri suggested. "They both had opportunity. One of them must have been mighty displeased to discover it wasn't the church register."

Paul cautiously opened the ledger to the yellowed documents Mr. Corcoran had hidden there, then broke the seal and held up the pages of formal script for them to note. They were labeled *Last Will and Testament.*

THIRTY-TWO

PATIENCE PRACTICED PATIENCE WHILE SHE WAITED FOR HENRI and Paul to return, but it wasn't easy. Her mind spun in six directions at once.

Last night, Henri had *carried* great, gawky her out of the tavern. Yes, he was taller than she, and she'd never doubted his strength, but he'd carried her as if she were no more than a feather counterpane!

And then he'd held her as no gentleman should. Yes, she scolded herself, he was trying to keep her from hysterics. Gentlemen did not appreciate hysterics. It meant nothing that he'd put his arm around her and whispered soothing phrases in that marvelous accent of his. But it had felt like so much more. . .

She was being a daft looby. He was a charming, elegant gentleman, son of a *count,* and he was just doing what a gentleman does.

So she turned to better subjects, except they didn't ease her mind at all. She chafed over not knowing whether the bearded Mr. Bergstein was innocent and might be asked for rootstock for the orchard. She prayed fervently that they found evidence to prove grouchy Mr. Bartholomew's innocence so his family might go home.

Only, that might mean Paul's father/uncle was guilty of murder, and that would be perfectly horrid. She supposed leaving a killer on the loose would be worse, but she couldn't wrap her willful thoughts around it.

In the meantime, she sang nursery songs, read books, and tried to teach the youngest Bartholomews the rudiments of the alphabet—anything to stay out of sight.

After luncheon, the carriages arrived. Her mother went into frantic mode sending their very limited staff to complete the final tasks to ready rooms for a baroness and a marchioness. They hauled hot water, arranged bouquets in vases, and provided newly aired towels while Clare and Hunt greeted the guests.

Patience continued hiding in the nursery. She was accustomed to being invisible, even if she fretted to be in the garden and orchards. If she fled Gravesyde and the manor. . . She might never have the opportunity to garden again.

She had nearly bared herself in public and sang like a tavern wench for a room full of men! No one had denounced her yet, but there hadn't been time for gossip to spread. She felt like a criminal awaiting her sentence.

A maid knocked timidly on the nursery door, bobbed a curtsy, and waited for Patience to acknowledge her. "Miss Knightley asks that you tidy up and join the guests in the family parlor."

To meet Hunt's noble relations? Why, to pass sentence on her as Hunt would on his prisoners? Aflutter with nerves, she still had the sense to ask, "Have Henri and Paul returned?"

The maid bobbed another curtsy. "Yes, miss, they're with the captain now."

At least, if she was thrown out, Paul would be there to pick up the pieces.

With trepidation, Patience left the children to the care of

their distraught mother. She ran down to their below stairs rooms, changed into a clean apron and cap, tidied her hair, and hastened out. The arrival of a marchioness and baroness had turned the kitchen into her notion of Bedlam.

Emerging from the noise and confusion, Elsa slammed a tray into her hands before Patience reached the stairs.

Fine. She'd pretend she was an invisible maid. She'd go quite mad if she had to stay down here with steaming pots and slamming knives and fish guts. How an earl's daughter *enjoyed* this madness was beyond understanding.

She hurried upstairs and slipped into the cozy family parlor through the connecting door from the dining room. The parlor's brocade chairs and flowered needlepoints were faded and fraying, but the walnut tables gleamed with polish. Bouquets in lovely china vases adorned multiple surfaces. Her mother had done an amazing job preparing for their aristocratic visitors.

Patience set the tray of pastries on the low table between Clare and their guests. Lavender and Meera had taken a corner table to converse with a sour-looking young woman. Lavender sat stiffly, her back turned toward the old ladies. A boy in rumpled jacket and linen played on the hearth with pieces of wood he appeared to be taking apart. Intriguing, but she'd rather flee.

Before she could hope to escape, Clare gestured to the seat beside her. "Lady Spalding, Lady Lavinia, this is Miss Patience Upton, the curate's sister and the expert gardener I mentioned."

Patience bobbed a curtsy and reluctantly took the seat indicated. Was she on trial already? With wariness, she studied her elderly interrogators.

In her seventies, Lady Lavinia Marlowe was the late earl's daughter, a baroness, and Lavender's grandmother, even if from the wrong side of the blanket. Judging by Lavender's unusual silence, the relationship was not progressing well.

Slender and haughty, with a large mole on her lip, the lady wore her gray hair in a pompadour much like the old-fashioned wigs in portraits.

Elaine, Lady Spalding, a marchioness and the late earl's granddaughter, was a matronly woman in her early fifties, with kind eyes hidden behind heavy lids and jowls. She was knitting what appeared to be an infant cap. She studied Patience with a degree of interest, nodding her head to her thoughts.

"A gardener, indeed." Lady Lavinia lifted her teacup in frail, spotted hands and observed her with narrowed eyes. "I thought that was the task of your companion. . . Mrs. Abrams, was it?"

Meera didn't even lift her head at the mention of her name.

"Mrs. *Walker* now. She and the captain's friend married. Meera knows herbs and is learning vegetables, but the property is extensive. She is an apothecary and physician, remember, and cannot be expected to handle an estate. I am hoping Patience will take charge of the landscaping, as she has at the chapel." Clare turned and winked at Patience under cover of handing her a tart.

Ladies did not work in orchards, but they might trim roses. Perhaps she had lowered her reputation sufficiently to be considered a common gardener suitable for employment. But then, why was she sitting here?

Not giving her time to reply, Clare nodded at the sour young lady ignoring her tea in the corner. "I'd like you to meet Dorothea Reid Talbot. Miss Talbot, this is Patience Upton, who I understand is your cousin, as well as mine and Lavender's."

Patience thought her teeth might fall out. Cousin to the aristocracy? Well, Lavender was illegitimate, so Clare was being generous. She clenched her molars, ignored the family reference, and turned to acknowledge Lavender's companion.

"A pleasure, Miss Talbot. Dorotay is a lovely but unusual name."

"It's spelled with Thea at the end, but Mother likes to believe she speaks French." The young lady finally picked up her teacup and sipped.

"Your mother speaks lovely French," Lady Lavinia sniffed. "If she would only bother visiting here, she might read Lady Reid's journals for herself."

Patience hid her confusion behind her teacup, waiting for explanations.

Miss Talbot's expression was pained. Her blond hair was more pale champagne than yellow, and if she had the Reid thumb, it was confined by her gloves. Blue eyes and dimples were common, but the odd Reid ear. . . appeared to be present, although disguised by earrings. Patience refrained from tugging at her own quirky lobe.

"If Mother understood French, she would have known the Comte Avignon was a fraud. London is littered with phony French aristocrats looking for titled spouses. But my parents were determined to sell me to the highest bidder." Abandoning the tea table, Miss Talbot stood to examine paintings darkened by decades of smoke. "One cannot entirely fault Avignon for playing to their greed. Gentlemen are inclined toward competitiveness."

Lady Lavinia offered a strained smile. "Miss Talbot cast aside a charming suitor, and she and her parents are now at odds. She and her brother have been staying at one of my older estates, where she discovered her great-aunt's diaries. We thought they might be helpful in your research, so we decided to bring them with us."

Poor Lavender's back stiffened even more. Learning this cousin was allowed to stay on her grandmother's property, where she'd never been welcomed, could only fuel resentment. Patience had heard the sad tale from Lavender's other grandmother, the former maid who preferred the kitchen.

"I should like to read Lady Reid's diaries, if you do not mind." Miss Talbot spoke, while continuing to the next painting. "Do I correctly understand the earl's will? He left this manor to the descendants of his *siblings* as well as his children?"

"Child, sometimes I wonder if your mother taught you civilized converse," the elderly baroness complained. "This is no place to air your nonsense."

Patience bit back a smile as Clare merely reached for a teacake and answered pragmatically, "That is what Captain Huntley and the solicitors have determined. We have sent notifications and invitations multiple times. Your mother should have received one."

Hundreds of letters had been sent, few were answered, Patience knew. Clare ought to be irritated beyond imagining, yet she calmly accepted being ignored by her wealthier relations.

Miss Talbot appeared appeased. "Excellent. I believe both ladies can vouch that my great-grandfather, Lord David Reid, was the earl's younger brother. He died young and only had one daughter, my grandmother."

Ah ha, the *David* the late Blackstone had claimed as grandfather. But Miss Talbot was definitely not an impostor.

The plump marchioness, Hunt's aunt, nodded over her knitting. "It's all in the family archives. My mother died before she could add Dorothea's name to her tapestry. It's possible she did not even know of Dotty's birth. Living out here, she relied on gossip, not any formal communication with family."

Patience could think of nothing to say to this. She had not studied the tapestry that the late viscountess had created while abandoned by her husband's family. She waited to hear about being a cousin. Embarrassed by her illegitimacy, her mother had denied her heritage and never spoke of it.

Lady Spalding set aside her needles to produce a book

from her knitting bag. "This is the old diary Dotty found. I knew nothing of ancient scandals, of course. We were all much too young to know what the earl's generation knew."

Clare, the historian, eagerly took the book and read the title aloud. "The Diary of Harriet Reid Abbott Nelson, although the *Nelson* appears to have been added at a later date."

Nelson? Patience bit back an exclamation. Her mother's name was Henrietta Nelson. Patience had thought Nettie's last name had been that of the vicar who'd raised her, but. . . *Harriet*? Henrietta? The Reid family had a tradition of naming daughters similarly to their mothers.

"I found the diary in a secret drawer of an exquisite Chippendale desk in Lady Lavinia's attic. I like antiques." Pacing the dark corners of the parlor, Miss Talbot ran a gloved finger over an old writing desk. "This piece is of no consequence. I assume a gentleman, perhaps the late viscount, purchased and abandoned it here."

"It's a pity *my* mother did not leave a diary," Lavender murmured from the corner. "Perhaps then my existence might be verified."

"Your mother could not write, dear," Lady Lavinia said stiffly.

Patience thought she might go quietly mad. Or could she go noisily? No, she disliked drawing attention to herself, although no one seemed to pay her any mind now.

"Sit down, Miss Talbot," Lady Lavinia continued in irritation. "One does not critique the furnishings of one's hostess."

The young woman smiled faintly at the admonition and slipped into her chair without comment.

Patience wanted to stamp her foot in frustration. What had been found in the diary of whoever this Harriet person was?

At least this was distracting her from whatever Paul and Henri were discussing with the captain for so long. Although it was a pure wonder the children hadn't escaped the nursery to slide on banisters by now.

Clare opened the diary to a page marked by a feather. "This passage is dated in May of 1767."

Her mother had been born in September of that year, if Patience remembered correctly. She started doing mental math. Forty-eight years ago. Wide-eyed, she bent forward to hear every word.

"This may be my last entry. I shall lock my childhood diary in my desk after I complete this note. Mr. Nelson and I are leaving for Scotland tonight," Clare read aloud. "I know my father will never consent to our marriage, but the child I carry must have a name. I think I shall call it Henry, for him, if it's a boy, or Henrietta, for him and for family tradition, if it's a girl."

That was it? There was no more. *Henrietta Nelson*, her mother. Patience bit her lip and waited.

"A great scandal, of course," Lady Lavinia said in satisfaction, her pompadour bobbing. "My Aunt Helen, Harriet's mother, died young, and my father and her husband were estranged. One wonders if Wycliffe even knew of the elopement."

Patience made a quick trip through her memory—Lady Lavinia's father was the last earl of Wycliffe. *Helen* must have been one of the earl's many sisters whose portraits adorned the gallery. Runaway Harriet was the earl's niece?

Lady Lavinia continued, "As I remember, Aunt Helen married a veritable nobody. My father disapproved of the connection. I never met her, but I suppose I must have been aware that I had a younger cousin. Harriet didn't live long enough to be presented."

"We had the solicitors search after Dotty found the diary." The plump dowager spoke almost apologetically as she knitted. "They have Cousin Harriet's death certificate. The poor child was only seventeen when she died in childbirth. That was the same year as my father drowned. The family would have been in terrible turmoil at the loss of the earl's only heir. The solicitors have uncovered a marriage certificate from a vicar in Scotland, and the birth register for her daughter, Henrietta Nelson, in that same year, 1767. Harriet's husband was a lieutenant in the army, called overseas to deal with the unruly colonials."

"And he left his wife with the vicar," Clare murmured, following the family details better than Patience—even though Patience realized with shock that they talked about her *mother*. And grandmother. She had never known grandparents. She had a whole family out there?

"According to the solicitors, when the new Mrs. Nelson died giving birth, the vicar brought the infant to Mr. Abbott, my cousin's disapproving father," Lady Lavinia said, nodding again, disturbing a diamond pin in her gray pompadour. "Abbott refused to have anything to do with the child."

Patience finally recognized the horror that had been her mother's unwanted life. "What happened to her father, this Lt. Nelson?"

"He died fighting the rebels, from all we can ascertain." Lady Spalding picked up her knitting and met Patience's wide eyes. "I believe your grandfather died with honors. Your mother really should acknowledge her parents. She is a Reid, after all, and a family as unfortunate as ours must stick together."

The last Earl of Wycliffe was her great-uncle. Patience had no notion how to respond.

"I don't suppose that includes me?" Lavender asked with an unusual degree of cynicism.

The quiet boy on the hearth shouted "Eureka!" and held up his puzzle for all to see.

THIRTY-THREE

STARVING AFTER THE MORNING WITH MR. CORCORAN AND explaining events to Hunt, Henri snatched a handful of bread, cheese, and meat from the remnants of the cold luncheon buffet and sent a frustrated glance to the parlor door where the women were closeted. He wanted to see Patience, make certain she hadn't taken it in her head to flee. At the very least, she should know Paul stood to inherit his grandfather's rather valuable investments. Perhaps that would convince her to stay.

But Hunt was determined to rid the house of prisoners, so a trial must be held. Henri didn't know how the captain would persuade the ladies to stay away from potentially dangerous criminals—unless he held court in the wine cellar with the spiders and mice.

Walker, Arnaud, and Hunt had gone off to arrange the great hall for the trial. Henri pondered bringing in Bartholomew's rambunctious family from the nursery to speed events, but Hunt would fling him out on his crown. The captain was increasingly testy about any obstacle on his road to matrimony.

Released from Hunt's machinations for the moment, Paul

loaded up a more polite plate of fruit and cheese. "How do I go about locating my mother in this immense edifice?"

He'd be wanting to break the news about his grandfather's wealthy American family. The curate still seemed thunderstruck by the knowledge that he might one day have a modest income.

"We'll need to ask the ladies for her whereabouts. Do you dare enter their lair?" Henri nodded at the closed parlor door.

To his relief, that door opened as he spoke. Clare led out a fair-haired lad of about Oliver's age, although much chunkier, and steered him toward the library. A round-faced young woman he'd never met emerged behind them, followed by the aging aunts. Where was Patience?

Telling himself that Paul could ask his sister for directions, Henri led the curate across the hall.

She was cleaning up, naturally. Their few maids were all above, preparing for their guests, so Meera and Patience loaded tea trays.

While Paul inquired into his mother's location, Henri took the tray Meera held. "You shouldn't be carrying anything. Go forth and heal. I shall accompany Miss Patience to the kitchen."

"I would object to the insult to my ability to be useful, but I know you wish to be alone with Patience, so I thank you." Meera bobbed a curtsy and sailed off toward her infirmary, her colorful shawl blowing in the breeze of her efficient steps.

The lady was much too perspicacious.

"I can carry them both," Patience said, transferring cups from the tray Henri held to her own. "I am sure you have important business you must be about."

Paul agreeably abandoned his sister and aimed for the door.

Henri couldn't tell her the most important business in his life was her, not while her brother was right there. Before he could find his tongue, furious shouts echoed down the corridor.

Merde, that had to be the prisoners. He gestured for Patience to stand back, then joined Paul in blocking the doorway. Meera had just gone that way! Damnation, he couldn't. . .

Intelligently, the little apothecary darted into Clare's sitting room and shut the door.

The three prisoners, with ties binding their wrists, emerged from the back hall, cursing the company of stalwart soldiers, stable hands, and the towering young footman. After their night in the cellars, the prisoners were scruffy and antagonistic, brushing off any help if they stumbled. Naturally gaunt, Bartholomew appeared as if he'd been living on a desert island for months. He elbowed Corcoran, who kicked and struggled against his bonds. Bergstein, the big, black-bearded giant, shrugged off any attempt to push him forward and strode down the corridor as if he owned it.

Corcoran, although of a similar age to the other two, seemed to have shrunk to a wizened, belligerent old man. He'd been locked in the filthy crypt, away from the others. With his tailored coat covered in dust and spiderwebs, he lost any hint of polish he'd once possessed. Unshaven, a nasty bruise on his chin, with what remained of his lank hair falling in his face, he shuffled along, twitching away the grasp of his guards.

If this was Paul's natural father, Henri hoped the young curate took after his grandfather. Although, if he understood the documents rightly, Teddy was not related to the old man. He was Bridget's boy and a Corcoran only by adoption. Paul must have inherited his generous nature through his mother, the old man's only child.

Probably not a good idea for Teddy to see Paul right now. Still holding the empty tray, Henri elbowed Paul backward to join his sister, out of sight and range.

He was too late.

Corcoran saw them. His red-rimmed eyes widened with fury. Yanking free of his guards, he rushed from the rear corridor, bellowing like a demented bull. "You! I should have killed you at birth!"

With time only to react, Henri stepped into the hall and rammed the corner of the empty tea tray into Teddy's gut as hard as he could. Combined with the prisoner's velocity, the blow doubled Corcoran up in pain.

Paul snatched the empty tray away and whacked his unnatural father over his balding crown. Corcoran collapsed into a groaning ball. So the curate wasn't entirely a man of peace. Good to know.

At the commotion, Arnaud and Hunt emerged from the great hall to shout orders. The tall footman and one of the stable hands ran to reclaim their prisoner.

Looking stunned, Paul handed the tray back to Henri, then knelt beside the gasping prisoner, who cursed and shoved away any offer of aid.

Weeping, Patience took Henri's arm and buried her tears in his coat sleeve.

This was not exactly how he'd planned to court the lady.

Sorrowful at his father's continued rejection, Paul returned to his feet and bent his head in prayer.

Striding down the corridor, Arnaud grasped Corcoran's collar and yanked him up, giving Henri a look of concern. "I had not thought you a fighter, *mon frere*. Well done."

Henri scoffed. "Normally, I *talk* villains to their knees."

Arnaud glanced at Patience, clinging to Henri's arm, and dragged Corcoran away without a word.

Henri knew he was no coward. He had long ago learned that fighting took up precious time better spent elsewhere. But his big brother's admission that he might be a little worthwhile boosted his confidence. Arnaud's lack of objection to Patience on his arm meant his brother was a fool, and Henri felt no guilt in pursuing her.

Hunt limped up to warn them, "You're witnesses. Proceed to the courtroom."

Right. Henri squeezed Patience a little closer, just because, then stepped back. "If we go in there, you won't beat anyone up, will you?"

She peered up at him through tear-drop lined lashes. "You truly are the smartest man I know. I love that you stay out of brawls. . . and keep me from them."

Henri laughed. She made him feel twelve-feet high, even though he knew he simply did what needed to be done. That she recognized his not-always-obvious value gave him a worth he hadn't felt until now. Perhaps he might be a little more than a man who understood how to make money. "If I am so smart, I wouldn't take a boot-wielding woman like you into the courtroom. But I think you have as much right to know what's happening as your brother. Am I wrong? Would you rather retreat to the nursery? It sounds as if they're becoming a little loud up there."

Bartholomew had cast anxious glances up the stairs as he passed, but the guards hustled him on. Prisoners and witnesses were now safely installed in the great hall, where Hunt probably had pistols on his podium and Walker standing guard with a musket.

"If the captain won't be too angry, then yes, I would like to hear what is said. I wish to know what happened at the Corcorans today." She took his offered arm and followed him down the corridor.

"I will tell you all later," he whispered, thrilled to have her at his side.

He raised his eyebrows upon entering the great chamber to find the elderly aunts and Clare already ensconced on the scattered settees. They must have entered through the library.

Hunt glowered at them from the makeshift podium near the fireplace.

On his arm, Patience giggled. "They cannot resist passing judgment."

Paul entered without Mrs. Upton. He sat with the other witnesses in one corner, on the opposite side of the immense room from the prisoners.

The stolen ledger they'd just acquired from Corcoran, the clean murder weapons from Bartholomew, and the jewelry box from the grave rested on a table in front of Hunt.

The bearded giant saw the box, shouted "Desecration!" and stormed to the evidence table to grab the trinkets with his bound hands.

The eldest of Bert's children slammed open the main doors and ran to her father, weeping. Patience squeezed Henri's hand, then abandoned him to join Clare in reining in the others following suit.

Not to be delayed, Hunt pointed at the furiously struggling Corcoran. "I charge you with assault with a deadly weapon for last night's knife fight and attempted assault for this recent incident. Since the stolen register was found in your residence, placing you on the scene of the church vandalism, I'll also charge you with murder of Archibald Blackstone Jr. Given your propensity for violence, would you care to make it easier on yourself and confess to the death, accidental or otherwise, of the late Mr. Isaiah Upton as well?"

"I didn't do it," Corcoran screamed. "She did! The old hag killed the lying sot. Blackie meant to turn her in, so I *had* to stop him! A man's got to defend what's his!"

This might be more dramatic than a night at the opera.

"CONFESSION SIMPLIFIES JUDGMENT CONSIDERABLY," HUNT declared, sitting at the formal dining table and sipping his grandfather's—or possibly Lady Reid's—fine brandy over dinner. After a day like this one, he had earned brandy.

"It's still awful." Clare caressed his hand. "Paul's *grand-mother* killed poor Mr. Upton."

They'd had to pick up Mrs. Corcoran and install her in a locked attic room until Henri could transport her and her son to assizes on the morrow. Paul was making arrangements for his grandfather's care. The tragedy had to haunt their poor curate.

"Even if she only meant to hit Mr. Upton and not kill him," she continued, "Bridget Corcoran had a temper as bad as her son's! And with an example like that for a mother, how could Teddy not kill for her sake?"

"Well, he did it for his own hide as well. Blackstone knew what he'd done to Paul's mother. Teddy thought he'd steal any evidence in the register, except Blackie got there first and taunted him. I suppose I have to believe him when he says Blackie had already drunkenly ripped up the chapel and hit Paul with the register before running away with it. The thatching tool was all he had to stop him."

Clare sighed in despair. "And now mother and son must be sent to trial. Surely, they will not hang an old woman? What makes people that way?"

"Greed, in this case." Hunt assumed others at the table listened, but the clergyman and his small family had retreated to the parsonage, allowing him to reply without circumspection. "Teddy Corcoran knew his stepfather favored his own flesh and blood over him. He may even have ruined Paul's mother in hopes of turning the old man against her, although I suspect baser reasons and temper over rationality. Killing Blackie certainly wasn't the act of a rational man."

"Is Daniel Corcoran mean enough to turn out his stepson in favor of his daughter?" Clare asked.

Hunt shook his head. "Daniel Corcoran promised his wife and Teddy that they'd have the farm. But without the investment income, Teddy would have to actually work the land to make a living. I'm not certain he ever worked a day in his life. I'm sure he hoped to convince his stepfather that Paul was lost to him, so he'd leave the American family holdings to him."

"And later, Corcoran threw both weapons in the brook by Bartholomew's farm, implicating a man he hated?" Elsa slathered butter on a roll and took a delicate bite to test it.

"The brook was convenient. I believe him when he swears he did not mean for Bert to be implicated. Corcoran is just not that smart, but he is lazy." Jack glanced up from his own meal to regard Hunt. "Thank you for letting Bert get away with not telling us about the tools. He's a hardworking man doing what he can without a proper education. Paul has agreed to help him with the thatching."

"We really need to do something about those children. They're a handful already. Without schooling, they'll end up like all the other lay-abouts, getting into trouble." Elsa forked her chicken a little harder than necessary.

"Education is a necessity," Lady Lavinia agreed, not glancing at Lavender, for whom she'd provided an expensive boarding school. Not that Lavender appreciated it.

Jack nodded thoughtfully. "I'll begin asking around about a teacher and if we have a building that might serve as school."

Hunt thanked the heavens above that someone else had volunteered for that difficult chore. There were only so many hours in the day.

Elsa fed her fiancé a choice morsel in gratitude. "Thank you. Now tell me of Bergstein. Are we to believe him when he says Blackstone beat and killed his sister, then claimed it was an accident and refused to bury her? And the poor brother had to place her in the orchard because he could not afford a grave?"

Lady Lavinia frowned, which tugged her mole downward

in a disapproving moue. "This is not a topic for dinner conversation. It seems this place fosters drunkenness and violence. I cannot approve."

"Henri, we may need to close down your tavern." Hunt said to wake up his cousin, who was pushing food around on his plate.

"You don't own it." Henri flung a wadded roll at him. "You can take back your chairs, if you like. I'll find others."

Amazingly, Hunt caught the roll, despite his limited vision.

"I think the tavern should have entertainment nights for the whole family." Clare hid her grin with a forkful of beans, but Hunt knew his intended was simply following his lead and teasing Henri out of the doldrums. "Patience could sing. We could play cards."

"I can't throw food at you," Henri complained. "It's unfair that Hunt uses you as shield. Patience will *not* be singing in a tavern again."

"I daresay the girl will do as she pleases." Lady Spalding, signaled for a second serving. "Why should the tavern not serve as a school during the day? And it wouldn't hurt to take Sundays off from drinking. If the weddings are on Sunday, it can be used for a reception room for wedding breakfasts. Much simpler than carting everyone up the hill."

Hunt chuckled at his cousin's groan. "This is what it is like to stay in one place and live with family. You can always hit the road again." He dodged another flying roll. Lavender's mop-pup chased after it.

"Leadership," Lady Lavinia, his great-aunt, said in a sonorous voice, her pompadour bobbing. "A community needs *good* leadership. That is your responsibility as landowners. Without good leaders, the bullies take over. They crush the less fortunate and hopelessness prevails. Once that happens, crime and violence follow, as you have seen."

"I'm not a leader," Henri growled.

"You're a peddler," Arnaud taunted from the other side of the table, then dodged a flying fork.

"*Good* leaders pull a community together by sharing what they can, whether it's wealth or skill or knowledge," Clare interceded, picking up the lady's thought. "*Bad* leaders keep power and wealth to themselves. One offers opportunities so people may all prosper together, the other sucks out everything valuable for their own benefit and leaves a shell. Lady Lavinia, you make a most excellent point. It is our task to build Gravesyde Priory into the village it once was."

Hunt wanted to kiss her and run far, far away at the same time.

Resurrecting Gravesyde from the dead was a monumental task that could take several lifetimes.

THIRTY-FOUR

"I AM A JEWELER, NOT A FARMER," BERGSTEIN COMPLAINED, digging a hole for a sapling. "Wrap that trunk in linen to keep the bucks from rubbing their antlers on it," he added, putting the lie to his declaration. "You need fencing or the deer will eat everything."

"Your knowledge is the reason your orchard is thriving, while this one is dying," Patience remonstrated. "If the village is to survive, it needs these trees. It's the least you can do after Paul built a casket and buried your sister beside your parents. That's how civilization works."

"My father, *he* wanted to be a farmer," the bearded man griped. "He sold his jewelry from a caravan, only mama wanted a home. But staying here. . ." He gestured down the hill at the village. "It killed them. I live where I am wanted, in the city, with my own kind."

"You still have land here. You return to tend it." Henri snapped off a dead tree branch. "Patience has a carpenter for a brother. He can help you fix up your caravan. In return, you can help Patience understand what the orchard needs."

Patience loved Henri's ability to trade anything with anyone. She pulled the tender sapling from its life-giving water and gently set it in the newly dug hole. "The orchard needs love, just like people. Do you have a wife, Mr. Bergstein?"

The bearded giant fell silent and started on a second hole while she mixed Elsa's kitchen compost with Jack's stable manure. It was amazing how much the land provided when people gave it a chance.

Henri grabbed a second shovel to stir her mixture and add it to the tree roots. He'd borrowed old breeches, coat, and shirt from anyone willing to lend them. Patience tried not to stare too hard at his straining muscles as he dug into a dirt pile.

Bergstein was silent for a long while before reluctantly responding. "She is a good woman. Her husband mistreated her. We have had children together. They are grown now, but we cannot come back here."

He did not say who *she* was or say that *she* was his wife. Which might explain why he didn't think they could return. They lived in sin.

While she tapped the dirt mixture around the tree roots, Patience did a quick mental calculation and a leap of logic. "Teddy Corcoran's wife, Sally, ran away nearly twenty-five years ago, about the same time you did. You said she's fine and doing well. The captain meant to send someone to Birmingham to verify that, but since you've confessed the bones belonged to your sister, he didn't. What would he have found in town?"

Henri raised his expressive eyebrows. She adored the way he did that. She wasn't entirely certain why he was here and not Arnaud, but she was glad of it. After all they'd been through, she'd forgotten to be self-conscious. And even though Henri could charm a snake from an apple tree, he let her talk and didn't interrupt.

Bergstein hit an old root and drove his shovel into it. "I took her to friends of mine. I could not let Corky do to her what Blackstone did to my sister. This is not how family behaves. Men do not beat wives!"

Patience sought a way to voice what needed to be said. She wished Paul were here, but she was satisfied that she could speak for him. "The law is cold. It does not accept human behavior, does it? The people who write laws think only in white and black and not shades of gray. But we live in a gray world."

Bergstein responded with a perplexed glare and returned to digging.

Grasping the conclusion she'd reached, Henri said the hard part. "Corcoran stabbed and killed a man. He will hang. The law is clear and makes no exception for weakness of character and temper."

"Paul says he will go to the trial and ask for transportation for Teddy and his mother. However horrible the circumstances, they are his family." Patience appreciated that her brother could forgive. Killing for killing did not seem logical.

"The *law* does not forgive," Henri reminded her. "He will hang, without doubt. They may be more lenient with an old woman and manslaughter, but I doubt it."

Bergstein finally caught their drift. "Teddy Corcoran's wife will be a widow."

"Paul would be happy to perform a quiet ceremony, as he did for Meera and Walker. Then your wife can visit her family without shame. I am sure Mr. Bartholomew would love to see her again." Patience tugged the next sapling from its bucket of nourishment. The orchard would take time to recover, but ten years from now. . . It would flourish.

She smiled up at Henri as he shoveled dirt around the roots. The look he gave her caused her to flush from head to foot.

∾

CLARE ADMIRED THE SECOND GAS LAMP HUNT HAD MANAGED TO install midway down the central corridor so that the door to the formal dining room and the study across from it were illuminated. "For a medieval keep, this is marvelously modern, my brilliant captain."

He rested his big arm around her shoulders and examined the effect with his one eye but merely nodded agreement.

"Probably more Jacobean than medieval," their new guest, Dorothea, corrected. "The monks might have built the original priory during the medieval era, but not much remains of that structure. I daresay the earls, being rural, built more in the outdated Elizabethan style, however."

Clare buried her snicker in Hunt's coat sleeve. Dorothea was definitely a bluestocking.

"I take it we need a larger retort to provide enough gas for upstairs?" Walker asked, admiring the new lamp on his way to elsewhere, as always.

"Or better science," Hunt agreed. "My efforts were merely experiments. Bringing the manor up to modern standards will take fortunes we do not possess."

Arnaud coughed and nodded his head toward the library. "Come look at what we've found."

A clue to the jewels? Clare glanced at the stoic Frenchman's expression but it revealed nothing. She tried not to let her hopes rise as they proceeded into the library. Mr. Birdwhistle had established a small schoolroom upstairs in the nursery now that it had been cleaned up and he had two students. That left the library to adults. She was amazed that Oliver did not escape with regularity, but he seemed content with the books the tutor provided.

She hoped Dorothea's family would contribute to the tutor's salary. Her little brother had worse learning problems than Oliver. The men of the Reid family were often brilliant but not exactly *normal*. She was waiting for a report on what was needed to help him before petitioning for aid.

In the library, Jack's bookworm father and Arnaud had lined up several large volumes and a scattering of papers. Henri and Patience were already there, puzzling over them. Jack and Elsa were indifferent to the library and the search for jewels once Jack solved the original puzzle. They were off with their horses. And billing and cooing, no doubt.

Lavender preferred sewing and waited for jewels to magically materialize so she might buy more fabric. Hers was a simple world. Clare was thoroughly grateful that the beautiful adolescent turned her mind to fashion and work and not men. Yet.

The baron handed a paper to Hunt. "We have located a new message from your puckish earl. It appears we should have discovered an order to his codes. We have apparently missed the first messages and the one between this and the other you found."

Hunt handed the missive to Clare to read aloud. *Congratulations on finding the fifth map. You are not far from your first prize. Now, you need to be creative.*

First prize? She frowned and looked to the baron for explanation.

He shook his head and held out a similarly yellowed document. "It is little more than another square, I am sorry. It is possible that Wycliffe was losing his mental faculties at the end."

Hunt gestured for the first odd map they'd found, donned his monocle, and held up both to the light. Squares did not indicate *map* in Clare's mind.

"The X's are outside the blocks in both cases," Arnaud explained for everyone else. "We seem to be missing the main map that would explain these."

"But it does seem that there actually *are* jewels and more maps, and it's not wishful thinking." Henri tried to brighten the gloom. "We simply need to sit down and apply ourselves to decoding the remaining codes."

"I think the earl just wanted someone to clean his old artwork." Arnaud set a small painting of an infant in what appeared to be an early Georgian gown on an easel. "There are codes sketched into every family portrait I have found, and there are dozens. This, I believe, is the last earl as an infant." He pointed at a patch of color not quite matching the blue coat on the child.

If she squinted, she could see the letters and numbers. Clare sighed in exasperation. "Wycliffe must have been enormously bored to waste his days like this. As his first letter indicated, he wants us to earn his fortune."

More pragmatically, Hunt handed the papers back to the baron. "Would you be willing to remain here and continue the search after the weddings, if necessary?"

The baron tucked his own spectacles back in his pocket. "This is the most fun I've had in decades. Of course, lad. I'm enjoying the correspondence over the auction. I already have a select few bibliophiles arriving for the first sale." He gestured at the stack of books they'd sorted as too valuable to keep. "After they see your riches, you will soon have museums and collectors at your door. I will enjoy meeting them all."

Clare hugged Hunt's arm as the possibilities opened. "We will bring London here! Oh, this will be diverting. I'll tell Mrs. Upton that we may need to open *both* wings. I wonder if we can persuade anyone to bring a schoolteacher for the village? May I help write the letters responding to requests?"

"You have a book to finish, remember," Hunt whispered in her ear. Aloud, he gestured at the document-strewn table. "All hands on deck, let us find our fortunes! Castles in the air are always entertaining, as long as work continues in reality."

"A book and a *wedding* to plan," she murmured back. "Are you ready?"

"More than ready." With a bow to the baron, he caught her waist and nearly carried her from the room. "Want to choose

299

a bedroom?" He leaned over and kissed her in the glow of the new gaslights.

She threw her arms around his neck in reply. Less than two weeks to go. Surely, there would be no more murders to interfere.

CHARACTERS

George Reid, Earl of Wycliffe—deceased, left Gravesyde Priory to all his family

Captain Alistair Huntley—engineer US Army; great-grandson of Earl of Wycliffe

Clarissa (Clare) Knightley—spinster; great-granddaughter of Earl of Wycliffe

Oliver Knightley Owen—Clare's seven-year-old nephew

Daniel Walker—Hunt's friend, steward

Arnaud Lavigne— Hunt's artist cousin, eldest son of Comte Lavigne

Henri Lavigne— Arnaud's younger brother, a peddler

Meera Abrams—druggist/apothecary; Clare's best friend

Lavender Marlowe—illegitimate great-granddaughter of Earl of Wycliffe

Lt. Honorable John (Jack) Cecil de Sackville—retired soldier, son of Baron de Sackville

Lady Elspeth (Elsa)—great-granddaughter of Earl of Wycliffe

Benedict Bosworth Jr.—banker for Wycliffe Manor Trust; illegitimate grandson of Wycliffe

Terrence Birdwhistle—tutor

Archibald Blackstone—former bartender's son

Isaiah Upton—garrulous curate
Henrietta (Nettie) Nelson Upton—curate's 2nd wife
Paul Daniel Upton— curate's eldest son by first wife
Patience Upton—curate's daughter by second wife
Bert Bartholomew—farmer with ten kids
Abraham Bergstein—planted manor's orchard
Bridget Corcoran—Paul Upton's maternal grandmother
Ted Corcoran—Paul's uncle
Mary Corcoran Upton—curate's first wife, Paul's mother, deceased
Daniel Corcoran—Paul's grandfather
Lord de Sackville—Jack's father, baron; bibliophile
Lady Lavinia Marlowe—baroness, Wycliffe's daughter; Lavender's paternal grandmother
Elaine, Lady Spalding— marchioness, Hunt's aunt; Wycliffe's granddaughter
Dorothea (Dotty) Reid Talbot—granddaughter of Wycliffe's brother David
Bar flies: **George**- tavern authority; **William Oswald**-postmaster's brother; **Charley Jones**- deacon

GRAVESYDE PRIORY MYSTERIES

Secrets of Wycliffe Manor
Book #1

Be wary of what you wish for. . .

In Regency England:

The descendant of adventuring—dead—aristocrats, Clarissa Knightley supplements a modest inheritance by penning gothic novels that cost more than they earn. Upon learning that she has mysteriously inherited a share of an earl's estate, she rashly packs up her household. In remote Gravesyde Priory, she hopes to find a safe haven and family who will welcome her and her young nephew.

Instead, she discovers a drunken American army captain, his African servant, and ancient, surly caretakers. Terrified, prepared to flee, Clare is lured to linger by the prospect of secret diaries, hidden jewels, and an increasingly intriguing man. Then a killer strikes.

The crumbling manor's ominous and baffling history offers fascinating fodder for Clare's horror novels—if only she can survive real-life madmen and a spectral murderer who may seek the jewels at any price.

To Buy, Please Visit
https://patriciarice.com/books/the-secrets-of-wycliffe-manor/

∽

The Mystery of the Missing Heiress
Book #2

Wycliffe Manor, a magnet for murder...

On a long-delayed errand to remote Wycliffe Manor, ex-Lieutenant Jack de Sackville stumbles across the murdered body of London dandy, Basil Culpepper, in the hedgerow, a long way from his usual haunts. To Jack's dismay, he discovers the earl's daughter Culpepper ruined hiding in Wycliffe's kitchen.

Disguised as a lowly cook, Lady Elspeth Villiers may have liked to shoot Culpepper for ruining her life, but she dropped out of sight for more immediate reasons than an old scandal —her wealth has become the focus of greedy men. The arrival of Jack, the man she's adored since childhood, along with Culpepper's corpse, mean her hiding place is no longer safe.

But once Lady Elsa reveals herself to the unconventional inhabitants of Wycliffe Manor, they become the protective family she has never known. Outraged to learn the beautiful woman he once loved and lost has become a target of greed, Jack joins the investigation into Culpepper's death.

With a murderer on the loose, the amateur sleuths must unravel a deadly tangle of kidnappers and counterfeiters or the Manor's eccentric inhabitants will be in as much danger as their cook.

To Buy, Please Visit
https://patriciarice.com/books/the-secrets-of-wycliffe-manor/

The Bones in the Orchard
Patricia Rice

Published by Rice Enterprises, Dana Point, CA, an affiliate of Book View Café Publishing Cooperative

Book View Café
304 S. Jones Blvd. Suite #2906
Las Vegas NV 89107

BOOK🍵VIEWCAFE

ABOUT THE AUTHOR

With several million books in print and *New York Times* and *USA Today's* bestseller lists under her belt, former CPA Patricia Rice is one of romance's hottest authors. Her emotionally-charged contemporary and historical romances have won numerous awards, including the *RT Book Reviews* Reviewers Choice and Career Achievement Awards. Her books have been honored as Romance Writers of America RITA® finalists in the historical, regency and contemporary categories.

A firm believer in happily-ever-after, Patricia Rice is married to her high school sweetheart and has two children. A native of Kentucky and New York, a past resident of North Carolina and Missouri, she currently resides in Southern California, and now does accounting only for herself.

ALSO BY PATRICIA RICE

The World of Magic:

The Unexpected Magic Series

MAGIC IN THE STARS

WHISPER OF MAGIC

THEORY OF MAGIC

AURA OF MAGIC

CHEMISTRY OF MAGIC

NO PERFECT MAGIC

The Magical Malcolms Series

MERELY MAGIC

MUST BE MAGIC

THE TROUBLE WITH MAGIC

THIS MAGIC MOMENT

MUCH ADO ABOUT MAGIC

MAGIC MAN

The California Malcolms Series

THE LURE OF SONG AND MAGIC

TROUBLE WITH AIR AND MAGIC

THE RISK OF LOVE AND MAGIC

Crystal Magic

SAPPHIRE NIGHTS

TOPAZ DREAMS

CRYSTAL VISION

WEDDING GEMS

AZURE SECRETS

THE GENUINE ARTICLE

THE MARQUESS

ENGLISH HEIRESS

IRISH DUCHESS

Regency Love and Laughter Series

CROSSED IN LOVE

MAD MARIA'S DAUGHTER

ARTFUL DECEPTIONS

ALL A WOMAN WANTS

Rogues & Desperadoes Series

LORD ROGUE

MOONLIGHT AND MEMORIES

SHELTER FROM THE STORM

WAYWARD ANGEL

DENIM AND LACE

CHEYENNES LADY

Dark Lords and Dangerous Ladies Series

LOVE FOREVER AFTER

SILVER ENCHANTRESS

DEVIL'S LADY

DASH OF ENCHANTMENT

INDIGO MOON

Too Hard to Handle

TEXAS LILY

TEXAS ROSE

TEXAS TIGER

TEXAS MOON

Mystic Isle Series

MYSTIC ISLE

MYSTIC GUARDIAN

MYSTIC RIDER

MYSTIC WARRIOR

Mysteries:

Family Genius Series

EVIL GENIUS

UNDERCOVER GENIUS

CYBER GENIUS

TWIN GENIUS

TWISTED GENIUS

Tales of Love and Mystery

BLUE CLOUDS

GARDEN OF DREAMS

NOBODY'S ANGEL

VOLCANO

CALIFORNIA GIRL

Historical Mysteries

Graneside Priory Series

THE SECRETS OF WYCLIFFE MANOR

THE MYSTERY OF THE MISSING HEIRESS

THE BONES IN THE ORCHARD

Urban Fantasies

Writing as Jamie Quaid

Saturn's Daughters

BOYFRIEND FROM HELL

DAMN HIM TO HELL

GIVING HIM HELL

ABOUT BOOK VIEW CAFÉ

 *Book View Café* Publishing Cooperative (BVC) is an author-owned cooperative of professional writers, publishing in a variety of genres including fantasy, romance, mystery, and science fiction — with 90% of the proceeds going to the authors. Since its debut in 2008, BVC has gained a reputation for producing high-quality ebooks. BVC's ebooks are DRM-free and are distributed around the world. The cooperative is now bringing that same quality to its print editions.

BVC authors include New York Times and USA Today bestsellers as well as winners and nominees of many prestigious awards.

Made in the USA
Las Vegas, NV
25 March 2024

87715467R00187